THE
BALLROOM

Praise for *Wake*

'A compelling and emotionally charged debut . . . I loved it.'
RACHEL JOYCE, author of *The Unlikely Pilgrimage of Harold Fry*

'A tender and timely novel, full of compassion and quiet insight.'
CHRIS CLEAVE, author of *The Other Hand*

'*Wake* is powerful and humane; a novel that charms and beguiles.'
SADIE JONES, author of *The Outcast*

'Hope's unblinking prose is reminiscent of Vera Brittain's
classic memoir *Testament of Youth* . . .'
New York Times

'A masterclass in historical fiction.'
Observer

'A moving novel about the aftershock of the 1914–18
conflict . . . unlikely many will prove better . . .'
Sunday Times

'Absorbing and timely.'
Daily Mail

'Wise and insightful.'
Sunday Express

'A hit, we think!'
Simon Mayo Bookclub

'Superb . . . beautifully crafted.'
Irish Times

'Affecting.'
Times Literary Supplement

'Intricately researched and beautifully written.'
HANNAH BECKERMAN, *Huffington Post*

Also by Anna Hope

Wake

THE
BALLROOM

Anna Hope

Doubleday

LONDON · TORONTO · SYDNEY · AUCKLAND · JOHANNESBURG

TRANSWORLD PUBLISHERS
61–63 Uxbridge Road, London W5 5SA
www.transworldbooks.co.uk

Transworld is part of the Penguin Random House group of companies
whose addresses can be found at global.penguinrandomhouse.com

Penguin
Random House
UK

First published in Great Britain in 2016 by Doubleday
an imprint of Transworld Publishers

A CIP catalogue record for this book
is available from the British Library.

ISBNs 9780857521965 (hb)
9780857521972 (tpb)

Typeset in 11/15pt Palatino by Kestrel Data, Exeter, Devon.
Printed and bound by Clays Ltd, Bungay, Suffolk.

Penguin Random House is committed to a sustainable future
for our business, our readers and our planet. This book is made
from Forest Stewardship Council® certified paper.

1 3 5 7 9 10 8 6 4 2

To John Mullarkey, my great-great-grandfather,
1863–1918.

And for Dave, who proves, every day, that magic is real.

'The hall is 104 feet long and 50 feet wide, and is fine alike in dimensions and general arrangement. There are dado and frieze in Burmantofts work, string courses, and above these arched windows, which form a further decorative feature. The windows are filled with cathedral glass, and long sprays of bramble with birds flitting about are painted upon it with charming effect. The ceiling is panelled and coved in light brown and gold, and picked out with various tints, all harmonising with the rich hues of dado and frieze, as well as with a magnificent arcaded gallery in walnut. At the opposite end is a large stage, fitted with all requisites in the shape of wings and flies, and accommodation for the band behind the foot-lights.'

Ilkley Gazette, 1882

'The garden of humanity is very full of weeds . . . nurture will never transform them into flowers.'

Karl Pearson

Prologue

Ireland 1934

THE DAY WAS FAIR AND WARM. She walked slowly, careful on the rutted earth. On either side of the lane were meadows, and the meadows were filled with cattle, lazy in the sun. Summer flowers grew wild from the cracks in the tumbled stone walls. The land was green. Somewhere at the edge of things she could smell the sea.

Rounding a corner she saw the house: low and long, with three windows at the front. Whitewashed. A house that someone had taken care over. Around it lay a plot of land, where the tall stalks of vegetables grew in rows, ready to be gathered in. Close by stood a barn, where a man was working at the top of a ladder, the sound of his hammer bright on the air.

She stopped. Caught her breath. The man had his back to her, absorbed in his work. He had not seen her yet.

She had not expected him to be here. Somehow she had thought there might be time to see the house, to sense his presence, to wonder if it really was the place.

As she watched him, the ease of his movement, the rise and fall of his arm as he worked, she felt herself grow fearful.

Would he know her, after all these years? Would he thank her, for disturbing his peace?

She looked down at herself. She had taken such care as she dressed this morning, but she was all wrong suddenly: her shoes too tight, the colour of her dress too loud. Her hat too smart for the warmth of the day. It was not too late to turn back. He would never know she had come.

She closed her eyes, the filtered light of the sun flickering against her lids.

She had waited for this moment for too long.

The man's hammer had stopped. She opened her eyes and the day burst in upon her.

The man had seen her. He was standing on the earth now, facing out, his gaze steady. She could not read his face. Her heart stalled.

She lifted her chin. Took a breath. He would not see her falter.

She walked towards the gate, and when she reached it, she opened her mouth and spoke his name.

Book One

1911
Winter – Spring

Ella

'ARE YOU GOING TO BEHAVE?' The man's voice echoed. *'Are you going to behave?'*

She made a noise. Could have been yes. Could have been no, but the blanket was pulled off her head and she gasped for air.

An arched hall stretched before her, lit with lamps. The thin hiss of gas. Plants everywhere, and the smell of carbolic soap. On the floor were tiles, reaching out in all directions, polished till they shone, some in the shapes of flowers, but the flowers were black. She knew then that this was no police station, and started shouting in fear, until a young woman in uniform appeared from the darkness and slapped her on the cheek. 'There'll be none of that in here.'

Irish. Ella whipped her head back, tears in her eyes though she wasn't crying. She knew those Irish girls. There were plenty at the mill. They were mean as hell.

Another woman came, and they put their hands beneath her armpits and began pulling her towards two doors. Ella dragged her feet, but they slapped her till she walked for herself. Both of them had sets of keys at the waist. There must have been twenty, thirty keys there, clanging away. They pushed her through the doors, locked them behind her, and then they were standing at the top of a corridor so long the end was impossible to see.

'Where am I?'

No reply. Only the wheeze of gas and the corridor, stretching. They turned to the left with her, through another set of doors, marching her between them, uniforms crackling as they walked. Everywhere the same hard smell of soap, and something else, something wrong underneath.

Then, a last door, and a large room, with a stink like a pigpen, where they dragged her to a narrow, metal-framed bed and shoved her down. 'We'll deal with you later.'

Other beds showed themselves in the greyish light, hundreds of them lying end to end. On each a person, but man or woman she couldn't tell. Heavy furniture lined the walls, which were painted dark. She could see the large double doors she had come in from. Locked.

Was this prison then? Already?

She crouched at the top of the bed, breathing hard. Her cheek was throbbing. She lifted her fingers to it; it had split where the men had punched her earlier, and was pulpy and thick. She pulled the rough blanket up over her knees. Someone nearby was singing, the sort of song you'd sing to hush a baby to sleep. Someone else crying. Someone muttering to themselves.

A humming started up. It seemed to be coming from the next bed, but all Ella could see of the woman in there were her feet, soles like peeling yellow paper, until she sat up straight like a jack-in-the-box. She was old, but wore her hair in bunches like a little girl. Thin, tallacky flesh hung slack on her arms.

'Will you come with me?' the woman said.

Ella inched a little towards her. Perhaps she knew a way out. 'Where to?'

'Germany.' The woman's eyes were wet and gleaming. 'We'll dance there, we'll sing.' And she started up a word-less tune in a cracked childhood voice. Then, 'At night,' the woman said, in a loud whisper, 'when I'm sleeping, me soul comes out – creep creep creep like a little white creature.' She pointed at Ella and smiled. 'But you must let it be. It comes back in the morning, right enough.'

Ella brought her fists over her eyes, curling away from the woman into a small, tight ball. Someone was banging on the walls:

'Homehomehomeiwantogohomehomehomeiwantogohome.'

She would have joined in. Except she didn't know where that was.

She stayed awake through the night, but couldn't have slept if she'd wanted to. Her cheek flamed, and as soon as one of the women stopped bleating another one started up, bawling, singing, chelping to themselves:

'Andhewasthe'

'Wouldyoutaketheelectricity'

'Reek!reek! didmeagreatfrightand'

'But that's it, where the spiritscomeintome'

As the sky started to lighten, the chorus got louder, and Old Germany in the bed beside her was the loudest of the lot, a terrible songbird greeting the dawn. A bell clanged at the top of the room. But there was movement at least, something happening, Ella could see a woman at the far end, dressed in uniform like those who had brought her here last night, and she slipped out of her bed, walking fast down the middle of the room. 'I've to speak to someone.'

'What's that?' The woman was plump, her face thick with sleep.

'Someone in charge.'

'I'm in charge.' The woman smoothed her uniform out over her belly. She lifted her watch, began to wind it up.

'Where am I?'

17

'You don't know?' The woman smiled at the round face of her watch as though the two of them were sharing a nice little joke. Another bell rang, louder, somewhere outside the room. The women began to swarm and press themselves into lines. Ella put her thumbs in her palms. For a moment she was back at work – seven in the morning and everyone rushing up the hill so as not to be late, not to have their pay docked – the metal-tasting panic in the mouth. Jim Christy, the pennyhoil man, standing at the gate, waiting to shut it in your face on the stroke of seven.

'You should wait till you've eaten something.'

She turned to see a tall pale girl at her elbow.

'Never fight on an empty stomach.' The girl had a quick, easy smile. 'Come on.' She touched her on the arm. 'I can show you the way.'

Ella shook her off. She didn't need friends. Especially not in here.

She followed the crowd into a large, echoing room, where the women were taking seats on benches set before long wooden tables. One side of the room was all doors, and at each of the doors stood a woman with one of those sets of keys. The other side was all windows, but the panes were tiny, so even if you broke one you'd only get your wrist through.

'Sit down.' She was given a shove by a passing woman in uniform. A bowl clattered on to the table before her.

'Porridge,' said the pale girl, who was sitting on the other side of the table. 'There's milk. Here.' She lifted a large pitcher and poured some for herself, then did the same for Ella. 'The food's not so bad.'

A young, dark-haired woman sitting beside Ella leant towards them. 'It's mice,' she said, pointing towards the porridge. 'They put them through t'feeder.' Her face was grey and sunken. She seemed to have no teeth.

Ella pushed her bowl away. Her stomach was cramping with hunger, but if she ate here, then it was inside her. It was real. And wherever this was, it wasn't real.

'You've hurt your cheek,' said the pale girl.

'I know.'

'You should get it seen to.' The girl tilted her head to one side. 'I'm Clem,' she said, and held out her hand.

Ella didn't move.

'Your eyes look bad too.'

'They're grand.'

'They don't look grand.'

'Can I take yours?' Mouse-woman's breath was hot on Ella's arm.

Ella nodded, and the woman curled the bowl towards her.

There must have been five hundred women in there, and it was noisier than the mill with all the machines going. An old lady on the other side of the table was crooning to a rolled-up shawl, rocking it in her arms, shushing it, reaching out with a finger and touching it. A uniformed woman walking up and down the lines stood over her and rapped her on the shoulder. 'Give over with that rubbish and eat your food.'

The old lady shook her head. 'Not till babby's eaten first.' She began to unbutton her dress.

'There's no baby,' the other woman said, raising her voice. She grabbed the shawl and shook it out, holding up the holey piece of cloth. 'See? There's nothing.'

'Babby! You've hurt my babby!' the old lady screamed, and fell to her knees, scrabbling on the floor. The uniformed

19

woman hauled her up by her elbow. More women joined the commotion then, as though they'd all been given the signal to bawl. At the height of it, a bowl shattered on the floor.

'What did you want to do that for?' It was the same hard-faced woman from last night. The Irish one. Ella put her thumbs in her palms to grip them.

'You want the tube?' said the woman. 'You want the tube again?'

Baby-woman was shaking her head from side to side and crying as she was dragged to her feet and pulled from the room.

Across the table, Clem was eating calmly. When she had finished, she put her spoon to the side of her bowl and folded her hands in her lap.

Ella leant forward. 'Where did they take her? Where did they go?'

Clem's gaze flicked up. 'To the infirmary.'

'Why?'

'So they can feed her through a tube.'

'Where am I?'

'Sharston Asylum.' Clem's eyes were a still and steady blue. 'Why, where did you think?'

Ella looked down at her hands, clasped into fists; she stretched her fingers on the table: eight of them, two thumbs. But they did not look like her own. She turned them palms up and stared. She wished for a mirror. Even that old piece of cracked rubbish they had at the end of the spinning sheds. The one they'd all elbow each other out of the way for on a Friday. Even that. Just to see she was still real.

She looked up. Doors. Nurses standing at each like

jailers, carrying one of those big rounds of keys.

Sharston Asylum.

She'd heard of it. Since she was small. If you ever did anything stupid: the asylum. For the lunatics. The paupers. *They'll send you to Sharston, and you'll never come out.*

She stood, grabbing one of the passing nurses by the hand. 'Wait. There's been a mistake!'

The woman shook her off. 'Shut up and sit down.'

'No! You don't understand – there's been a mistake. I'm not mad. I just broke a window. I'm not mad.'

'Breakfast's over now. Get back in line.'

A scraping of benches. The clatter as several hundred women stood, lining up by the door. More uniformed women appeared, a huddle in the doorway. One of them was older, wearing a smaller headdress and badge. She was looking over. Now she was crossing the room towards her. There had been a mistake. They knew it now. Relief made her shaky.

'Ella Fay?'

'Yes.'

'I'm the matron here. You're to come with me.'

Ella clambered out from the bench.

'Good luck,' said Clem.

Ella didn't look back. She followed the woman, walking out into the corridor, and when the doors were locked behind her, her knees went, as though they had been kicked from behind. She put her hand against the wall to steady herself.

The matron clicked her tongue in the back of her throat. 'Are you ready then? Come with me.'

'Am I leaving now?'

The woman's jaw twitched, as though a fly had just

landed there and she couldn't brush it off. It didn't matter. Soon she would be outside. There were two shillings sewn in the hem of her dress, and she would spend them this time. Do what she should have done yesterday. Take the train. Far away – to a place where the land stopped and gave way to the sea.

They marched through one set of doors – two, three, four. Every time they reached one, the silent nurse held Ella by the shoulders while the matron clanked around with her keys. They came to a lighter corridor and beyond it was the green of the entrance hall. She could see the plants, hundreds of them, and the thousand little tiles on the floor. She was marched past the front door into a stuffy room with a couple of chairs and a table and not much else.

The nurse shoved her into a seat, put down the papers she was carrying, and Ella was left alone. The windows had no bars in here. Through them was a wide gravel drive. The door opened, and a man entered. Humming. Fair hair. A long moustache, pointed at the ends, ears that stuck out and were pink at the tips. He eyed Ella briefly before coming to sit, and his eyes were blue and pale. He reached out and slid the papers towards him. He wrote something down and then read some more. He carried on humming as he read.

The man looked up. 'My name is Dr Fuller.' He spoke slowly, as though she might be deaf. 'I am one of the assistant medical officers here. It is my job to admit you.'

'Admit me?'

'Yes.' He sat back in his chair, fingers touching the edges of his moustache. They were sharp, as though you might prick yourself on them. 'Do you know why you are here?'

'Yes.'

22

'Oh?' He leant forward a little. 'Go on.'

The words fell from her. 'I broke a window. In the mill. Yesterday. I'm sorry. I'll pay for it. But I'm not mad.'

The man's eyes narrowed as he held her gaze. He gave a brief nod then looked back at his paper and wrote something down. 'Name?'

She said nothing.

His tongue clicked against the roof of his mouth. 'What is your name?'

'Ella. Fay.'

'Thank you. Occupation?'

'I'm not mad.'

'Occupation, Miss Fay.'

'Spinner.'

'And for how many years have you worked as a spinner?'

'Since I was twelve.'

His pen scratched out over the paper. 'And before that? Did you work as a child?'

'Yes.'

He wrote it down. 'Since what age?'

'Since I was eight.'

'And what did you do then?'

'Doffer.'

'And, remind me, that is . . . ?'

'Doffing rolls of thread when they're full. Tying up the ends and that.'

He nodded and wrote some more.

'Are you married, Miss Fay?'

'No.'

'According to the papers I have here, you still live with your family, is that correct?'

'My father. His family. Not mine.'

23

'And what about your mother?'

'Dead.'

More writing, more scratch scratch scratch.

'And what's your father's address?'

The room was quiet. Outside, clouds raced each other across the sky as though they had somewhere better to be. She saw the house she lived in. The house where she had grown up. That her mother had died in. A black house that was never safe. Her father, his new wife, their children. And her. Like one of those fents of cloth that were left over, that fitted nowhere, were just chucked and left to fray.

'Fifty-three Victoria Street.'

The doctor nodded, wrote and then stood and crossed the room towards her. He took her wrist in his fingers and pressed lightly. With his other hand he took a pocket watch out and stared at it. 'Tongue.'

'What?'

'Put out your tongue.' He spoke sharply.

He peered at it, then went back to the other side of the table and wrote some more. She watched the letters spooling from his pen, marching from left to right like a line of ants she saw once on a baking summer afternoon, crossing the path on Victoria Street. She had been small, sitting with her back on hot stone. Inside, she had heard the rasp of her father's voice, then the thud of fist on flesh. the thud of fist on flesh. Her mother crying, a low, animal sound. She had stared at the ants. They looked as if they knew just where they were going. She wondered what would happen if she followed them. Where she would end up.

'It says here, Miss Fay, that yesterday morning you broke a window in the factory in which you are employed.' The doctor was looking at her again, a keenness to him now.

'That doesn't make me mad.'

'Do you deny you did this?'

'I . . .'

How to explain? How to speak of what she had seen – of the women and the machines and the windows that blocked everything out. It had been so clear then but would muddy before this man, she knew.

She shook her head, muttering. 'There was no damage. Only the glass, and I'll pay for that. I've already said. I'll find a way.'

He bent down and wrote in his book.

'I'm not mad,' she said, louder now. 'Not like those women in that room anyhow.'

He carried on writing.

The room got closer then, darker. Pulsing. Her face was hot. Bladder hot.

'What are you writing?'

He ignored her.

'What are you writing?' She raised her voice. Still, he ignored her. The only sound the scratching of his pen. The furniture, heavy and silent, watching her too.

She hit the table in front of him. When he didn't look up, she hit it again, stood and smacked her hand right down on his papers, his pen clattering on to the floor. The ink splattered over his hand. He snapped back in his chair. Took a bell and rang it, and two nurses appeared, as though they had been waiting in the hall just for this.

'It appears Miss Fay is feeling violent. Please take her downstairs. We can finish the assessment when she's calm.'

The nurses grabbed her, but she landed a bite on one of their arms and wrested herself free. And then – the door

25

– not locked, running across the entrance hall, the black flowers. The big front door, unlocked too, and her outside on the steps, and the fresh air smacking her face, and her gasping for it, sucking it down, pelting across the gravel. Whistles blaring, shrill and hard. A nurse making towards her. Her turning to the left, to the far side of the building. Then only more buildings, and running from them too, out across the grass. A cricket pitch. Tall trees. Lungs burning. This way only fields, brown and muddy, stretching out, and sheep, and a lane ahead. The top of a small rise. Two men, standing in a hole. One of them waving his arms, shouting. Turning, seeing the nurses behind her, gaining on her. Swerving to miss them, but slipping in the mud, her ankle turning over and her falling, hard on to her front, pitching and rolling down the hill.

The fierce slap of mud. Everything red and black. A hot wetness spreading between her legs.

A face before her, a dark man – hand stretched out, palm open. 'Are you all right there?'

People around her. Upon her. She on her hands and knees, spitting black earth to the ground. Her arms, yanked behind her back. Pain tearing as she was pulled up and made to stand by people she couldn't see.

The dark man there still. Standing, watching her. A little way apart. Looking as if he pitied her.

No one pitied her.

'What?' she screamed at him. '*What are you looking at?*'

John

'COLD ENOUGH FOR YOU, *mio Capitane*?'

'Aye.' John took his place beside Dan in the line. 'Cold enough.'

Eight of them out here in the low tin light, waiting for their shovels, their breath meeting the air in vaporous clouds. The men coughed, blew on their hands, moving their weight from foot to foot, and went up one by one to Brandt, the attendant, to give their name and be told where to dig. It was always the same faces out here; not so many could be trusted with something hard and sharp.

'Mantle Lane,' said Brandt, when it was John's turn, passing the heavy shovel over. John could just make out the thin lines of the man's face.

He hefted the spade on to his shoulder and followed the grey outline of Dan's bulk down the gravel path that led behind the main buildings, over the railway bridge and then out to the furthest reaches of the grounds. Their boots crunched on the frosted grass, and John hunkered into his jacket. It was a raw morning all right, with the wind coming down off the tops and finding the gaps in your clothes. When they reached the graveyard, they made their way to the hole they had been digging last week, covered over now with thick wooden boards. Dan crouched beside it, lifting one of the planks and peering inside. 'Two of them in there.'

'Aye.'

Four more deaths then until it would be full.

It was a little lighter now, and John could see the frown on Dan's face as he brought two thin, sappy twigs from his pocket, twisted them into quick knots and laid them carefully in the hole, speaking a few low words as he did so.

There were always six to a grave. No headstones, just patches of earth raw with soil that had been dug and put back in.

John traced a rectangle on the ground with his shovel, marking the plot of a new grave. Dan soon joined him, and when the two men lifted their spades the metal struck the ground with a high, ringing sound.

They did not speak as they worked. It was always like this at first: silence until you got your rhythm up. Your boot finding its place on the lug. The shaft against your knee. Your breath finding its way. Only the sound of your shovel cutting into the ground and the odd grunt of effort. The cold no longer bearing on you, as all of you went into the digging, making the sides sharp and smooth.

They were good at it, and the hard jobs were the good ones – the ones that made you forget.

Occasionally there was a shout from one of the other men and the high shriek of the train as it arrived on the branch line from Leeds, casting a trail of smoke above the trees, but mostly there was silence. It took a day for the two of them to dig a grave: twelve foot deep, to fit as many as possible in the hole. That was fair going. Even though the tools were useless. Not like the ones from home, the narrow *loys*, which were made to fit a man, to fit the job, whether it was cutting turf or digging potatoes or sod. These shovels were factory made. They were fast enough though, since John had cut earth since he was old enough to grasp the spade and Dan was the strongest man there.

They dug on, the heat rising in their bodies, while the sun smeared its late-winter dawn over the black buildings at their back and then hid itself behind thick grey cloud. While Brandt paced on the top of the rise, with the long stick that all of the attendants carried, keeping his beady eye on them and the other scattered working groups, ready with his whistle should anything occur.

'Here,' said Dan, when they were a good couple of feet down and standing in the hole. He palmed a bit of shag from his pocket, jerking his shoulder towards the fence that hugged the field. 'Wouldn't take much to climb that now, would it?'

John rubbed his forehead with his cuff, a sweat on him now. Beyond the fence the land rose a little – not the high rise of the moor that could be seen from their ward, but gentler. A few houses dotted the horizon. He glanced at Brandt and, seeing the man had his back turned, leant in, took a pinch of Dan's tobacco and rolled a quick thin cigarette for himself. Dan was right. The fence was just the height and a half of them. A leg up and they would both be over and away.

'Where would I go?' said Dan, in answer to a question unasked. 'If I did a scarper? Well now, *mio Capitane*, let's see.' He struck a match, the flare of it licking the hollows of his face.

John leant in to the small flame. He never knew how Dan managed to find and smuggle his lunts, but he had the knack of it. And a small piece of pride was always saved in not having to beg the attendants for a light.

'Know what I wouldn't do.' Dan spat a stray piece of tobacco on the ground. 'Nothing like them daft buggers who went wandering round the village.' He gestured to the

29

houses in the distance. 'You wouldn't want to do that. Not in this clobber.'

Everyone knew about the four who'd escaped. They were out for less than a day and did nothing worth the effort, wandering around Sharston in the daylight, going into a newsagent's, visiting a barber for a shave. The man read the labels on the eejits' fronts while they were sitting in his chair.

He and Dan were both wearing suits made of rough grey tweed, *Sharston Asylum* sewn on the outside of the jacket. Dan pinched the cloth of his label in his fingers. 'I can't hardly read, but even I'm not daft enough to think they wouldn't brand us like sheep. No . . .' He stepped back, eyes half closed now, smoke curling from his nostrils in the low winter light. 'You wouldn't head for the village. You'd head for the wood.' He leant his weight back, gestured over to the west. 'I've friends in the woods. They'd help me. They'd help you too, *chavo*. They always help an honest man.'

John took a draw on his cigarette. He never knew quite what sort of friends Dan meant.

He liked his stories, did Dan, looked like some strange sort of story himself, with his slab of a face and his strongman's chest and his arms like great hams, inked all over with tattoos of birds and flowers and creatures that were half woman, half beast. He had been a sailor – *twenty years of it* – and called John his Captain, since he reminded him, so he said, of an Italian skipper he'd had: *a right handsome omi, just like you.* He'd sailed until he'd lost his registration ticket, then become a pugilist, knocking down lads for money in the fair. But he had many stories, and you never knew which ones were true.

Most of the men in there had faces marked with something John knew – poverty, or the fear of it. Dan Riley's face was different – the only marks a nose that had been broken many times and creases made by laughter and sun. In two years, John had never come to know quite why the man was in there.

'And then I'd head to sea,' Dan carried on. 'The sea, *mio Capitane*. South Shields. That's where to go. You turn up with nothing, and they'll take you on a merchant ship. No questions asked. I'd travel by night.' Dan gestured a winding way with his cigarette. 'Keep away from the roads.' He slowed up a little, savouring. 'And when I got there, I'd go round Norah Carney's house.'

Norah Carney. The legend of Norah Carney had passed many an afternoon's work.

'I'd knock on her door, and she'd appear.' Dan stepped back as though to make room for her between them in the hole of the half-dug grave. 'She'd take me in, like she always does. First thing we'd do, we'd burn this lot o' clobber in the grate.' He gestured at his suit. 'Then we'd up and off to her *lente*, and I wouldn't get up till—'

A high whistle sounded in the distance. Over Dan's shoulder John could see Brandt waving his stick. Dan laughed, a ripe cackle that shook his body as he rubbed his butt out between his fingers and threw his cigarette on the ground. 'What about you? Where'd you go, *mio Capitane*?'

He had a way of asking questions, looking at you straight, as though he wished for an answer. As though he were interested in the answer you might give.

The edge of a dress.
A woman. A child.
Before.

31

'Nowhere,' said John, and brought his shovel back down to cut the earth.

They dug for the rest of the morning and were left to it. Dan hummed and sang while they worked. He sang to suit his mood: sometimes a murder ballad, verses of blood and revenge, or scraps of wandering songs from the road, but most often a song of the sea:

I am ragged love, I am dirty love, and my clothes smell
  much of tar,
I have silver love in me pocket love and gold in great store.

I am frolicsome, I am easy, good tempered and free,
And I don't give a single pin, me boys, what the world
  thinks of me.

Then he changed the words, making them filthy, adding verses about slippery, lusty lasses called Norah, making himself laugh.

And though the work was bleak – this digging of graves twelve foot down to be filled six deep – when the smell of the earth rose fresh to your nose, and someone was singing beside you, and the digging was hard and the sweat came, blinding you from time to time and stinging your eyes, the world was simple enough.

Some time after the main clock had struck eleven, when they were a good few feet down, there came a commotion. Whistles, not one but many this time, being blown over and over again. They looked up and saw a figure coming towards them from the far side of the building, small, dark and hurtling.

Dan let out a low whistle. 'Would you look at that, *chavo* . . .'

It was a woman, moving fast, heading right for where they stood.

'Well I never,' Dan grinned, 'a *dona* in the morning.'

John stared. Women were ghosts. They shared the buildings with them but were never seen. Other than on Fridays: the dancing. And he didn't have anything to do with that.

Dan pushed his cap back on his head. 'Go on, lass,' he said, under his breath.

The girl was coming closer, arms pumping at her sides, face dark red with the effort of it. A wildness in her. A freedom. It pitched and turned in John's gut.

'Go on, lass!' roared Dan, throwing his shovel to the ground and flinging out his arms. '*Go on!!*'

Behind the girl, on the rise of the hill, not twenty feet away, was Brandt, his thin black shape gaining on her, and behind him, nurses: three, four, five of them, skirts flapping, arms flapping, useless birds that could not fly. John scanned the distance to the trees, breathing fast, as though it were him running, not the girl. She might make it. She might.

'Stop her. *Stop her!*' Brandt was shouting, mouth open, face twisted as he ran.

'Did you hear that?' said Dan.

'Hear what?' John spoke softly. Neither of them moved.

Go on, lass. Go on.

But the girl looked up then and saw them. And though both men put their hands in the air to show they meant no harm, there was terror in her eyes and she swerved in her path, stumbling, falling badly, rolling towards where they stood.

For a terrible second she was still. John moved – did it before he thought – hauling himself from the hole and starting over to where she lay. He knelt on the mud beside her. 'Are you all right there?'

The girl was not moving. He reached out and touched her arm, and she rolled to her back. Her eyes were red and swollen, her cheek a painful sight. Her wet dress covered with mud and grass. He put his hand out to help her up, and she reached for it, but it was smacked away with such force that John was felled, sent spinning on to the ground himself. And when he stumbled to his feet he saw that Brandt was on her, his knee in her spine, her arms already pulled behind her back.

He watched, helpless, as the girl was pinioned and trussed, a rabble of nurses around her, squawking and squalling. Throughout it all, the girl's red eyes were fastened on his, and he could not look away.

'What?' she snarled at him, as she was pulled to her feet. '*What are you looking at?*'

He shook his head. 'I'm sorry,' he said, half to himself, and turned away.

Dan was thigh-deep in the grave, his cap pushed back on his head. He let out another low whistle. 'Thought she was going to scarper it good and proper then.'

'Aye.'

She had been running fast. She had been going to make it to the trees. She could have outrun Brandt. And then she had seen them and fallen, and now she was taken.

The moment had stained the morning. As yet, its colours were unsure.

John lifted his shovel to the hard winter earth. And he thought of where he was. And how long he had been there.

And what was simple broke apart and became a shattered, sharded thing.

Charles

IT WAS ALMOST A relief when the call came; late afternoon and he was on the far side of the men's quarters, over in ward five, playing Mozart sonatas to the epileptics.

A young attendant tapped him on the shoulder and gave the news, 'The superintendent wishes to see you now,' and he was forced to break off in the middle of the Adagio of the C major, K545.

A queasy feeling assailed him as he hurried down the long main corridor, unlocking and locking doors as he went. He knew what this was about: it was about that girl. He should have gone after her. It had made him look weak. To have such a breach of security on his watch was not good.

As he approached the superintendent's door, Charles took a couple of deep breaths before rapping on the wood with what he hoped was a confident tone.

'Come!' The superintendent's voice was muffled by the heavy door. 'Ah . . . Fuller.' Soames was seated behind his desk. 'Sit down.'

Charles felt the man's eyes on him as he crossed the room.

'All well, Fuller?'

'Very well, sir,' said Charles, taking his seat.

'Good, good.' Soames's black-rimmed spectacles, perched as they were on the tip of his nose, gave the impression that he might be looking at him with multiple eyes. There was, in fact, something distinctly spidery about the man, tall and thin-limbed as he was; he rarely moved from this office, set at the centre of this web of corridors, but he missed nothing that occurred beneath his care. The superintendent gave a brief nod. 'We have more music in the day rooms now, I hear?'

'Yes, sir. I've just come from the piano, in fact.'

'Indeed? And how goes the new *regime*?'

'Ah. Well . . .' Charles tried his best to make his voice light. 'I believe the patients seem to like it. I've . . . experimented a little with the different composers. It's almost becoming a . . . prescription, if you like.'

'I see.' A brief twitch of the lips that could almost have been a smile. 'And whom do they like the best?'

'Well, it rather depends.' Charles leant forward. 'I tend to favour Mozart for the epileptics. Or Bach. They seem to appreciate the order it brings and, then . . . Chopin, Schubert, the impromptus – for . . . well, for their . . . beauty, I suppose.'

'Beauty?' Soames raised an eyebrow.

Charles's blood quickened. He decided to brazen it out. 'Yes, sir. I find them the most beautiful of all the music for solo piano.'

Soames made a non-committal noise. 'And the orchestra?' he said. 'Not too much for you? We can always find someone else to take up the strain.'

'No, sir.' Charles laughed. He had meant for it to sound easy, but it came out instead as a congested bark. 'Not at all. Coming along well, sir. We have a viola now and a trumpet, so as of last week we are a full complement at last.'

'Very good.' Soames leant back in his chair, index fingers

steepled beneath his chin. 'How long have you been with us now, Fuller?'

'Five years, sir.'

'Five years.' Soames sounded thoughtful.

'Sir . . .' Charles fretted his fingers together. 'About the girl. I'm terribly sorry, I should have seen the signs, but she has been sent downstairs now and I believe—'

The superintendent held up his hand. 'Did I ask you to speak, Fuller?'

'No, sir.'

A heavy silence filled the room.

'Tell me, Fuller. How did the girl appear to you?'

'I – she . . .'

She had smelt of engine grease, urine and wool. His only thought while taking her pulse had been to wish the interview were over soon.

'Her notes were scant. Birth date approximate. Family, but estranged.'

Soames nodded. 'And physically?'

'Physically she was . . . below par.'

Well below par. He had expected one of the lower examples of the female, but she was quite a sight: eyes so swollen as to be almost deformed, skin pink and stretched above and below the eyeball, the conjunctiva inflamed and weeping, the edges crusted and yellow. Below them was an open wound, recently made, a punch to the upper cheek, which had split the skin.

'Here's the thing, Fuller.' Soames's eyes met Charles's. 'We don't want any more escapees. Diminishes our reputation. Scares the villagers. You understand? We cannot be seen to be . . . out of control.'

'Yes, sir. Absolutely. Quite so.'

'I hope your recent promotion will not be found to have been too presumptuous. Can't have you taking your eye off the ball.'

Charles nodded and shifted in his seat. 'I do see, sir. And I sincerely hope not.'

'Very good, Fuller.' Soames lifted his hand in dismissal. 'That will be all.'

Charles stood. Took a few jellied steps towards the door, then hesitated. It was rare enough to have an audience with the superintendent. Who could say when the next one might be? 'Sir?' He turned back.

Soames looked up as though surprised to find him still standing there. 'Yes?'

'I know you will be aware, sir, of the Feeble-Minded Control Bill the government hopes to introduce this coming year.'

Soames gave a small inclination of the head. 'If I weren't, Dr Fuller, I think I might come within its remit.'

Charles felt himself colour. 'Of course, sir, I didn't mean to suggest—'

'Never mind, Fuller.'

'Yes, sir. Thank you. Well, I'm sure you're also aware of the existence of the Eugenics Education Society.'

'Indeed I am.'

'Well, sir, I am a member and receive their quarterly review.'

A flicker of irritation crossed Soames's face. 'Where is this heading, Fuller?'

'There is to be a Congress, sir, next summer, in London.' Charles reached into his pocket, taking out the small piece of paper he had been carrying around for the last week, straightening it, laying it on the superintendent's desk.

'And, I . . . well . . . I had the idea that I might write a paper.'

The superintendent leant forward, peering down at the advertisement on the desk.

Call For Papers
First International Eugenics Congress
Subjects of Wide Importance and Permanent Interest.

'I thought I might use my new programme of music in the wards – trace its beneficial effect on the patients, so to speak. I thought, sir, with your permission I might—'

'Fuller?' The superintendent stared back up through his lenses.

'Yes, sir?'

'*You* may have time for idle musings on the very best manner in which to improve the lot of our patients, but I for one am too busy to countenance such diversions. May I remind you that you are not a man of leisure? If there are any further slips such as this last, then I will be forced to reconsider your position. At the very least I should be forced to conclude that the extra musical duties you seem so keen to perform and write about are detrimental to your role. So, please, no more talk of papers or congresses.'

'Yes, sir. Of course.'

'And now.' Soames swept his hand before him in the direction of the door.

'Thank you, sir,' said Charles, when he had crossed the floor, but this time Soames did not look up.

Ella

ONLY HER LEGS WERE FREE. Those and her voice. At first she had kicked the door and shouted so hard she ripped her throat, before she slumped, head between her knees. Cold rose from the stone beneath her. A thin grey blanket was folded beside her, but with her arms tied like this there was no way of opening it out.

A sound came, as though someone was throwing themselves up against something soft, over and over again. Voices too, distant and thin like ghosts. On the way here there had been other doors, each with round holes in them, so other people must be here too, locked in their own damp cells. Was this where they had brought the old woman with the shawl? Was she down here now, rocking her woollen, holey baby to sleep?

Then, behind everything else came a deeper sound, a clanking, as though the building were a machine and she was near the heart of it: close to the workings, the grinding of its gears. She put her head back against the stone chill of the wall.

She had failed. For a brief green moment she had thought she was free, but she had failed.

Yesterday.

Was it only yesterday?

Ten o'clock in the morning. Spinning room number four, five floors up above Lumb Lane. A morning like every other in the twelve years she had worked there. They had just had their break, and her mouth was sour with the taste of tea and mash. She must have fallen asleep, because she was woken with the smack of the alley strap across her back.

'Watch yer bleeding thread,' the overlooker screamed in her ear.

Panic flashed through her. Fifty machines clattered. It could only have been a second.

'Next time,' the man's lips said. 'Next bloody time.' Then he moved off with his strap down the row.

She tried to concentrate, but the threads thinned and blurred before her eyes. She could feel her head going again, nodding, as if she was a puppet someone was forgetting to hold up. Dangerous. It was dangerous to fall asleep. There was the sickly, animal smell of the wool. The scorched metal of the machines. The lint, burning and swelling her eyes.

She wished for air, but the windows were closed, clouded and mottled, and there was no way to see the sky.

She had asked once, on her first day there, when she was small and frightened and eight.

Why are the windows all covered up?

And one of the older girls who was showing her what to do – how to scurry on the slippery floor beneath the looms and tie the threads together and tuck your plaits in so your scalp didn't get pulled off – had laughed and clouted her on the back of the head. *Why d'you think? You're not here to admire the view.*

So the windows were clouded in spinning room four, but there was nothing new in that. And the noise. She sometimes thought that was what the place made: noise and cloth, but mostly noise; so much it drowned your thoughts, so much you heard it ringing and buzzing in your ears all the way through your day off.

But yesterday morning Ella had seen the children, with their pinched, frightened looks. Seen the older women, hunched over like half-empty sacks. The young ones steadying themselves against their frames as though offering themselves up in the din and the lint to the gods of spinning and metal and wool. She saw the life that was in them passing into the machines, as they gave themselves away in spinning room four. For what? For fifteen shillings at the end of the week and giving half of it away to your father and only all of the days to come while everything leached from you and falling asleep and getting beaten for it and the windows so clouded you could never see the sky.

She wanted to see the sky.

So yesterday, the same as every other day, but not the same any more, Ella slid a skep of empty bobbins out from under her feet, picked one up and launched it at the window beside her. The clouded glass shattered, and she stood, gasping – giddy with the cold slap of air. She could see the horizon beyond. The dark, crouched promise of the moor.

She turned, walking down the centre of that long room, past the gawping faces, past the machinery still going, going, heart racing, through the lint snowing around her head, and when she got to the door she began to run, down five flights of stairs, out into the yard, away from the gate, through the scrubby grass, and out the back way on to Lumb Lane. The day was bright and clear and cold. The street empty. The sweat drying on her face.

She lifted her brown, oily hands to the sky, as though seeing them in a dream.

She should have kept on running.

Had she thought they would not come after her? They came. Of course they came. Feet pounding on the metal stairs.

They called her mad when they dragged her off the

street: Jim Christy, the pennyhoil man; Sam Bishop, the overlooker. Called her mad when they took her into a small room by the gate of the mill and she had screamed and kicked and spat. 'What did you want to do that for, you mad bitch?' And they might have been right, since she knew she had reached a point when she could stop, but then she was past it, way past it, and had become the screaming, become the kicking, become the spitting: a river that had burst its banks. She had hurt them, she knew that, could tell from the sounds they had made. Until a punch split her cheek and silenced her, and there was only the raw red beating of her blood. Until they chained her to a pipe and left her there.

But the feeling part of her was far away by then.

Then the men in uniforms came.

The light from the window turned on the ceiling, and the small room grew darker. Sounds faded as the night took hold. Cold rose from the stone beneath her skirts, and fear crouched beside her in the darkness, ready to crawl into her lap.

They'll send you to Sharston, and you'll never come out.

Was she mad then, for breaking a window? Mad, for kicking and biting those men? Was that all it took?

She jostled herself to sit. Rubbed her arms on the wall behind her so the pain might keep her awake.

She was here. Arms tied behind her back. Only the clothes she sat in left. There was a room in a house on a street in Bradford, where a narrow bed faced a window above a yard; there was a change of clothes there, in that room she had slept in since she was a child but which meant nothing to her.

43

She felt a power in her then. The same feeling she'd had in the mill, but now it took root, lifting her spine. It was dark, she was alone, but her blood was beating; she was alive. She would study it, this place, this asylum. Hide inside herself. She would seem to be good. And then she would escape. Properly, this time. A way they wouldn't expect. And she would never go back.

Be good.

That was what her mother had said to her – *be good* – pressing Ella's face into her chest so she couldn't breathe. Her hand the claw of a drowning woman.

Ella knew about being good. Had known it since she was small. Being good was surviving. It was watching while your mother was beaten and staying quiet so you wouldn't be next. Feeling sick because you were a coward and didn't do more. Taking the blows once she had gone and never crying, or showing how much they hurt. Tucking in your plaits, shutting up and working hard. Day after day after day.

But being good was outside only. Inside was different. That was something they could never know.

Charles

IT WAS PAST SEVEN before he had finished his rounds, and as he made his way outside, night had fallen, blustery and cold. The family of rooks that made their home in the bell tower, disturbed by the weather, circled and called above his head. The wind had picked up and rain fell in small squally blasts. He was aware of a frayed, hangnail feeling as he set off across the damp grass. It had hung about him all day. He was glad to reach the low stone building that made up the male staff quarters. Inside, all was dark – it was a peculiarity of the asylum that there was no electricity, the junior attendants taking it in turns to light the gas. Often these buildings were the last to be lit. Charles groped his way down the murky corridor to his room, which was darker still. Closing the door behind him he fumbled for a match, striking and holding it to the gas sconce on the wall.

He breathed out as yellow light lapped on to familiar things: the mantelpiece with his charcoal sketches of the patients, a few small volumes of poetry, his desk, where his papers were stacked in a neat pile, the violin and music stand in the corner by the washbasin. He was in the process of transposing the aria from the *Goldberg Variations* from piano to solo violin, and the music, half finished, was laid out on the stand.

He shrugged off his rain-spattered jacket and hung it on the back of his chair. His fire, at least, had been lit for him and a good poke and a few lumps of coal roused it nicely. Easing his feet gratefully from his shoes, he unbuttoned his collar, laying it also over the back of his chair.

At the corner of his desk was a heavy palm-sized stone, grooved with markings, with a small depression at its centre – a relic of one of his walks on Rombald's Moor, that swathe of land whose heights lay due west of here, named for a giant whose path across it was said to have left great granite stones in its wake. He picked it up, letting its cool weight possess his palm, feeling the pressures of the day disperse. *Perspective.* That was what was needed. He had spoken too early. He would have to be more careful in future.

Sounds came from the room adjacent: the opening and shutting of a door and then muffled music. Charles smiled;

Jeremy Goffin, practising his trumpet with the silencer in. It would be orchestra practice tomorrow night, and Jeremy was a charming new addition to the band, a young assistant from the Midlands, burly, built for the sports field and the restraint of troublesome patients, but with the sweetest and most disarming of smiles. Not, perhaps, the best of musicians, but Charles had made room for him nonetheless. A trumpet was rousing. Good for morale.

By now, with his five years of service and his promotion through the ranks, Charles could have chosen to 'live out', finding lodgings in the village, as many of the married men did, but, not being married, he saw no point in this. His hours were long and the Barracks, as the male staff accommodation was known, were only a short evening stagger over the grass. No call to waste money on rent when he was more than provided for here. Besides, he liked the room's monkish charms, the excellent views of the sunset from its westerly aspect over the moor.

He cast a glance to the window, where the wind, fiercer now, threw itself against the glass. Sometimes, on rough nights like this, with the wind blowing and the moor so close, the asylum could feel like a place out of time, a place where the old gods might yet hold sway, but tonight, tucked here, with the sounds of Goffin next door, and his fire burning happily now, Charles was content.

Five years since he had first seen this room, five years since he had paced its limits – the whole not more than ten steps long and five steps wide. But what he had felt that first day was not confinement but liberation. He had *escaped*.

As escapes went, it had been a narrow one; after four years of medical school, he had barely scraped his final exams, not nearly enough of a pass to take up the place at

Barts his father had worked so hard to secure. He had been summoned home to Yorkshire.

The reckoning had come in the drawing room after supper once his tearful mother had taken her leave. His father stood before the polished fireplace. Charles, sitting before him, felt twelve again, his mouth tacky, lacking spit.

'How has this occurred?' His father's jaw was clenched, hands clasped behind his back.

'I don't know.' Pathetic. But it was the best he could come up with by way of reply.

But he did know.

Boredom. He had been bored. By turgid, indigestible tracts of information delivered by desiccated lecturers with half of the students asleep by the end. Lectures he skipped in favour of music practice or lunchtime concerts at the Wigmore Hall. Only Karl Pearson had interested him. Pearson, who stood at the front of the lecture theatre and studied his pupils like a hawk, who spoke of Malthus. Population. Empire. Disease. Charles still remembered the question Pearson had posed to the room: *I ask you, gentlemen, to consider, do we not take more care in breeding our animals than we do in breeding our men?*

During his lectures, Pearson spoke of many things, but alongside the danger of the inferior man he spoke of the superior man and of the need for these superior men to *populate the world*, and Charles's seat, over the months, had drawn ever closer to the front, so by the time the lecture series had finished he had an inviolate place towards the middle of the second row. Sitting there, listening to Pearson talk, it had seemed inevitable that he too would become one of these superior men; just by sitting close to him it would occur.

But standing before his father, he felt just about as far from the superior man as could be imagined.

'This is what I have decided,' his father decreed. 'One, you will take your meals at home; two, your days will be spent in the Central Library studying for your exams, which you will retake at the end of the summer and in which you will *excel*; three, your allowance will be stopped.'

The law laid down, Charles was left alone to contemplate his fate. He stared at the aspidistras, rampant as jungle plants in the clammy, overheated air. 'I cannot stay here,' he said to them. 'I will suffocate. I will die.'

But the aspidistras, in that smug, silent way of theirs, had nothing in the way of reply.

At the library he found himself a desk at the back of the reading room and dutifully opened his textbooks, but staring at the pages, at their cross-sections of liver and lymph and bone, he felt only creeping despair. He missed London. He missed his concerts. Even if he were to survive the summer and pass this exam, the future only contained more of them. In truth, he did not know if he had any real wish to become a doctor at all. He would rather, much rather, have found some way to pursue his music instead. He knew he had talent, perhaps not *great* talent, but talent enough to play in an orchestra perhaps, not first violin, not by any means, not even second, but enough to be a dedicated fiddler amongst the ranks.

The beginnings of a headache prowled around the edges of his skull, and he built his textbooks into a defensive wall on the edge of his desk, put his head on his hands and went to sleep.

*

Later that evening, when the family dinner had been served and cleared and there was nothing to do but to retreat to his room and 'study', Charles opened his window, climbed out and sat on the ledge. He took out his violin, lifting it to his chin, feeling the bow balance in his hands, and fiddled a Bach partita to the suburban lawns of Roundhay. And when he played, when he poured out his soul to the flaming June air, Charles was no longer himself, no longer the lonely ten-year-old who made up friends to play with, no longer the twelve-year-old who was sent away to school and cried himself to sleep, no longer the twenty-two-year-old who had returned in disgrace to a house that he hated. When he played, he was something other, something that reached, something that did not disappoint.

This became the pattern of his days: he would play his violin till late, sleep a little, or sometimes not at all, then take himself to the library, where he would doze, textbooks unopened, and catch up on the sleep lost to practice in the night. If he focused only on the matter and the moment in hand, life was tolerable, but if he looked ahead, the future closed upon him like claws. He would fail to improve his exam results – this much seemed certain. What then?

Then there was the question of money. His allowance had not been much, but now there was nothing, nothing for a magazine subscription, or a concert ticket, none of the myriad inexpensive things that made a man's life tolerable.

He began to read the newspapers in the library, taking particular interest in the advertisements for jobs, copying out the names of those that took his fancy. *Circus Performers Wanted!* (he circled the exclamation mark, which seemed to encompass a world of adventure and risk) or *Trainee Pastry Chef.*

He drew stick figurines of himself in costume in the margins of his notes: dressed as a ringmaster, or in one of those outlandish chef's hats. But often the jobs he came across conjured futures even more depressing and constrained than his own: countless clerk's appointments – a desk among many other dusty desks, men bent over ledgers, totting up columns till the day they died. Nonetheless, he would mark the rate of pay and imagine how it would be to have money, making lists in the margins of his notebooks of the things he would do:

1. Visit London once a month.
2. Attend Pearson's public lectures.
3. Stay in a hotel, and visit the Wigmore Hall.
4. Never set foot in a lecture theatre again.

Then, one hazy morning in high summer, when he was one of the only people left amongst the stacks, and the dust the only moving thing, his eye was caught by a few spare lines:

> *Nursing Staff. Both male and female.*
> *Able to play an instrument.*
> *Sharston Asylum.*

The rate of pay was meagre, but it was more than his father had ever given him, and food, accommodation and uniform, as well as a 'beer allowance', were included in the sum. They were looking for people to start immediately, holding an open interview in Leeds the following week.

Charles launched himself from his seat and, once home, took the stairs two at a time, locked himself into his bedroom and practised his fiddle for five hours straight.

In the waiting room at his interview were two men and one woman, their clothes patched many times over: the working poor. He waited a fervid hour, during which the sounds of warbling alto voices and honking clarinets escaped from the room next door, and when his turn came, sat nervously before three pale-faced and serious men. He began to tell them the story of his education, of University College, of becoming a doctor but not quite doctor enough, until one of them, a man with a shockingly bulbous nose, waved his hand to silence him, as if all of that were of no consequence at all.

'Thank you, Dr Fuller.' He spoke in a thick Yorkshire accent. 'That will be fine. Now, if you wouldn't mind fiddling us a waltz.'

Charles stared, then coughed. 'Certainly, sir.' He bent to his case and, bringing his violin beneath his chin, played them a few bars of Strauss.

The men exchanged looks. They asked him for another. He gave them a little Morelly. They offered him a job on the spot. 'But with your skills, Dr Fuller, we feel Second Assistant Medical Officer will be closer to the mark.'

His mother cried at his leave-taking, chin wobbling over the tight collar of her dress, handkerchief bunched in her hand. 'It is a terrible place. I have heard stories of its horrors for years . . .'

And yet. Sitting here now, with the wind outside, Charles smiled.

His mother had been wrong.

Nothing could have prepared him for the splendour of that first view. He had approached from the south along the main drive, the curve of Rombald's Moor rising to the west, and the buildings appeared before him like something from a dream, so wide his eyes could not encompass them all at once, hewn from the same gritstone as the Yorkshire mills, but the whole, with its turreted outline and its bell tower ten storeys high, seeming more like a fairy-tale castle or a vast country house.

It was high summer, and the beds were fringed with lavender, bursting with roses in fullest bloom. Men were dotted evenly over the grass, working on their hands and knees. At first sight they seemed to be gardeners, but the attendants standing close and watching showed them to be patients. Charles studied their faces with fascination as he walked up the drive; there were some who appeared ill but many more who seemed possessed of their faculties and who nodded and smiled politely as he passed. The front door was large and freshly painted, with a single day bell set into the wall. It was answered by a hall porter dressed in morning coat and watch chain, cravat and enormous tie-pin, who bowed from the waist and enquired in a sonorous voice, 'What is your business, sir?'

He made himself known and thence began a tour of the asylum, to which the porter made a most knowledgeable and agreeable guide. The scale of the place was staggering – corridors of which Charles could barely see the end ('The finest example of the broad arrow system, sir'). A cool room devoted entirely to bacon, one to milk and one to cheese ('We have our own flock of Ayrshire Heifers, you'll see them when you visit the farms'). A room for the preparation of vegetables ('six hundred acres in all') and one filled with hanging meat ('our own slaughterhouse'). One filled with the sweet, yeasty scent of loaves upon loaves of bread ('all of the corn and all of the wheat come straight from our fields'). Kitchens with ovens that were themselves twice the size of his mother's scullery; a butler's pantry; a china closet; a library; special rooms for the assistant medical officers to take their meals; finely appointed ones for the medical superintendent and the other doctors to receive patients in; and a committee room, twenty by thirty feet across.

'*How* many staff are there?'

'One superintendent, sir. Four assistant medical officers. Four second assistants like yourself. One hundred and seventy nurses and attendants, and eighteen administrative staff.'

Then, on to the patients' quarters ('all the wards face the south'), the men's day rooms, the wards ('eleven of them'), the vast dining rooms.

'And how many male patients have we . . . ?'

'About a thousand, sir.'

'And the women?'

'More or less the same.'

Washing rooms for patients led from the wards, with four baths in each, fully plumbed WCs and marbled washstands with brass taps ('The water is all from our reservoir, sir. Spring fed').

Not only was the scale astonishing, but the detail was remarkable: the miles of corridor half-tiled and dadoed. ('Burmantofts faience, sir, you see, the glazed terracotta tiles? World famous, but made in Leeds'). Polished oak used for skirting boards and doorframes, the vaulted ceilings of the corridors studded with skylights, and, in the entrance hall, an exquisite mosaic floor tiled with marble ('Specially imported from Carrara. I believe that's in Italy, sir'). And, then, sitting at the dead centre of the asylum, forming, in so many ways, Charles had come to feel, its *heart*, something entirely unexpected: a magnificent ballroom, a hundred and fifty feet long and fifty feet wide, with a stage at one end.

Fine stained glass was set in the sixteen high, arched windows. Birds and brambles painted upon it. Summer light pooled upon the sprung wooden dance floor. Above, an arcaded gallery stretched the length of the room; the ceiling, gently curved, was panelled with gold.

'And all this, for the *patients*?'

'For the patients, sir, yes.' The man's voice rang with pride.

Charles was dumbfounded. It hardly seemed possible.

By the time he reached his quarters and was left alone, he had walked for miles, his feet were aching, and he was almost ready to collapse. The room he was taken to that first day was the room he sat in now: spartan enough but lacking nothing of necessity, and as he touched his hand to the coarse regulation coverlet on the bed, Charles was filled with an overwhelming sense of relief. He had escaped his family. Wrested the rudder of his life from his father's hands.

And now here he was, five years later, first assistant medical officer, with a salary of five pounds a week, and newly appointed bandmaster and head of music. It had been his first action in his new post to institute a programme of pianism in the day rooms: an hour a week in each, carried out by himself. He believed he was already seeing a positive effect amongst the patients. He had great plans for the orchestra too; under his care he was determined to see the ballroom thrill and live as never before.

Charles stood, brought out the *Call for Papers* from his pocket, smoothed it out and placed it on the desk, weighting it down with his moorland stone.

Patience.

There was something coming; he felt it. A chance, perhaps, to take his place in the pantheon of superior men.

Ella

ON THE SECOND DAY, when the small room was filled with pale morning light, footsteps stopped outside her door. Ella pulled herself up from where she had been lying. Her legs were stiff. She had hardly slept.

'Ella Fay? Come with us.'

She tried to remember their steps, tried to fix the route they were taking in her mind: along the dark underground corridor, past the doors with holes in them, then upstairs into the greenish light. Down another corridor, with high, strutted ceilings above, but soon they passed through too many doors to count. It was hard to walk. Several times she tripped, but the nurses caught her before she fell, yanking her straight, pinching and nipping at her skin. Eventually they reached the room she had been in that first night, the ranged beds empty of women now. Only a small group were there, hunched on hands and knees, scrubbing the floor. She was marched past them, into a side room where four baths stood, one of which was half filled with water.

The nurses moved behind her, unlacing her ties with quick, hard fingers and pulling the jacket up and away.

Ella fell forward, sinking to her knees, her arms heavy and useless at her sides. They did not seem to belong to her. She cried out at the strangeness of it all.

'Take off your clothes.' The Irish nurse dragged her to her feet.

'I can't move my arms.'

'Here.' The nurse leant forward and unbuttoned her dress with rough fingers. It fell, pooling heavy on the floor. Her stays and petticoat were yanked up and over her head and her knickers pulled down, and she was made to stand, arms hanging, shivering in her nakedness, the vinegar smell of her body sharp on the air.

'Get in then.'

Hunched over herself, Ella stepped into the water. It was warm around her heels.

The nurse made an irritated sound. 'All the way. You won't get clean standing like that.'

She managed to crouch down.

'Ten minutes,' said the nurse. 'And make sure you use the soap.'

Her heels clattered back over the tiles. Ella stared after her. The door did not seem to be locked behind her, but that way led only back to the ward. Ahead of her the windows were large but covered with bars.

She inched gradually further into the bath, flexing her swollen fingers in the warmth, gritting her teeth against the pain. Bit by bit she stretched herself out. She looked down, curious; she had never seen herself like this before. Her legs were filmed with grime, and there were cuts on her knees where she had fallen, from which blood curled through the water like thin red smoke. The rest of her skin was white, blue nearly, something made in the dark and meant to

56

stay there. Where her legs met her body, her hair floated, a black river plant in the water. On her upper arms were the purple-brown smears of bruises. She reached her fingers to her cheek, wincing as she touched the swollen skin.

Beyond the windows was green, mucky-dark in the low winter light, but green all the same. Hills in the distance, covered by a thin haar of mist. She stared out at the green, not moving for a long time, and the water had grown cold and scurfy by the time the nurse came back.

'Hurry up. You've to put this on.'

The woman carried a uniform with writing on the pocket. Ella knew what it said. *Sharston Asylum.*

It was hard to dress with the feeling not yet back in her arms. The nurse watched, impatient, then pushed her hands away and stepped in to button the jacket herself. The clothes were clean but faded and soft with use, and Ella wondered how many people had worn them before her.

The nurse bent to shove her feet into cramped boots, then, 'Sit down,' she said, pulling out a needle and thread from her apron. 'This will hurt.'

Ella bit the inside of her cheek as the needle passed through her skin. But the woman was quick at least.

'How long?' she said, when the nurse was done.

'Till what?' Standing again now, the nurse yanked Ella's collar into place.

'How long till I leave?'

The nurse lifted her upper lip. Her teeth were grey. 'Depends. Most get moved. Chronic ward. And then you stay there.'

No.

Not me.

57

She was taken to a room and the nurse stood by while a man pushed her down into a chair from which straps hung on either side. When she was strapped in, he went and stood behind a camera, which blinded her with a sudden burst of light.

Back in the ward, five women were on their hands and knees, scrubbing. Ella looked, but Clem wasn't amongst them.

'Take this.' The nurse pointed to a brush beside a bucket.

She did as she was ordered, dropping to her knees and joining the line. It was hard to grip the brush, but she wet it, bending her head and setting to scrubbing till the floor around her knees had darkened with damp. She could feel the nurse standing behind her watching. But she knew what she was doing, knew how to be good, knew how to work hard, and after a while the nurse went away.

After dinner, they were shunted together into the day room, which was painted brown; the windows had bars, and it had a thick reasty stink to it, even worse than the ward. In the far corner was a piano and a thin yellow bird in a cage. Fires were lit in the grates, but they were covered with a padlocked guard. Clem was there though, and Ella felt a small lift at the sight of her, sitting by the piano bent over a book.

Close to where Ella sat someone was muttering. *'My head. Head is boiling. My head is boiling, my head, my head.'* The speaker kept reaching up to pluck at herself. Patches of her scalp were so bald they shone. In her lap lay a tangled bird's nest of hair.

One woman stood before her chair, gaze fixed on a

point just ahead of her, arms and hands making the same movements over and over again. Ella's eyes passed over her and then were pulled back. She watched the woman reaching out – plucking the fibres to test the strength of the thread. She was performing the actions of a spinner at the mill. Forward and back. Forward and back. Searching for the broken threads. Watching the thick, fluffy wool get thinner and thinner, till your eyes couldn't see straight any more.

'Why are you here then?'

She turned. On the other side of her sat an older, ill-thriven woman with greasy hair like rags. A red mark stained the side of her cheek. She had a small table in front of her and appeared to be sorting coloured beads into different piles: red, yellow, green.

'I smashed a window,' said Ella. 'Why're you?'

'I took a gill of ammonia.' The woman spoke in a thin and listless way. 'I felt like someone else.'

I felt like someone else. It made a sort of sense.

'Who've you got?' the woman said.

'What do you mean?'

'Outside? To ask for you? I've got my girls. My girls'll come and get me soon.'

Ella shrugged.

'Careful then.' The woman left off what she was doing and leant closer. 'You don't want to go in with the gawbers. You only go out feet first. If no one comes for you, they put you in the ground in a hole with five others. No name. And that's where they kill them. They kill the babbies in there.'

The woman's eyes had changed; they were glassy and dead now, like the fish at James St Market when they'd been left out too long.

The chair beside Clem was still empty, and Ella stood and crossed swiftly towards it. 'Can I sit here?'

Clem looked up, eyes distant, then, 'If you like,' she said, before turning back to her book.

Ella watched her read a moment, then, 'I went downstairs,' she said.

Clem didn't respond.

'They put me in a room with a window, there were—'

'Two holes in the door.' Clem put a finger to her place and looked up. 'I know. You weren't there for very long though, were you?'

'A day and a night.' Ella bridled.

'Yes, well. Like I said. Not very long.'

Clem looked away again. As she lifted her hand to turn a page, Ella caught a glimpse of her wrist, where red marks, like scratches, crosshatched her skin. As though she felt her watching, Clem pulled down her sleeve and covered them up.

Later in the afternoon, the doctor appeared, and a stillness came over the room at his entrance, the chelping chorus of women quietening to a low, anxious hum. He spoke to the nurses, extending his finger every so often to point at one or two of the women, *What about her?* he seemed to be saying, *or her?* And the nurses would nod and smile or shake their heads and say something back.

He began moving around the patients then, asking them brief questions, feeling their necks, noting things down in his book. When he reached their side of the room, he spoke to Clem. 'Reading again, Miss Church?'

Clem nodded as a small red flush clambered up the side of her neck.

'Be careful.' The doctor wagged his finger. 'Or one day you might never come out of those books.'

Clem seemed about to say something back, but his gaze moved quickly on to Ella. 'Miss Fay.' The man frowned. 'I hope you're feeling calmer now.'

Ella's heart was drumming, but she copied the way Clem sat, putting her hands in a quiet fold in her lap, sitting a little straighter in her chair.

He eyed her for a long moment, then, 'Good,' he said. 'Very good.' He scratched out some notes and pocketed the book. 'Time for a little music, I think,' and he moved to the piano, where he seated himself with his back to the room and lifted the lid.

Music came, gentle at first, pooling out from the instrument and lapping at where they sat. Then the doors to the ward opened and two male attendants appeared: short and stocky, poured tight into their jackets. They were the men who had brought her here.

'Who are they?' She turned to Clem, whose head was up; she was watching them too.

'They've come to take people to the chronic ward.'

'Who goes in there?'

Clem shrugged, but there was a new tightness to her voice. 'We don't know till they go.'

On the other side of the room Old Germany, her hair still in bunches, rose from her seat, making her way with determined steps to the middle of the floor. At first Ella thought that she was offering herself up to be taken, but then the old lady closed her eyes and began to sway, hands fluttering like two small birds at her chest. She was dancing. Dancing to the piano.

The men were making their way towards where they

were sitting. Ella's stomach clenched, but they passed her by, heading instead to a small woman with short-cropped hair, sitting shrunken in her chair with her face screwed tight. The music from the piano grew in volume. The men bent down, and the woman began to cry, softly, calling for her mother as she was hauled from her chair.

Old Germany's movements were larger now, limbs lifting and falling, lifting and falling, turning on the spot.

The men came back, and the nurses pointed to the spinner. The men lifted her, and she yelped like an animal, twisting to be free: 'They'lltekemestomachapart. There'sapartitionthere. That'sit. Where they get in. That's where the spirits get in.'

Raw fear flashed in the woman's eyes as she was carried past.

The music finished when the men were gone, the sound of it still trailing in the air as a thin spatter of handclaps came from the top of the room.

'Thank you, Doctor.' It was the Irish nurse. 'That was gorgeous. Wasn't it just gorgeous, everybody?'

'Chopin,' said Clem under her breath, shooting the woman a murderous look. '"Raindrop". Not that you'd know.'

The doctor stood, gathered his music, then gave the room a funny little bow. Somewhere in the distance a clock struck three. Ella looked down. Deep marks gouged her palm where her fingernails had dug into the skin. How long had she been here for? She looked up and around the room: at Clem, deep in her book; at women plucking at themselves, women staring into space.

Panic sent its dark root deep inside her.

John

THE WEATHER CHANGED – rain slamming in off the moors
and pelting the windows so there was no outside work to
be done, not even the digging of graves, and they were
shut up in the day room with the dark-painted walls that
swallowed the light.

He stayed in his corner, as far away from the others as
he could get. In this long, thin day room there was a rule:
the far-gone ones were wheeled in each morning and set in
one half, where they stayed for the rest of the day. Ruins of
men, faces eaten by disease, many of whom did not know
their own names. As the day wore on, the smell in the
room thickened: sweat and tobacco, and the heavy linger
of those who could not look after themselves. It made your
eyes smart. Clagged up the back of your throat.

There was a line in the middle of the floor, invisible, but
stronger than any painted in tar, and those on John's side
would not cross it, not even if a billiard ball had fallen from
the table and rolled away. On this side, stretching from the
middle fireplace, were the rest of them. Not so bad as the
others, perhaps, but that was not saying much. There was
the old soldier who talked only of the Pashtun and spent
hours attempting to blacken his boots to be ready for battle.
A toothless old-timer named Foreshaw, of whom it was
said he had been in there since the place opened, almost
thirty years ago, and that he had once drunk the blood of a
sheep. A scattering of Irishmen, one of whom, by the slant
of his accent, could only have been from the same side of
Mayo as John himself. And though John did not know the
man from before, he knew the brokenness on his face, the
restless eyes – as though the world were a trap ready to

spring upon you – had seen it on too many faces to count. And on most of them too, the same bafflement, as though unable to understand that this was where they had ended up.

He did not look at any of them if he could help it, not on either side of the room, staying in his corner by the canary instead. It was darker here, quieter. He always tucked a bit of bread from breakfast in his pocket for the bird. Close to where he sat was a shelf of books, some old newspapers, a worn-out billiard table, a few cues with no tips, and a piano that no one ever really touched.

John turned the pages of the papers; they were days old, and the leaves were crispy, but it was something to do, even if there was nothing there he wished to know about: old football matches, Ireland, a Fenian murder not five miles from where he grew up. He knew the family name. He pushed the paper away.

'Tell us again, Dan.' John looked up, saw Joe Sutcliffe speaking. He was a new one in there, young and skinny with a tremble on him like a sapling in a high wind. 'Tell us about the running girl.'

'Oh, she was a beauty all right.' Dan was standing in the middle of the room, feet planted wide, holding forth to a small clutch of men. 'She came towards us so fast I thought she might fly. Long hair like snakes around her head. First thing I thought was she was a Spanish *dona*. Or an Irish queen. Isn't that right, John lad?'

John said nothing; they didn't need stoking from him.

As the day wore on and the weather did not lift, the men played cards, hunched over the folding table in the middle of the room, betting for tobacco, or matches, or both. The assistants turned a blind eye as Dan shuffled and dealt the stained old deck, the cards rifling from his fingers. From where he sat, John saw what the others did not: saw the cards tucked up Dan's sleeves, ready to be brought out for a royal flush.

Occasionally, after much cajoling, John would join in for a brief hand or two. While they played, they smoked. They smoked as if they were paid to do it; they ripped the old well-thumbed books to shreds to use as papers. They smoked their tobacco packets down to the last crumb and then they traded for more.

On Thursday, the doctor visited the ward, making his way around the patients, and then, when he had done with touching necks and taking pulses, came back over to John's corner of the room. 'Dark old spot you've chosen here.' The man thrust his hands in his pockets, staring out at the rain splaying itself against the window. He looked at John sideways. 'What's the name again?'

'Mulligan.'

'Mulligan. Ah. Yes. I remember now. Do you like music, Mr Mulligan?'

'Well enough.'

'Well enough.' He gave a smile. 'Well. That will do for me.' He sat himself at the piano, pausing with his fingers above the keys before lowering his hands to play.

As the music began, many of the men turned their heads towards it. A stillness seemed to come over the far-gone ones on the other side of the room. The card players put down their cards and leant back in their chairs.

John closed his eyes. Behind them was a road, curving through hills.

Morning.

Rain stopping. Clouds shifting and the sun sliding free. The gorse singing yellow after the rains.

He breathed in the scent of the wide sky, the road. And when the music came to a stop, he stayed where he was, eyes shut, wrapped in the feel of it still.

'Are you feeling all right, Mr Mulligan?'

He opened his eyes. No road. Only the end of all roads. Only this room, and these men. Only the doctor, sitting in his seat before the piano, looking over at him, a small smile about his face.

'Schubert,' the doctor murmured. 'Impromptu, G flat major. It often has a similar effect on me.'

By Friday evening, though the rain was still lashing against the windows, the mood in the day room lifted, because tonight, as every Friday, there would be a dance. Two hours in the ballroom, and those that had behaved during the week and not cheeked the staff and eaten all their food and could stand on their own two feet and put one in front of the other and keep their hands to themselves were allowed to go.

By half past six the usual commotion had started up. The men on John's side disappeared off to the washrooms, and when they came back they had scrubbed faces and hair spat on and smoothed down. You could taste their excitement, thick and sticky, filling the air and leaving room for little else. It disturbed the far-gone ones on the other side, who got restless in their chairs and moaned and shouted out. John sat himself in the corner and took small, shallow breaths, trying not to let it in; it was a terrible dangerous contagion, hope.

Someone came up behind him, rubbing his cheek on his, and John jumped back, lifting his hand, ready to strike.

'Whoa there,' Dan laughed as he moved around to John's front. 'You all right there, lad? It's only a bit o' cheek. Smooth as a baby's arse that.' He took John's knuckles and rubbed them against his skin. 'Took the best part of half an hour: *Riley's bristles*. You could melt them to make iron.' His eyes were glittering. He smelt of soap.

'Will she be there, Dan? The running girl?' It was Joe Sutcliffe speaking, sidling shyly up to the pair of them. 'Will she be there then?'

'Aye, lad. Reckon she might. You ever danced the lancers, John?' Dan clapped his hands together, banging out a rhythm with his heel on the floor. Several of the men laughed and began clapping along, and Dan was off, scooping up Sutcliffe and hauling him at a racketing pace around the billiard table, until one of the attendants had to grapple him to a stop. 'Any more of that, Mr Riley, and you'll be given the long sleeves.'

By a quarter to six they were all lined up, pushing and jostling for space like schoolboys, holding their palms out for the attendants to check. Old Foreshaw was there, standing proud, a smart blue tie tight at his chin. Dan beside him, with Sutcliffe on the other side, the young man's eyes popping with excitement, elbows sharp, hands jiggling in his pockets. 'Not coming then, *mio Capitane*?' Dan yelled over.

John made a gesture: no. Dan knew he never went.

'Good,' crowed Dan, clapping the backs of the men on either side. 'You stay here with the rest of the *meshigeners*. We don't want you spoiling our chances, do we, lads?' He took Sutcliffe under one of his arms and knuckled his scalp.

Then they were gone, their voices fading down the corridor and the air empty and hanging. John the only man left on his side. It was like this every Friday. The other men jiggled and gibbered a bit, and then settled back to whatever sort of nothing they were doing before.

He stood, going to the window to look out, but only his face came back to him, blurred and shadowed in dark and rain. *The ballroom.* He had gone there once, when he didn't know what was what. A vast space with eight fires roaring and a band up on the stage. And women. That had been a surprise.

Was the running girl there then? Or was she downstairs? She'd have to have been put there after a stunt like that. He had been downstairs himself – a long white corridor and rooms off it, tiny cells the size of a man, only a blanket and a bucket inside, and a lone high window, impossible to reach.

He felt it again, standing there, the soaring that had filled him when he saw her run and the ashy bitter feeling when she fell. The furious face she had, the swollen eyes. She was no beauty, but a fierce, frightened girl.

But she had been right, at least, not to take his hand. He was not the man to help her. He would only have pulled her further into the bog.

He went over to the canary's cage, calling to the bird with a low clucking sound, fiddling in his waistcoat pocket for a piece of bread, breaking it into crumbs and then holding them to the thin space between the bars. The bird hopped over and nipped from his hand. He felt the scratch of its beak, brief against his fingertip. The bird's black eye was bright, but there was something listless about him. He hadn't heard him sing for days.

Charles

As THE MUSICIANS FILED out of the mess room, Charles hurried to catch up with Goffin. 'Well done,' he said, as he came alongside him. 'You made a fine fist of that!'

'Oh. Thank you! Was it really all right?'

'Rather,' Charles averred.

In truth, Goffin's playing had been a little strident on the top notes and had squeaked terribly on the national anthem at the end of the night, but on the whole the chap had done a good job.

'Well – thanks,' Goffin gave him a flash of that sweet smile, 'for giving me the chance, I mean. It's an honour to play with a musician as talented as yourself.'

Charles gave a brief shrug – *nothing to it* – but the compliment bloomed in his chest as he and Goffin walked in companionable silence across the grass towards the Barracks. 'So, how are you finding it? This old place, I mean? Been keeping you busy, have they?'

'Just a bit.' Goffin grinned, holding the door open for Charles. 'They're a good bunch though. Although the weather's a little . . . bleak.' He grimaced as he shut the door behind him and they began to climb the stairs.

'Ah, the moors! Not what you're used to?'

'Not so much.'

'Well, I'm glad you're settling in. Lucky to have you, I say.'

They had reached their respective doors now. 'Well,' said Charles, 'see you tomorrow then.'

Once inside his room, Charles put down his violin and music case and slid his post on to the desk. His head felt pleasantly warm and muzzy – it was always like this after the dances: a sort of glad tiredness that came from long playing, from the companionship of the other players. After the last patient had left the ballroom, there was always a late meal laid waiting in the attendants' mess room: bread and cheese and jugs of ale, and although he could easily have requested a cold supper to be put out for him in the assistant medical officers' dining room, Charles always preferred to take beer and break bread with the men. He was not much of a drinker, but a glass or two of ale was always a pleasant way to round off the evening's work.

He shed his jacket, unlaced his bow tie and unplucked his cufflinks; he always made an effort with his dress on a Friday night and expected his players to do the same.

The week, which had started so badly, had ended rather well; his leadership of the band seemed to be progressing favourably, and the musicians seemed happy enough. Since the meeting with Superintendent Soames he had been careful, working harder at his ordinary duties so he might carve out the time to play for the patients, and the programme already seemed to be bearing fruit – the other day, for instance, he had been playing the Schubert G flat when Mulligan, an Irish chronic, had brought his chair forward to listen. When Charles had finished playing, there was a look on the man's face that was . . . well, beyond words really.

A new charcoal portrait stood on the mantelpiece. Charles went to pick it up: Mulligan, in the moments after the Schubert. The likeness was not bad. The Mulligan on the paper was one anyone would recognize: square-shouldered, slim but well muscled. The hair close cropped to a finely shaped skull, a steady brow, eyes the colour of flint. But the man's expression – its very inscrutability – had eluded him.

Having not been the admitting doctor, Charles knew little of the particulars of the case. He had a mind to check the man's admission papers as soon as possible, see what had landed him in here. He placed the portrait carefully back on the mantelpiece then went to his desk, where he shuffled through his post. A slim brown envelope with a London postmark lay within the pile. Taking his letter knife he sliced quickly through the card, and felt a pleasurable quckening as a light-green pamphlet fell into his hands. *The Eugenics Review.*

It was always a treat when the quarterly arrived. A glance at the clock showed it was after ten, but Saturday mornings meant a slightly later start. Plenty of time still for reading. He brought his chair up to his desk and sharpened a pencil, before bringing his notebook towards him. As he opened the pamphlet, a coal popped and cracked on the fire.

The first of the articles was a tribute to Sir Francis Galton, first cousin of Charles Darwin and erstwhile president of the Society, who had died last month at the age of ninety-three. Pearson had always hailed Galton as the man who had taken his cousin's findings and applied them to society; the man who dared to pose the question of how better people might be made. After due observance of Galton's polymath genius (explorer, meteorologist, statistician), the end of the piece looked forward to Major Leonard Darwin's forthcoming presidency. Another scion of the Darwin line, the great man's son this time; he was due to give his inaugural address in the summer. Charles scribbled the date eagerly in his notebook. It had been far too long since he had visited London, and this would be a happy hook to hang a trip on. He was allowed seven holiday days a year and had taken none so far. He would have to make sure to book the day off soon.

Aside from the usual calendar of meetings and talks, the main body of the journal was taken up by the transcript of Dr Tredgold's recent address to the society at the Caxton Hall in London, rather grandly entitled 'Eugenics and Future Human Progress'.

Charles knew Tredgold had been the chief doctor of the Royal Commission of 1908. It had been reported in *The Times* that Dr Tredgold's findings on the matter of the Feeble-Minded had been passed to Parliament, and as such would be vital in shaping the debate over the coming bill.

Tredgold's argument began simply but was elegantly and persuasively expressed.

Man today stands on a much higher plane of development than did his palaeolithic ancestor. The human race has undergone a progressive evolution . . . If the race is to develop, it must give rise to individuals who can do more than mark time, who can advance.

Charles nodded in agreement. It would be a fool who would seek to refute it.

Tredgold went on to argue that, throughout this evolution, disease had played a vital part in 'purifying the race of its weaker members', but that now:

I have no hesitation in saying, from personal experience, that nowadays the degenerate offspring of the feeble-minded and chronic pauper is treated with more solicitude, has better food, clothing and medical attention, and has greater advantages than the child of the respectable and independent working man. So much is this the case that the people are beginning to realize that thrift, honesty, and self-denial do not pay.

Charles shifted in his chair. Such rhetoric always made him uncomfortable; *feeble-minded and chronic paupers* were the mainstay of Sharston's ranks, and they did indeed have good food, clothing and medical attention; what man living in the crowded backstreets of Bradford had his milk from a flock of specially selected Ayrshire heifers, ate fresh meat and vegetables with his supper most evenings and was played classical music as he rested for the afternoon? But the asylum was not a prison; the aim of its treatment was not punitive but restorative.

He glanced over at his charcoal sketches, catching the eyes of Mulligan. Shouldn't a man like Mulligan be treated with *solicitude*? Shouldn't he hear and respond to Schubert? Wasn't there *potential* in the man? And then there were the dances; if he closed his eyes he could see the ballroom as it had looked this evening – the fireplaces lit and blazing, the orchestra – aside from the odd squeak from Goffin – sounding fine, but suggestive of greater things to come, the patients clapping and smiling and turning together on the floor. If the good burghers of Bradford and Leeds had not wanted their pauper lunatics to have some pleasure and – yes, why not say it – *beauty* in their lives, would they have built such a magnificent space for them to meet?

He turned back to the pamphlet, where Tredgold's argument was reaching its crescendo:

The stream of degeneracy is steadily increasing, and is threatening to become a torrent which will swamp and annihilate the community. It is quite clear that we are face to face with a most serious problem, one, indeed, of vital importance, not merely to our future progress, but to our very existence.

So. Here was the nub of it. And while absolutely seeing the problem – Sharston itself was bursting at the seams with the poor and mad – Charles was not so sure of the means by which to address it.

It seemed certain that the feeble-minded should be prevented from breeding. But how to proceed from this – how to define that category and how to go about that prevention – was something about which Charles was unsure. It was the idea of enforcement that sat uneasily with him.

The sexes could easily be kept apart in the sort of gentle segregation that was practised at Sharston, and while here they could, perhaps, with the help of good food, good behaviour and good, honest work (not to mention good music), *improve*. Become better specimens.

In truth, Charles thought, it came down to this: one either believed people could change or one did not. And Charles was, by nature, an optimistic man.

He glanced back at the *Review*:

I unhesitatingly affirm that if measures of social reform are not accompanied by others to prevent the alarming multiplication of the unfit which is now going on, the end will be National Disaster.

Charles let out his breath in an irritated sigh; there was something so *joyless* in the man's rhetoric. He tapped the end of his pencil on the desk. The Eugenics movement was split between those who believed in sterilization and those who argued for the merits of segregation, and here was the chief doctor of the Royal Commission, the man who had the ear of the Prime Minister and of Home Secretary Churchill, who, while he did not come right out and declare for sterilization, did all but.

Charles stood and went to his window, hands thrust into his pockets. In the small wood that bordered the buildings, tall trees waved their branches to the moon. Soon, although spring came slowly to these moors, they would be coming into leaf. Beyond the wood lay the farms that would provide food for the thousands within these walls. Soon, it would be time for planting – six hundred glorious acres of self-sufficiency.

He knew that Churchill had recently given a speech in Parliament on the idea of labour colonies for mental defectives. Well, Sharston was a labour colony by any other name. What if Charles might have Churchill's ear?

He glanced over to the *Call For Papers*, lying where he had left it.

Call For Papers
First International Eugenics Congress
Subjects of Wide Importance and Permanent Interest.

Tredgold needed answering.

He bent over his notebook and scribbled:

One of the main arguments against Segregation is expense, Tredgold's 'taxed and taxed heavily', but the amount needed to keep Sharston going, contrasted with other such institutions (schools and hospitals for instance), is negligible – testament to the self-sufficiency wherewith the patients are employed in growing their own food, caretaking their own cattle and washing their own clothes. At present our death rate is high, running at around 15 per cent. The more men we get out into the fields, the healthier our population will be.

The patients here are a ready-made workforce, one that finds its therapy, moreover, in the good and honest work it does. In the future, there could be more farms like Sharston's – more patients put to work, an excess produced. We already produce enough meat to sell on to local butchers – imagine if enough meat and vegetables were produced to feed half of Bradford and Leeds!

It is clear from the shortest of my walks in the villages hereabouts that the countryside economy is shrinking – anyone with anything about them is eager to move to the towns. Let us then give over these jobs to our pauper lunatics! Let us do so in great and greater numbers! Let us see our countryside flourish again!

(N.B. The root of the word Eugenics comes from the Greek, meaning of noble birth. Is it not most noble, indeed, to work towards the highest good for all?)

Charles read back with mounting exhilaration – yes, there was something there. He particularly liked the last sentence. He underlined it, and as he did so a thought slid into his head.

He *would* write a paper for the Congress.

He would write such a paper that he would convince Superintendent Soames, and Dr Tredgold, and Churchill, and all of the others, that sterilization was unnecessary – that there was another way, a way that did not tax the ratepayer too greatly, and that, moreover, allowed for the possibility of improvement: of culture, of music, of – yes – *joy*, why not say it, in the lives of the pauper lunatics in their care.

He scrabbled in his drawer, brought out writing paper and an envelope and then, flipping back through the pages of the *Review*, he stopped; on the first column was the name of the secretary, a certain Dr Montague Crackanthorpe.

Dear Dr Crackanthorpe,

I was very interested to read your *Call for Papers* in the latest *Eugenics Review*. You ask for work which discusses the relative merits of Segregation and Sterilization.

I should like to put myself forward as a candidate.

If chosen, I will present on the benefits of music and segregation at Sharston Asylum in the West Riding of Yorkshire.

Yours sincerely,

Dr Charles Fuller

First Assistant Medical Officer

John

THERE HAD BEEN AN incident in the ballroom. Dan had been too boisterous, it seemed, and was confined to the day room for a week.

So John was sent out to dig with young Joe Sutcliffe instead.

The mornings were a little lighter now, and a pale-orange
strip lit the sky as they walked out towards Mantle Lane.
Sutcliffe seemed steady enough on the journey out, but as
soon as they came in sight of the graveyard, and the grave
they were to finish, he started shaking. 'How many go in
there?'

'Six,' said John.

'No.' He stood by the side of the deep hole, staring down.
'They're making me dig it. I won't do it. No.'

'What do you mean, lad?'

'The grave.' Sutcliffe pointed at the raw gouge of earth.
'It's mine. I know it. They're making me dig it. And they'll
put me in there when I've done.'

'No, lad.'

'They say you never get out.' Sutcliffe lifted his panicked
face. 'Not when you're where we are. Not on the chronics.
They say that's it. That you'll die here. That you'll get
thrown in a hole like this with people you don't know, and
no one'll find you again.'

'Come on, lad.' John put a hand out to the lad's shoulder,
felt the tremble on him, the thin bones like blades beneath
his palm. 'Calm yourself.' He climbed down into the hole.
When he held out his hand, the boy clambered awkwardly
down alongside him, but, once there, Sutcliffe stood frozen
and useless.

'Sit yerself down a while.' John gestured to the lip of the
hole. It was clear there would be no good work from him.
'I'll get on by myself all right. And it's not your grave I'm
digging, lad. I can promise you that.'

Sutcliffe hauled himself out and sat on the side of the

hole. He shoved his hands in his armpits and stared down at the earth. He looked no happier than before.

'Why don't you turn round? Look up there instead?' John pointed to the brow of the hill, the place the girl had come from when she ran.

Sutcliffe raised a grey, grateful face to him. 'Can I?'

'Aye.' John nodded. 'Do that.'

The young lad stood, turning three times on the spot, and then, like a dog fussing over its bed, set himself down on the earth, facing away. John could hear him muttering away to himself as he began to dig.

After an hour or so, when sweat was pouring down his face, and Sutcliffe had grown quiet and, from his bent head and thin, bowed back, looked as though he might have fallen asleep, a whistle blew, and the figure of Brandt appeared on the brow, swaggering down the hill.

'What's happening here?' The attendant came to stand before Sutcliffe. He kicked the lad hard in the knee. Sutcliffe sounded a frightened yelp. His face, when he raised it, was panicked, puffy with sleep.

'Get up. Go on.' Brandt kicked him again. 'Get up and get down in there.' He pulled Sutcliffe up by the elbow and shoved him backwards into the grave, where he sprawled in the dirt.

'If you don't start digging, I'll start digging,' said Brandt. 'And I'll bury you in there.'

Sutcliffe began whimpering. 'No. No. It's not for me. He promised it's not for me.'

'If you don't shut up, when you're finished I'll send you downstairs.'

'Please, no . . .' Sutcliffe gasped, pointing to John. 'He said . . . he said . . . it weren't for me.'

'What's that?' Brandt's ratty little eyes came to land on John. 'So you're giving orders, are you, Mulligan?'

John shook his head, lifted his spade, carried on with his work.

'Hey.' The man's stick thwacked him on the upper arm. 'Hey. I'm talking to you. Can you not hear? Or are you deaf as well as daft?'

Brandt crouched on his haunches, and their eyes were level. 'Do you know what?' The man had no front teeth and he hissed as he spoke. 'I've always wondered what you were in here for. What is it then? Being a stupid Irish fuck? I know you lot.' His spittle landed on John's jacket. 'You come over here. Sit on your arses. Expect to be looked after. And now you're telling people what to do?'

The man's breath stank of cheap liquor. The edges of his eyes were yellow, but their pupils were beady and black.

'Why are you never in the ballroom? Don't they have dances back in Ireland? Can't lift your feet up out of them bogs? Or is it you don't like women?'

'Aye,' said John.

'Aye you do or aye you don't?'

He said nothing more.

'Don't they teach you to speak English over there? *En-ger-lish?*' Brandt made his mouth slack, tongue hanging, like some of the men in the ward. 'En-ger-lish, you fuck.' He waved his stick in the air, as if deciding which of the two of them to beat with it. 'Tell you what,' he grinned, gesturing towards Sutcliffe, 'I'll let this lad off his trip downstairs if you say it. Say, "I'm a stupid Irish fuck." And you can dance while you do it.'

Sutcliffe had stopped his moaning. John could hear him panting like an animal behind him.

80

'Say it.'

John's hands twitched on the handle of his spade.

There was a stirring on the hill above them. A small procession coming down across the railway tracks to Mantle Lane: four men, carrying a plain coffin, and a vicar, all in a line. Brandt twisted to look and then clambered up to attention, his hat pulled off his head and held in his hand. The funeral party stopped at the unfilled grave. One of the men took the boards from it and laid them to the side, and the coffin was lowered in. John could see its pine lid peeking out. Space was tight in there; the grave was full.

The vicar looked uncomfortable, long skirts flapping in the cold and the breeze. One of the men stepped forward and put something else in the hole, a small box this time, just a foot long, and when he saw what it was, John's stomach clenched.

The vicar held his Bible, said a few words, bent for a handful of earth, which he threw on the coffin, then looked over to where the three men stood. 'Fill this in,' he said, before he turned and led the small procession back across the lane.

John took a spadeful of earth from the side of the new grave to the other and tipped it in.

'You know why they do that, don't you?' Brandt had come up behind him. His tongue rested between his missing teeth. 'Put little'uns in't bottom.' He reached down with his stick and rapped it on the wood of the smaller box. 'So as they won't be lonely.' He snorted. His mouth was a black pit when he laughed.

John moved away quickly, back to the other grave, digging a fresh load of earth.

'What about you?' Brandt called after him. 'You ever had a little'un?'

John's load rattled like sharp rain on the lid of the small wooden box. If he covered it fast enough, Brandt couldn't touch it again.

But Brandt was crouched before the grave now, rocking on his haunches. 'I always heard babbies were born in here, but I never seen one myself.'

He struck his stick, harder now, on the wood of the tiny coffin. It gave off a small dull sound. Then, tongue between his teeth, Brandt edged the end of his stick between the wood, beginning to ease it open.

John roared, launching himself towards Brandt. He grabbed him by the collar and twisted, wresting him around, bringing his face up to his. Brandt coughed, gasping for breath, hands flailing before him, face reddening from the lack of air.

'No!' Sutcliffe was behind him. Thin fists rained on his back. John let go and Brandt fell, gasping, to the earth.

John shook Sutcliffe off and knelt beside Brandt, a knee on his chest, shovel still in his hand. 'Leave the dead alone. You leave the dead alone or I'll send you to join them, I swear.'

He stood, shook himself right. Below him, Brandt curled around, gathering his breath, coming to a slow stand, hands on his knees. He spat on the coffin, and blood mingled with phlegm on the wood. He gave a low, black laugh. 'You stupid Irish cunt,' he said. 'You'll pay for that.'

That night, in the ward, Dan told a story.

It was a habit of his, when the lights were turned out. He would begin low, almost in a whisper, and everyone would fall still and listen.

Tonight it was one John had not heard before, the story

of a giant who kept a woman prisoner in his castle on the top of a hill.

'A hill, my friends, which was white with the bones of the champions who had tried in vain to rescue the fair captive.'

'At last' – Dan had a knack: he could make his voice grow, while keeping it quiet, make it travel to the four corners of the room, without waking the sleeping attendant – 'at last the hero, after hewing and slashing at the giant, but all to no purpose, discovered the only way to kill him.'

Dan paused, and in it John heard the soft breathing of the listening men around him.

'And this was to rub a scar on the giant's left breast with a certain egg, which was in a pigeon, which was in a hare, which was in the belly of a wolf, which dwelt in the wild lands many thousand leagues from here . . . And so what do you think the hero did? He found that egg, and slew the giant, merely by striking it against the scar on his breast.'

The men breathed out, and Dan chuckled softly to himself.

After a while, John heard the sounds of the men sliding into sleep. Soon Dan was snoring too. But John lay on his back, staring up at the dark above him.

He did not want to sleep. Knew what was waiting for him there: a woman and a child. Dan's stories did not frighten him, neither did Brandt and his threats; it was what was inside him that did.

If he closed his eyes, she was there, just as he had seen her first. A shawl held up to a mouth, covering a smile: Annie.

Would you like to dance?

The slither of her skirt. And him rising to her, as though he had no other choice but this.

And then, a lilting tune. A slow turn. Her throat. The swell of her breasts. The brush of her cheek on his. The taste of her mouth.

Her mouth.

A woman he had thought to be refuge but discovered to be the storm itself.

And then a child, with skin like a song.

And then illness, and a tiny box.

Burying the child himself in the dark, sucking ground.

And Annie's mouth, a red wound now, framing the words. *You. Everything you touch dies.*

You're nothing.

You're no man at all.

Ella

SHE WAS MOVED TO work in the laundry – a huge grey-lit room beneath whose high ceilings women moved to and fro. Large puddles of water stood on the ground, and the stench of dirty clothes was sharpened by a harsh, chemical smell. Ella's eyes scanned the room, but, despite its size, there was only one door in and one door out. The only windows were set in the ceiling. There would be no way of reaching them.

'Go and work with her.' The nurse who had marched her there pushed her in the direction of someone who was bent over a large metal drum. 'She knows what she's doing. She'll show you what's what.'

It was Clem, sleeves rolled and face glossy with sweat. She surveyed Ella coolly through the damp air. 'Careful with your feet,' she said, as Ella picked her way over the wet ground towards her. 'You don't want to get them wet. You get all sorts of blisters and it's hell for weeks.'

The air was damp and heavy. The huge steel drum Clem was standing beside was shaking and whining. Elsewhere, women's voices were drowned by the rattle and hum of other machinery.

'So,' said Clem, raising her voice to be heard. 'There's different types of laundry in here. Clothes . . .' She turned and gestured to where linen lay in great drifts at the side of the room. 'It's our job to sort them into types: shirts, skirts, blouses, underwear. You put a mask on for that. Then there's flatwork: sheets and pillowcases. That's the stuff that really breaks your back. Here.' As the steel drum before her came to a shuddering stop, she bent and yanked open the lid. 'We put the laundry in these machines and then a bucket of soap in there too. These sheets are done, so we need to take them out and put them through the mangle. Go on then.'

Ella reached into the drum, trying to lift a sheet, but they were all cluthered together and heavy with water.

'You won't get far like that. Here.' Clem elbowed her out of the way and, reaching into the water with quick, deft hands, unravelled a sheet from the knot within. 'When you've managed to get one free, you give it a first twist.' She worked as she talked, squeezing the sheet so that grey water poured back from it into the tub. 'And then when you've done that, you carry it over here.' And she looped the still-dripping sheet over her shoulder and carried it to the other side of the room where a huge mangle stood.

The machine was about the same size as the double share Ella minded in the mill. There were even belts running around the ceiling to operate the machines. It was a factory. Not so loud as the mill, but a factory for all that. She took a corner of the sheet as Clem walked a few paces so the wet material grew taut between them.

'You feed it in between the rollers so it catches. Slowly. That's it. The next bit is dangerous. You have to make sure you've stepped back and your hair's tucked in before you make it start.'

Make sure your hair's tucked in.

Clem pulled down on a lever, the mangle started up with a shuddering movement, and Ella was eight again, watching the belts tightening, feeling her life contract. She shook her head to clear it. 'How do you stand it?' she said.

'Stand what?' Clem's eyes were fixed on the mangle as the sheet fed itself through the rollers.

'All . . . this.' Ella threw out her arm. 'Does it not make you mad?'

Clem glanced up. '*Much madness is divinest sense,*' she said, and gave a small laugh. 'There are plenty of mad women in here. I'm not sure I'm one of them though.' She shrugged. 'You'll get used to it.'

The words sank to the bottom of Ella's stomach as though she had tied them around a stone. She wanted to tell Clem she wouldn't get used to anything, not any of this, that she'd be out a long time before that, but even though the desire to speak was salting her tongue, she held it. It was safer to say nothing for a while.

Clem moved to the other side of the mangle, where the sheet was ready. 'Come on. We need to peg this lot out to dry.' She threw the sheet on top of a wicker basket, gestur-

86

ing for Ella to take the other side. The basket was heavy, but Clem lifted it with ease.

They passed into another room – this one filled with lines and lines of hanging laundry. It was hard to tell for certain, since any number of people could have been hidden behind the clothes, but for the first time, there did not seem to be any nurses watching over them.

'It's all right in here,' said Clem, as though reading Ella's thoughts. 'You're left to yourself a bit. I always make it last as long as I can.' She pulled a small book from the pocket of her apron and gave a swift half-smile. 'Sometimes I'm here for hours before they remember to look.'

It was much quieter in this white dampness, where sound seemed to be gathered by the hanging clothes. The smell was not so bad either – sharp starch and bleach, but none of the thick rammy stink of the room next door. Here, too, were only two doors that Ella could see – the one she had entered from and one at the far end of the room.

'I don't think it leads anywhere exciting,' said Clem.

Ella looked back and coloured.

'Maybe the kitchens, but you can bet it's locked. They miss nothing, you know.'

As Clem reached up to peg a sheet, Ella saw those red, ridged marks again, all the way down her wrist until they disappeared into the fabric of her blouse. They were too thin and regular for burns. The rest of Clem's hands were chapped and raw, the skin bleached and baggy, as though it had been held in water for too long. Again, as though she had caught her watching, Clem brought down her sleeve.

Ella stepped over to help her. After a moment, she spoke. 'Who are the gawbers?' she said.

'The gawbers?' Clem looked over. 'That's what the

women in here call the chronic ward. They believe that when you're on the chronic ward, you don't get out. Unless you're dead, that is.'

'But people do get out before that?'

'Yes, often enough. Look,' Clem sighed, crossing her arms and looking at Ella straight. 'There are three ways out of here. You can die. That's easy. People die all the time. You can escape. Almost impossible. Or you can convince them you're sane enough to leave.'

'Which one are you doing then?'

A quick colour flared in Clem's cheek, and she bent to pick up another sheet. 'None of them yet,' she said. 'I'm still deciding what I want.' She was silent a moment, then said, 'Where would you go then? If you got out?'

'I don't know. Away.' Ella thought of a picture she had seen once, a poster of the seaside up on the wall of the Co-op – of the green land ceasing, giving way to blue. 'The sea.'

'Have you ever seen the sea?'

Ella shook her head.

'Well, *I never saw a moor*,' said Clem. '*I never saw the sea, And yet I know how the heather looks, And what a wave should be.*'

'What's that?' asked Ella.

'Just a poem.' Clem shrugged, and bent down and swiped up the next item in the basket.

'What about you?'

'Me? University,' she said. 'And I'm going too. I'm just . . . waiting.' She held the piece of clothing out to look at. It was a man's cotton shirt, large and stained at the cuffs. 'My brother's about to go to university,' she said, 'to Cambridge, to study English. And he's so stupid he thinks Kipling is the finest poet there is. He probably thinks Dickinson is our grocer.' She looked up, a half-smile on her face. 'Well, he *is* our grocer, but that's not the point. Do you know, I said to him once, *"There's a certain slant of light. Winter afternoons. That oppresses, like the heft of cathedral tunes."* And he just stared at me like this.'

And Clem pulled such a gawping, vacant face that Ella had to laugh. 'He had no *clue* what I was talking about,' she said. 'No clue.'

Neither had Ella, but the feeling of the laugh remained, softening the air between them.

'Men,' Clem said under her breath, gazing at the garment in her hands. 'You can never get the stains out. Here.' She chucked the shirt at Ella, who caught it.

'Are there men in here then?'

'Not *here*, obviously, but on the other side of the buildings. We never see them though, apart from Fridays.'

'What happens on Fridays?'

'Don't you know? There's a dance, in a ballroom. They have a proper stage, and an orchestra, with violins and trumpets and . . . well.' Clem reached down for another shirt. 'You should see it, before you get out of here. It's all right. The doctor leads it. You know . . . the one who plays the piano.'

'How do you get there? To the ballroom? Who's allowed to go?'

'I don't really know how they choose. They call your name on a Friday, and if they call your name, then you go. Those who've been good, I s'pose.'

Be good.

Ella stretched the shirt in her arms.

*

After that, things were different between them. Not friendship perhaps, but something like it. Ella took the seat beside Clem's in the day room, and walked with her at recreation, which was hardly worth the name: half an hour every day of nantling up and down a thin stone yard – two by two like in Sunday school – with echoing walls on either side.

Otherwise, she kept her mouth shut and worked hard and watched. When she wasn't hauling sheets or feeding them into the mangle, she was in the sorting room, low-ceilinged and so filthy-smelling she had to tie a cloth over her nose and mouth just to stand it. Her hands were raw from the chemicals in the laundry, and the skin between her fingers had grown soggy and stinging and split. One of her fingernails had broken as she twisted cloth. Her feet grew so swollen from the heat and from standing all day that it was hard to take off her boots before going to bed. But she did not complain.

In the day room, in the afternoons, while Clem read her book, Ella looked out of the window.

She could see the path she had taken when she ran, across the short grass and then curving round the buildings to the left. She remembered the feel of wind on skin, running at the edge of her lungs.

On Fridays after dinner, the Irish nurse came in and rattled out a list of names of the women who were allowed to go to the ballroom, and Ella always listened, breath bated, for her own, but the weeks passed and it was never called. She saw the excitement of those who were though: donning themselves up as best they could, tugging their clothes straight, brushing at the oily white flecks that clung to their shoulders. They would help each other – standing in front of one another and acting as each other's glass. Old

90

Germany always badgered Clem till she brushed out her hair and put it up in fresh bunches for her. Often, when the women were all ready and jostling with excitement, but it was not yet quite time to go, Clem would get up and play the piano for them, just a few bars, and they would hold hands and dance on the spot.

They put her in mind of the women and girls in the mill, that same elbowing to get a glimpse in the bit of mirror at the end of the spinning shed on a Friday night, the same flashing hopefulness as they turned and patted and sucked in their cheeks, as though they were covering themselves all over with hooks that might land a catch.

She had never wanted to see herself in that mucky bit of glass. Knew what she looked like well enough, with her red and swollen eyes. Besides, even if she'd managed to make herself look nice, what would it be for? She had been out promming on Manningham Lane and Toller Lane with the rest of them in the summer, on Friday or Saturday nights – in amongst so many young people that the police had to come and shout to keep the crowds moving. Great dense girl-packs all arm-in-arm and clavering away and swooping looks at the lads. She had never walked with them though. They made her feel trapped, those packs of girls, taking up the middle of the road.

But she saw the way the attendants looked at the patients, sniggering sometimes behind their hands. She had heard the Irish nurse the other day, chattering to another in her harsh magpie voice: *Aren't they just animals? Worse than animals. Filthy, aren't they? And the way you have to watch over them all the time? Aren't they? Aren't they just?* She knew Clem was right, that people were let out of here. She had seen it for herself – the way their faces changed when they knew.

But now, sitting there in the day room as the Fridays passed, watching the women get ready, she felt afraid. Did they still think her mad?

Who would know the things inside her if she stayed in this place? She had no one to speak for her here, no creature to echo her, nothing to say who she was or might have been.

Charles

THE NEWS CAME ON a Friday, by the second post: a single letter in a thick envelope bearing a London postmark with the address 6, York Buildings, Adelphi.

When he lifted the flap, saw the name of the Society printed at the top and read the first line – *'We should be happy to accept your paper for the Eugenics Congress of 1912'* – Charles was so delighted he couldn't help himself dancing a little jig on the spot.

'All right there, Dr Fuller?' The old porter was regarding him with something approaching horror.

'Yes! Gosh – yes! Quite all right.'

Charles's first instinct was to take the letter straight to the superintendent – to see, perhaps, a glimmer of approbation on Soames's face. But he restrained himself. He was learning to be measured. It was better by far to be politic. To bide his time.

Now, his work took on a different cast. He kept a notebook on him at all times, and as he passed through the corridors and wards, scribbled down anything in thought or deed that seemed of relevance to his case.

He began to indulge in a small fantasy, and each time furnished it with a little more detail. It was this: he imagined Churchill and Pearson and Tredgold – even Superintendent Soames – sitting in the audience at the Congress as he gave his speech, listening intently, his words swaying their opinions, and afterwards Churchill approaching him, the Secretary, Dr Crackanthorpe, making the introductions: *'Home Secretary, may I introduce Dr Fuller, who has done such fine work with music with his lunatics in the north.'*

And Churchill nodding, his handshake warm, that handsome baby face of his sporting a smile. *'Interesting, Fuller. Very interesting paper. Lots to think about. We must come up your way and see for ourselves.'*

Life was hopeful; the air had lost the keen edge of winter and the evenings were getting visibly lighter now. The grass on the lawns had recently had its first mowing and felt soft and spongy underfoot. Snowdrops had come and gone, and now daffodils were pushing themselves up in great clusters from the soil. Charles had a new duty too: it was his job to escort the female patients from the acute wards to the reception room and oversee them on visiting days – Wednesday afternoons, Saturdays and Sundays. On the one hand he thought it might be a good thing – a sign the incident with the girl had faded and the superintendent was trusting him more, but on the other, it might be an attempt by Soames to weight him so heavily with work that he had no spare time. Regardless of the motives, however, it was proving to be a useful little role.

The visitors' room was a large, sparsely furnished hall just off the main administration block, and Charles always made sure to pack his notebook and pencils for these sessions; from his desk at the top of the room he had a fine view of the proceedings and was able to make copious drawings and notes. Most of the patients received visitors only rarely, and they were a sorry sight in the main, rigged up in whatever patched and over-mended black stuff constituted their Sunday best: Tredgold's Chronic Paupers to a woman and man. Sometimes they would bring small presents – a homemade cake perhaps, or if they were religious, an improving pamphlet might be passed over the table – but mostly they sat mute. Often, it was difficult to differentiate the lunatic from the visitor, but whether it was poverty or feeble-mindedness that had marked them both it was difficult to tell.

Here for instance was a young woman of twenty-five, a chronic patient – hair cropped short to her head to stop her plucking at it but still sporting scabbed patches where she had managed to pull out the shorter lengths. Opposite her sat a woman – her sister? – who looked to be of a similar age; the sister's hair, though lank and greasy, was long and at least seemed to be in place. A scruffy child played silently on the floor while the women whispered to each other. Charles estimated the depth of their respective brows as he sketched them quickly in the margins of his book. Pearson had been fascinated with the depth of the brow – had always insisted the measurement denoted the mental capacity therein.

His eye fell next on one of the female acutes – a handsome woman of forty or so. He had been her admitting doctor and could well remember the particulars of the case: ten children and the last an idiot. She had been driven mad by the boy's appearance and tried to murder him. The courts had ruled that she had not been in her right mind, and she had escaped gaol, being sent to the asylum instead. Charles was glad of it – after a month of sleep, food and time away from work and offspring, the woman looked rested and fed; well enough to return to her family. This was not unusual; many women suffered a temporary post-partum insanity. A short spell in the asylum's care and most were restored to themselves. But what would be the consequence when she was released? More children? Her husband sat opposite her now, an anxious, fretful-looking man. Here was an instance in which Tredgold's view might have some traction. If there were some ready method of birth control . . . he was sure that the women themselves might queue up to take it.

He cast his eyes further around the room; in the far corner, conspicuous amongst the mass of grey and brown and black, sat a family group of strikingly fair colouring: the father a tall, scholarly-looking man, the son stouter, fuller-figured. Charles recognized the young woman before them, a certain Miss Clemency Church, a young female acute. A private patient, as was obvious from her own clothes, today a rather fetching dress of pale spring green.

The father's low voice was sonorous and carrying, and it was impossible not to catch snippets of what he said. Talk of a school, the weather, and then, in lower tones, of a visit to a mother's grave. Miss Church nodded now and again, in a listless sort of way, but in the main did not move, hands folded in her lap and head bowed. The brother appeared restive, uncomfortable, twisting in his chair. A small stack of books lay on the table between them.

Charles began to draw, rendering Miss Church's posture in quick, simple lines. An undeniably attractive specimen: the hairline high and clear, the pale green of her dress complementing the colour of her eyes. Scandinavian. Must be. Somewhere along the line.

The brother was speaking now, his voice a harsher version of the father's. There was a high scraping of chair legs, and Charles looked up in time to see that Miss Church was standing, arms windmilling in the air. 'Alone!' he heard her say. 'Just *leave me alone!*'

He scrambled to his feet, but two nurses were there, and before he could cover the ground, they had grabbed Miss Church by either arm and pulled them behind her back. The brother was standing now too, shouting, jabbing his finger in his sister's face. 'You' jab, 'ungrateful' jab, 'little' jab, '*bitch.*'

'All right over here?' said Charles as he reached them. He tried to make his voice low and reasonable.

'All right?' The young man's face was puce. 'No, I should think we're just about not all right.'

'Enough, William.' The father placed an arm on his son's.

William turned away, ruffling his hands through his fair hair until it stood on end.

'Put Miss Church back in her chair,' said Charles.

The nurses did so, and the father shook his head, as though his daughter's behaviour saddened but did not surprise him. 'Come along, William,' he said. The pair of them threaded their way through the tables of staring faces, the son going first, the father more slowly, with the loping gait of a wounded lion.

'Now, now, Miss Church,' said Charles, taking the chair recently vacated by her father. 'What's this?' High colour flushed the girl's cheeks and she was breathing fast. 'You seem upset.'

'I'm not upset.' Her face was defiant.

Charles checked his watch. There were still some minutes left of the visiting hour. 'Make sure she doesn't move,' he ordered the nurses, before hurrying out. Thankfully, both father and brother were still in the visitors' waiting room, buttoning their coats to leave. 'Mr Church?' he called over to them.

The man's head was large, the wavy, silver-gold hair swept up and off the brow. In his youth, no doubt, he would have sported the same fine colouring as his daughter and son. 'Yes?' His tone was weary but not unkind.

'Are you . . . quite well, sir?'

The brother was still spitting. 'Quite well? Of course he's not bloody *well*. Did you *see* that little charade in there?'

'William.' The father, sighing, put up his hand. 'Please.'

'Who are you anyway?' William turned to Charles. 'I've not seen your face here before.'

Something in the young man made Charles queasy: the ruddy skin stretched tight across the flesh, as though he were a sausage roasting on a spit.

'Fuller,' said Charles, holding out his hand. 'Dr Fuller. I've recently been given the job of—'

But William didn't wait to hear the rest, turning and pacing off down the corridor, muttering to himself about 'twenty shillings a week for *this*'.

'Forgive my son.' The father spoke again in that same low, unhurried voice. 'He does tend to get rather exercised by his sister's position. You'll understand? It is only, I believe, from an excess of love. A desire we all share to have our Clemency back with us.'

'Of course,' said Charles, inclining his head.

The father put out his hand. 'Horace Church.'

'Dr Charles Fuller. How do you do.'

'I'm glad to meet you, Dr Fuller.' The man hesitated. 'I wonder . . . if you might tell me . . . I'm rather keen to know how Clemency appears during the week?'

As he spoke, Charles watched that great head of his, the deep brow.

'In what way, sir?'

'Is she ever cheerful? Anything about her behaviour that might bring me hope?'

He thought of the young woman's face in the day room when he played the piano, a pale petal reaching for the light. 'She . . . seems to like music, sir.'

'Oh?' He passed his palm over his forehead, his face suddenly weary.

'She seems to enjoy the piano. And her books, of course.'

The father nodded. 'Well. You seem a good sort of chap, Doctor. I'd appreciate it very much if you could keep an eye on her for me.'

'Yes, sir, indeed. I'll make sure to tell you if she seems happy and well.'

The tentative joy on the older man's face was almost too much for Charles to bear.

The case captured his imagination. The girl carried a mystery, a contradiction. The two halves of her did not fit: her outward grace contrasted sharply with her outburst in the visitors' room. Then there was the obvious antipathy between the brother and herself, and another thing too – the family was a clear cut above the vast majority of those who had patients in the asylum. The brother had spat out the fact that they paid *twenty shillings a week* to keep Miss Church there – the amount any private patient must pay. There were plenty of private patients at Sharston, but most of them were the sorts of people that families wanted to forget. Miss Church was far from amongst their number.

But she was obviously not well – the scars on her wrists were testimony to that, scars she took pains to hide but which showed whenever she raised her arms, not the large marks of a single suicide attempt, but the livid cross-hatching of multiple cuttings. And yet she appeared to be in full possession of her faculties.

Why had she not been admitted to a private asylum? And why, when she had been at Sharston for as long as she had, was she still in the acute wards?

Charles took himself to the library at the earliest opportunity. It was the following Friday afternoon, an hour before the dance, while the patients were taking an early tea, and he had an hour to himself until he was required on stage.

The library, like the visitors' room, was in the main body of the asylum – a medium-sized room in which the casebooks and a selection of medical texts were kept. He asked the librarian for the casebook for both males and females for the previous year.

The male volume he set to one side, but he propped the female casebook on the stand, turning the pages until he reached Miss Church's photograph and notes. When he reached her page, he drew in his breath. It showed a wild thing, dangerously thin, the bones of her cheeks protruding so far it was possible to see the shape of the skull beneath. The sharp line of the collarbone jutted from beneath her dress. The hands, which the photographer had presumably asked her to show to the camera, were held in front of her chest and bandaged so they looked like hooves. But the gaze – the gaze chilled him. She was staring straight down the lens of the camera with those pale eyes – eyes that dared the observer to look away.

He tried to read her notes but found it hard to concentrate.

All he could sense were those eyes, so he took out his handkerchief and covered them up.

Here were interviews, one each with the father and the brother, William, giving the particulars of the case. As was usual, the father – the headmaster of a boys' school not far away – was questioned about any previous illness in the family, and there was a brief relation of the nervous illness of his wife, the girl's mother, now dead. According to the interview, she had been subject to 'nerves and fits' but never hospitalized. She died young, a suicide, at thirty, when the girl was seven years old.

As Charles read, he felt the pleasurable sensation of pieces of a puzzle slotting into place. So the neuropathic taint had passed down the female line, the mother the transmitter of infection. Nothing the helpless father or brother might have done to prevent it. Nothing, in fact, the girl herself could have done to escape her fate. He sharpened his pencil and wrote: 'Contagion from womb to womb, the very essence of hysteria. *Hystera* = uterus – from the Greek.'

It made perfect sense: she was one of the few patients of the middle classes – and displaying a typically middle-class disease. It was a strange fact, but the working classes tended not to be hysterics; with them the strain of madness was pushed underground, becoming something deeper, stranger, harder to root out – delusional, fantastical. A woman from the working classes displaying a hysteric illness would be laughed at.

Underneath, he wrote: 'Is it too late for Miss Church?'

He thought again of her face in the day room – her face upturned, a book held open on her lap.

A *book*. Yes, she was always with a book.

He bent and scribbled:

One thing strikes me immediately – chief amongst the many qualities the young woman possesses is her love of reading. She is allowed a book at all times. Her father even left her a pile of them when he came for his last disastrous visit. Presumably this is a regular event.

Unlike music, excessive reading has been shown to be dangerous for the female mind. It was taught in our earliest lectures: the male cell is essentially katabolic: active and energetic; and female cells are anabolic: there to conserve energy and support life. While a little light reading is fine, breakdown follows when woman goes against her nature. Perhaps it would serve Miss Church to have a break from her books?

Closing the page on Miss Church for now, he reached for the male casebook, and as he slid it towards him over the table he felt a release of saliva in his mouth, as though anticipating a long-deferred treat. He flicked through its pages slowly, holding his breath until he found what he was looking for: *Mulligan*.

The man stared out from the page, chin level, with that veiled, impenetrable gaze. The skull was perfectly formed, the brow deep and true. Three inches perhaps? A beard of around two weeks' growth shaded the contours of the chin but did nothing to obscure the startlingly fine face, which would have been almost excessive were it not held in check by the austere line of the jaw.

'Pearson:' Charles wrote, 'the link between physical prowess and mental.'

Pearson had made much of this in his lectures, stating the finest judges and lawyers would undoubtedly make fine athletes too. But did the equation ever work the other way about? Might this fine specimen carry an innate intelligence within?

Quickly, Charles noted the particulars of the case: Mulligan had been admitted from the Bradford workhouse, the admitting interview having been conducted with a warder there who stated he was a 'good worker' and 'quiet'. Indeed, he had 'hardly spoken two words since being there'. Before the workhouse, as far as anyone could make out, he had come to England from Ireland, held various jobs, and had a wife and child, but had seemingly lost both job and wife upon the death of his daughter.

Charles paused. So Mulligan had lost a child. It was sad, certainly, but odd it should have caused his life to unravel. Children died all the time, especially Irish ones, and there always seemed to be plenty more where they came from.

According to a very brief interview conducted with Mulligan at the time of his admittance, the only words he spoke were that he felt 'there was a great curse upon him'. He had been living outside for weeks before he turned up at the workhouse, and was 'emaciated, destitute'.

Destitute: the phrase rang a bell. There had been a recent article on the dangers of the destitute in the *Review*; it had been a striking piece, and he had copied sections of it out; he flicked back through his notebook with eager fingers:

It is the view of the Eugenics Society that destitution, so far as it is represented by pauperism (and there is no other standard), is to a large extent confined to a special and degenerate class. A defective and dependent class known as the pauper class.

> Lack of initiative, lack of control, and the entire absence of a right perception are far more important causes of pauperism than any of the alleged economic causes. How do you propose to deal with it?

Charles looked up. It hadn't seem so when he had written it down, but now this last seemed to be a challenge directed solely at him.

How do you propose to deal with it?

He underlined the phrase. 'I don't know,' he murmured. 'At least, not quite yet.'

There was a last paragraph:

> The pauper is shown to be a person outside the considerations which move the normal person. As Dr Slaughter has said, 'He was born without manly independence . . . he came into the world with his mainspring broken.'

Charles clicked his tongue against his teeth. Again, it was the *pessimism* that jarred. If the article was right, and pauperism was indeed hereditary, then it was impossible for a man like Mulligan to change. Mulligan did not *look* like a man with his mainspring broken, but, then, it was impossible to tell. And the facts of the case were so scant! It was like reading the first chapter of an intriguing book but then realizing it was out of the library on indefinite loan. It seemed belligerent, somehow, to give away so little of oneself.

There had been a recent incident between Mulligan and an attendant. A rather nasty piece of work: Jim Brandt. An ex-patient with a propensity for violence, kept on to keep the chronics in line. Apparently Mulligan had attacked him, though Charles was sure it was not unprovoked. He had taken it upon himself to look into the case, but had yet to decide what an appropriate punishment might be.

His eyes flicked back to Mulligan's – those twin shards of flint. Was not flint the precursor to fire? It was clear from the incident with Brandt that the man might be roused, with little kindling, to a blaze. If it were true of his violent side, might it also be true of his finer side? What of his face, that afternoon, listening to the G flat major? What if his response to the Schubert was the first green showing of a crop in spring? The man obviously had a feeling for music, but he had never, or not as far as Charles could remember, attended the dances on a Friday evening.

What if this Mulligan, rather than being consigned to the chronic ward, might be shown to *improve*?

> Appeals to his manliness, his courage, or his self-respect will fall on barren ground, because there is nothing in him to respond.

Had anyone yet appealed to Mulligan's manliness? To his courage or his self-respect? Man to man, as it were? Charles wrote this down, underlining it, <u>man to man</u>.

'Sir?' The librarian was standing behind his desk. 'I'm awfully sorry, but I have to close up now.'

Charles took out his watch – a quarter to six. The orchestra were due to gather at half past, and it was a long walk back up to his room to fetch his violin. 'Thank you.' He carried the two large books back over and set them on the librarian's desk, drumming his fingers against the wood. As he did so, he began to smile: an idea was forming, beautiful in its simplicity. Here they were, working all hours to offer enlightened care, and here was this stubborn man *refusing* to participate in his own recovery. Mulligan had been in the chronic ward for months – presumably no one cared whether he recovered or not. Well, Charles cared. And he was not an advocate for letting someone rot. Not at all.

Mulligan would dance! And Charles would write about him for the Congress. He would make a case study of the man's redemption!

John

HIS WORK HAD CHANGED. With no warning, he and Dan had been moved. No longer digging graves, they were out in the fields instead.

The weather had softened; it still rained, but the cold had lessened now and the earth smelt damp, of stirring things. Daffodils were blooming in great clusters in the beds. He tried not to look at them as he passed. There was something about them, the way they pushed up from the earth, reaching out to the light. The blind hope of them. It made him uneasy, that was all.

To reach the farms, the men walked a path that ran from the chronic blocks between paddocks and a belt of woodland, where trees were coming into bud, their branches covered with a light furring of green. A large old oak marked the corner of this wood, and each time they passed it Dan would salute, as though it were a general or priest. The land was more open here, at the west of the grounds; with the wood behind, you could see the crop fields stretching ahead, giving way to pasture and then the low tussocky rise of the moor. The fields had been ploughed and harrowed and spread with dung, and the dung had been dug in, and now the men walked in lines for the planting, each with their share of seed to spread.

As a child in Ireland at this time of year, John had watched his parents sow, an apron tied around each of their waists, held and heavy with seed. He would watch each dip into the apron, each toss of the wrist, and pray the harvest would be good, that they would have enough. He did not pray to the Virgin, or to God, but to the earth, since it was clear the dark earth itself was the thing to wrangle with. But the earth was fickle, and though some years she was generous, often she was not, and did not respond to his mother's cajolings, or his father's hours bent in ministration to her sod.

Now, standing in a line with the other men, casting his seed to the ground, he prayed for nothing. Between digging holes for death and sowing life, he did not know to which he belonged.

He was called in to see Dr Fuller: a visit that was not in the ordinary way of things, since they were only seen every three months or so in the chronic wards.

'Mr Mulligan!' The man's arms were open and he was smiling. 'Do sit down.' The doctor looked over to the window, where the rain had begun a fresh, battering assault. 'I expect you're used to it.' He gave a brief grimace. 'Coming from Ireland and all that. How are the natives this morning? Restless?'

'Restless enough,' said John, taking his seat.

'You've finished the planting now?'

'Aye.'

'And you're . . . enjoying your work in the fields?' The man looked eager. He had the big book open in front of him, the one they wrote everything in, and John could see his own photograph, upside down. He remembered when that picture was taken: the first day he arrived. They had held him on a chair while a light exploded in his face, and it had felt like the end of the world.

'Now, ah, Mr Mulligan.' Fuller tapped his pencil on the dark wood of the desk. 'There has been some . . . *disquiet* . . . about the incident with James Brandt.' He put the pencil down flat. He seemed nervous. It made the air strange. 'Would you like to smoke? I'm going to smoke. You're welcome to join me if you like.'

John pulled a twist of shag and paper from his pocket and rolled himself a cigarette. Fuller lit a match and the smell of sulphur filled the room.

'Here.'

John leant to his flame. The doctor's fingernails were clipped and clean. A sharp smell of soap hung about his hands. Fuller shook out the match and it fell with a clatter into the ashtray. He sat back, puffing on his pipe, and pulled a single sheet of paper towards him.

'According to Mr Brandt,' he read, '*If he had not been stopped in the act, John Mulligan would have strangled me.*' The doctor looked up, an eyebrow raised. 'Is this so?'

John felt it again – the twist of the shirt, the man's face changing – as though his own darkness might swallow him.

He had wanted to do it.

Fuller frowned. 'I'm sure you realize this is a very serious allegation?' He put down the paper and leant forward. 'Mr Mulligan, between you, me and these four walls,

James Brandt is as nasty a piece of work as we have here, and I'm sure whatever occurred was not unprovoked. But when anyone makes a complaint, we must take it seriously.' He opened his hands. 'So here I am. Taking it seriously.' He hooked his pipe between his teeth and smiled.

Something in that smile made John think of the music. The doctor's face when he had opened his eyes. As though they had shared something. As though he had been seen. He wanted to share nothing with this man.

'Mr Mulligan, I would like to help you, but I cannot do so unless you also want to help yourself. Do you see? And to that end, I really cannot stress enough how important it is that you try to talk.'

When John stayed silent Fuller brought his hands to the table and looked at them, frowning now, as though the answers to his questions might lie in his knuckles or his wrists. Then he looked up, saying in a softer voice, 'I read your notes recently, Mr Mulligan. I was interested to learn more about your case. I read about your . . . tragedy.' His eyes were wide and slightly watery.

John took a long, slow drag of his cigarette.

'But to speak the truth, Mr Mulligan, I was a little surprised.' Fuller smoothed his moustache. 'I understand that life can . . . mark us. But you are a fine, strong man. Tell me, how did you let yourself be so cast down? Hmm? Don't you think the world needs fine strong men in it?'

Smoke hazed the air between them.

'All right, Mr Mulligan.' Fuller sighed. 'Since you're here, I might as well give you your examination now. It'll save time later in the wards.' He stood and crossed around his desk, so he was leaning against it and John's eyes were level with his waist, where the doctor's stomach bulged slightly over his belt and seemed to pulse with the beating of his heart. 'Tongue.'

John put out his tongue. Fuller nodded, then leant forward and placed his fingers either side of his neck, pushing slightly into the skin, before, 'Take off your shirt, Mr Mulligan,' he said, his voice low, as though he did not want to be overheard.

John shrugged off his jacket, then unbuttoned his waistcoat and overshirt and pulled them off until he was sitting in his vest.

'You might as well take that off too.' Fuller gestured to the vest. 'I'll need to listen to your lungs.'

John did so. There was a short silence in which he caught Fuller's gaze – saw a look there, the same he had seen on farmers back home when the cattle were brought into the ring, before the doctor turned and fiddled with his stethoscope, looping it over his ears and sliding the cold metal round on to John's flesh. The man was close now. John could see the hairs on his skin, a thin pasting of sweat over the bridge of his nose, the nostrils of which flared with his breath. A faint trace of yellow stained the edges of his moustache. Outside, the weather had changed. The rain had stopped and a bright sun shone through the clouds.

'Good,' Fuller murmured. 'Very good. You really are in perfect health.' He straightened up and moved behind. John closed his eyes, feeling the sun on his lids, the beating of his heart against the skin-warmed disc that Fuller held to his back. 'I should like to see you at one of our dances, Mr Mulligan,' came the doctor's voice.

A clenching in him. John opened his eyes. 'No.'

'Excuse me?' The stethoscope was jerked away.

'I won't go there. No.'

There was a small, incredulous laugh from the doctor as he moved back to face him. 'You seem a little unsure of your status here, Mr Mulligan. You are a patient. I am a doctor. I am inviting you to attend the dance for your *own good*. The invitation could easily be an order. Would you prefer that? Besides.' He frowned, moving back to his side of the desk and packing his instrument away. 'I wouldn't want to revoke any of your privileges. I certainly wouldn't want to see you confined to the day room for the duration of the summer.' He snapped shut his case. 'I don't suppose you'd like that much, would you, Mr Mulligan?'

John was silent. What could he say? That this not going was the only choice he had left?

'Mr Mulligan?'

'No.' He pushed his cigarette out in the ashtray with his thumb.

'No. Good. Well, I'm glad we can agree on that at least.'

Fuller bowed his head, began writing in his book. 'Thank you, Mr Mulligan.' He waved his hand in dismissal. 'That will be all.'

But when John stood, Fuller was looking up at him again – the sort of look people have when they think they've done you a favour. The sort of look Annie would have towards the end, if she condescended to look at you at all.

He knew what was required. 'Thank you,' he said.

Fuller's face softened. He was eager again now. 'That's quite all right, Mr Mulligan. Quite all right. Do you know, I think, perhaps, you might surprise yourself. Who knows, you might even enjoy it.' The doctor grinned. 'I only hope our little band will not disappoint.'

*

110

He stared at his face in the speckled washroom mirror.

Another dance then.

There was a time when dancing had been easy enough: on summer Friday evenings, when the cows had been brought back into their byres, when he would drag an old bucket from the stream and wash at the back. Change his shirt and walk the few miles to Claremorris with his friends, elbowing and pushing each other along the road, faces eager and smooth and awkward, their shadows long behind them in the evening light.

There was a hall there, plenty of fine musicians, and they would dance polkas and lancers and reels until they were footsore, and all the talk was of America, and who was going, who had gone, and who was coming back. There were plenty of women too, younger women, those that had not gone yet to America, or were too shy to go, and some of them lovely enough.

Plenty of times he stood outside with one or other of them and felt the low, leaping pull of desire. And when they yielded and pressed themselves against him he knew he might easily do more. But he did not. Because to do more was to be caught. And he was good, in those days, at not being caught. Good at leaving. Good at walking far.

But here he was, on Friday night, getting ready with the rest of the poor eejits in the washing shed.

He cast up his eyes to meet his reflection.

It had been a long while since he had looked in a glass.

It was a wary face he had on him. As though its owner might punch you if you looked at him the wrong way.

111

Ella

IN THE WASHROOM, Ella scrubbed her face in the sink and wet her hair so it would stay in place. She avoided her gaze in the mirror though. Didn't do anything to don herself up.

It had happened that morning: in amongst the rattle of the other names the Irish nurse read out, there it was, 'Ella Fay'. She had spent the day framelled and clumsy, her mind far away from her work.

At half past six, all the women were made to line up, two by two like in recreation. Ella stood beside Clem, and Clem's cheeks were red, and there was excitement in her eyes. 'Ready to dance then?' she said.

'Does everyone have to dance?' She hadn't thought of that.

They walked in a long line through the corridors, and this time there was no locking and unlocking of doors; they had all been flung open one after the other, all the way along, so you could see right through to the end.

The noise grew as they walked, as more women came out from their wards and joined the march, till it seemed to crest ahead of them and curve back again, a great rolling wave of sound.

'Keep to the side,' the Irish nurse screeched, stalking up and down the line. '*Keep to the side!* I don't want anyone out of the line.'

They were held waiting in the corridor while the women before them went inside. And when it was their turn, Ella's breath caught as she passed through the double doors. The room was the size of two of the spinning floors at the mill at least – there were windows, but they were high and set with coloured glass like you might find in a church. There would be no way of reaching them. Arching above their heads, the ceiling was painted brown and gold.

'Beautiful, isn't it?' Clem touched her arm. 'Have you seen the stage?' She pointed to the other end of the room, where a group of musicians sat. The doctor was up there in the middle of them all, a violin tucked under his arm. As they watched, he lifted it and placed it beneath his chin, drawing his bow over the strings. The crowds cleared, and on the other side of the room the men were revealed. Hundreds of them. At first they were just a black, gawping, smoking mass, until one in the front row, a small man with red hair, stood up and shouted something across at the women, then put his hand inside his trousers and started jiggling away. An attendant came and smacked him on the arm, then carted him off. There were howls and jeers from some of the other men.

Clem rolled her eyes. 'Come on,' she said, 'we can sit over here,' and she began making her way over to the benches at the front.

'No. I . . . I think I'll just . . . go further back.'

Ella slipped away through the crowd until she found a seat close to the very back of the room, near where a fire was lit in a huge fireplace. Odd snatches of melody floated down from the stage. Close to the front, Old Germany was already up, clapping her hands like a girl.

The nurses were dragging people to their feet now. Ella saw Clem making her way towards the middle of the floor. She was easy to spot, so much taller and straighter-backed than anyone else. Men were bunching, jostling, hustling to be picked to dance with her, but Clem seemed unaware; she kept throwing glances up at the stage. She seemed to be looking at the doctor, but the doctor wasn't looking back; instead his eyes raked the crowd, he seemed to be searching for someone in particular – until his gaze landed on a man sitting almost opposite to Ella in the back corner of the room.

Ella leant forward. It was dark over where he sat, but she felt a jolt pass through her at the sight of him: it was the man who had been there when she ran; the one who came towards her, who had tried to help her. The one she spat at. This man had not seen her though; he was sitting, smoking, staring at the ground.

A strange sound started up, a low drumming. At first, she couldn't light on what it was, until it grew faster, and louder, and she understood: it was the men, beating with their boots on the floor. Something stirred in the pit of her stomach. It was wild in here. Dangerous. Anything might occur.

The nurses clapped their hands for quiet, as up on the stage the doctor and the other musicians lifted their instruments to play. The music began, a slow melody, and the couples began to move, forward and back, bumping into each other, most of them mazzled by the music and the steps. Some people were moving well though: Old Germany for one, dancing with a man in a blue tie. She had her eyes closed as she moved, the lilt of the music was in her, and from this distance her body could have been that of a girl.

Ella searched for the dark man again, craning to see him through the forest of dancers. He was still there, sitting in the corner, smoking his cigarette in slow, deliberate drags.

As the music came to an end, there was a tap on her shoulder. 'Your turn.' She turned to see one of the nurses speaking, a young, pleasant-faced woman, someone she had not seen before. 'Everyone must take their turn on the floor.'

'But I . . . can't dance. I don't know how.'

'Go on,' the woman said with a smile. 'Go and find yourself a partner. It's not so bad as all that. I promise.'

And so she stood, threading her way out towards the dance floor. The first person she came to was a pale, fluthering boy.

'Do you dance?' he stuttered.

'No,' she said.

'I don't know how to either,' he said, and, stricken, stared down at the floor.

The music started up, and the two of them were pushed and jostled towards each other.

'Here.' She reached out and took his trembling hands in hers. 'It can't be so hard, can it?'

But it was hard enough. Shoving each other round, trying not to bump into anyone else. As soon as the music was done, Ella pulled herself away from the lad's clammy grip and began making her way back to the women's seats when someone caught her wrist.

'My *dona*! My Spanish queen!'

The man's face was brown and creased, and his hair stuck up all around his head. 'Done much running lately?'

She remembered then. He had been there too.

He pulled her hands up into his. 'I loved to watch you run,' he said, as his smell enveloped her: sweat and meat and earth.

'Don't worry, lass,' he said in her ear. 'This is a fast one, but you can just follow me.'

And when the music started, a rapid, kicking rhythm,

he threw back his throat and hollered, half pulling, half dragging her around the floor.

By the time the music had finished she was breathless, limbs pulled and feet sore, but the big man didn't let go of her hands. 'Here,' he said. 'Come and meet *mio Capitane*.'

The man's grip was strong, and she had no choice but to follow in his wake, back across the hall, away from the musicians, over to the far corner of the room, where the big man put his fingers to his mouth and whistled, and the man sitting in the corner looked up.

She twisted against the big man's arm. She didn't want to have to dance with this other man. Didn't want this man thinking it was she who wished to disturb him, or that she had asked for this. She wanted to go back to her seat and count the doors and think of slipping through them, down those corridors and away.

The big man loosened his grip, and she shifted but he caught her, his fingers wrapped around her wrist. 'Now, now, my queen,' he said, in a low, coaxing voice. 'I don't want you to do anything you don't want, but we all have to dance. Even my old *chavo* over there.'

The dark man was on his feet now, making his slow way out through the lines. She saw him properly then: he was older than her but still young. A beard shadowed his chin. As he came close, his eyes searched hers and she looked away. His face. The way he had come to help her, hand outstretched. The way she had shouted at him, spat at his feet.

'You don't have to dance with me,' she said to him, looking back. 'Not if you don't want.'

But in response he just reached for her. Taking her hands in his.

Charles

The fire stubbornly refused to be roused, and after a while he gave up, coming to sit listlessly on his bed. His usual glad tiredness was absent.

His gaze strayed to the portraits on the mantelpiece. *Mulligan*. It was Mulligan's fault. Something about him stung.

What was it?

The way he moved.

The way he danced.

In truth, Charles had expected him to flounder, a little, at least, at first. But so far as he had been able to tell the man hadn't floundered at all. In fact, he had danced as well as any man faced with a paucity of decent partners might. He could see the effect the Irishman had on the women in there too. Not that Mulligan seemed to notice himself. The man had moved so well that Charles had been a little ashamed at the music they were offering. He danced, in fact, like a *superior man*. But to whom was he superior? The other inmates? That would not be hard. To Charles himself? Of course not. Where, then, did the man fit in the scale of things?

The thought of Mulligan was like juggling with something slippery and liable to sting – one of those jellyfish he used to poke with a stick as a child on the beach. He had been excited by the prospect of the Irishman in the ball-room; now he felt . . . what? It was the same sensation he had had when reading the man's notes. Thwarted.

Perhaps, if he was truthful, he had wished for something more. Not much: a look, a glance, an acknowledgement. But there had been nothing. The Irishman had not looked up at the stage once. And this despite the fact that Charles himself was the reason he was there! Did he have any idea how he had intervened on his behalf?

Goffin was moving in the room next door – shuffling around, humming a few bars of the Strauss waltz that had ended the evening. Charles winced. The music had rankled with him tonight too: Strauss. Lehár. So stiff, so upright, so little room to *move*. Would they be playing these tunes for ever? It was the twentieth century, for God's sake, something had to change. He was bandmaster. It was up to him.

He turned to the mirror, regarding himself in the half-light: the curve of his skull, the incipient double chin. He jutted his face out, pulling at his skin so it hugged the line of his jaw. *Take off your shirt.* Mulligan's torso hovered before his mind's eye, the finely etched musculature, the V-shaped groove where the stomach met the groin – the inguinal ligament – just the place that a thumb might fit.

'Inguinal ligament.' Charles spoke it out loud as he unbuttoned his own cuffs and pulled his shirt over his head, placing it on the chair and pulling off his vest, so that he was naked from the waist up.

He turned from side to side, regarding himself with a frown. His own chest tended to the concave, his shoulders rounded from hours of playing the violin, and the puppy fat of his childhood still clung to his haunches in spongy lumps. Fair tufted hairs grew in a small clump above his belt. No inguinal ligament to be seen. A chill memory slid into his mind: standing at the side of a river, eight or so, a schoolboy. Hands tucked under his armpits, teeth chattering, classmates diving, and he, unable to, standing, helpless, watching the water slide from their slick wet bodies, watching their open laughing mouths.

You coming in, Fuller?

And him, shivering. Trying not to cry. No. No. He couldn't swim.

He faced himself in the glass, saw his hazel eyes, the softness of his frame, and pale revulsion filled him.

Here he was, determined to create a better world, eating Yorkshire pudding and steamed pies and believing himself to be on the way to becoming a superior man. It was laughable. He was a disgrace. As much as it was his duty to write a paper for this Congress, it was also his duty to change his shape, to embody the superior man in *all* his aspects; as Pearson had said, the finest minds must be cased in the finest bodies. There was a new body waiting, surely, beneath this blanket of flesh. He had only to carve himself free.

Charles hurried over to his notebook and scribbled:

1. Exercise.
2. Music. New.
3. Mulligan???

He took down the *Yorkshire Evening Post* and scanned through it. On the second page was an advert for dumb-bells. He pulled out his chequebook and ordered them on the spot.

Book Two

1911
Spring – Summer

John

THE BIRDS APPEARED. Only a couple at first, in the dark grey of the morning, the sudden flash of white at their breasts flickering and gone before you were even sure what they were, and then the sky was full of them.

John's stomach twisted at the sight. 'What do they call them then?' he asked Dan; he only knew his father's word for them, the Irish word, *fáinleog*.

'Swallows, *mio Capitane*,' said Dan, as one swooped low above their heads. 'A *bona* omen.' He licked his fingertip and held it to the breeze. 'Smell that, *chavo*. Direction's changed. Wind's coming from the west.' His face creased into a smile. 'Summer's on its way.'

John stared up doubtfully as the birds spiralled into the sky. They were no good omen to him.

'Here.' Dan halted amid the calf-high grass and unbuttoned his shirt. 'You seen this?' He pointed to a tiny blue bird etched on his right chest. 'For my first five thousand miles. And here.' He pulled the other side down to reveal another, facing towards the first. 'Sailed round the horn for that little beauty. When you're out at sea and you see the swallows, you know you're close to land.'

They were outside almost every day now. Sometimes John was put to helping with the horses, or they might be humping warm kerns of milk and sacks of grain to the kitchens, or carrying the carcasses out of the slaughterhouse and sluicing the bloodied benches down, but mostly they were in the fields, planting and hoeing, turning the

123

earth. The weather seemed to be set fair, but while the men bent to their work, the farmers gathered in small close packs, casting worried glances at the sky. John knew what those looks meant – the balance of it all. It was never good to have such fine long stretches in May; for the crops to thrive, the farmers wanted rain.

It was a strange, light feeling, to observe this and not to have the carrying of it – not to care. Not to have to think always about the weather and too little rain or too much.

At dinnertime they were allowed to take their breaks in the shade of trees, and if they were close enough, he and Dan lay beneath the old sentinel oak at the corner of the wood.

'All right, fella?' Dan greeted it like an old friend now, touching the bright new growth with a caressing hand. 'Like being a lad again, in't it? Like coming new.'

Dan seemed younger too now the fine weather had come, face like tanned leather, the bald patch in the middle of his hair shining like a conker's skin. His stories coursed from him, oiled and easy in the heat.

Reminds me of the tropics, mio Capitane. Did I ever tell you about the Maui girls?

One of the last great whaling ships. Six months in the freezing south, the chase, and then blood and blubber and oil, and the money, and the soft southern seas with water like glass, and the soft southern girls, all wandering the sandy shores with nothing to cover their breasts at all.

At all, mio Capitane. At all.

His crackling, catarrh-laced laugh was like lightning striking the ground.

Sitting there beside him, on his own patch of warm earth, John only half listened. His skin was tight and throbbed with heat. A white mark showed where his rolled-up sleeves stopped, and, below, his hands and lower arms were brown. Dr Fuller had been right: *It looks like being rather a fine summer already, don't you think?*

But the women were pale.

He had been to the ballroom every Friday. The dances were easy enough: similar to ones he had learnt at home, but simpler versions, instead of the fine weaving of four-handed reels, the fiddlers' bows scraping low and hard, there was Dr Fuller, leading a steadier, more English sort of playing altogether. Though they were similar enough for all that: a polka, a lancers, a march.

But the women there troubled him: those whose faces loomed, terrible in the lamplight; frail women who giggled and clutched at themselves like girls; women who jabbered like parrots and had hard bright eyes like a bird might. Women with yellow skin who gripped too tight, whose sour breath was a poisonous cloud he could not wait to escape. Silent women covered in a pale sheen like wax, so far inside themselves they hardly seemed to know he was there.

She was there too – the running girl – pale and watchful in amongst it all.

That first time, when Dan had brought them together, John was careful, touching her warily, as though she were an animal that might bite. But she was not the fierce, spitting thing he had first seen. Her eyes, so red and swollen before, were clearer now. The wound on her cheek had healed, and only a scar, thin and silver, showed where it had been. You had to look hard to see it. She moved clumsily, and it was clear she knew none of the steps. It roused a tenderness in him, this awkward movement, and as the music ended he bent so she might hear. 'What do they call you then?'

'Ella,' she had said, as though handing him something she did not think he would want to take.

Later, sitting watching from a distance, he searched for her in the crowd. She was almost opposite him, eyes darting, as though danger might approach from any side.

Where had she come from that day, wild eyes on the horizon, until she saw him and fell? He thought he could feel it still, when they danced together, her desire to run, coiled and tight, still beating at her skin.

Now, sitting beside Dan, his back leant up against the trunk of the oak, John bent and rolled himself a cigarette. 'Have you a light there, Riley?'

Dan, eyes still closed, brought a box from his pocket and chucked it towards John. John lit his cigarette and stared out towards the green swathe of the wood. 'Do the women not get outside then?'

'Whassthat?' Dan opened a lazy eye.

'Do they not go out at all then, the women? Do they not let them out?'

'Nah.' Dan shook his head. 'Keep them damsels lily white.'

'But do they not get any air?' He was impatient now. 'Are they locked up all day?'

'S'far as I know. Aye. Why?' Dan's mouth lifted in a crooked half-smile. 'Is there one you're thinking of, *mio Capitane*?'

John shook his head as a whistle blew and they hauled themselves up off the ground, making their way back to the acre of potatoes they were weeding.

As he worked, the thought of her and of the other women

trapped inside was like a stone in his shoe, a small one, one you might walk a few miles with without breaking your stride, but there nonetheless, making itself known.

It was with surprise that he began to think of her when he stepped outside in the cool of the mornings; mornings that carried the sweet dank dewiness that came before warmth. A smell that lifted him and put him in mind of times on the road when he had walked all night, when the sun rose and people came out of their cottages just to stand and greet the day.

He began to notice things more closely: the brightness of the old oak's new leaves; the way the swallows flew in the sun, more sure now, as though they gloried in it, their breasts flickering like silver as they span, weaving light.

It did not seem fair that he should see these things and she, and the other women, should not.

And so he began to store up the sights he saw so he might have something to tell her on Friday, in the ballroom, something smuggled from the bright world to the dark corridors inside.

But when they danced together it was late, and she seemed tired, and smelt of harsh soap and closed spaces, and had wary, shadowed eyes. They marked their brief circles on the floor, and the words dried on his tongue and he was dumb and useless, telling her nothing. When they had done, he took his seat in the furthest corner and did not look out again, turning his cap over in his hand.

Useless.

Useless.

Is that all that you can do?

*

That night he dreamt of Annie, and in the dream she held their daughter in her arms, and both of them were ragged, like a garment chewed by moths.

He reached for his daughter, but she had no face, it had been eaten away, and he could see right through her to the vastness and the howling space beyond. When he woke, he was pasted in his own sweat and turned on his side, breathing fast into the darkness.

He saw his dead daughter, laid out in her box.

So few people had come to wake her. Those that did ducked into the room and stood awkwardly, not taking the chairs he had laid out or the whiskey he had bought, and leaving as soon as they could. There was no snuff by the body. No clay pipes to smoke. Annie had wanted none of it; it was Irish, she said, and part of his curse. So there was no music or wailing. Where were the women who could have wailed for him, who could have sung their *caoines* over the body of his child? They were back in Ireland, and he had left them, left the land he had promised his father to protect.

When the few people had gone, Annie stood, moving past him. He caught her wrist as she went.

'Don't touch me.' She slapped his hand away.

So he sat and drank the whiskey. It was the first time he had been alone with death. In Ireland, death was not a time to be alone. He reached for his daughter. Let his finger trace the edge of her ear. Let it linger over her mouth. He remembered the feel of her warm gums, when sometimes, when she was crying and Annie was sleeping, he had given her his knuckle to suck.

As he drank, he felt it: the claggy pull of the land, reaching out, even from this distance, pulling him and his small family back down into it, because he had broken his promise. He had walked away. He was no man at all.

At the end of the whiskey was blankness. At the bottom of the bottle was a cold bare morning in which his wife was gone, tucked away in a back bedroom of her parents' house as though their marriage had never been.

He buried his daughter and went out into the country, looking for work on the land, but the harvests were over and the jobs were thin. He found his way to the edges of the towns, ragged places where ragged men stood in lines, waiting for those who might hire them for a day.

He looked for his father wherever he went. Sometimes, for a second, he thought he saw him: that way he had of putting his hands in the pockets of his trousers, or shaking those pockets for coins for a drink. His heart lurched at the sight – he wished to tell him he was sorry. But when he looked again, it was never him.

He found the odd day of work. Sometimes, if he was lucky, a week of digging in thick November mud. But once the farmer had his turnips and swedes safe in, once his beet crop was cosy for the winter, then the hired men were turfed off. He became ill, too fevered to move from the barn where he was sleeping until the farmer chased him out with dogs.

He wandered then, too weak for labouring, finding what food he could. Stealing if he had to, while the illness took root.

He remembered little for a long while after that. He knew he had been taken to a workhouse, where he sweated on a mattress in the corner of a room full of hundreds of other men, like living ghosts. When he became well again, he found he could not speak, as though all the words inside him had been pushed to the bottom of a dark well.

One day doctors came, examined the men. Took many of them away at once in carts. They stared at him, asking him questions, but he had nothing whatever to say to the world.

They kept repeating one word. *Melancholia*, they said to him, *melancholia* – a litany, an incantation, over and over again.

He lay now, curled around his memories, and thought of the things he had wished to tell Annie: how he had felt when their daughter was born, as though part of him was born again too. How he loved to watch them both when things were still. How when their daughter was feeding he would close his eyes and feel her, like a small fire lighting the room.

He remembered how, when her time was near, Annie wished to have the child out of her – screamed to have it out. Now, lying there on his narrow bed, the sleeping men around him, he felt the same; he could feel words inside him, clamouring to come out. He had been too full for too long.

He knew why Annie had come: she had come to haunt him. For wanting to speak to that girl.

He turned on his bed. Pushed the image of his wife away.

He would write to her. To this Ella. This odd, lonely girl. Write to her of what he saw outside.

It was one small good thing he could do. And if she didn't want to read it, he would write it nonetheless. He had had a book once. A commonplace book. He had lost it somewhere along the way.

Ella

BEYOND THE WINDOW THE season was changing. The grass was bright, and the sun, streaming through the day room in the afternoons, filled Ella with a bitter longing she could taste. But inside, everything stayed the same. Each Monday the doctor still played his piano and the dog men came and carried someone away. Last week they had taken the woman with the red-marked face – shouting about her girls, about how her girls were coming to get her, and how they wouldn't find her now.

In the laundry it was always hot, and it always stank, so badly it made your eyes water. But something had changed there at least: there had begun to be grass stains on some of the men's clothes. A small knot of anger lodged in her chest at the sight of them, and she looked up to where the sun burnt an oblong shape on the wall. Were they outside now, these men? Why should they be outside when she was locked in here?

She thought of the dark one, the one who had come to her when she ran. John. He had asked her name and told her his, but other than that he did not speak. He was holding on to something, she thought, a secret, or many secrets. Closed around them like the hard shell of a nut.

She pressed armfuls of laundry into the drum of water, added a bucket of soap, then swirled the washing with a stick. As they sank, an arm of a shirt rose up, filled with a sudden dancer's grace. She watched as it fell again, claimed by the knot of clothes. She had no such grace when she moved. She wasn't the worst – there were plenty who could hardly put one foot beside the other – but there were plenty too who seemed to know just what to do: Old Germany

131

for one, and John who, despite his silence, danced with lightness and ease. Clem might have been the best of all; she never jerked or stumbled, but moved like water and seemed to know all the steps. Many of the men fought to dance with her, and when they did so, even though they tried their best to gain her attention, they didn't seem to touch her. Their gazes slipped off. Ella thought she knew why that was: that it was the doctor Clem liked, the one who played the piano in the day room and violin in the band. She had seen the way Clem's eyes would search him out.

She caught him sometimes – the doctor – dropping Clem a smile from the stage in a quick, absent way. And she saw Clem gather that smile like so much treasure, putting it away somewhere safe. Ella imagined she would bring it out later, turn it this way and that and wonder what it meant. But she saw the smile fade as soon as his eyes moved on, and she thought it didn't mean what Clem wanted it to. And that was a secret too.

The only time they were allowed outside was at recreation, but there was little to look at there – only the high-sided walls of the echoing yard, only the other women fratching as they were kept in line, only Clem, who walked with her book held up at eye level, so she could read it while she moved. Although she had a new book every week, there were two she seemed to read again and again: the small, red-covered one she had that first day in the laundry, which she carried with her everywhere, and another, thicker book, brown, with gold writing on the spine.

Once she was reading, Clem never looked up; she had disappeared as surely as though a hole had appeared and she had crawled through it, and watching her, Ella thought she would have liked to disappear too. She read Clem's face instead, imagining it was possible to tell what the story was like that, from the way Clem bit at the edges of her nails or the skin around them. The way she turned the pages fast or slowed down, eyes moving fearfully, almost as though she didn't want to reach the end.

One afternoon, when Clem was close to the end of her book, Ella saw silent tears standing on her cheeks. 'What is it?'

Clem rubbed at her face with her cuff and gave a quick, rueful smile. 'It's just so sad. It's the umpteenth time I've read it, and I always think it will have a different ending. But it never does.'

'Why, what happens?'

'Oh . . . she loves the wrong man. Or the right man, at the wrong time. He persuades her to marry him, and then leaves her. And at the end she's lying there, lying like a . . . a sacrifice, and . . . she doesn't seem to mind.' She stared at the book in her hands. 'When I go to university,' she said, 'if I write an essay about it, then I'll talk about the ending. How I want it to be different. But how it's still the right ending after all.'

Clem was silent for a whole length of the yard, then, 'Have you ever wanted to get married?' she said, tucking the book under her arm.

Ella gave a small, shocked laugh. 'No.'

'Why? Did no one ever ask you?'

She shook her head.

Clem put her head on one side. 'Well, I can understand not wanting to get married, but not that you've never been asked. You're such a striking-looking person. Especially now your eyes have cleared up.'

You're such a striking-looking person.

'What about you? Did anyone ask you?' said Ella.

'Once,' said Clem.

'And what did you say?'

'I said no.' Clem's nose wrinkled. 'Even if I'd wanted to get married, I didn't love him. I didn't even like him. And he was old.'

'How old?'

Clem shrugged. 'A teacher at my father's school. He was young when I was a child. He saw me grow up. He used to take me out for walks, just after my mother died. And my father used to let him.' She grasped the book against her chest. 'One evening, when I was seventeen, he came to our house for supper. We all sat around the table – my father, my brother and he and I – and all the men kept looking at me and smiling between each other. I remember my brother's face. How pink it was. He had been drinking wine, and I thought he looked like a pig.

'The next day, my father called me into his study. He told me that the teacher had approached him, that he was a good man. But I knew different . . . he had cruelty in him. I had seen him hitting the children if I ever visited the school. And when I was a child, when we walked together . . .'

Clem broke off, something frayed and dangerous hovering at the edges of her words. 'Well, I knew if I married him I would be unhappy.'

'Did you tell your father that?'

'I tried. He didn't listen. I think he was glad to get me off his hands. I think he thought no one would want to marry me because of the way I am.'

'Why? What way are you?'

'Oh. All wrong,' said Clem with a brief smile. 'I'm all wrong.'

Ella stared over at her. Clem was tall and fair. She knew how to dance and play the piano. She had a mouth that turned up at the sides and seemed to be made for smiling. If she was all wrong, then what was anyone else? 'What did you do?' she said.

'I stopped eating,' said Clem, a tinge of pride to her voice. 'For weeks. Till they thought I would die. Till I thought I might die. I don't remember much about it. That's when they brought me in here. They fed me from the tube. They gave me the tube every day.'

She remembered then how Clem had talked of the tube that first morning, the dullness in her voice. Her voice wasn't dull now though – it was fierce and alight.

'Twice a day they would come in. Four, five, six nurses and two doctors. One pushed my hands down at my hips. Two opened my mouth with a gag. The doctor held up the red rubber tube. I fought then. Struggled and fought, but they forced it down. I got fat. They gave me milk and eggs. I couldn't taste it properly, but I could feel it.' She grimaced. 'Lying in my stomach afterwards. I used to make myself sick to get it all out. But then they started staying with me. They would stay for an hour after the treatment, and if I tried to vomit they would hold me down again. So in the end I stopped.'

She fell silent. Ella remembered her words in the laundry. *There are three ways out of here. You can die . . . You can escape . . . Or you can convince them you're sane enough to leave.*

'So . . . *why*?' said Ella. 'Why do you stay here?'

Clem turned to her. 'I've been thinking about that since you asked me. And it's because I'm only here while I think

135

of what I'm going to do. I'll get out one day soon, and I'll get to university. But I'll stay for now. And it will be better than being at home or being married to . . . that *man*. Have you heard of the women in Holloway?'

'No.'

'Well, they're behind bars too. Being fed with tubes. And whenever it gets bad in here, I think of them. Locked up too, because they want something else, something more. And I think, if they can stand it, I can. I'll stay here and belong to myself. Not to my father, or brother, or any man. So that's what I do, I stay. And my family pay to keep me here, and I get my own clothes, and I have my books, and every time that they let me out, I make cuts on my wrists so they'll send me back.'

Clem rolled up her sleeves, so that what had been hidden before was displayed, a livid badge of courage.

'I have a razor,' she said. 'I took it from my father's house. I keep it sewn in here.' She gestured to her sleeve as she rolled it back down. 'No one knows. Except you.' The look on her face was half pleading, half proud. 'My father thinks I'll break. But I won't break. And now you're here,' Clem was smiling now, 'I can bear it even more.'

That night, when the ward was quiet, Ella slipped from her bed.

Behind was the window, stretching to the floor. She knelt on the cold tiles, reaching out and feeling for the edge – the place where glass met frame, imagining levering it open, the warm smell of the night outside, stepping out and on to the grass.

She could see herself reflected in its tiny panes, her hair dark and straight in the middle, so that the line of the parting was a sharp slash of white; her eyes large and serious-looking. Clem was right about one thing though: they had cleared up. For the first time she could remember there was no sign of the swelling, and they hadn't itched for weeks.

She touched her fingertips gently to her lids, then moved her finger down to her mouth and ran it along her lips, which were set in a tight line.

She passed her hands lower, cupping her breasts. She brushed them with her thumbs, feeling herself stiffen beneath the rough fabric of her nightgown.

If she had been touched before, she had carried bruises afterwards. As a child at work, if she had not tied the broken ends of the thread fast enough, she had been beaten with the alley strap, the thick brown leather paddle the overlookers slapped to clear the ways of lint. Her mother though – her mother had touched her gently. Had stroked her hair. She could remember it, just.

She whispered her name to the girl in the glass.

'Ella.'

It sounded odd. She wasn't sure it matched the person before her.

The ward was quiet for once, only the small soft sounds of women snoring or turning in their sleep. She thought of Clem. The look on her face when she had shown her scars, the secret she had shared. Ella felt the knowledge of that razor inside her, a small, silver hidden weight.

'Now you're here too, I can bear it even more.'

It was the first time anyone had ever said they needed her. A strange new warmth had filled her when Clem had spoken. And yet she was not sure she wanted to be needed. Not in here.

Beyond the glass, the moon lay on its side, half full and yellow. An unseen bird called across the darkness.

On the other side of these buildings were the men. He would be there.

John.

Was he sleeping? Or awake like her? What had brought him here, with his secrets and his silences? Last Friday, when they danced together, something had felt different, a crack in the shell of him – almost as though he were readying himself to speak.

You're such a striking-looking person.

Was it true? She loosed her hair and let it fall over her shoulders, where it lay, heavy and dark. There was too much of it, too much for working at least, and she had only ever worn it pulled into the same tight braid down her back. The girls at the mill wore theirs pinned up, had sometimes put coloured ribbons in it, or come to work of a morning with it tied in damp rags so it would curl. She had never done any of that. She lifted it now and plaited it, but more loosely, so it was not so tight. It didn't look right though, and so she did it again, looser still, till strands of it framed the pale round of her face.

There was an odd feeling in her stomach, as though a fish was trapped in there, flapping away.

Charles

HOW GLORIOUS THIS WEATHER was at the beginning of May! One sweetly warm day following the other, and in each a new and pleasurable change to observe in the landscape. And how verdant everything seemed, as though the very sap were singing – as though the season had progressed from winter to summer in one heady leap.

It was a Friday and Charles had risen early as was his wont (as was almost, he thought, his *duty* when the mornings were as light and beautiful as this), and it was not yet seven o'clock as he walked down the main, raked driveway. Turning to the right, he found himself on a path that wound through wild grasses thick with cow parsley and thistles and led to an old iron gate, rusting at its hinges. He passed through it into a thick belt of woodland. Outside, all was light and song, but inside the world was a dense, deep green.

It was a pleasing size this wood, and a favourite haunt of his; not small enough to see the edge when one was standing in it, and not large enough to have a name. No patients were allowed inside, and no other staff seemed to take their walks in here, so it was rare he did not have it to himself. After a few minutes he came to a clearing, where he perched himself on an inviting-looking log to pack his pipe.

There was such a great deal to look forward to, not the least of which was the Coronation in not so very many weeks; amongst other celebrations a special Sports Day was planned: a fancy-dress afternoon of revels capped by a tug of war, in which the attendants and doctors were to pull against the men. Goffin had been put in charge of picking the team, and there had been some amusing discussions already in the staffroom as to what costumes they might find for the job. Charles had a small, burgeoning hope he would be chosen to be amongst their number. He believed he was growing fitter by the day.

He stood now and stretched, lighting his pipe, moving

through dappled sunlight as he walked, the sweet smell of tobacco trailing in the air.

His dumb-bells had arrived just last week. They were there when he stopped off at the porter's office to check his mail.

'Ah, Dr Fuller,' said the porter, pointing to a large cardboard box behind his desk. 'A parcel came for you today.'

At first, Charles had no idea what might be inside, since it had been weeks since he had ordered them, but then, remembering, he made his way over to the box and tried to lift it. It was quite impossible to raise from the floor. He tried again but could feel himself growing flustered and straightened up. 'I wonder if you wouldn't mind sending them to my room?'

'Yes, sir, right away.'

By the time he had finished his rounds the parcel was waiting outside his door. He pushed it over the threshold with the side of his foot, opened the box and peered inside. They looked rather terrifying, crouching there. The first pair was easy enough to lift – once – but the second needed both hands to manoeuvre out.

Rooting further, Charles saw, tucked into the bottom of the box, a helpful note showing a stick man curling the weights up towards his arm. The stick man's biceps bulged alarmingly, making him look like a picture Charles had once seen of a snake swallowing a rat. He shrugged off his jacket and waistcoat and took the piece of paper and the smaller of the two pairs over towards the mirror. Positioning himself in front of the glass he began to lift, tentatively at first:

One

Two

Three
Four
Five

His arm hardly bulged, but it burnt rather pleasantly when he put the weight down. After a moment he bent and lifted again – ten on each side this time. Beneath the tiredness of his limbs he had felt something stirring. Something formless as yet, but exciting nonetheless. Strength. Will. Since then, he had got up to twenty. Perhaps he might pull in this tug of war after all!

At the edge of the wood he emerged into bright sunlight, making for the Home Farm, where the first crops were showing themselves properly in the raked vegetable beds, lambs were in the fields, and all around the cow sheds was the sweet smell of grass and dung and milk. The treble chattering of small birds surrounded him, and, somewhere nearby, a wood pigeon sallied bass notes with a low, insistent coo. Faintly, very faintly at first, Charles heard music, so vivid and clear that it was a moment before he understood it was coming from his inner ear. It grew, and he recognized it, unmistakeable, those first fizzing bars of the final movement of Beethoven's Sixth, that delicious melody passed between strings and wind, music that seemed to rise from the ground drenched in cuckoo spit and dew.

'Da *da* da! Da *da* da! Da *da*-da *da*-da *da*!'

He began to sing, beating time on the ground with his cane as he walked.

He was not the first up by any means; men were everywhere, engaged in raking, sowing, planting, and over everything lay the optimism of the new season, and everything felt so beautifully aligned with purpose and with harmony, and underscoring it all was this glorious, swelling music. If only Churchill could witness this scene! Charles could almost see him, keeping pace beside him now:

'See, sir. Should the government, as I believe it must, vote against compulsory sterilization, then with proper investment and right management we might build more colonies such as this.'

He passed fields of cows, the heifers with their calves close by:

'There are four farms here and over six hundred acres of land. Our herds of imported Ayrshire heifers produce 1,600 pints a day. Our men too are rarely idle. See! Here we have little need of the manacle and the rope – the chains of Bedlam have been all but banished. Instead, we have our hoes and our spades.'

Work on his paper had continued in secret. Charles had said nothing to anyone, but as his case notes mounted, his sense of transgression had been tempered, had been replaced by a great, growing excitement. Mulligan's transformation, which was undoubtedly occurring, from taciturn melancholic to . . . well, it was not yet clear quite what, was to be the main focus of his paper. He had made various sketches of Mulligan dancing. He thought they might be useful to accompany his talk.

'Here in our colony we have a weekly dance. Let me describe it to you . . .'

When he gave his paper to the Congress, there would undoubtedly be time for questions in the immediate aftermath; he was almost certainly likely to be probed as to how exactly a weekly dance contributed to and helped to promote a healthy segregation. He would have to have an answer ready. In his heart, he knew it to be a good thing, but how to quantify that positive effect? How to *measure* it in a way that was scientifically verifiable? That would persuade Churchill and the audience a dance ultimately contributed to an *efficient* approach to care of the mentally ill?

What would Pearson have said?

Come, come. We must deal only with what is measurable.

Numbers.

Statistics.

Quite.

He wished there were some sort of formula – some mathematical equation – that could be carried out to display it:

Let x equal the state of mind of the patients on a Friday evening.

Let y equal the delight they feel in the music and dancing, and the escape from the humdrum routine.

Let z equal the combined good of a weekly dance.

But there was no such equation. All he could say was he *believed* it to be a good thing. And that was not enough. He was a scientist, was he not? He must be able to *prove* its worth.

This spiky thought was in danger of puncturing his mood when in the distance he saw a figure he recognized as Mulligan, standing in a nearby paddock with one of the shire horses, walking it slowly around the perimeter of the field. Charles veered from his path and came to stand before the low, three-barred wooden fence.

The animal appeared to be limping. Every so often Mulligan would step back to watch its gait. Only one attendant was close by – busy with another animal at the top of the field. Otherwise the Irishman was alone. He had not seen Charles; indeed, seemed to see little but the horse itself. After a while, he called with a low whistle and the beast turned its head and came directly towards him, whereupon he caught at its bridle, leant in and put his hand flat against the side of the animal's head. Now man and horse were facing each other nose to nose. Mulligan appeared to be whispering something in its ear. With his other hand he began to softly stroke the animal's neck.

Charles leant forwards – stupid, really, since it was impossible to hear anything from where he stood. The Irish had an affinity for horses: this was common knowledge, particularly the lower of their race, but there was something else at play here – a rare absorption, tenderness even. It was the same absorption Charles had noticed the man brought to his dancing. There was a quality to it that perplexed him. Where did Mulligan fit?

'Hello there!'

Mulligan raised his head.

Charles lifted his gloved hand, beckoning him over. Mulligan turned, tying the horse to a nearby post before walking over the field towards him. The Irishman had discarded his jacket and stood in shirtsleeves and waistcoat, shirt open at the neck. He seemed larger out here amongst the elements; he seemed almost elemental himself.

'So.' Charles felt suddenly, unaccountably shy. 'It's a lovely morning, is it not?'

Mulligan reached up and wiped his forehead with his cuff. The man's pulse beat amongst a small tangle of hair at his neck.

Charles lifted his hat, felt the sun warming the crown of his head. 'Summer appears to have arrived.' As he smiled, he was aware of the tightness of his cheeks. Somewhere in the distance, the final movement of the *Pastoral* was reaching its crescendo, the strings sawing away.

The Irishman's gaze slid back over towards the horse,

and Charles felt a pang of irritation: the man's part of the bargain was not being kept up somehow.

'Tell me, Mulligan, how have you found the dances?'

The man's expression hardly shifted. 'Fine.'

'Honestly now.' Charles dropped his voice, leaning over the gate again and speaking in a conspiratorial tone. 'What do you think of the music?'

Mulligan crossed his arms over his chest. His flint-coloured eyes levelled with Charles's. 'Oh, good enough, I'd say.'

Charles gave a small laugh, pointing his finger at the man. 'I can see you're being polite, but I don't believe you are being honest. I only ask, you see, because I've been feeling a little . . . frustrated with it myself. I keep feeling a sense of . . . constriction.' He touched his fingers to his throat. 'No space to breathe.'

Mulligan planted his feet wide on the ground, looked down between them and back up again, hands grasped in his armpits now. 'Honestly?'

Charles smiled. It appeared he had the man's full attention at last. 'That's what I asked.'

'Well, I'd say it's . . . very English music.'

'I see,' said Charles. 'Well, it's not, I can assure you. It's mostly German, in fact. But . . .' He gave a barking laugh. 'Would you have us dance like Irishmen, Mr Mulligan? Would you have us playing jigs?!'

'I wouldn't go that far, now.'

Was that the glimmer of a smile on the man's face? Whatever it had been, it had already gone, but Charles felt a small surge of victory.

In the distance, the bell of the clock tower was chiming the half-hour.

'Well, Mr Mulligan.' He lifted his hat again, gave a slight bow. 'I can see you have work to be getting on with, as do I. So I bid you good day.'

The smile may have been infinitesimal, but it was the most he had ever managed to eke from the stony Irishman, and, as he walked back to the asylum buildings, Charles found it had lodged in his chest like a small shard of May sun.

Ella

THAT FRIDAY IN THE ballroom she sat in the second row, just beside Clem.

Everything was closer here, louder, and the bulky presence of the men was just a few yards away across the floor. Their looks stuck to her like flecks of hot lint. She brought her hands up to touch her hair. She licked her finger, rubbing at a stain on her ill-fitting skirt.

Up on the stage the orchestra were readying themselves to play. She searched for him and found him in his usual position at the back, head down, as though he wanted to be anywhere else but here, and a strange disappointment filled her.

The first dance came and went, and she remained where she was. John stayed in the corner, not looking up. But when the second dance was called, she saw him rise, weaving through benches of men, and as he reached the front of the male lines he looked up and caught her eye.

She felt herself colour. She stood up, hesitantly, but someone had slipped in front of her – Old Germany, plucking John by the sleeve and asking him to dance with her instead.

'All right, girl?'

She turned. The tattooed man had his heavy hand on her arm. 'Will you dance with me? I'm a poor second, I know.'

As she moved around the floor with the big man, she looked for John from the edge of her eye. Old Germany had her eyes shut. He held the old woman close.

'You like him then?' said her partner.

She jerked her head up.

'Him,' he said, tipping his head towards John. '*Mio Capitane.*'

'No.' She shook her head. Heat scalded her cheeks.

The big man bent to her ear. 'You know you have to gamble, don't you, to get what you want? So what are you prepared to lose?'

She gave him no answer but as soon as the music was finished, pulled herself away, moving as fast as she could to the benches at the back of the room, where she caught sight of herself in the mirror above the fire: cheeks flushed, hair askew. She had been seen. Seen in her wanting. And if this man had seen her, then who knew who else had too? *Stupid.* Stupid to think that she was worth dancing with. Stupid to think she was worth touching. Stupid to have put her hair like this. She undid it and yanked it tight, so tight it stung her scalp, then brought her arms around herself and did not look up again, staring at the patch of floor beneath her feet until she knew each whorl and knot in the wood, until the whorls and knots turned into spiders, dancing to the music, until, at the end of the evening, with a clattering of benches, everyone was made to stand, and she stood with them, desperate to get back to the ward, where no one could see her or believe that they had.

But the patients were being corralled into lines for a last dance, one in which they all moved together, and there was no way to sit it out. When she took her place, she saw him standing, his dark presence further down on the opposite line of men. He caught her eye and her stomach flipped, and she knew in the way of these dances that he would soon be dancing with her. It was too late to move to another set, the music already beginning, the doctor's fiddle high and giddy, skittering over the thick, hot air.

First came the old man with a blue cravat tied at his chin, who led her gently around the clapping crowds, and now John was four dancers away. Then, a young man, who smelt of sour milk and shook as he took her arm, and did not stop shaking as they completed their circle, and he was three dancers away. Next, a man who held too tight and pinched her waist, so she stood on his foot and he cursed her for it, and he was two dancers away, and her skin was so hot she thought it would blister, and the last man was a brown dank-smelling blur, and then it was him, and he was leading her in a circle around the other dancers, with his hand held low on her back, and he was speaking, but that was not like him, not like him to say things, and everyone was clapping, and she couldn't hear, and perhaps she was imagining it, but then, as they parted, he bent to her ear. 'You're too pale,' he said. 'It's not fair.'

He let go of her and she span, breathless, back into her line: she with the women and he with the men, and the dance still continuing, another partner to the right, and the next man coming towards her as though in a dream.

She flicked her head this way and that, trying to see

him amongst the other dancers. She was near the end of the line now. The dance would be over soon, and she could recover herself. But there was a whooping, clapping, a rising from the floor, and up on the stage the doctor was grinning, lifting his bow, signalling, *the music would go on.* Her stomach tumbled. There would be another set; she would dance with him again.

This time, when he took her, he was quick, leaning down and speaking close to her ear. 'What can you see?' His voice travelled through her, lifting her skin like wind on water.

'When you look from your window. Tell me, quickly, which window is yours? What can you see?'

Her tongue was thick, her mind slow. 'I . . . don't know.'

'Close your eyes.'

His gaze was fierce.

'Close your eyes.'

She did as he said, and he held her closer, his hand shifting and lowering against her back. 'Now,' he said, 'you are in your day room. Looking out. Tell me what you see.'

'Two big trees.'

'Yes?'

'Side by side at the bottom of the hill.'

'And?'

'Their branches grow together.'

'In front of your window?'

His heart was beating against her back, against her own heart, which felt swollen, too big for her now. 'Yes, yes, but quite far away.'

'All right,' he said, when she opened her eyes. 'I'll find it. I will write a letter and bring it to you. Look for me. And I will come.'

He released her. Her dress was damp where his hand had pressed against it. She was dizzy, drenched, as she stumbled to the right.

Later, in the ward, when the gas had been turned out, she thought of the thing he had said, took it out and turned it around as though it were a lighted thing in the dark.

There was kindness in him. He was a different man to her father. A man whose palms were held open. Whose hands touched things gently, as though he knew they might break. She had felt it in the way he held her. Seen it in the ballroom, in the way he danced with the other women, with the old ones, like Old Germany. As though they were worth as much as any other partner to him. So what if he was kind to her? Did it mean anything at all?

And then the other man – the big man, with the tattoos on his arms. *You have to gamble to win.* What had he meant by that?

She had nothing in this world to lose.

Two beds over there was a soft moaning. A bed rattling against the wall. The matchbook scratch of fingers in hair, until the rattling stopped with a sigh.

'Jesus will punish you,' came Old Germany's wavering voice. 'He'll punish you for that.'

'Fuck off.' The other woman's voice was clotted and heavy, already halfway to sleep.

Ella turned the other way in her bed, a queasiness rising in her. Who did that woman think of when she touched herself like that? One of the men? John? It could be; it could be him. Her skin felt itchy. Her blood hot. The air had been breathed by one hundred women already.

As dawn began to break and still she had not slept, she

turned to the window, where the dark blue of night was lightening, and small birds dipped and rose across a pink-streaked sky.

She should be out there. Not waiting in here. There was no use, anyway, for a letter from him.

He didn't know that she could not read.

The day was close and sticky. Behind the iron bars, the window of the day room was open a tiny way, but no breeze seemed to come through it. The heat played tricks, rising from the ground in wavy lines, which danced as though they might be people.

The only truly moving things were two small birds, who had their nest up above the window: a rounded cone of mud with an opening like a surprised mouth. The weather didn't seem to bother them at all; they were tireless, making journey after journey, each time coming back with something new: a piece of twig, a beak full of earth.

Once, in the middle of the afternoon, a figure of a man did walk across the edge of the fields, wobbly in the distance, and Ella rose from her seat, hands pressed against the glass. But the man did not turn or come close to the buildings, and she saw he pushed a roller before him and was there to press the grass flat.

She put her thumbs in her palms to grip them. Behind her, the women's chorus was louder than ever:

'Setmeonfire! Setmeonfire! Fireiscoming. It'scomingcoming.'

'Andthedevil'shere.'

'That'swhattheysaid. Burn out the devil. Burn him burn him.'

'Oh! Oh please! Oh please help me!'

'Why will you not? Will you not?'

151

She put her hands over her ears and pressed them so all she could hear was the whoosh of her blood.

She was like them. She had made it all up: his touch on her back, his mouth. The words he had spoken. She had been in here too long and now she was mad. She made things up to make things better, and no one was coming to find her at all.

You are too pale. It's not fair.

He only said that because he pitied her, because she was trapped.

The close afternoon wore on, sagged and stretched to snapping all at once. Eventually, she leant her head against the hot glass and dozed.

She woke to a scratching at the window. He was there – pushed almost flat against the wall, holding a folded piece of paper towards her. Her breath caught in her throat. Their fingers grazed as she took it from him. She said nothing, and nor did he speak but touched his hand once to his forehead and then was gone, running in a low crouch along the buildings until he disappeared from view.

She pushed the letter down the front of her dress, heart hammering. Behind her, everything in the room was as it was before: Clem reading her book, most of the other women sackless, slumped in their chairs, mouths open, asleep. When she stood, her legs felt full of a strange, sluggish liquid, heavier than blood. Somehow she managed to reach the nurse on duty. 'Can I go to the toilet, please?' Her words seemed to hang, heavy and dangerous in the air, but the nurse just waved them away with a lazy hand.

The toilet block was empty. The thin paper of the letter was already damp from her body when she pulled it out. Something dropped into her palm as she opened it: a yellow flower, the colour of it startling, like a messenger from another world. She brought it to her nose. Brushed its petals back and forth with her fingertip, then placed it in her lap and opened the letter properly, blood pounding as she searched the page. There was her name, Ella, written at the top, and the letters that made up his name at the bottom, but she could make out nothing of the jumble in between. She put her head in her hands, felt the dull throb of her heart.

There had been one hundred of them in a class, and she was always so tired, working in the mornings and school in the afternoons, or school in the mornings and working in the afternoons. She sat at the back and her eyes were bad and all she ever wanted to do was to close them and sleep.

No one had noticed her much.

She knuckled her eyes with her fists. When she lifted her head, she knew what she had to do.

She went back into the day room and wove her way over to Clem.

'Clem?'

'Hmm?'

'Will you read something to me?'

'From this?' Clem flicked the page of her book.

'No, from a letter.'

Clem looked up from the edge of her eye. '*Your* letter?'

Ella nodded.

'From whom? One of your family?'

'No . . . from someone else.'

'Well . . . why don't you read it yourself?'

'I can't.'

Clem looked up properly then. 'Ah,' she said, closing

her book and tucking it under her arm. 'I see.' She tilted her head to one side, as though Ella looked different somehow. 'Can you not read at all, or only a bit?'

'Not much.' Ella shrugged. 'My name. A few other words. Hardly anything really.'

Clem's face contracted, as though in some sort of pain. 'You poor thing,' she said. Then, 'Of course. Hand it over then.'

Ella pulled the tightly folded square from where she'd hid it in her sleeve. 'Thank you.' She passed it to Clem's palm. 'But . . . please.' Her eyes scanned the attendants on duty. 'Please just . . . put it in your book. Quick, so as no one sees.'

Clem nodded and did so, smoothing it with her hands and closing the book a little to hide it as she read.

Ella took the place beside her, seated forward, watching Clem's eyes, the way they moved from one side of the page to the other, her bottom lip, held between her teeth, which she rolled back and forth as she read.

She wanted it to be her, taking her time as Clem was doing, letting her eyes roam where they pleased over the page.

When Clem had finished reading, she didn't look up straight away; instead, she stared at the bottom of the letter for a long while as though trying to understand what was there.

'What?' She couldn't wait any longer. 'What does it say? Is it bad?'

'It's from a John.' Clem looked up, her eyes narrowed. 'Which John is it?'

'Why? Tell me. Is it bad?'

Clem shook her head. 'No, it's not bad. It's just . . .' she gave a quick smile, '. . . surprising, that's all.'

154

'Please.' Ella could hardly catch her breath. 'Will you just
. . . *read* it to me?'

'All right,' said Clem, and began to read.

Dear Ella,

I have not known how to begin this letter and so I begin by
saying that I feel badly that I and the other men are outside
in this weather while you and the women are not.

There is a flower in here as you can see. They are wild
these flowers and do not grow in the beds that are tended
and clipped so carefully growing instead in the grass that
will be cut to make hay. They make a great display in the
fields so that the fields seem almost to be made of gold.
Yesterday Daniel Riley who is somewhat of a friend of
mine (you will know him I think a strong brown-haired
fellow – his skin covered with ink) took off his shoes in the
morning. He unlaced his boots and put his bare feet on the
grass and laughed as he did it – he has a laugh that would
burn the hairs from your head if you caught it sideways –
and I followed him and did the same.

The feeling made me think of when I was a boy when I
walked with my boots tucked under my arms to save them
from the road.

We walked with our boots in our hands and our feet in
the dew. The attendants did nothing. They are lazy in this
heat I think. Soon it will be time for the first cutting of the
hay. It grows high already and is as I said gold. Though
there are other colours too but the gold is the best of it. I
think they are most beautiful just before they fall.

I will stop now and send you best wishes

John

His words coloured the air. She wanted to hear them again, more slowly this time. Wanted to imagine her own hot feet bootless in the damp green of the dew. But Clem was already folding the paper up.

'Open your palm.' Clem put the tight square of the letter back in there. 'Now.' She clasped Ella's hand into a fist. 'Which one is John?'

'He's . . . Irish. He . . . dances well.'

'My goodness.' Clem let go of her hand. '*You're* a dark horse.' She became thoughtful. 'He *is* a good dancer,' she said quietly, 'but who would have thought he could write like that?'

A burning started up in Ella then, deep at the base of her spine, and her eyes raked Clem's face, but then she remembered the doctor, and the way Clem looked at him, the way her face turned red when he spoke to her, and the burning eased. 'Clem?'

'Mmm?'

'Will you help me?'

'Help you what?'

'To write back?'

'Yes.' Clem's eyes were alive with mischief. 'Oh yes. I should think I could manage that.'

John

THE MOWER – A STRANGE, ungainly contraption – was harnessed to two of the shire horses. A farmer clambered up to ride on the saddle, and the machine bumped off across the ground, its blades turning behind it. The riot of colour that the meadow had become – buttercups and cornflowers and poppies – was felled in seconds, and the men followed behind with their rakes. John moved along the swathes, spreading the cut grasses across the field to dry.

He had been a fool.

It was not the writing of the letter. That was all right, or all right enough once he had begun it. It had taken a few attempts – a few crossings out and wasting of the paper he had pulled from the back of books – but once he had managed to begin, it came easily enough. No, it was not the letter. It was the delivering of it that had been madness.

What can you see? he had asked her – as though it were the easiest thing in the world for him to go where he pleased. As though he were the postman himself.

And yet her face when he had said he would. Startled, as though astonished anyone would do such a thing for her.

And foolish or not, he was bound to it then.

He had done it when a break was called. Had to ask Dan the way, who raised his eyebrows and told him, a path through the wood, then a secluded lane, and then the stand of trees that edged the playing fields.

From there you see the women's side.

And John had taken the path, and hiding behind a great sycamore, lungs raw from the running, had seen the women's wing for the first time – the mirror image of his own, stretching three hundred feet or so wide. Somehow he had done it: had found the trees she spoke of, found her framed in her window, managed to slide the letter through the tiny gap, deliver it into her hand, run back without being seen.

Ten minutes. No more. But it was there still, the feel of the running in his lungs and limbs. The shock of it.

The foolishness.

As he raked the grass, he saw there had not been enough rain after all. What greenness was in it gave itself up quickly to the sun, and what remained was thin and brittle. The horses would not eat well this year. He said the names of the grasses in his head – the thick fronds of *féar caorach*, the stumped cat's tails of *féar capaill*, and *féar garbh*, with its reddish feathers – but still his mind would not calm.

There was this business of the flower. He should never have put it in there. He was a fool for that too. If a man gave a woman a flower it meant he was courting her, and he was not courting her and did not wish to be mistaken for one who was.

It only took a day for one side of the grass to dry, and then it was turned and given a day for the other, before being shovelled into the small humps of cockeens, and once they were fully dry, the men were set to building haycocks. John and Dan worked together. They were fast and knew what to do, how to build the field cocks tall and wide, the height and a half of a man; how to twist and draw the *sugans*, the hayropes, to secure them, weighting the fragrant loads with heavy stones in case a wind should come. But no wind came. The days were dry and breathless.

He gave himself to his work, and his mind quietened.

He was at home here, out on the land; had made the same movements since he was a boy, in him so deep they were a natural thing. Had stood in fields in sun and wind and rain, hands chapped and callused from the scythe and the ropes. In Ireland, he would have checked the sky continually for the clouds that came from the sea, but there was no need to do so here. The ground was parched and the cows were fretful, their udders hanging slack. The air filled with the sweet burnt smell of the mown fields.

The heat grew, and the mower unearthed things that had been hiding in the long grass. You had to be quick, to save what needed saving: a shilling piece, flashing briefly in the afternoon sun, a thrush's nest full with five pale-blue eggs. Creatures fled in all directions from the machine – mice and snakes and rabbits and rats. But most of them sheltered in the diminishing patches of grass, and when the last patch was left, the farmers let their dogs free. The terriers ran squealing and yapping in delight, emerging bloody-muzzled and crazed with killing.

Once, in the hot, still afternoon he came upon a creature that had not run in time, a hare with a slashed belly, wild eyes staring as its body panted with fear. John knelt by the dying animal, its hot entrails splayed on the ground. He stroked it briefly with his fingertip and then he broke its neck.

There were plenty of men out here now – every man that could be useful, it seemed – and as he and Dan worked, forking hay or throwing and lashing the ropes, Dan cast glances over the other men, juggling names: 'The one who thinks he's Jack the Ripper, the one with the hobble, the fat one from the fitters' ward . . . they'll be good pullers, *chavo*, what do you say?'

'Aye,' said John. 'Good enough.'

A Sports Day was coming. Coronation Day. The men were set to pull a rope against the male staff, a *tug of war*. Dan had already anointed himself the general of this war and talked of little else. When he had done with his lists, he sang, sea songs, shanties, to help with the pull:

Well they call me hanging Johnny,
How-way, boys, how-way,
Well I never hanged nobody,
And it's hang, boys, hang.

Well first I hanged me mother
Away, boys, away
Me sister and me brother,
And it's hang, boys, hang.

One long afternoon Brandt appeared, darker since last they met. Face burnt from the sun. 'So this is where they keep you then. Cunt.'

The attendant's eyes were yellow slits against the light. Violence hummed about him like bees in the still air.

'A gyppo and a cunt.' Brandt stepped up and poked their haycock with his stick, shaking hay over the ground, but the pile was steady and did not fall.

John wiped the sweat from his brow.

'Oi, gyppo,' Brandt called to Dan. 'I hear you've been saying you're going to win this tug of war.'

Dan grinned. 'I think that's right. That's what I reckon. Pull you ladies over just like that.' He snapped his fingers.

'That's not what I heard. I heard they're only doing it so they'll be something to laugh at.'

'*Mio Capitane?*' Dan turned to John. 'Why don't we show this *cartso* what we can do with a rope?'

So John tossed the heavy hay rope in a clean arc over to Dan, who caught it with one hand and pulled it taut, securing it with a stone.

Brandt turned, spat on the ground. 'I told you you'd pay.' He lifted his stick towards John. 'And you will. You too, gyppo.'

Dan whistled through his teeth as he watched him go.

'We'll get the bastard, *chavo*,' he said, coming to stand beside John. 'Just wait. What does he think? He thinks gyppos and trampers and Irish don't know how to work ropes? He'll see.' He shouted after Brandt now: 'He'll see what we can do with a rope all right.'

Friday came.

In the ballroom, he took his place and watched for her, restless in his skin.

Every so often he could not help but cast his glance towards her, and when he did he saw that there was a high colour to her cheek. That she moved, perhaps, with a touch more grace than she had before. And as he watched her dance with other men, there was a hunger on him that was painful and new.

When the heat of the evening and the heat of the dancing was at its height, he made his way towards her. Her face was flushed with sweat and in the candlelight seemed to shine. He felt a shifting inside him at the sight of her, something falling, finding a new place.

When they danced, he could see only the white strip of her parting and the paleness of her forehead beneath. He caught the sharp-sweet scent of her as they moved. He wanted to ask if the letter had pleased her. If it had been the sort of thing she wished to hear. But he felt raw, his body become an unwieldy thing. Now it was he who was clumsy, he who forgot the steps.

She said nothing to him, and he did not speak, only felt a growing disappointment, and as the music faded he released his grip.

'Here,' she said, lifting her face to his. With a fugitive

smile, she tugged a folded piece of paper from her sleeve, and in a quick, darting movement, pressed it in his palm.

He opened it in the ward, when there was only the small lamp burning over where the attendant slept.

> To John,
> Thank you for your letter. I liked to hear it.
>   When I look out at the green, I wish I were outside too. But I do not wish to be outside and come back in here at night. I wish for freedom, only.
>   It is true that people act strangely in this heat. But I wish they acted stranger still. When you are a woman, and you work in the laundry, no one lets you take off your boots. You keep everything on and you keep your boots on till you go to sleep, when your feet are swollen and they hurt.
>   I think there are rules for the men and rules for the women in here.
>   Yours,
>   Ella

He folded it back and placed it in his pocket, from where he took it and read it several times that day. One thing was a relief – it did not sound like the letter of a woman who had been courted, and for this he was glad.

Still.

He would have liked to have known what she thought of the flower.

One late afternoon, when the sun was slanting sideways over the field, John uncovered a feather in amongst the hay, deep blue and white.

He knew which bird it came from, a *fáinleog*, a swallow. And he knew what it meant all right; it meant his father, and a broken promise, and everything that came after.

He thought of his father now, of the closeness he had felt to him as a boy, when he would sit with him at the front of the cart, on trips to the coast to collect seaweed and sand for their fields. Crossing the blue rush of rivers on to the sea. Scouring the shore by his side, pulling at the knotty wrack and moss and slimy weed. His father singing while they worked, Irish songs, full of words that were forbidden at school, where speaking in Irish got you beaten. Sleeping on the shore beside the mules and the sound of the waves.

Then, one evening in spring, when the fields of the farm had been harrowed and raked and spread with the green weed, his father calling him over, telling him he was leaving.

'To England. And you'll be glad that I do. And if the weather is too good there and the hay does not thrive, I'll be back. But you won't want that, because there'll be nothing for the shop and nothing for your mother or your sisters, and nothing for the pigs, and you'll end up on the roads, or I will. So pray for showers and rain, and then there will be work and plenty of it.'

His father took him outside and pointed to the sky, which was full of birds, small ones with forked tails. 'D'ye see them? The *fáinleog*? They fly a long way. And they come back. Every year they come back. And that's what I'll do. But you must look after the farm while I'm gone.'

John stared round at the low, thatched farmhouse, the uneven yard, the outhouses, the land stretching away to the bog where the turf was cut.

'Say it.' His father gripped him. 'Say you promise. I want to hear you say it.'

'I promise.'

'In Irish. Say it in Irish, lad.'

'Gellaim duit.'

He watched his father leave, along with a large group of men, all with their sharpened scythe blades glinting in the pale spring sun. All of them walking out to take the boat to Liverpool. And it seemed to John his father was part of a great army of men, and he was proud of him, and his father lifted his hat and waved as he walked away.

When the summer ended, John watched for his father's return. On his knees, cutting turf from the patch at the back of the cottage. Cleaning out the pigs. Sitting with his back against the gnarled and knotted tree at the front when the work was done, he stared and stared at the bend in the road.

The other men returned, but his father was not with them.

Some of those men came and stood in the cottage with his mother and put their hands on her arms and murmured things John could not quite hear.

His mother wept and hunched and dressed in black. The priest came and they knelt, he and his mother and sisters, saying rosaries for his father's soul. There was no body to wake, but the neighbours all came and took their snuff, and the men stood about and touched him on the shoulder.

'You're the man now, you're the man all right, you'll be looking after the place. You'll be looking after your mother now.'

But he did not believe his father was dead.

He watched for him still. He sat amongst the roots of the

164

gnarled oak and stared at the road, until the *fáinleog* were long gone and the air was pinched and frost crusted the blackened grass.

As he grew, he kept his promise, but came to hate the weight of it. Often, he imagined slipping into Confession, the darkened grille, the priest's sour breath: *'Bless me, Father, for I have sinned. I want to torch it all.'*

He walked out his hate, and he could walk far, twenty miles a day in the summertime: passing barefoot women, turf on their backs, children running after them. Past fields of black earth bounded by loose stone walls, where great drifts of sheep blocked the roads.

Sometimes, in the middle of nowhere much at all, when all that was around him was heather and bog and mountains, he turned the corner and there was a group of people, backs bent, breaking stones.

Plenty of young men were amongst them, some of whom he vaguely recognized from the dances in Claremorris, or faces in the crowd at the horse fairs. A ganger moving up and down them, shouting, making them hurry. And his father's voice echoed in his head: *'You'll end up on the roads, or I will.'*

But he saw beauty too, as he walked: saw the gorse, singing yellow after the rains. Felt a tugging that was happiness and sadness mixed together and made from the light and dark and the morning and moving and all of it rising inside him. Sometimes there were women, or girls, standing in their doorways, staring out. He saw them and felt he understood their loneliness and their wanting.

Once he approached one, walked right up to her and asked for a glass of milk.

'I've such a drought on me.'

She was beautiful, standing just in her petticoat and shawl. She fetched a cup for him and waited while he drank, her pulse keeping time at her neck, her feet bare on the earth floor. He imagined her taking him inside the cottage, lying on the bed. Giving her pleasure in the darkness. Spilling the things he had seen into her ear. How the beauty of life and the world struck him like a fever sometimes, but how it was all mixed up and mangled with the hate. But he said and did none of those things, only, when he had drunk down the milk, handed the cup back, thanked her and walked on.

He kept on the road until he reached the sea, staring at the place where the horizon blurred and the west carried on to America.

Beyond.

He could get there on a boat, from Ballina, from Sligo, but you needed money. The best way to get there would be Liverpool first – he had heard there was plenty of work in the docks there – and save the money for the passage.

And so that was what he wished for, standing at the place where the land gave way to the sea. But when he had wished it, he always turned back. He had promised his father he would.

Until his mother died and the men clustered around him, their voices a low, insistent swarm. 'It's your farm now, John Mulligan; you'll be after marrying now.' Their daughters staring at him over the coffin. The sour-milk smother of them, and all the time his feet itching to take him back on the road. He had to hold himself in his chair to keep from jumping out of it. Kept taking pinches of the snuff laid out beside his mother's coffin, his foot rattling on the floor.

He dug her grave himself. Made sure the sides were pared and smooth. He threw his sod on the top of the box, and when it was done they went back for the eating and the drinking. He could see his sisters inside the house. Knew they would be sweeping the floors, setting the clock going again, moving the hands from where they had been halted when his mother died. He wanted no part of that slow, silted time.

So he walked.

He walked away from home. Away from his father's land. Away from his promise. Walked to Kiltimagh and to Claremorris, and from there he walked the road to Dublin. He could get to Liverpool, and America from there.

There was a great lifting in him. There was only the road ahead.

He wrote of this to Ella. Or parts of it. Not the women and the imaginings, or the broken promise. He wrote the things he believed she would like to hear. She was like those women, he thought – standing at the doors of their cottages, in their toughness and their loneliness. Staring out.

He felt lighter when he had written it. He slipped the feather in the folded letter when he was done. For not all feathers were tainted with blood, were they? It was such a light thing, to have to carry so much. Could a feather not be just a feather after all?

Charles

CHARLES HEADED NORTH UP Bishopsgate, weaving to avoid a throng of labourers outside a pub. From their manner and bearing they had just been released from their Saturday morning's work and were drinking lustily in the afternoon heat.

It was a fine day, radiant in the way only early June can approach, and he would have far preferred to have been walking up on the moor than in Leeds, but it was his mother's birthday, and he had to make the obligatory visit to Roundhay for lunch.

Many of the drinkers had discarded their shirts, and their torsos were exposed and beginning to broil, their laughter ringing out raucous on the city air.

The sun did strange things to people. It made them regress. It was obvious from just these last weeks of heat that it was harder for everyone to concentrate on work. He was dressed in light flannel trousers, jacket and boater, and the cotton of his shirt felt deliciously cool against his skin. Such a relief! The asylum staff were forbidden to take off a layer of their stiff black uniforms, however hot it was. These last days Charles had taken to noting the temperature on the thermometer that was nailed to the wall of the kitchen garden. As the column in his notebook grew, the figures remained remarkably steady; the mercury had hardly dipped below seventy-nine for the last two weeks.

If he approached it scientifically, it helped to quell his own irritability with the heat: once the temperature veered towards eighty, ordinarily quiet people became fractious, less biddable. Troublemakers were more extreme. The stench on the wards was noisome. Surely the weather must break soon?

How few great empires had sprung from the places where the sun shone? The African, the Indian, the Aboriginal in Australia . . . what did these races have in common? They were less guided by reason. Surely it must follow that the closer you were to the sun, the more your animal nature was uppermost? It certainly seemed so in Leeds today, where these men, drinking, with their rough voices and their skin so flagrantly displayed, seemed little more than cattle, brawny and red.

Work on his paper continued, although a little less urgently, he had to admit, in the heat. He had sent away for a copy of Dr Sharp's publication *On the Sterilization of Degenerates*, thinking to acquaint himself with the arguments for sterilization that he might the more fully refute them in his own work. Dr Sharp was the chief medical officer of the Indiana Reformatory, a man who had already sterilized many hundreds of patients. It was said that Home Secretary Churchill held him in extremely high regard. But the pamphlet – slim as it was – had lain on his desk unopened for a week.

Charles pulled out his pocket watch as he headed up Kirkgate – there was a little time in hand, and he'd had the idea that he'd like to visit Spence's music shop. Since making his list in the spring he'd had no time to address the relentless round of Strauss.

The bell rang as he entered, but the shop appeared to be deserted. The interior was welcome and cool though, all dark-brown wood and shaded blinds. He stood for a moment in the entrance, letting his eyes become used to the dim light. One side of the shop was taken up with instruments, violins mostly, while the other walls were lined with racks of music. There was no one behind the counter and only one other customer, an elderly gentleman bent over some sheet music on the other side of the room. A dark passage led through to the back. Charles wandered over to the music stands and set himself to browsing, but it was with a distracted manner that he fingered a stack of piano music – Mozart, Chopin, Liszt – before putting them peevishly aside. Whatever he was looking for, it was not that. Not today.

A soft call came from behind the desk, and he turned to see a young man, not more than twenty, with a head of improbably thick, sandy hair.

'Hello there,' the young man said. 'Can you see all right? I closed the blinds for a bit of cool.'

Charles nodded. 'Quite all right, thank you.' He recognized the sound of an educated Yorkshireman, an accent not unlike his own. Upon regarding him, the strangest thought slid into his head: that this man was the opposite of Mulligan, the light to his dark; where Mulligan, despite his relative youth, was hewn from something old and hard, this young man was made from something softer, newer altogether.

The young man said that he was sorry, he had just been sorting through a delivery. Could he help with anything at all? He had a wide, easy smile. There was the sound of a bell, and Charles turned to see the door being shut behind the other customer.

He felt suddenly, unaccountably nervous now they were alone, stammering a little over his request, which was simply to say that he played in a small orchestra and wondered if there was anything *new* to dance to.

That smile again. The young man thought he had just the thing. They had been sent a fresh batch of tunes from America, the very consignment he had been unpacking when Charles arrived. Perhaps he would like to see?

Charles followed him into a small, untidy room at the back, stacked floor to ceiling with musical scores, with an upright piano at the far end.

'You'll think us very messy. It's a family business, you see, but my uncle is quite as disorganized as I am, so that's all right.'

The young man moved towards a bundle wrapped in brown paper, chattering all the while, saying there was one tune in particular that was already something of a hit in London. He pulled a folded sheet from the bundle, took it over to the piano and started to play.

Charles stood in the doorway, half in, half out of the room, holding on to his hat. He felt his breath change. The music was extraordinary: like hearing something from a dream. Where Strauss was airless, this was oxygen. It bubbled with life. The time signature was fractured, but what should have been disturbing was intoxicating, fresh.

When the young man had finished, he swivelled round in his seat. 'Do you like it?' For a moment he looked even younger, unsure.

'I do,' Charles managed, taking a step towards him. 'Very much.'

The smile was back, wider now. 'Why don't you try?' He jumped up, vacating the seat, indicating that Charles should sit.

'If you're sure.' Charles placed his hat on top of the piano and saw that the straw had made painful grooves in his palm where he had gripped it. He took his place on the stool. He could feel the young man behind him, could smell tobacco, but sweetly, and something else, brighter than that. He thought of the sea.

A little light-headed, he lifted his hands and tried a few bars, but his fingers were clumsy; the young man had played a syncopated rhythm, but Charles seemed stuck in a regimented four-four. He gave a quick, embarrassed laugh as he pulled his hands away. 'I can't seem to get it.'

He twisted, as though to stand up, but the young man touched him gently on the shoulder, gesturing that Charles should make room for him on the stool, which he did, inching to the left, until one buttock was all but hanging off, hardly daring to breathe, unable to decide whether the experience was pleasurable or painful, as the young man played through the first few bars again. 'There are lyrics too,' he grinned, and began, rather unselfconsciously, to sing:

Oh ma honey! Oh ma honey!
Better hurry and let's me-an-der,
Ain't you goin'? Ain't you goin'?
To the leader man, ragged meter man . . .

'You have to *swing*, you see.' The young man lifted his hands and turned to Charles. 'They say that Negroes play it best. Down in New Orleans.'

This last was spoken in an approximation of an American accent, and Charles, understanding it was supposed to be amusing, nodded and laughed. 'Yes,' he said. 'I suppose they do.'

The young man wrinkled his nose, as if to show that he was no actor and he knew it, and Charles found himself smiling back.

Just then the bell rang in the front of the shop, and Charles scrambled to his feet, banging his knee on the underside of the piano.

'Gosh. All right there?' As the young man reached out, his hand grazed Charles's arm.

'Yes, I'm . . .' He took a step away. 'I'm fine.'

The young man nodded. 'Well, it seems I have a customer. Please.' He gestured to the piano. 'Do stay. Take your time.'

He disappeared into the front room, from where his voice soon sounded, alongside those of a woman and a child. Charles stared at the sheet music, his knee throbbing, hands stinging. The air felt rearranged. The young man's laughter sounded behind him. The woman's then too. Whatever he had said she sounded pleased. He was nice. A nice young man. Good at his job. That was all.

He made himself breathe. Stayed there, swaying a little, until he felt he had mastery of himself. Then he lifted the music from the stand and took it through to the front of the shop.

The woman and her child were bent over, the child testing out violins for size. The young man was standing close.

'I'll take it,' said Charles.

'Very glad to hear it.' The young man looked up with a smile. He took it back behind the counter, where he slid it into a brown paper bag before ringing it up on the till.

'What do I call it?' asked Charles. His palms were slippery as he handed over his coins.

'Ragtime. It's a rag. Perhaps you could come back and let me know how you get on?'

Charles nodded, half tipsy as he made his way back out on to the street.

He could feel that rag burning a hole in his music bag as he took a tram across the city to his parents' house. *Oh ma honey! Oh ma honey! Better hurry, and let's me-an-der.* It was as though he were smuggling something colourful and rare and contraband.

He could hardly sit still as he endured a particularly long and tiresome lunch. He was seated across from his mother, who picked at her food, reaching up and plucking repeatedly at the collar of her dress. It occurred to him that in those repetitive, unconscious movements, she looked for all the world like one of their patients. She could not hide her perspiration, only took out her handkerchief from time to time and dabbed at herself. Her smell, of which Charles caught occasional wafts over the table, was a miasma of the female body and lavender water – as far from the fresh scent of the young man at Spence's as it was possible to get.

His father, dressed as usual in a suit of black stuff, looked lumpy and uncomfortable, his skin the colour of steamed suet. Even the meat on Charles's plate seemed offensive, everything redolent of death and decay: the room itself, the corner table, the aspidistras, the endless ornaments that covered every spare piece of surface – china dogs and china girls, with tiny china parasols – and china, china everywhere and none of it of any practical use at all.

Purge.

'Purge,' said Charles.

'What was that?' His father's head snapped up.

'I'm sorry?'

'You said something.'

'Did I?'

174

'Sounded like "purge".'

Charles shook his head. 'I'm sorry. I didn't mean to.'

Silence fell, punctuated by his father's rigorous chewing and his mother's softer, more troubled endeavours.

Charles tugged at his tie. It was true: he wished for something to come and cleanse this house, to get into the corners and shine a light. He imagined a great electric light in the middle of the ceiling, imagined the young man in Spence's holding it up: how all of the darkened, murky, female corners would be lit by the certain, unblinking light of the future. How his parents would shade their eyes and shrink away.

His mother was saying something.

'I'm sorry?' Charles dragged himself back to the room.

'The Coronation?' she was saying. 'What are your plans? At the . . . asylum. Will it be marked at all?'

He pulled a piece of cabbage over his half-eaten meat and placed his knife and fork together on the plate. 'Of course. I have no doubt that there will be a special tea. A Sports Day too. We'll be having a tug of war. Patients against the men. I believe I might be pulling myself.'

This last was not true. Indeed, it was a flagrant lie. The team had been picked, and Charles had been extremely disappointed to see his name was not on the list. He was down for 'referee' instead.

His father snorted. 'I'd like to see that.'

Charles's skin flared.

His mother gave one of her special rictus smiles. 'Well,' she said. 'Won't that be nice?'

Charles said nothing. In other times, very recently even, he might have dug in his heels at this juncture, given ever more florid descriptions of the day to come, the splendid cakes and pies that would come forth from the kitchens, made by the patients' hands, the fancy-dress costumes the staff would labour over, but today was different, today was . . . rearranged. Today, all he could hear was a tune in his head: 'Alexander's Ragtime Band'.

When the dessert spoons had been cleared, he leapt up, went over to the old upright piano in the corner, lifted the lid and picked out a few choice chords of 'Alexander', humming the tune over the top.

'Stop!' His father banged the table. 'Stop that infernal noise!'

But Charles did not stop. He played as much as he could remember, drowning his father out. When he had finished, he turned, breathless, back to the table and saw his father had left the room.

'What,' said his mother, the expression on her face for all the world as though the family cat had deposited a dubious-looking parcel at her feet, 'was *that*?'

'Ragtime, Mother!' said Charles, jumping up, almost knocking the aspidistra from its perch on the occasional table. '*Ragtime!*'

And then it came to him in a great golden rush: he didn't care if his father disapproved. Didn't care what his mother thought. They would see what he could do soon enough. He thought of the letter from the Society, waiting for him in his room at the asylum, tucked into his drawer. He thought of their faces when they learnt of *that*. He thought of the paper that he was to write, how he was to persuade Churchill of the merits of segregation, and music, and dancing, and work; how he was to save Miss Church from herself and from her books and deliver her to her family, and then – best of all – he thought of John Mulligan's face in the ballroom, when the orchestra played 'Alexander's Ragtime Band'. Because it was that very thing, in that very moment, that he had decided to do.

His paper.

The music.

The future.

He left the house humming 'Alexander', and the tune carried him all the way back, by tram and train and then by foot, through the bosky, scented evening lanes to Sharston.

It was late on Wednesday evening, towards the end of orchestra practice, when he brought out the music to the rag.

On his appointment as bandmaster he had made sure that the orchestra gathered for their rehearsals in one of the more pleasant of the spaces available – a large, airy meeting room with an aspect over the grounds to the west. As the evening had progressed, the men discarded their jackets and now sat in their shirtsleeves, doors flung open to the summer evening air. The last of the sun was lighting the tops of the wood beyond, turning the green to gold.

Their rehearsals followed a similar course, each of them taking turns to suggest a number, which they would then stagger through. Tonight they had begun, as usual, with a few bits of Strauss and Lehár, stopping after the first few numbers for a break and a smoke. Jeremy Goffin had taken it upon himself to light candles, forgoing the usual gas lamps, and now the whole scene had rather a timeless, enchanted air.

Charles brought his music bag on to his lap, fingering the papers inside. During the week he had copied out each instrumental part for 'Alexander'. They had been pleasingly taxing to transpose; it had been satisfying to watch the dots cluster across the page and to imagine the sounds from each instrument combining to make a whole. He had heard the young man's voice in his head as he did so: *You have to make it swing.* That odd little accent he had put on, as though performing a show just for Charles. *They say that Negroes play it best. Down in New Orleans.*

He had tried to swing, moving forward and backward in his chair:

> *Oh ma honey! Oh ma honey!*
> *Better hurry and let's me-an-der.*

It made no sense – and yet it made a delicious sort of sense all the same. And it suited the weather too, something about the laziness of great heat: *meander.* What a wonderful word that was!

> *Ain't you goin'? Ain't you goin'?*
> *To the leader man, ragged meter man?*

Ragged meter man – this surely meant the time signature, a ragged meter, not strict, not straight-edged.

> *Let me take you by the hand,*
> *Up to the man, up to the man,*
> *Who's the leader of the band!*

And that was him: the leader of the band. It was too delightful!

Now, when the men had finished their cigarettes and their pipes and drifted back from outside to take their place in the small semicircle of chairs, Charles cleared his throat and spoke. 'I have something here you might enjoy.'

His hand was not altogether steady as he passed the sheets around. There were some mutters as he hummed tentatively through the first few bars. When he had done so, his fellow players stared, as though he had taken leave of his senses, and Charles's courage threatened to fail him. But then he thought of the young man in Spence's and the swinging, easy way he had played, and, emboldened, beat out the syncopation on the top of his music stand. One by one the men took up their instruments.

By the end of the session, when the moths were flapping around the candles and singeing their wings in the flames, and people's faces were swimming rosy in the candlelight, they had made a fairly decent fist of the piece.

It was, however, a very *English* fist, thought Charles, when the rehearsal was over and he was folding away the music stands. Upright and stiff-jacketed, as though a gentleman's club had been tipped unceremoniously on to a paddle steamer on the Mississippi. They were far from capturing the true *spirit* of the music, that sense of swinging ease.

They say that Negroes play it best.

He could well believe it. There was something so utterly foreign about the sound. He should try to obtain a copy. Perhaps a gramophone record, if one existed? Perhaps he should ask the young man in Spence's where he might find one? Or if he might play for him again? Certainly he should return, sometime soon, to purchase more music like that. It was so . . . intoxicatingly fresh.

He moved around the room, finishing the last of the music stands, humming, extinguishing the candles. When he reached the last one, he paused; catching his reflection in the window glass, in the candlelight his face looked different. The cheeks hollowed, his eyes harder, as though lit by an internal fire.

Good.

Let the fire come. Let it transform him. Let it temper him.

The future was coming. Even here. Even here in this island ship of souls, cast away on the green-brown seas of the moor, even here it would find its way through.

Ella

Dear Ella,

This is a feather from a swallow. I believe it must have travelled from Africa. Or so says Dan Riley who knows such things as he was out on the ships and that as he says is thousands of miles from here and a mighty unknown place. A place of jungle and of heat. And yet they choose to build their nests here and return here each year.

They make me think of freedom. But also of home. They put me in mind of my home which was in the west of Ireland which is rocky and full of grey sea and grey sky. But sometimes there is a great softness and greenness to the land there also.

There is something in those birds that makes me think of you. I hope you will not mind me saying so. Something small but wild. Something made for flight.

I will stop now,

And send you best wishes,

John

Ella held the feather in her hand. It was deep blue in colour, almost black, with a round spot of white on it. If she stroked it one way, it was smooth, almost oily, the other way was rougher to the touch.

She looked up, to where Clem was reading the letter over in her head.

'Which ones are the swallows?' she asked.

Clem folded the paper and jumped to her feet, handing the letter back to Ella. 'Wait a moment.' She went over to the set of bookshelves that were ranged along one wall. There was a row of books there, on the bigger shelves at the bottom, each the same large size and shape and edged in gold. Clem trailed her hand along their backs. 'This,' she said, 'is the *Encyclopaedia Britannica*.'

Ella made her way to join her. 'What's it about?'

'Oh . . . everything,' said Clem, 'that's the point. It's extraordinary that they have it here at all, really. I must be the only one who ever opens it. The entries are arranged alphabetically, so . . .' she ran her hands more slowly now, stopping at one of the spines, 'here's S . . . but this volume ends at Subliminal Self, and though I'd love to know what that means, for our purposes we need the next book, which begins at Submarine and ends with Tom-Tom, so Swallow should be in here, d'you see?'

'I think so.'

Clem lifted the book from the shelf and carried it over towards the table. She opened the covers, passing the pages through her hands, as though she were some sort of stage magician, words and pictures flying past until, '*That*'s a swallow,' she said triumphantly, stopping at a picture of a bird with a white throat and forked tail.

'I know those birds!' Ella put her hand to the page. 'There are two above the window over there.'

Clem nodded. 'They're everywhere at this time of year. Shall I read out what it says?'

'Yes!'

'*The swallow is the bird which of all others is recognized as the harbinger of summer in the northern hemisphere.*' Clem wrinkled her nose. 'Harbinger means . . . a sort of messenger, so, the bird that tells you summer is here. *In summer it ranges all over Europe, whereas in winter it migrates south, reaching India, Burma, the Malay peninsula and the whole of Africa.*'

Clem began raking through the book again. 'Here,' she opened it at the front, smoothing the page out, 'this is a map of the world. You've seen one before?'

Ella nodded. She saw a huge room, one wall taken up with a map; they had been ushered in there once a year to be addressed by the owner of the mill. He would point to where Bradford was, and then all the many places that their wool was sent to, picked out with red, looping thread.

'D'you know where we are then?'

Ella leant over the map, found Britain. 'There,' she pointed.

'Yes. So now,' Clem said, 'you must imagine a bird . . . A bird with a wingspan no bigger than *this*,' she reached for Ella's hand, turning it over and opening her palm, then she took the feather, and with the lightest of touches traced a line from Ella's thumb to the tip of her little finger, 'making the journey all the way across Europe, down to Africa, or even all the way to India and further east.'

Made for flight.

Ella felt her skin lift as though the wind had passed over it.

For a moment the two of them stood, unmoving, until Ella curled a soft fist over the feather and drew her hand away.

'I'd love to see India,' said Clem, moving back towards the book. 'The highest mountains in the world are there.' Her hands hovered over the map. 'This bird has probably seen more in a few weeks than I'll see in a lifetime. Can you imagine – being born here, right here, in the grounds of this place, and then spending the winter in India, or Africa, and then coming back here, to the very place where you were born, to find a mate? How on *earth* do they do it?'

Later, Ella looked for the two swallows in the eaves outside the window, watching them even more closely now. The thought of them flying all that way, across mountains and seas and returning here, because this was their home – of them knowing how to find it – changed things. It was a new way of seeing; this was no longer just the place where women and men were kept, but the home of other creatures too, ones that had travelled far and still chosen it, because this, above all other places, was the place to bring their families into the world.

The next time they met they moved in silence still, hardly looking at each other, but it was a different man she danced with now. Someone whose insides, she knew, spanned miles, even if his outside was closed and shuttered as before.

Facing him in the ballroom, her eyes only came up to his chin, and so she let them roam over his neck, tracing the dark hairs at the soft fold of his collar, the clear line where the sun-brown stopped and the white of the rest of him began. There were marks of the fields left on him: a stray piece of grass, a trace of dirt. Knowing she could not be seen, she closed her eyes and drank his scent: the heavy sweetness of tobacco clinging to his jacket, the freshness of the outside air, and his own, headier tang beneath, light at his neck, stronger when he lifted his arms, but none of it bad.

When the music finished, he handed her a folded square of paper, which she hid in her sleeve.

After the dance, as they filed back to the ward, Clem sought her out as soon as she could. 'Have you got it?' Her eyes were large, her breath coming quickly. 'The next letter? Can I see?'

Ella shook her head. 'Wait,' she said. 'Not here. Not yet.'

She wanted to sleep with the letter beside her, just one night, before she gave it to Clem to read.

The letter held a leaf – full-green and fleshy, waxy to the touch. Ella traced the ridge of its spine and the thin lines that came off it. If she held it to the light, the leaf changed, the thin tracery of lines coming clearer still.

She folded it into her dress along with the feather, wrapped in a handkerchief she had stolen from the laundry. It had appeared one day in amongst the grey linen, a white square with coloured flowers sewn at the corner, so lovely she couldn't resist tucking it into her sleeve. The buttercup, which was turning brown, she put between the pages of the encyclopaedia, in the book of B.

The next afternoon, in the day room, she handed the letter to Clem.

Dear Ella,

At the far side of the field we have just mowed for hay is a wood. I think you cannot see it from your window. I will try to write it so you can picture it. The trees are tall. The wind lifts the leaves and the sound is that of water over rocks.

Beside this wood is an oak. It has low branches and offers good shade and if we are allowed to then we rest beneath it.

Dan Riley has a strange way with trees and this is his favourite – so big it would take ten men to clasp around it hand to hand. He bows towards it. He takes off his hat and waits as though for some signal before he sits.

Do you know says Dan this was the land of oaks Mio Capitane and the oak was the great god of these lands and that this land was covered in oaks like these before we cut them down to make the ships.

And I remember then how in Ireland in the village where I grew up there were few trees remaining but a ballad singer who passed through there every once in a while sang of the land and of the trees that had been cut. There was a grove nearby. There were trees there whose branches you could take to bless a marriage or those that women would tie charms to if they wanted a child or didn't want a child. Or wanted a man or didn't want a man. And many other things too. The trees were covered with these hanging wishes that caught the light and wind.

Listen.

Dan puts his ear to the bark and closes his eyes till a smile comes over his face. Listen, he says. We have all forgot to listen.

I put my ear to the bark. I can feel the warm wood the soft brush of the moss.

Can you hear that? Dan says. Wild wood.

Dan says he can speak with trees. But they take a long time to answer. That's why you have to learn to listen. If we listened he says we could not cut down our friends. Their jokes are too good for that.

Then he laughs his great laugh and I no longer know whether he is telling stories or not.

Yours,

John.

Ella was standing by the window, her hands pressed against hot glass. Ahead of her was the stand of tall trees, the two with their branches growing together. She had watched them as they grew greener day by day, and now they were in the full glory of their leaves.

She had never seen a wood. Trees upon trees. How would it be to lie on the earth – to have nothing to do but lie and look up into the green?

There was a small sound, and she turned to see that Clem had come to stand beside her. She brought her hands up so that they mirrored Ella's – placing her palms flat on the glass. For a long time she just stayed there, not speaking, then, 'If I tell you something,' she said, in a low voice, 'will you promise you won't breathe a word?'

Ella half turned towards her.

'*Promise?*' Clem's face was tight.

'I promise.'

'The doctor . . .' said Clem. 'The one who plays the violin, and the piano in the day room . . . What do you think of him?'

Ella looked back at the browned grass beyond the window. 'He . . . plays the piano well.'

'Doesn't he?' said Clem, and then her face contracted. 'He's lonely. I know it. I can feel it when he plays. Sometimes, when he's finished, he sits for a moment with his hands on the keys and it's all I can do not to go to him. Just to touch him. To say I'm here. That I'm living too. That he's not alone.' She was quiet, and there was only the high, fast sound of her breath until she spoke again. 'Have you ever been with a man?' she said.

'No.'

'Neither have I.' Her hands whitened. 'I haven't even been alone with one. Except for the teacher when I was young, and I don't want to think about that.' She leant forward, her breath misting the glass. 'Sometimes though, when I'm in the ballroom, and there's someone who has touched me gently, and knows how to dance – the big man with the tattoos – it was him the other day. I looked at him and I thought – what would it be like? What would it be like to be with you? And I imagine it. In that moment I imagine it. And it's not ugly,' she said. 'It's not.'

Ella turned to her.

'But mostly,' said Clem, 'I think of him. The doctor – of his loneliness. And then I think – what am I thinking of *him* for? There are better, finer things to do with a life than think about *men*.' Her voice faltered and dropped. 'But there are women who die, aren't there, without ever knowing what it feels like. Women in here, in the chronic wards, who will die without ever knowing that. Sometimes I think that will be me. That I'll wither and rot before anyone knows any part of me.'

Ella inched her hand towards Clem's on the glass, till

187

the edges of their little fingers touched. 'That won't be you, Clem. That can't be you.'

'But it might.' Clem turned to her now. 'What about John? Do you think about him? About how you can be with him?'

'I don't know.'

'*Liar*.' Clem lifted her hand and placed it down, trapping Ella's own against the glass. 'You're lying. Don't lie.'

'Yes. Yes, I do.'

'I know you do. I know.' Clem pressed harder. '*Listen*, Ella, listen to me. You should go to him. You should meet him.'

'How?' She tried to pull away, but Clem was gripping too tight. 'How can I do that?'

'You'll find a way.' Clem's eyes were stretched wide, and a bright flush scalded the side of her neck. 'You have to. It's the Coronation next week. It's Midsummer. We'll be outside. You'll be able to find a way to him then. Be with him. Taste him. Let him know he's not alone.'

Ella stared at her hand, pressed in Clem's, and felt a green wildness pass between them, the current of it loosed and dangerous, and she didn't know if it was her, or Clem, or the letter, or the summer itself outside the walls that had conjured it first.

John

THE FOOTBALL PITCH WAS chalked into long straight lines. John stood on one side of it, he and a thousand other men, penned in like cattle behind ropes, waiting, sweating in the heat. His shirt was plastered to his back, and they hadn't even started moving yet. Every so often a light drizzle spattered the ground. The sun was only visible as a pale-grey disc behind the clouds.

Beside him, Dan was gripping the rope, practising for the pull. On his head he wore a great swathe of ivy fashioned into a crown, leaves taken from the sentinel oak twisted amongst it. 'Midsummer's Day,' he had winked, as he put it on his head.

John kept his eyes on the baking field, waiting for the moment the women would appear.

A movement on the top of the small hill signalled their coming, then a great straggling line of them poured out of the asylum buildings, down the slope that led to the cricket grounds, and then across that expanse of grass, their attendants yelling, fanning them out so that they took their places behind a rope, on the other side of the football pitch, opposite the men. Their bodies were slightly hunched, their movements jerky and uncertain, as though unused to such things as space and sky. He thought he caught her briefly, walking with the tall, fair girl, until she was swallowed by the roiling crowd and hidden from view. He touched the edge of the letter in his pocket.

> There will be many people there.
> Perhaps we can meet then?

There was no chance now while the ropes were up, but later, when the games began, perhaps they might.

Beside him, Dan sent up a low whistle. 'Here we go. Would you look at these jesters then?'

A clutch of the attendants was trooping over the grass in the wake of the women; they were dressed in costume and wearing a forced and jaunty air. Jim Brandt led the pack, dressed as a policeman, a truncheon in his hand. Others had their faces blackened and were wearing frizzy wigs. Clowns with little hats on the sides of their heads had costumes covered in red spots, drummer boys in full uniform beat the instruments that hung about their necks. There were Chinamen in pointed hats, men made to look like monkeys, and near to the back, Dr Fuller, in a strange mixture of a costume, wearing top hat and frock coat, his face made up as a clown's, but dressed as a horse below, his bottom half clad in brown. Strange little-man legs flapped uselessly either side of the horse's flanks as he walked.

A chorus of jeers and whistles went up from the men. 'All right there, Doctor!' Dan roared. 'What have you come as then?'

'Good afternoon, gentlemen!' Fuller came to a stop before them; his make-up looked greasy already. 'Happy Coronation Day!' He lifted his top hat to them, showing hair stuck to his head with sweat. 'Are we ready for our revels? A little Midsummer madness before our tea? I see you're already anointed, Mr Riley?'

Dan rolled up his sleeves and threw his big arm out over the rope, hand outstretched in challenge. 'Those fellas in London aren't the only ones who get to wear a crown, eh, Doctor?'

Fuller ignored the hand, busying himself instead with his papers. 'I see you two gentlemen are down for the tug of war. Let's hope the rain holds off till then, eh?'

'Aye.' Dan's hand curled into a fist. 'Let's hope so.'

As Fuller made his way down the line, Dan's face changed. 'That's not a horse,' he lobbed after him. 'It's an ass. The arse end of an ass.'

The men whooped at this. John saw Fuller pause before mustering his dignity and carrying on, making his way over to a high chair facing the grass and calling out names for the egg and spoon.

'Midsummer.' Dan turned to John. 'Did they used to light bonfires in Ireland then, *chavo*? Midsummer's Eve?'

'Aye.'

'He'd make a good Guy, wouldn't he?' Dan jerked his shoulder after Fuller. 'To put on top of those fires?'

A shrill blast sounded on Fuller's whistle and the games began, the first men picking their way out to take their places on the grass.

John's gaze slid back over towards the women, and with a jolt he saw her – facing him at the edge of the crowd, her pale face steady and intent. The sky was lightening a little, and she tipped up her chin to receive a shaft of sun. His heart clenched at the sight; looking at her now, her face bright, he could not believe he had ever thought her funny-looking, could not believe he had ever thought her plain. She was beautiful. She blazed with it. He wanted to go to her, to climb over this rope and walk across the grass, while these idiots were prancing about in their costumes. Desire welled within him, a wave powering him forward, and he almost moved, before it broke in his chest and raked back across his belly, and he stayed where he was, shuddering in its wake.

'All right there, *chavo*?' A smile creased Dan's brown face.

John ducked his head, rolling himself a cigarette. 'Get to fuck, Riley,' he said, 'and give me a match.'

The rain did hold off, but barely, spitting sometimes but never falling with much force. There was no wind. It was as though they were all simmering under the great grey

191

lid of the sky, like water almost brought to the boil. The afternoon rumbled on: race after race, and all of them as tame as children's games. He would not have minded a game of hurley, throwing the ball and running, letting his body take him where it would, but this was nothing like it; this was being pushed and prodded and corralled into lines and whistles and races and no freedom at all.

He concentrated on her instead. Not letting her from his sight. It was not hard, as she stayed in the same place, always just across the grass, but as the afternoon stretched and sagged, he began to wonder if she was real; she seemed insubstantial somehow, in her paleness, as waves of heat rose from the earth and blurred her outline, a changing creature, made of water, not of flesh and blood. If he crossed the grass towards her, if he tried to touch her, would she slide through his fingers and be gone?

When the races had finished and the ground was dusty and the fag end of the afternoon only wanted a heel to put it out, it was time for the tug of war. Dan, who had been dozing on the patchy grass, launched himself up as soon as it was called, the general again now, beckoning the men he had chosen out of the pen, placing them into position on the rope, shuffling them like a deck of cards, muttering to himself.

John was the last to be placed, right at the front, facing Brandt.

'I knew you'd have wanted to be here, *mio Capitane*,' said Dan.

John gave a swift nod. Brandt was smirking over at him.

'I'll hold us steady, *mio Capitane*.' Dan clasped John on the shoulder. 'You at the front, me at the back. We'll show them. We'll show the bastards all right.'

Dan trotted back down the line, and once there wrapped the end of the rope three times around his body before taking up his place at the rear. He sent up a loud whistle to say he was ready.

The crowd had come to buzzing, chattering life. Dr Fuller waddled his horse into the middle of the field and held up a hand for silence. 'Ladies and gentlemen,' he shouted, 'on my whistle, the men will commence pulling.'

She was watching. He felt the knowledge of it lift his skin.

A memory filled him – playing hurley, or pitching on the crossroads, the women sitting in the fields beside the road, wrapped in their shawls, their red petticoats bright against the green grass, their high chatter like the sound of small birds. Every young man growing a little taller in the gaze of them.

A different sort of heat rose in him as the sinews of hemp grew taut in his hands.

Fuller stepped up to the middle of the rope. His make-up had melted and his mouth was an ugly, smeared gash. 'The team who are the first to pull the first man from the other team, over *this* line,' he bent to the ground, drawing a bright chalk mark on the browned grass, 'will be declared the winner. Are you ready, men?'

Brandt nodded. John nodded. Fuller blew his whistle and stepped away. Immediately, John felt the pull from the other side. He leant backwards, as though into a strong wind.

'*Allez, chavos!*' Dan's voice came from the back of the line, tight with the pull.

He dug his heels into the parched earth, the rope's dry fibres twisting in his hands. His feet stumbled a little, and he was at such a low angle that for an awful second he feared he would fall, but he found his balance and stayed upright. His palms pricked then burnt. Sweat fell from his forehead, stinging and blinding him. He was leaning far, far back now. A stillness came over the pullers, the stillness of great effort, evenly matched. A stillness over the silent, watching crowd. The air taut now too. Little give on either side. Nothing in it.

'*Allez, chavos!*' A roar from Dan Riley ripped into the air. '*Pull now! Pull!*'

John grunted with effort, felt the rope move towards him, a little, a little further. Brandt's smile was gone, his face was distorted with the pull, and John had him; he began to walk backwards, slowly, slowly backwards, and he was groaning, all of them were, lowing like cattle with the effort of it, and his forearms were bursting, but he felt the strength of the men behind him, felt Dan, although he could not see him, holding the back steady, and Brandt was coming closer to the line, grimacing, cursing with each step, a filthy black fish flapping its last, ready to be caught.

Something to laugh at.

Brandt was almost up to the white chalk line, and his face was the face of a man who had lost, but then there was a great shrill whistle from Fuller, and in the surprise John felt the rope yank from his hands, watched helplessly as it twitched and loosened like a living thing, and his hands were empty, and he was on the ground.

He scrambled to his feet. Brandt was moving towards the doctor, who had his hands over his head as though to shield himself from a blow. Then, after another quick blast from Fuller's whistle, the doctor stretched his arm out to-wards the attendant's team. 'The staff are the winners!'

A great bellow came from the back of the line, and Dan barrelled past John, heading straight for Brandt.

John bent, gathering his breath. He cast his eyes towards the women, saw with a start that Ella had moved – that somehow, in the commotion, she had managed to break free of the women's lines and was waiting by a stand of high fir trees curving close to where he stood. She was alone, not twenty feet from him. As he watched, she disappeared into the trees. His heart battered his chest. He turned from the mayhem, slowly at first, then covering the distance in great, gathering strides.

'Mulligan!' A shout came from behind him. 'Stop! Stop now!'

He ignored the voice, carrying on until a blow halted him, clumsy and splayed across his shoulders.

'Where do you think you are going?'

He turned, breathing hard. It was Fuller. The doctor was holding his hand to his chest as though it were painful, as though he himself was surprised by what he had done. *'Where do you think you are going?'* The man's voice was shrill. A vein pounded at his neck.

John stared at him. At his ridiculous make-up, half smudged, his horse's head, heat sagged, drooping off to one side.

'I need a piss,' he said, and his voice was low and hoarse.

Fuller's eyes bulged. 'Excuse me?'

'I need a piss.' John gestured with his arm towards the clump of trees. 'Would you want me to do it here on the grass instead?'

'No,' Fuller barked, his neck crimson. 'No, I most certainly would not.'

John reached up and wiped his forehead with his cuff.

Over by the tug of war, the patients were being rounded up by the attendants. Dan was still shouting. Brandt had his arm twisted up behind him. The afternoon was over. The bastards had cheated and won. Just as they would always cheat and win. The game was rigged from the first.

He glanced over at the trees but could no longer see her. His mouth felt sour, as though the bitter dregs of something were held there. He swallowed. He and Fuller seemed to be alone in the middle of this heat-scoured field. A strangeness hovering in the air between them. He recognized it, though he could not name it. 'D'ye know what?' John fumbled with his trousers. 'It's a fair way to those trees. I think I'll do it here after all.'

He heard the shocked intake of the man's breath. '*Mulligan—*'

But his piss cut the man off, ripping on to the thirsty ground, arcing and pooling between their feet.

'Mulligan! I will not allow this. *Mr Mulligan! It is CORONATION DAY!*'

'This is what I think of your rules.' John was enjoying it now. 'This is what I think of your *coronation*. And this is what I think of your *fucking* king.' Hot piss splashed over the doctor's boots.

Fuller stared down, panting, but still he did not move. It was as though some enchantment had rooted him to the spot.

When John had finished, he took his time, shaking himself off, tucking himself back in. There had been a decent amount. He had needed it after all.

Charles

HE COULD NOT THINK of it, and yet he could think of little else. It colonized his thoughts. Had anyone else seen? He didn't think so, but it was impossible to tell.

Following the Sports Day there was to be a Coronation Tea, and Charles's plan had been to debut 'Alexander' while the patients were eating; there was a last rehearsal scheduled for three o'clock. But as soon as he entered the room Charles saw that the meeting was ill judged: half of the players were missing, and those that were there were sweaty and hectic from their exertions. Goffin arrived still wearing his athletics gear – his great thighs on flagrant display.

Trying to keep the atmosphere light, trying to quash the sight that threatened to insert itself continually in front of his eyes, Charles smiled as he brought out the music and handed it around. 'Just the thing for this sort of weather!' he said. 'They say the negroes play it best,' he attempted an American accent, *'down in New Orleans!'*

There was a strange, strained silence at this last, until Goffin, seated to Charles's left, his trumpet resting against one of those thighs, snickered, 'Yes, well, it helps if you're a nigger, I suppose.'

Charles tried a laugh to show he had a sense of humour too, but it sounded hollow and peevish.

'Actually,' he said, after the band had stumbled once through the piece, 'I'm not feeling at all well. I've a headache from the heat. All this syncopation is making me a little queasy. I think it might be better to stick with something simple. The Trio from *Pomp and Circumstance* will do.'

And so it had been. A steady two-four time signature. Elgar for the Coronation Tea.

Later, when the patients had been put to bed, the staff gathered in their quarters, a few bottles of ale were opened and the new King and Queen were toasted once more. It was nine o'clock and bright as noon outside. The grey of the day had given way to a fine evening, and a jostling little group of the younger men had formed, readying themselves to walk out across the fields to the pub in Sharston village.

'Fuller! Hey, Fuller!'

Charles looked up.

'Are you coming with us then?'

It was Goffin, washed now and changed from his sports kit into a pale cotton suit. A high colour to his cheeks, grinning as though nothing untoward had occurred, giving off the air that young men do when they have tasted alcohol and know there is more to come. Charles felt his cheeks sting all over again. He gave a wave. 'Thank you. I have some work to do.'

He picked up his *Times* and turned to the back pages, where the paper had recently begun to run a column entitled 'Deaths by Heat'.

Where was the shy young man who had been so happy to be included in the band? Gone in the heat of athletic triumph and a couple of ales. And really, thought Charles, it was disputable whether the men deserved their victory. He supposed it was his fault if there had been an injustice. The patients had been winning, but he had blown his whistle too soon. Confusion had reigned. Perhaps he should have been tougher, rather than declaring the victory for the staff. But tensions were high, and Brandt was a threatening fellow at best. It had seemed the orderly, sensible thing to do.

He looked up and saw Goffin standing before him, his face a little blurry with drink and heat. 'You sure?' He waved a bottle of ale in Charles's face.

'Yes. Thank you. I have, as I said, some work to do.' Charles felt brittle suddenly, as though he might crack.

'Ahh, but . . .' Goffin looked a little unsteady on his feet. 'Seems a shame. Shaaame to be working on an evening like this.' He waved a hand towards the windows.

'Yes, well,' Charles said. 'There we are.'

As he mounted the stairs to his room, he could hear the young men singing:

> *It was a lover and his lass,*
> *With a hey, and a ho, and a hey nonino,*
> *That o'er the green corn field did pass . . .*

Inside his quarters the sun still blared through the window, relentless. Outside, it fell on the scorched grass. It was an official heatwave now, twenty days straight without proper rain (the ragged sprinkling of that morning could hardly be counted). He longed for darkness, for shadow. He reached up, prodding uselessly at his window, even though he knew it would not open far.

He could see Goffin and the clutch of men below, pushing and ragging each other as they headed out over the grounds. A couple of them had obviously raided the hay stores and fashioned rude torches, which were burning brightly as they walked, casting long dancing shadows behind them. Charles flinched at the sight; it looked as though giants were abroad.

199

Midsummer Night, but he did not feel any joy – everything felt upside down. He caught a glimpse of his reflection in the mirror, saw that despite a hurried washing earlier in the day vestiges of his clown make-up still clung to his skin. He bent to his basin and scrubbed until the stains were gone and his face was raw, then closed the curtains a little way, unthreaded his laces and sat on the edge of his bed. He pulled *The Times* listlessly towards him, tugging at his collar as he read that evening's offering in 'Deaths by Heat': a young couple whose motor car had skidded on melted tarmac and ended their days impaled on railings. He was glad he had not been the doctor at that particular scene. He leafed through the paper for some light relief but found none: industrial unrest was growing, coal heavers and dockers were on strike. Seamen had struck again to join them. Home Secretary Churchill would have his hands full.

Where was Churchill then, right at this moment? Not stuck in a tiny room, alone and musing. He would be out. At his club perhaps, relaxing after the exertions of the day, surrounded by the great and the good, cigar in one hand, and in the other a glass of champagne, or hock, or something that Charles had never heard of but Churchill knew intimately, a French white, crisp and clean, to wash away the mugginess of the day. He would be taking the bottle himself, topping up his companions' glasses. Holding forth. Toasting the King.

And the others, in the pub in Sharston? Their laughing faces, fists clinking tankards of frothing ale. He should have gone, it was Midsummer Night after all, a time to be abroad. It would have been the best thing to do. Show there were no hard feelings. Make sure they did not think him a prig. But the day had stripped him some-how.

It helps if you're a nigger, I suppose. He drew Goffin's comment forth like a splinter from beneath his skin.

The thing he wished, most fervently of all, was to see the young man in Spence's again, to step into the cool of the shop, feel his propinquity, catch his oxygenated scent. The easy way he played. His lightness. What wouldn't he give for a draught of that lightness now?

Had they wanted him to go with them, those men at the pub, or were they simply being nice? Or worse – had they wished to humiliate him further? And why could he not tell the difference?

And Mulligan. *Mulligan.* After all he had done for him: the music, the dances, the moving him to work in the fields; all the hope he had placed in his recovery.

Good God.

Charles groaned. Finally, he gave way to it. The memory, the sight of the Irishman's organ: red-tipped, half engorged, the pace arc of liquid soaking his boots. He peered down at them now. He had rinsed them thoroughly, there was no sign of the man's depredations there. But the stain was not to the leather. It had been a Saturnal, out there on the cricket field. Not just Mulligan, but Riley too, in that ridiculous green crown, ordering his troops like the Lord of Misrule. Anger welled within him and he understood; *that* was why he had blown his whistle – Mulligan's strength, the puckish grin on Riley's face as the rope edged towards the line. It should not be allowed.

He lay back on his bed and closed his eyes, but a hectic energy invaded his limbs. He swung himself up and over to his desk, brought out his papers and shuffled

201

through them until he reached Mulligan's notes. There were pages of sketches there: Mulligan – his shirt removed, that particular, maddening hinge where the torso met the groin.

He saw it again, the man's member, held in his hands. The red, slightly swollen tip. His penis. His *cock*. The man was filthy. Soiled. Everything was soiled. The season, which had seemed to hold so much, curdling as though a canker had entered a fruit. *Midsummer night.*

Nothing was as simple as it seemed.

What would Churchill say?

He imagined the great man, standing beside him, peering over his shoulder.

Tell me about him. Churchill pointed with a stubby finger at the pictures of Mulligan. *He's a fine specimen. He interests me.*

'He . . . he is . . . a delinquent.'

I see. And this is a man you wished to make your argument for? For segregation? For the improving benefits of music? This is the man you hoped would improve? Sedition, Fuller, lurks in the Celt! We cannot weed it out.

'Yes.' Charles stared at his papers. 'Yes, I see.'

Imagine, Fuller! Just imagine if Mulligan were to chose a mate in here. You must entertain it. It is the logical extrapolation of the future you propose. If men like Muligan believe their right to choose a mate and procreate remains inalienable, what dangers are posed to the race?

Read this, Fuller.

If you wish to see sense, then read this.

Churchill pointed to a pamphlet on Charles's desk.

ON THE STERILIZATION OF DEGENERATES
H. C. Sharp. Indiana Reformatory.

Charles edged it gingerly over towards him, opened it at random and read a page:

> Since October, 1899, I have been performing an operation known as vasectomy, which consists of ligating and resecting a small portion of the vas deferens. This operation is indeed very simple and easy to perform. I do it without administering an anesthetic either general or local. It requires about three minutes' time to perform the operation and the subject returns to his work immediately, suffers no inconvenience, and is in no way impaired for his pursuit of life, liberty, and happiness, but is effectively sterilized. I have been doing this operation for nine full years. I have two hundred and thirty-six cases that have afforded splendid opportunity for post-operative observation and I have never seen any unfavorable symptom.

He pushed it away again and put his head to the desk, breathing wood and resin and ink.

Exhaustion. He had hardly slept properly in weeks. And the heat. His nerves were strained to breaking.

He needed sustenance. He had been adrift from the great world for far too long. Next month was Major Leonard Darwin's Inaugural Address. It was to be held at the meeting rooms of the Eugenics Society in London and nothing – not even the train tracks melting and warping in the heat – would keep him from being there.

And Mulligan?

Charles lifted his head and took a long, last look at his sketches, before tearing them in two.

Sedition lurks in the Celt.

Churchill was right.

He would have to punish Mulligan properly this time. He had been far too lenient for far too long.

John

IT HAD COME, as he had known it would. Not in a summoning, nor in a visit to the doctor's office, but quietly, on a Friday evening when they were lined up for the dance. Just a shaking of the head, a pushing back from the line.

'Not you, Mulligan. Not you, Riley.'

John stared at the attendant. 'How long for?'

The man shrugged.

John turned, hands in his armpits to still them, or he would have taken a swipe at the man, and went and stood by the canary's cage, breathing hard, only looking up as the other men filed out.

It was Fuller. He knew it was.

He thought of her, of the men she would dance with to-night. The greasy hands she would have to pass through. A wasp buzzed, furious against the windowpane. Somewhere behind him, Dan slammed his fist repeatedly into the wall. John looked over towards the door. The attendant on duty was one of the older men, slumped in his chair, arms clasped over his chest, face puffy and nodding in the heat. It wouldn't take much to knock him sideways. Take the man's keys. Free himself from this stinking room. Open the doors all the way to the ballroom and lead a troop of the poor benighted fuckers out of here.

Then what?

Then he would be put downstairs until the wintertime.

So he stayed there, taut and unmoving, hemmed between the canary and the wasp, until the men returned from the ballroom. And when they did he searched their faces, greedy for a glimpse of her, as though she might have gilded those she danced with by her touch.

It was a sour, stagnant weekend. They weren't allowed out for recreation either, so John spent his days pacing the day room, with the windows that hardly opened, and the foul stench simmering, staring out at the sun-bleached grass.

He wished they had put him downstairs. At least it would be cool there, and quiet, and he would be left alone with his thoughts.

He waited for Fuller to come and play the piano on Monday. He wanted to see him – have the doctor look him in the eye and know the shame would be too great for him to speak a word about what John had done. There would be satisfaction in that at least. But Fuller did not appear, and so his anger brewed, strong and dark.

Then, Tuesday morning early, they were woken and hustled outside.

A ragged collection of men out there – he counted sixty or so huddled in the yard. He and Dan, some of the other stronger men from the ward, and others he did not know, faces he could hardly make out in the early blue light.

Even at this time it was already warm, with only a small freshness to the air, the heavy heat of the previous day just giving way to the heat of the day to come. But it was a freshness John gulped, taking great lungfuls after three days locked in that foetid ward. They were doled out a bowlful of porridge and a mug of tea, while a clutch of farmers stood before them, faces tight, dogs yapping by their heels, impatient for the men to finish. When they were done, they were led out to the fields while the sun cast a pale thin line across the sky. They were each handed sickles: bowed knives with small, serrated blades.

'So the bastards are not so proud they won't have us work for them then,' said Dan, turning his blade round in his hand. 'Not so proud not to give us these.'

'Aye.' The weight of the sickle was good in his palms. 'Not so proud as that.'

The first of the swallows were out, skimming the ears of wheat, their forms grey against the slowly lightening sky. The farmers hastened them into their rows, John and Dan in the first of them, as the sun rose and the dawn became streaked with blue.

'All right there.' Dan reached out, speaking softly, touching the crop, which shivered in the dawn air. 'All right there.'

A shout came from the farmers, the signal to move.

'Low and clean, *chavo*,' said Dan. 'Low and clean to the living earth.'

John bent, grasped his first fistful of the crop, and cut low and clean. At first he was awkward, but then found his stride, working out anger, working up a rhythm of hate.

By eleven the heat was raging and they were allowed to rest, and sought what shade they could beneath thorn trees that marked the borders of the fields out here. The farmers sat apart and watchful, faces creased with worry for the crop.

'They need us.' Dan nodded over towards them. 'We are more than we were to them. There'll be no shit from them for a while now.'

A strange sort of truce hung over them all, as birds of prey coasted in the high, arcing currents overhead.

The farmers brought them water to drink; cups were filled and passed around the men. Dan called for more, for a bucket, and not one of them said a word as he took off his shirt, dunked it in the water, and then wrapped the sodden garment around his neck. John followed, twisting his shirt to wring the wet from it and tying it in a blessedly cool crown around his head.

As the day passed, John's hate was swung out of him and gave way to something else in which there was only breath and the movement of his body, only the blue-gold dazzle of the light. Only walking forwards, one foot before the other across the field.

She was there before him, hand trailing through the ears of corn. Hair unbound. Sun glimmering on her skin.

She was there when all the other thoughts had fallen away.

A letter. He needed to get a letter to her somehow.

This became the pattern of their days: woken before dawn and led to the fields before the heat began to rage.

The farmers would stand by, shouting at the men to get them to work faster, but Dan was the one who kept them going. In the afternoons, when the heat was at its raging worst and the men were beginning to lag, he would start up a song: a sea shanty, lewd and salty in the mouth, with a chorus that everyone, even the men who forgot their own names, could learn. John joined in. At first his voice was parched and cracked, like the earth they walked upon, but it soon found itself again in the ripe and yeasty songs.

When he lay down to sleep, she was there, wound around his thoughts. He imagined her wound around his body. Her length of black hair. The weight of it. The paleness of her. Her sharp scent. He felt himself stir in response.

When he slept though, he slept dreamlessly, his body heavy, skull scraped clean by work.

Another Friday passed. Another Friday he and Dan were left behind while the others went off to dance. Another weekend locked in the day room.

John took paper and wrote to her – letters in which he poured out words he did not know that he would ever dare to send.

And then – another week of rising before dawn.

Even so, even working at the pace they were, they did not cut the crop quickly enough. The farmers cast dark faces to the sky and muttered to one another, and they were woken even earlier, and there was no respite and no rain. The fields were a torment of dust. At the end of the day they were all covered in it, strange creatures: eyes swollen, lids weeping and raw.

Once, in the dry, cracking afternoon, smoke rose from the rise of the moor ahead, a thin wisp of purple, and then the gorse and heather raging. The men downed their tools and watched, laughing at first, before standing in silence and awe: the burning enough to scorch your skin even at that distance, the fire moving quickly, leaping from bush to bush, roaring into the still afternoon, the moor shivering in rising waves of heat.

The farmers, panicked, scuttled to and fro, shouting uselessly, attendants clustered around the pump house while the old red fire engine was filled up and wheeled out and strapped to four horses, then clanked its way up on to the moor. But there were no roads up there, and the fire engine got stuck, and the hoses did not reach.

John watched it rage, glad it had not been tamed, since it answered the raw burning in himself. It seemed to him the heat had become a living thing with its own hungers now.

It was hours before they controlled it, hours in which the men lolled in the shade, as black gorse snow scattered and settled on their hair and skin. John lay back, felt the pull of the hot earth beneath him. Above, the leaves of the oak filtered the sun. They were hardly watched by the attendants at all. If he had wanted to, he could have just walked away. But he could not walk and leave her here.

Where was she now? How was she faring in this heat?

There was still no sign of Fuller. No more appearances in the day room on a Monday. The piano remained stubbornly unplayed. It was as though a combatant had retired early from a fight.

There was a movement beside him, and John turned his head to see Dan, squatting, his face filmed with black flakes, frowning with concentration as he fiddled with an ear of wheat.

'Here.' His eyes were gleaming.

'What?'

'Hold out your hand.'

John leant towards him, and Dan dropped the thing he had made into his palm.

A tiny corn doll. It was Fuller. There was no mistaking it; by some strange skill of his battered hands Dan had caught his likeness, the way he had been when they last saw him, riding his ass.

'You want him out of the way?' Dan edged closer, his voice low. Danger plucked the air around them.

'Who?'

'You know who.' Dan sat back on his haunches, nodding to the tiny figure. 'I can keep him out of the way. If you like.'

John looked around him; the men were all lying down, snoring, most of them, asleep. 'How?' he said.

'Easy.' Dan spoke in a soft, coaxing voice. 'Easy now, lad.' It was as though he was talking to an animal. Soothing it. But John did not want to be soothed. His blood was fired. Jumping.

'No. Tell me, Riley. How? What would you do?'

'There are some things that can't be spoke of. But I'll do it for you, lad. I'll do it for me too. I'll make him burn.'

John looked at Dan, at his face smeared in black gorse snow. Clear rivulets where the sweat had coursed through.

He nodded, slowly, once, and Dan grinned, grasping him by the shoulder. 'That's it, lad. That's it.'

Then Dan plucked the figure between finger and thumb, slid his box of matches from his pocket, struck one and touched it to the edge of his effigy. He held it as it burnt, first slowly, and then grinning as the tiny man was licked and swallowed by flames. When the fire reached his finger-tips, Dan tossed the corn to the earth and ground it out. 'Burn, boy, burn,' he said.

Then he spat on it. Then he laughed. Then he took the ashes and smeared them on his cheeks.

Ella

She scanned the ballroom with spiralling unease for his shape, but he was gone.

'Where's John?' said Clem, when they gathered at the end of the evening. 'He wasn't there. Where is he?'

'I don't know. I don't know any more than you.'

Clem's face was naked in its wanting, peeled raw. Ella didn't like to look at it; it looked like she felt.

As the week passed, she avoided Clem's gaze, which was half desperate, half accusing, as though it were her fault John had disappeared.

Her thoughts circled the moment she had seen him last: he had been coming towards her over the field, the doctor behind him in that daft costume, throwing out his arm with one ungainly blow and stopping John in his tracks. She had seen little more after that, moving back through the trees to safety and then losing herself in the crowd. But there had been the feel of trouble out there, the doctor furious, his arms flailing in the air.

And now John was gone. And she might have asked his friend, Dan Riley, where he was, but he was gone too.

Illness was rife on the wards: perhaps it was that?

Old Germany had been taken to the infirmary, coughing and shivering, her eyes huge in her head. There was talk of deaths. In the laundry, as Ella went about her work, the air was so hot it was hard to breathe without burning your lungs. You had to take small sips of it. Women fainted all the time, especially the older ones; last week one had slipped and cracked open her head, blood puddling with soapy water on the laundry floor.

What if he should die? Die in the same building as her, and she not know it? What if he were dead already and had been taken out and buried in one of those graves? Buried along with people he did not know, and she did not know, in a hole she might never find?

The next Friday he was not there either. Panic swirled as she danced, the men were more visible to her now, and she to them it seemed, their wants more greasy, their hands more restless than before.

'Give me the letter,' said Clem in a tight voice the next morning at recreation. 'The last one he wrote. The one about the trees.'

'Why?'

'Because I want to *read* it. I want to remember it. Because I'm forgetting it already.'

'But . . . it's mine.' Ella heard her own voice, high like a child's.

Clem stared at her for a long moment, then took her book out from under her arm and flicked through the pages with quick, angry fingers. Ella's heart rattled. Clem wasn't really reading though, because her eyes didn't move, just stayed staring at the same spot, until she blew out her breath and looked up again. 'What's the point of walking beside me,' she said, 'if you're not going to share your letter?'

The question was like a slap.

'If you don't let me read it again,' said Clem quietly, 'next time, I won't help you write back.'

They walked in silence, but it was a silence noisy with unnamed, dangerous things. After one turn of the yard, Ella reached into her dress. 'Here.'

Clem snatched for it, almost tearing it from her hand and

reading it with ravenous eyes. She did not read it aloud. When she handed it back, she seemed calmer, restored to herself. 'I'm sure there's an explanation,' she said with a smile. 'I'm sure he'll be back soon.'

But as Ella folded it into her dress the letter felt sullied.

The sky above was blue, deep blue, but it hummed and buzzed, as if the blue were only a sheet and behind it, waiting to be rent free, lay black and boiling weather.

And the doctor still came every Monday and chose the women to be taken off. And the dog men still came. The doctor still played the piano, and Old Germany still danced while the women were carried away. And whenever the doctor was close, Clem's cheeks were red and scalding in the heat.

Sometimes one of the women would beg the nurses to open the windows – just a little more. But the Irish nurse just laughed and shook her head. 'What do you think this is?'

One sweltering afternoon, an old woman died. Her neighbour began poking and prodding her and then screaming, and Ella looked over and saw the woman's sunken face, the mouth open, the flies crawling in and around it and doing what they liked. The nurses came and tried to wake her, and when she wouldn't wake, she was carried out by the dog men too.

The only cool place was the toilet block. It was tiled, and the windows were much smaller in there. Ella would take as much time as she could whenever she visited it, splashing her face and her neck with the coldest water she could run, holding her wrists in a full, chill basin, watching the tiny bubbles rise to the surface and disappear.

One airless day, when it was almost two weeks since she had seen John, she went right to the stall at the end of the row, and once she had used it stayed there, her head held in her hands. She couldn't bear it. Couldn't bear the heat. Nor the heavy clothes they were made to wear. She unbuttoned her jacket, lifted up her blouse and her petticoat, and pressed the length of her bare back against the tiled wall. She stayed there a long moment, feeling the delicious touch of the tiles against her skin. She closed her eyes and saw the land giving way, the cold, blue sea stretching, as a small breeze lifted the hairs on the back of her neck.

She whipped her head around.

There was a broken pane of glass in the window above the stall. That was where the breeze had come from. She stayed there, staring up at it for a long moment, then crept to the doorway and looked out. No one in the whole length of the block. She turned back. The window was narrow, but wide enough perhaps for her to squeeze through. She clambered up on to the toilet seat.

Through the broken pane she could see a different part of the grounds, fields stretching, brown-gold in the afternoon sun, and to their left, the deep green of what must be the wood. In one of the furthest fields, a long line of bent figures was snaking over the earth. Two men were out in front, both of them shirtless, their skin exposed to the sun and blue sky.

There was a sound: voices raised above the fields. Singing. The men were singing, and the sound was proud and strong.

It was him. She knew it. Him and Dan Riley, his friend. She could tell it by the way he moved.

She stayed there watching them for as long as she dared,

listening to their distant song, taking great, deep gulps of air.

The next day was a Thursday and all she could think of was the broken window.

How long had it been like that? And how long would it be before anyone else saw?

She went to the toilet to check it as often as she could, stood staring up at it, blood pummelling in her ears.

She should go. Today. Tonight. Wait till it was dark and go. A chance like this would not come again.

But then she would climb up, and look out, and see him in the fields.

And the not running was a pain all over her body. But the pain of leaving was worse. And she was caught and pulled between the two.

It was Friday tomorrow. Perhaps he would be back in the ballroom then?

He was there. The sight of him snatched at her breath. She felt his eyes on her as she took her place on the bench beside Clem, and as she sat, Clem's hand grabbed hers and squeezed it tight.

He stood as soon as the first dance was called, crossing the room towards her, and she rose to meet him, moving through patterned light streaming through stained glass. He looked different: darker, his beard a thick haze across his face and neck. Yellow dust clung to him, crusting his eyebrows, his hair.

'They kept me inside.' When he spoke, his voice was dry and dusty too. 'And then I was in the fields . . .' He held out his hands to her, as though to prove his words; they were cracked and sore, with dirt worked into the creases.

'I saw,' she said. 'There's an open window. I saw the fields from it – and the men there and . . . you. I saw you.'

'An open window?' He grasped her wrists.

'Yes.'

'And no bars on it?'

'No.'

'Do you think you can get through?'

'I don't know – yes, I think . . . Yes.'

'Meet me.' His grip tightened.

'Where?'

'By the oak. A great oak, at the entrance to the wood. You'll know it when you see it. Find your way there. When the moon is at its fullest. In three days' time. Find your way and I will wait. I'll wait for you there.'

He held her until she nodded, and her blood pulsed wild against his thumb.

Later, Ella gave Clem the letter he had given her. She watched as Clem fell on it, but said nothing of what John had said to her. It bloomed inside her instead, rare and dark-bright.

From her bed, she watched the moon rise late and large over the grounds. *At its fullest*, was what he had said, *three days' time.*

Each day she checked the window. Each day she saw it was still broken.

Each night in bed she tried to lie still, but hardly slept.

Each hour she sent up a silent prayer:

Let it not be fixed.

Let it not be fixed till then.

Charles

THE MORNING CHARLES LEFT to visit London the mercury read ninety-five degrees in the shade.

'The dog days,' said the porter in heavy tones, as Charles passed by the front door.

'What's that?' Charles turned to him.

'T's not natural this heat, is it?' The man was mopping his brow with his hanky. 'We'll all be mad before the season's out.'

'We could well be!' Charles tipped his boater to him and laughed.

It was the first time he had left the asylum in over a month, a month in which the temperature had hardly dipped below ninety degrees. He was used to the seared yellow of the grounds but was astonished at what greeted him outside: even in the most sheltered lanes the leaves were sere, and the hedgerows were filled with crumbling dust. He could barely hear the sound of birdsong anywhere, but he had water in his knapsack, a pair of ripe apples and a book, and he was leaving Sharston for the day. He was sure his mood, that strange mood of curdled disappointment that had hung about him for so long, would lift. It was lifting already. It felt so wonderful to be moving, to be *out*. He was heading to London for the first time this year; he was going to see Major Darwin speak, and in his pocket he carried a ticket for the Wigmore Hall: four *Impromptus* and the *Moments Musicaux*. Dog days or not, nothing could dampen his spirits.

In Leeds, though, he arrived to find that his train, the train that would have got him to King's Cross in time for lunch and a stroll across town to the Society, had been cancelled. He wondered if it was a result of the strikes, some spilling over of the disturbances in London and Liverpool perhaps; for all he knew the railwaymen and dockers had downed tools across the land, but the harassed uniformed man in the second-class waiting room assured him that the next train to London – leaving at ten – would be running on time.

He stepped back on to the platform, which was already full of fractious people. If what the man said was true, then he would arrive in time to make the meeting, but the prospect of spending the journey down surrounded by the disgruntled masses was not appealing. Perhaps he should turn tail? Walk back to Sharston? He could feel a headache coming on. But as he stood there, pondering, he heard Churchill's voice in his ear:

'Turn back, Fuller? You will do no such thing!'

No. Quite right.

He would take a stroll through the city, leaving the platform to those with less initiative and more luggage. Taking out his pocket watch, he saw it was not yet nine o'clock.

Men in overalls were sluicing the streets, and market workers clustered around early coffee stands. He paid a few pennies for a small, bitter draught, drinking it straight, then carried on down Kirkgate, heading away from the market with no real thought of where he was going. As the coffee entered his blood he felt a lift, and he remembered a time, not so long ago, when he had walked these same streets with no money of his own. No sense of direction. When he had been trapped in that overbearing villa, not two miles north of here, where his father would be up already, sitting in his study or pacing the garden, his mother still asleep or pretending to be, suffering under blankets in her stuffy bedroom but too proud and too proper to sleep with fewer clothes or beneath a sheet.

How terrible it must be to be old! To have nothing pleasant or exciting ahead, only the contemplation of a past that may or may not have been what you had wished. And yet here he was, walking, on this beautiful early summer's morning, and despite the fact that his train was delayed and he had a long, hot journey to come, life, *life* was ahead.

He looked up and stared – *Spence's* read the sign above the door.

It was the strangest thing. He had not planned to come and yet here he was. He stepped up to the window and peered inside. The music shop was closed, the blinds pulled down. No sign of life within.

A form appeared behind him in the glass. Charles turned to see the young man standing, smiling, bearing a round of keys and sheaf of papers in his arms. 'Good morning!' He took off his hat in salute. A few strands of hair curled damply at his temple. 'This is a nice surprise.'

'Yes,' said Charles. 'I mean – for me too.'

The young man looked puzzled.

'My train. To London. Delayed. It's been delayed.'

'Ah.' The young man nodded. He lifted his sleeve and smoothed his hair away. 'Are you come for more rags then?' His tone was jaunty as he turned to the door, juggling his keys in his hand. 'I wondered if you might. How did Alexander go down?'

'I . . . no—' Charles broke off.

But the young man didn't seem to be listening; he was having trouble with the door. '*Damned* thing. Excuse me.' He turned to Charles, holding out the papers he was carrying, an apologetic smile on his lips. 'Sometimes I need two hands for the job.' He was successful this time, using his hip to push open the door before disappearing inside, leaving Charles alone on the sun-struck pavement.

The young man's head appeared around the door. He looked bemused. 'Aren't you coming in? Terribly hot to be standing on the street.'

That smile again. Charles took out his watch. Still half an hour until the train. The air was thick with heat, and yet it was as though he was standing in a high wind and being buffeted from all sides. The second hand moved. He looked up.

'Yes,' he heard himself say. 'I . . . suppose I might.'

'Good!' replied the young man. 'Just give me a moment and I'll be with you.'

Stepping over the threshold was like plunging into deep brown water. Already Charles could hardly see the young man in the gloom at the back of the shop. He had begun to whistle and Charles recognized the tune: 'Alexander's Ragtime Band'. Damp sprang into his palms. He stood in the darkness, feeling the syncopated beat of his own heart. The sign on the door was still turned to CLOSED.

Then the young man was back, opening blinds and windows to the morning light. And there was Charles, holding the papers he had been given, as though thrust on to a stage against his will. He would have been happier had the blinds been left drawn. But the light blared its insistence and he stayed standing there, and his body felt its awkward, puffy self.

'All right?' The young man turned to Charles.

Charles nodded, his throat too tight to speak.

'Shall I take those from you?' The young man stepped towards him. He flowed, his lightness spilling into the room.

He took the papers, stepped back again, but not too far. Close enough to touch. Close enough that Charles could smell him – tobacco and the sea. His unruly hair fell back over his eye. His teeth were gently crooked when he smiled.

'I'm glad to see you. You've crossed my mind, you see – more than once – and I was rather hoping we might play together again. The shop is rarely busy till ten on a Saturday—'

He turned, gesturing to where the piano lay in the room beyond.

Charles saw them, sitting in the cool, sequestered dark together, side by side at the keyboard as they had done before.

The young man reached out and his hand landed on Charles's sleeve. A dragonfly's touch. All lightness. All grace.

The moment swelled. Time seemed infinitely slow and infinitely fast.

Charles opened his mouth to speak. 'I can't,' he said.

He had not meant to say that. Who was speaking in his stead?

'Oh, really? That's a shame.'

The hand still there. His living pulse. An arm's breadth between them.

'I'm sorry.' His gut twisting now. 'I'm afraid I do have to go, after all.' He gave a small, sharp laugh. 'In fact, I never really meant to come. It was a mistake, you see. It was all a mistake. It's my train. To London. I don't want to miss it. I've a meeting this afternoon.'

'Ah.' The air between them pierced. The young man's face falling now. His hand sliding away. A burning where cool touch had been. 'How rude of me. I didn't realize you were in such a rush.'

'No, I mean . . . you're . . . it's me. I'm sorry. I'm awfully sorry.'

It was time to move. But Charles could not.

The young man was speaking still. 'Is there anything I can do for you before you go?'

What's your name? You could tell me your name.

And . . .

I could stay.

'No.' Charles shook his head. 'I just – *no*.' He turned and walked towards the door, wrenching it open. 'I'm sorry – I'm so sorry, I simply . . . have to go.'

Outside now. Fighting for breath. Pushing his way through the thickening crowds, through the jellied, un-forgiving air, to the station.

The train at the platform was already packed. He found a seat beside a large woman and her husband; tins of salmon and syrupy pineapple were already spread out on their laps, the sickly, pungent smell of their picnic heavy on the air.

He closed his eyes, trying to ignore the pressure building in his skull. But the chatter and wafts of noisome food coming from his companions kept him awake, and he gave up, burying his head in his copy of *The Times*, reading of the dockers continuing their strike in London. Of the tomatoes and other fruit and a hundred thousand pounds of Argentinian beef putrefying on the quays. Spoiling in the heat.

What a waste.

What a shameful, shameful waste.

London itself seemed changed, as though it were a fruit it-self, past its best and rotting in the heat. It was clear from

222

the first few moments in King's Cross that a pall hung over the city. It was grubby. Smelt rancid. And if Leeds had been hot, then London was an inferno.

The station was packed with policemen, long snaking lines of them, hurriedly moving goods from trains to a line of vans parked and waiting outside. Charles couldn't fathom what they were doing it for, until he overheard a fellow passenger stop one of the officers and ask him.

'It's instead of the dockers, isn't it? We've got to get this food out somehow, or we've all going to starve.'

His headache had only increased on the journey, and so he decided to hang the expense and take a motorcab across town. On another day it would have been a treat, but it took him a long, sweaty while to find one, by which time, should he have walked, he could have been halfway there. The streets were deathly quiet – only a small desultory trickle of traffic; it was as though a plague had come over the city. 'Where are all the cars?' He leant forward in his seat.

The taxi man turned. 'No petrol, is there? Strikes.'

The cab moved through almost deserted steets, crawling its way through the terraces of Bloomsbury, down the Gray's Inn Road and Chancery Lane to the Strand – streets Charles knew well, and yet today they seemed unreal: a stage set waiting for the people to arrive. The cab passed the Savoy, and he was close now, turning down a side street between the Strand and the river.

'Number six.' He leant forward again to the driver, his pulse thrumming at his throat.

Number 6, York Buildings turned out to be red brick, tall and rather grand, in the way of the area, but an otherwise unremarkable townhouse, with nothing to denote what or who might be inside. Charles paid the cabman the small fortune he asked for without demur, and then stepped on to the street. He was late. He took off his hat and smoothed down his hair, trying to control his breath. His light flannel suit, which had felt so promising hours ago, was crumpled now and covered with smuts from the train, and his shirt was stuck to his back with sweat. He thought he might be running a temperature.

The front door was opened by a smart, cool-looking man in late middle age.

'The Society?' Charles croaked. Something strange had happened to his voice. 'Major Leonard Darwin?'

'And you are . . . ?' The man raised an eyebrow.

'Charles Fuller.' A fresh outbreak of sweat on his back christened this last. 'Doctor. My name should be on the list.'

The man bent and checked and then, 'Upstairs,' he said to Charles. 'Committee Room. First floor.'

As Charles climbed the stairs, he was filled with a strange sensation of lightness, as though he was floating, somewhere a little above his head. The Committee Room, a large, double-windowed space overlooking the street, was packed; there were no seats remaining, and so he took his place standing at the back. He grasped his hat in his hands and smoothed out his hair.

The general nature of the gathering, from the cut of the suits to the sharp edge of the accents, bespoke a class and a dignity hard to find in Yorkshire. He tried to feel excited; he was here, in the heart of it: the heart of London, the heart of the Empire. In the second row, in the centre of a lively group, was a youngish man, fair hair escaping in unruly curls. *My God.* Charles leant forward. Could it be? It *was*. It was Churchill. Smaller then he had imagined him to be. He leant forward further, but had no more time to regard him since an older bewhiskered man had mounted the lectern, holding up his hand for silence, and everyone's eyes were turned towards the front.

'Thank you, Mr Crackenthorpe, for such a fitting tribute to Sir Francis Galton. And now it gives me the utmost pleasure to introduce to you Major Leonard Darwin; not only, as I know you all know, the son of Charles, but a most distinguished scientist and scholar in his own right, and our new president.'

The room erupted into applause as a man in late middle age stood and took to the stage. From his title, Charles had expected someone with a military bearing, but aside from his straight back, Leonard Darwin appeared more like a genial uncle than an army major as he stood at the lectern and smiled down at the crowded room.

'Well,' he began, his eyes sparkling with amusement, 'I always believed myself to be the most dunce-like of the Darwin brothers. And so it has taken me a rather long time and rather a few careers to find the thing I am purposed to do.'

There were chuckles at this, and shakings of the head.

'But I feel, at the age of sixty, I may finally have found it.'

More warm laughter, but now Darwin's manner shifted, and as he began to move into his speech the room fell quiet.

'Our task . . . in truth, at the Eugenics Society, is to study all possible methods of preventing the *decadence of the nation*; and when this is realized, it becomes obvious that not only will the struggle be long and arduous, but that our primary consideration should be to start on the right lines.'

'Hear, hear!'

'It is to be noted,' carried on Darwin, 'that those sections

225

of the community which are least successful in earning a decent living are reproducing their kind more rapidly than are those in receipt of higher wages; and, in the second place, that a considerable proportion of this poorest stratum are sifted out of it or fall into it in consequence of some innate strength or weakness in mind or body; with the result that the members of this ill-paid class are on average inherently less capable than are the better paid.'

Charles thought of Mulligan. His inherent capabilities. The man was a pain in his side. Why did he confuse him so?

'In order to stem the decadence of the nation thus clearly foreshadowed, the question whether any steps can and should be taken in the direction of placing restrictions on the marriage of those not earning a living wage, especially when young, is likely, therefore, to be more and more forced upon our attention.'

More agreement from the floor, and Charles saw Churchill was amongst those most vociferous in their response to this.

'As to those in receipt of poor relief and charity, their condition is frequently connected with an innate want of self-control, and any increase in the burden of taxation will be likely to produce but little effect on the rate of reproduction of those thus characterized. The more the self-respecting and prudent sections of the community are hit by taxation, the greater, therefore, will be the anti-eugenic effects produced; and every increase in the burden must do harm to the race unless indeed those who are incapable of bearing the additional strain are prevented from reproducing their kind.'

As Darwin's speech progressed, dizziness began to wash over Charles. He leant against the wall, but still he felt unstable. Nothing had passed his lips since the cup of coffee in Leeds. As Darwin carried on, his words began to warp and bend.

'Decadence.'

Decadence.

He closed his eyes, felt the dizziness abating somewhat, but his mind kept returning to the moment inside Spence's, as if to the scene of a crime. Again and again he saw the young man reaching out and himself pulling away, as though he were watching a moving picture, but one which had got stuck, looping at the same spot: the golden touch of a golden young man in a music shop in Leeds.

There was a sudden, surging movement, loud applause. Stones being hurled on to a beach. The crowd pressed around him, thick with the smell of bodies and hot wool. He snapped open his eyes, gasping. He was burning now. Burning. He pushed himself through the throng, heading for the stairs.

The crowd spilt on to the street outside, the men beginning to chatter and smoke. Shards of their conversations pierced his ears. Churchill was standing not five paces away from him. Lighting a cigar.

Now. Now was the opportunity. When would it come again?

Charles stepped towards him, and men made way to let him through. Churchill cast an expectant look, and his eyes were hard and piercing, and Charles opened his mouth to speak – but nothing came out except a parched croak. He closed his mouth again, felt heat sting his face.

Water.

Water quenches fire.

The river. The river was close. The river was what he

needed, the river would cool him, would wash this feeling clean.

Charles held out his hand in apology and turned, stumbling down towards the Embankment, the great roiling mass of the river below. There was a road in between which he didn't trust himself to cross and so he ducked into the gardens instead. His clothes were drenched. He was desperate for shade. He pulled off his hat and clawed at his tie, opening his shirt by a few merciful buttons and sinking on to a bench. A small green hut stood on the other side of the park, tables and chairs gathered in the shade. A sign for lemonade. But the queue was long and he seemed to have lost the strength in his legs. He closed his eyes and leant back against the bench as a shadow passed before the sun.

'You all right, gent?' A figure stood before him. 'Can I get you anything?'

Charles shook his head. He could hardly speak. 'Unless – perhaps – some lemonade?'

'Lemonade? Course. I'll get you some lemonade all right.'

Charles fumbled for change.

'Nah.' The man seemed to be moving. It was hard to keep track. 'You keep your money, Mister. I know the owner. Wait here. Won't be a tick.'

He felt he could weep with relief.

The man was as good as his word, returning in a moment with a cup of lemonade. 'Here you go, gent.'

It was warm, but it was wet. 'Thank you. But how—' Charles managed, when he had taken a sip. 'The queue?'

'S'all right,' the man said softly. 'We do each other favours round here.' And then, in a leisurely manner, he sat down beside him.

Charles turned stiffly, balancing his cup on his knee. The

man was not young, or not so young as the man in Leeds. He was about Charles's age. He was smiling. But his face was scarred. Red lesions clustered on the side of his cheek. Charles stared at them. He knew those lesions. He saw them every day.

Syphilis.

General paralysis of the insane. Far advanced.

'Sure you don't want anything else?'

The man's voice was light as he reached out and put his hand over Charles's knee, and Charles saw that the skin there too was covered in a rash.

'S'all right, gent,' the man said, coaxing. 'You don't have to pretend with me.' The scarred hand moved further up Charles's thigh.

'What are you doing?!' Charles stumbled to his feet.

The man held his hands up and gave a short, barking laugh. 'Nothing,' he said. The smile was back. 'Nothing that you don't want, anyway.'

And then it was upon him.

'Don't you *dare* tell me what I want.' He lifted his cane and brought it down on to the man's hands. 'You don't know me. *You don't know what I want.*'

'Don't!' The man was cowering, hands held over his face. 'Don't hit me. I'm sorry. I never meant any harm.'

But Charles did not stop. He lifted his cane, brought it down again. He was thrashing him now, and the man's face had changed, become his father, helpless before him, become the young man in Leeds, become Mulligan, become himself, he was hurting *himself,* until all of the strength had gone from him, and the man had run, and he was left clutching his cane, shaking, his cheeks wet.

What had he done?

He looked up. A young child was watching. Standing alone in the middle of the path. A girl. A large bonnet on her head like a black flower. Then she, too, began to weep.

Somehow he found his way to the station. Somehow he found the train to Leeds. A young woman sat opposite, a baby in her arms. She sent him a quick smile, and Charles attempted to smile back, but it felt crooked.

The young woman opened her clean red mouth. 'Filthy,' she said. *'Filthy.'* She spoke in his mother's voice.

'No,' said Charles feebly. 'I didn't mean it. I'm sorry. He came to me.'

The woman gathered her child to her. Charles looked around the carriage.

There was a sound beside him.

Fuller, it boomed. *Get a grip!*

It was Churchill. Churchill was here somewhere. He must have followed him.

The train lurched. Charles got to his feet.

Fuller! Churchill barked. *You're making a spectacle of yourself! Sit back down!*

Charles shook his head, blundering out into the corridor, people everywhere, every compartment full. Two carriages down was an empty WC. He locked himself inside. Leant against the sink. Had he messed himself? Was that what the woman had meant? *Filthy*. He pulled down his trousers but could see nothing there. Faces swarmed before him: the boy from Spence's, his face swollen; the man in the park, laughing; and then Mulligan – taking his shirt off before him, but this time, scattered over the etched shape of his torso were oozing sores, and when he looked up in fear, his face had changed; his nose was bulbous, horrible. His forehead was distorted. *GPI, far advanced.*

Far advanced.

Far advanced.

Depravity was everywhere.

Everything was spoiled.

Get a grip, Fuller.

Get a grip.

Get a grip.

Get a grip.

It was very late when he reached the grass at the edge of the asylum. He crawled towards the wide trunk of an oak and lay on the ground. There were sounds, but they were distant. A tumbling. Water. Or rain.

He was burning, burning. He wished to bury himself in the cool earth. Crawl beneath it. Pull it over his head. But the ground was hard as rock.

John

ON THE LAST DAY of the harvest, the sky was a still bowl of blue. In the morning, the men were silent, stunned by the heat and the fatigue that weighted their limbs, but in the late afternoon John sang: the only voice raised above those shorn fields, a song he did not even remember that he knew. One his father had sung, out on the kelp beaches when he was a boy, and when he sang it, he found he knew it so well that it was like putting on a garment worn by his father, and his father before him, and all the fathers down the line, so it fitted him better than any garment might.

He gathered a few stalks from the last sheaf he cut and tucked them into his belt.

The men were led to the farmyard, where a meal was laid out in the shade: long tables covered with food and jugs of ale. The farmers stood back, motioning for the men to sit.

'Bona mangarie!' Dan clapped his hands together and rubbed them. 'About time they showed us some thanks.'

John took his seat at the heaving table, where meat lay in the centre, not mutton in pies and stews, but a whole pig that had been killed and roasted on a spit and carved. Plates were piled high, and the men fell on them, eating with their hands, chins running greasy with the juice. The meat was sweet and tender; there was salty crackling, roast potatoes, bread. When the jugs of ale were empty, they were taken away and filled again.

John did not eat much. His blood was too high for that. He wove the corn stalks beneath the table instead, leaving the ears long and trailing, the way he had seen his father do it for his mother: a gift at the end of the harvest – after the *meitheal* – which his mother would put up above the hearth. He watched as the other men grew addled with beer and food, and he thought of Ella.

One of the farmers had a fiddle, and Dan jumped up, red and roaring with drink, hollering at him to play, clapping his hands and rousing the men to dance.

'Wake up the women!' he roared. 'Go on. Wake the women up!'

The farmers laughed – as merry as the men now, faces blurry, all differences dissolved by meat and drink and music.

'Not dancing then?'

John turned to see Brandt standing a little way behind his head.

The attendant stepped up towards him. 'Tomorrow,' he said, waving his arm at the table, the food, the drink, the dancing men, 'all this will be finished. They won't need you in the fields any more. Tomorrow you'll be back to digging graves with me.' He lifted his pint pot, bashed it against John's shoulder, sloshed the yellow liquid into his mouth, then wiped his hand over his lips and belched as he wandered off.

John knew he was right. Tomorrow, when the meat and the drink were cleared away and the men's heads were thick, when the crop was safe in the barns and the gleaning begun, things would be just as they were before. He had to take the night and stretch it, live inside it, make it his own.

As the evening passed, the attendants grew slow and sleepy. Everyone was heavy with food and drink, but John's own tiredness had left him. Everything was clear: the evening air, cooler now, the deep, rich smell of the meat, the hoppy ale, the ripeness of the men, all of it seasoned with the salt of anticipation on his tongue. When the fiddle was sawing and the music was at its height, Dan pulled out of the fray and came to lean over the table towards John.

'Here, *mio Capitane.*' His breath was dense with ale. He reached out and placed something in John's palm. 'You might need these tonight.'

John opened his hand to reveal a full box of matches. He looked up to thank him, but Dan was already off, boot stamping on the ground, fingers in his mouth to whistle the music on.

Now.

He stood, edging his way over to the place where the cobbled yard met the fields beyond. No one watched him go.

Now he turned and ran, keeping to the borders of the fields, making for the line of trees that was the wood, the evening air whistling around his ears, arriving, lungs raked. He climbed over the metal fence, and he was amongst the trees, where everything was quiet and cool and dim.

Far behind him, he could hear the distant skitter of the fiddle. The whoops of the men. He walked slowly, now feeling his heart grow calm, as he threaded his way through the trunks, making for the edge where the old oak stood. There was no one visible in the small patch of open ground, and he crossed it swiftly. When he arrived at the great trunk, he was filled with the impulse to put his hand on its wood, as Dan might, and when he did so, he was glad of the feel of the warm, rough bark beneath his palm. 'Now, lad,' he said. 'I hope you're after keeping me hidden tonight.'

Up ahead was a limb thick enough to hold him, and he pulled himself up towards it. The tree shivered and rustled around him and then grew still.

He was hidden now, but from up here could see the asylum buildings stretching ahead, the path she would take when she came, the clock tower, the buildings almost beautiful in this hazy evening light. The men approached, on their way back to the wards, and he held his breath as they passed beneath him, their chatter lower now, punctured by the earthy roar of Dan's laughter, the grey cloud of their cigarette smoke drifting lazily up to where he sat. They were drunk. All of them, ale-sodden and slow, and they would not bother to count heads tonight. He leant back against the solidity of the trunk.

His heart was thudding. His throat was dry. He wished he had brought some water with him. There was a long time yet to wait.

Small insects filled the air, and swallows swooped to catch them as they flew. He took out his tobacco and rolled a quick cigarette, then scraped a match against the hot bark of his seat, sending the smoke up through the leaves. The wood creaked. Small birds returned to the branches above.

Behind him, the sun cracked and spilt itself over the moor, and the light fell in pools of gold that turned to red, then purple and dark blue, and though the covering of the leaves was thick, he had a sense of the land beneath him: the buildings ahead, and then behind him the rest of the grounds, the farms with the animals put away for the night, the train tracks that led to Leeds and beyond and all the dark hills in between.

The dusk came, and the moon rose, golden, above the buildings ahead. Different shapes filled the sky – the whirling dance of bats – and when the edges of things were soft and the shadows began to merge he watched the path. He fingered the stalks in his pocket, his eyes on the trampled grass. The thought of her was like touching something hot.

He smoked cigarette after cigarette, and was grateful for the gift of Dan's matches. Now the space below seemed traitorous. Shadows flickered and blurred. He saw her twenty times and it was never her. Time passed and the night thickened and he was sure she would not come and he could hardly think above the pandemonium of his heart.

Ella

BREATHING OUT INTO THE dark, she was sick and slippery with fear and wanting. If she twisted her head, she could see the moon, full-bellied and high. Her heart thudded at her chest, in her throat, and the beat of it was strange, fast but halting, as though it might give up altogether.

You have to gamble to get what you want.

She peeled back her cover and swung down her legs, bare feet touching cool tile. The light was strong enough for her to see the beds ranged around, each with its humped shape of a sleeping woman on top. If anyone were watching they would see her clearly. A moan came from the opposite side of the room, and she fell to her knees, almost knocking her chamberpot over, catching it before it rocked and spilt.

She bunched her cumbersome nightgown around her and began to crawl over the floor as quietly as she could. When she reached the top of the room, she had the strange thought she might cry out and betray herself, and bit down hard on her lip as she crawled past the sleeping nurses and on towards the toilet block, and only when she reached it did she stand, running to the last of the stalls, arriving drenched in sweat. She didn't dare run the tap, so knelt and reached into the bowl instead, bringing out a handful of water, dashing it against her underarms and the back of her neck, until the smell of her fear was gone.

When she climbed up on to the seat, the window was in front of her, but the hole was much smaller than she had remembered, far too small for her to crawl through. She would have to break it further. She flailed in the darkness, grabbing the flush; on its end was a wooden handle, but it was trapped in a bracket on the wall and impossible to lift out. She wrapped the material of her nightgown around her fist, and the glass smashed with a high, traitorous sound. She stopped, arm half raised, blood pummelling in her ears, but no one came, and she could hear nothing from the wards.

She pushed the splinters out with her elbow, clearing the frame and then the ledge on the other side of the glass, then scrambled through the hole, felt cloth tearing, shards of pain. She landed on the grass and rolled.

For a long moment she stayed there, hunched in a small, tight ball, then slowly uncurled herself. She placed her palms flat against the earth. The grass was scarce, and the ground felt crumbly and dry, but beneath the smell of hard-packed earth she could sense the rich, dark tang of the soil. No light shone from the toilet block. They had not come after her.

As the thrum of her blood retreated, she could hear a small breeze in the leaves of the trees at the edge of the field, the close scratch of animals, the rustling night-sounds of nature all around. The light was that of twilight, and it was possible to see well and far: to the fields the men had sung in, to the dark outline of the wood, and beyond it all, the low rise of the moor. The air was sweet, and she gulped it down.

Free. She let the word fill her.

If she ran now, she would be miles away before anyone woke. If she ran now, she would never have to go back in there.

But then she thought of him waiting for her.

Would he come with her?

Would he run too?

She made her way along the narrow path that skirted the back of the buildings, and the earth was warm beneath the skin of her feet, the sweat cooling on her back. The air was thick, the temperature of blood.

She reached the edge of the wood, saw the single tree, standing apart, huge in the darkness, throwing its branches to the sky, and as she stepped beneath its spreading leaves, there was a rustling, and he was there, landing quietly on the ground beside her. The bulk of him. He seemed bigger here, with nothing else around him, only the trees and the sky. And her heart slipped and fear filled her and she thought that perhaps she did not know him at all.

'Ella.'

The sound of her name in his mouth made the skin on her arms lift and pucker. He reached for her hands and there was gentleness there, but she pulled against him.

'We are free,' she said. 'We can leave this place.'

The words beat and churned the air between them.

'Wait,' he said. His voice was low, like a drum covered by cloth. 'Wait a moment. Let me show you.'

She let him lead her to where a small, broken gate marked the edge of the wood. He went first, helping her through it, and then they were beneath the trees. She drew back. She had been outside where she was free, where she could see far and wide for the first time in her life, and this wood was dark and close – but 'It's safe,' he said. 'I promise.' And when they stepped forward she saw that the wood was not truly dark, but made of silver and blue, and was not thick, but full of wide clearings, where moonlight filtered through the trees and pooled against the ground. And as they walked, the grasses were long and cool. There was no dryness here. It seemed a space apart. She thought she saw eyes, quick animal eyes in the darkness, thought she heard the beat of small wings in the air.

They emerged before a rolling, stubbled field where corn stooks cast blue shadows on the ground and the moor rose gently behind. The moon swung high and ripe above it all, the air was heavy with the hot, sweet smell of the fields, and it felt to Ella, standing at its edge, like a new world and that she and the man beside her were the only people in it.

'Please.' He turned to her, spoke softly. 'Stay this night with me.'

And she was empty suddenly, and light, and the freedom was in her, was part of her, and the need to run had gone.

'Here.' He lifted her hand, placed something in it. In the moonlight she saw cornstalks twisted together, their ears fanning below. 'At home,' he said, 'at the end of harvest-time, the loveliest of all the women walks across the fields. It is her task to find a grain.'

Now, beneath this moon, nothing seemed strange to her at all. She stepped out over the field and the stubble was sharp beneath her feet, but the sharpness did not bother her. When she reached the centre, she knelt to the shaved earth, feeling with her fingers until she had lifted a fallen grain into her palm. She turned to see him come towards her. He dropped down beside her, put his thumb to the grain and closed his hand around hers, making a double fist. He put his lips to it, and she shivered, but not from any cold. Then he opened it again.

'Blow,' he said.

And she bent and blew the grain from her palm.

Then he dipped his face and kissed her. A long, sweet

239

kiss. He touched the skin on her neck, brushed her lips, passed his hands over her hair.

And she did the same, reaching up and touching his mouth. Tracing the line of it. She put her palms against his cheeks, felt the scratch of his beard. He closed his eyes, and she put her thumbs against his lids, feeling the light, living pulse of him there. She felt the creases in his forehead, the groove of his temples, put her hands in his hair, felt it rough with the blown dust of the fields.

She was learning him, out here in this blue night. Clem had her poetry, but she had this. She was learning him by heart.

'Your hair,' he said to her. 'Would you take it down?'

She undid her braid, letting her hair fall, and he kissed her again, and again, every kiss an unwinding, as though he were lifting off her, layer by layer, everything she had carried, revealing someone new.

He put his jacket on the ground, unbuttoned his waistcoat, his shirt, passed his hands beneath her nightgown, lifting it off. She was naked now but felt no shame. The warm air her only covering. The hot living breath of the earth all around.

They turned to each other, and when they moved together she cried out, colouring the night air with her sound.

Charles

WHEN SHE CAME, she was kind. And clean. She lifted his head. She changed his sheets.

She was an angel, and she had come to cleanse.

I am sorry, he whispered to her. *Forgive me.*
Will you forgive me? Can you hear?
They moved about his bed like moths. Silent moths with mouths that opened and closed. They could not hear him. They did not speak.
Why can't you hear me?
Listen to me.
Please! Listen!
I want to tell you what I have done.

'Nothing that you don't want.'

I want—

I want—

I—

'Shhh, no. Shhhh.'

Filthy. Filthy.

Water. I need water. Lemonade.
Can I have some lemonade? Please?
Please?

But it is hot. Everything is too hot.
Please come back.
Please
     come
         back.

A nurse stood at the end of Charles's bed. Her veil was bright.

'You've had flu.' Her voice was a metallic clang. 'And you're not the only one. You're in quarantine. You need to rest.'

He closed his eyes as a sour wave of fear rinsed him. He was filled with the horror of what he might have said.

Apparently he had been ill for a week.

He couldn't say how much this news disturbed him.

'A particularly nasty strain,' said Soames, standing at the end of Charles's bed. 'Lost five patients to it already. You take it easy, old chap.' He reached out and patted the taut cotton of his bedsheets. 'Lucky you're still here.'

Soames seemed pleasant enough. And yet. Charles thought he could detect something strained beneath his manner.

Lucky you're still here.

What did he mean?

Did he mean Charles was lucky to be alive? Or lucky to be kept on at the asylum? And if the latter, then lucky to be kept on after . . . what?

He had only been drunk once, but this reminded him of that: the waking with no recollection of the preceding evening, the horror that he had said or done something appalling, which everyone had witnessed but himself.

He could remember everything clearly up to boarding the train to Leeds, but then, little more. According to the nurse who was looking after him, he was found 'shaking and gibbering' on the grass in the morning.

Shaking and gibbering. On the grass??

Was that, then, where he had spent the night? Had he

lost control of himself completely? Of his bladder? His bowels?

Each time a nurse came to check on him, each question they asked – *Would you like some water? Would you like your pillows plumping?* – was infused with insidious intent, and whenever he saw two nurses speaking together, it seemed they were speaking about him.

He thought of that *thing* in the park (he could not call him a man). Had he gone to the police? He had not hurt him. Or not really. He had only given him what he deserved; the thing was depraved, and its mission was corruption.

Nothing that you don't want.

Why had he said it? What did he mean?

When Charles remembered how he had raised his stick, how he had beaten him, how the man had cowered in fear, it brought on sweating fits, and when the sweating was past he was left shaking, bones clattering, rattled shingle on a beach.

As the days passed, he began to feel a little better. When he was well enough to sit, he propped himself on pillows and asked for books to be brought from his room.

He began to read. He re-read Tregold's pamphlet. He read Dr Sharp's *On the Sterilization of Degenerates*:

Dr Barr, in his work, 'Mental Defectives', says: Let asexualization be once legalized, not as a penalty for crime, but a remedial measure preventing crime and tending to future comfort and happiness of the defective; let the practice once become common for young children immediately upon being adjudged defective by a competent authority properly appointed, and the public mind will accept it as an effective

243

means of race preservation. It would come to be regarded, just as quarantine, as simple protection against ill.

Charles made notes in the margin as he read, Darwin's words echoing in his ears:

To stem the decadence of the nation . . . poor relief and charity . . . innate want of self-control . . . prevented from reproducing their kind.

The infirmary, with its clean lines, pleased him, its white sheets and its white floors and its nurses speaking softly and bringing tea and water and food. The words he read seemed to rise up with a new power in that clean, clear space. It was a cocoon, and he was a chrysalis.

He left the infirmary on a Friday afternoon. He had been given the weekend off. He was asked if he wanted to go home, to have two days' leave instead of the usual one, to take some time away before resuming his duties, but the thought of visiting Leeds – even passing through the station, let alone walking those streets – brought on a revulsion so strong he feared a relapse. He did not want to visit Leeds again. Not for a long time to come.

After the high ceilings of the infirmary, his little bed-room seemed smaller than before. His sheets had been changed and a new blanket put on the bed, but otherwise all was as he had left it. His portraits on the mantel. His notes arrayed on his desk. He put his books back on the bookshelf and placed the grooved moor-stone beside them to prop them up.

He caught his reflection in the mirror and sucked in

his breath in shock. His cheeks were concave, and his moustache, which had been trimmed for him in the infirmary, looked enormous, covering half his face. His dumb-bells were on the floor beside the fireplace, and he bent to one, curling it tentatively towards his chest. It felt twice as heavy as before. He put it back and came to sit on the bed.

Two whole days to himself. Two whole days in which he might do as he liked. What might a man do in two days? Take the train to Scotland. Hike in the Caingorms. See a Test match in Nottingham. Travel to London and visit the Wigmore Hall.

He did not want to do any of those things. His place was here.

Outside, he heard the clock strike six. It was a Friday. Soon, the patients would be getting ready for the dance. His violin stood in the corner, unplayed. Two weeks. When was the last time he had left it for so long?

He wanted to be amongst people.

He picked up his violin case and made his way downstairs.

As he walked the length of the empty ballroom, footsteps ringing on the wood, his legs felt weak, but it was a pleasurable weakness, as though he were young again, or reborn. He made his way around the back of the stage, climbed it and then stood, looking out over the vast, empty room.

He had forgotten how high the ceiling was. The arched windows were those of a cathedral, their brown and gold panels catching and filtering the afternoon light so it fell in warm pools on the floor. He moved so he was standing in a tunnel of golden luminescence and bent back his head, following the pictures on the glass: the sprays of bramble, the birds that seemed to flit from branch to branch. It was hallowed, magnificent. It may have been his mood, a strange mood, hollow and yet full, but he began to cry. Just a little. He wiped the tears away with his cuff.

He made his way into the wings and brought out a seat, setting it away from the front of the stage, and sat, hands resting on his knees, filled with a sense of peace. Soon the other players filed in. They looked surprised. Lifted their hands in greeting. Enquired about his health. Complained about the weather. Loosened their ties as they took their seats. He was there and he was not. The conversation swirled around his edges.

It was good to be here, to be amongst these people whom he knew.

'We missed you,' said Jeremy Goffin, as he took his seat.

Charles turned. 'Did you?' The comment bloomed in his chest. Smiling, he reached into his case and took out his instrument, but as he did so he caught something: a look exchanged between Goffin and Johnston, the clarinettist, a small smile. A *smirk*.

The players began tuning up. The scraping of the strings was sandpaper to his nerves. A few minutes of holding the violin and already his arms were aching. He gritted his teeth. Sweat broke out on his brow. He took out his handkerchief, mopped at his face.

The patients began to arrive, first one, then two, then face after face trooping through the doors. So many. He had not thought there were so many. Hundreds of them, swarming over the floor. Where did they all come from? Were there usually so many as this? What if they came up here? Swarmed up to the stage, reaching where he sat, like vermin, like rats. He inched his chair further away from

246

the front. Tried to concentrate on his violin, but he could not seem to get it in tune.

Look at them.

Grinning and gurning. Turning in circles on the floor. Jumping up and down and clapping their hands. Like children. Like stupid children. Like the idiots they are.

The men put their instruments in their laps, waiting for the dancers to be ready to begin. The light had shifted, the sun shining through lower panels now, and the room was cast in a woozy haze. Charles searched for Mulligan, at the back, in the shadows, where the light was cool: that was where he would be.

But Mulligan was not there.

Charles's eyes raked the benches. The man was nowhere. He looked again, widening his search.

There.

At the front.

Charles stared. The man was transformed. His usual countenance had gone, the stone had dissolved and he was charged with something new. Mulligan's body was held taut, his eyes sweeping the space before him; he was looking for someone too.

A throng of women arrived, the air pounding with their voices. Mulligan almost jumped to his feet; Charles saw the effort it took the man to hold himself back. His eyes scraped the women, following Mulligan's gaze.

And then he saw . . . the small thing, the dark thing. Fay. Ella Fay. The Irishman's eyes were fastened on her, and he was hungry, as though he might cross the floor and devour her. And now the girl had seen him too and the man's face had changed. Softened. He looked . . . happy. Yes, that was it. Happy. It painted the air with its garish hue.

Who was he to be happy? This . . . man? He was not even a man. He was little more than a beast of the field.

And the girl . . . this *thing*. She had been one to haunt the shadows too, and yet here she was, taking her time in the sun as though it were her birthright, as though she deserved it, as though this whole spectacle – the ballroom and the carvings and the paintings and the fine Burmantofts work and the brambles and the ceiling reaching up, up into hazy space and the sun falling down, down, and lighting her, *lighting her* – was all here for herself and this man: a backdrop to their courting, to their *mating*, to their sordid match. A match forged here in this room, and this room, which not too many minutes ago had seemed to be a spacious cathedral, now appeared as nothing more than a stew.

Nausea gripped him. Before he knew what was happening he was on his feet.

'Dr Fuller?'

It was Goffin. He was staring. 'Are you ready?'

'For what?'

Down on the floor the patients were paired up and they too were looking up at the stage, waiting for the music to begin.

'It's time for the waltz,' said Goffin. 'Are you sure you're feeling well?'

'I'm sorry.' The tide of sweat broke again. 'I am sorry. I am . . . not myself.'

He could not stay. Not in this rank, corrupted place.

He hurried away from the ballroom, down the endless corridors, out of the front entrance, stumbling over the grass to the Barracks, and once in his room, he locked the door and hunched over the chamberpot, put his fingers down his throat and vomited, again and again.

Book Three

1911
Summer – Autumn

Ella

SHE MOVED SLOWLY, DELIBERATELY. As she dragged twisted cloth from the machines, she looked at her hands. Ordinary hands, rough hands, but they had not felt ordinary or rough that night. They had known where to go. How to travel across his skin. To read him. To understand.

And her own body – she had not thought she was capable of pleasure like that. Ella stared down at herself, encased in the heavy, black asylum uniform, and it was as though she carried a miracle beneath her clothes.

She looked up and jumped. Clem's eyes were following her from across the room. Ella bent to gather up a rope of clothes and haul it out of the washing drum, as Clem crossed the floor towards her.

'Here.' Clem leant in and took the other side, helping her to unravel the knot. Ella kept her eyes down but felt Clem's gaze spidering over her skin.

'You look different,' said Clem.

'How?' Ella risked a glance up. Could Clem see? Perhaps she could. Perhaps she could see right through her. Perhaps if you were to open her up then John would be there, tattooed across her insides, just like Dan Riley had his women on his arms.

Clem's eyes narrowed. 'I don't know,' she said, then she lifted a sheet free from the tangle and cracked it open between her hands.

*

At dinner they sat in silence, but every time Ella looked up, Clem was still watching, an odd look on her face. At first it was laced with humour, but as the meal went on it grew harder, and the air between them became twined and tight. 'You're going to tell me,' said Clem eventually. 'You know that, don't you? Whatever it is, I have to know.'

Ella felt a low panic in her gut; she couldn't speak of it. Not yet.

In the afternoon, sitting in the day room, it was harder to avoid Clem's accusing gaze, and so she closed her eyes and pretended to doze. It was so hot she slipped easily into sleep, not waking until the afternoon was almost past and it was time to eat. But at night, she lay awake long after everyone else was asleep. It felt safest to think of him then: the salt of his skin, the rake of his beard on her cheek. The places that his mouth had touched. She had not known what a hunger she had to be touched. His body – at first she had been shy of it, but then it was as though she were no longer there and something other than her was moving her hands, her fingers; someone who knew how to give pleasure, someone who knew how to take it.

She turned on to her back and almost cried out. A figure was standing at the foot of her bed, a dark mass in the shadow of the night, and for a strange, vivid moment she thought it was him, until she heard Clem's voice. 'Move over,' she hissed, 'and let me in.'

She moved to make room, and Clem slid under the thin cover beside her. The bed was so narrow it was impossible not to touch, and as Clem wriggled to find space Ella could feel the length of her, the sharp edge of her hip jutting up against her own. 'You've seen him, haven't you?' Clem whispered. 'You've been with John.'

Ella could still smell him, a low, rousing animal smell. Lying here like this, she was sure Clem must be able to smell him too. She nodded into the darkness.

'Oh.' Clem's hot breath touched the skin of Ella's neck. 'I *knew* it. I could tell.'

Beside them Old Germany moaned, and a thin spatter of words peppered the air. Both girls stiffened until she was silent again. This time, Clem spoke just on the edge of hearing. 'Why didn't you *tell* me?'

'I'm sorry.' Ella's heart began to race. 'I just . . . didn't know how. Not out there. It's all right now though,' she said quickly, and then wondered if it really was.

'Did you let him kiss you?'

His lips, tracing the skin on her arms, her legs, her stomach. Her breasts. The blue, not-quite-dark warmth of the night.

'Yes.'

'Oh.' Clem's voice caught in her throat. 'And . . . what else? Did you do anything else?'

She had to close her eyes as the force of it rose in her, and she was liquid again; this was how it had been: as though she were able to take on different forms, become an animal, a rising swarm of feeling, as though she were herself but not herself, something beyond, and he were something other too.

But all of this was impossible to say.

She could feel Clem beside her though, breath held, hungry for the scraps.

'Tell me, Ella, *what did you do*?'

Still Ella did not speak, but Clem seemed to understand and gasped then, her breath coming faster, as though she were struggling to catch it. 'Oh! Did it hurt? Was there blood?'

'I think so. I don't know. But then . . .'

'What?' The whole length of Clem's body was pressed up tight against Ella's now. 'Tell me. *What?*'

'I don't know. I don't know how to say it . . . it was . . .' She couldn't find the words and knew, in the end, that she didn't want to. Not pour it into words, where it might harden and set, where it could be given a name.

She felt trapped, Clem here, too close, her breath too hot, her need too strong. They both lay, breathing fast under the heavy blanket of the night air, until Clem gave a small unsatisfied sound, part anger, part hurt, and slipped away again as quietly as she had come.

Ella turned on to her side, hunched on the edge of the thin mattress, a thick black band tightening around her heart. Without Clem's help none of it would have happened; she should have given her more. But what? How could she share something that she could not compass herself?

Charles

AT NIGHT, HE DREAMT of rivers, of tides, of monstrous waves, and there was a man, one who menaced him, who stood in the shadows and watched. When he woke, Charles felt as though he had hardly slept at all. Sometimes, if he turned too quickly as he went about his day, he saw this shadow man, a blurred grey figure just at the edge of sight. He knew it was that *thing* from the park, showing him he was not yet clean. Not yet as pure as he might be. And he knew whatever it was that thing in the park had seen in him, he must erase it, and then the man would disappear. Thus he had a new list with a new title:

Cleanse.
1. If ragtime is redolent of depravity I will not play it. Ragtime belongs in Mazeland and Mazeland, like Louisiana, is full of swamps.
2. I will not think of the young man in Spence's again.
3. The issue of Miss Church. I have been lax in addressing the question of her books.
4. The future of the hospital. Sterilization? Mulligan. Ella Fay.

The first item on the list was easy; at the earliest opportunity he gathered in the sheet music for the rags. Goffin may have looked a little sheepish, but there was no objection amongst the players, and later that day, crouching before his empty grate, Charles crushed the pages into balls and burnt them. It was a small blaze and did not last for long.

He ceased playing piano in the day rooms. The ridiculousness of the act struck him anew. What had he been hoping to achieve? Some sort of *therapy*? The notion was laughable; as though Mozart and Chopin and Schubert might somehow cure these people of their hereditary taint. Galton was right, Pearson was right, Churchill was right: moderation in these things was the road to ruin.

And really, Charles thought, as he went about his rounds, he owed Mulligan a debt. If it weren't for the man's actions on the cricket pitch, he might never have seen sense. The incontinent and the intemperate must be brought to heel. It was manifest everywhere; everywhere he saw people unable to hold themselves back. Last week, for instance, during his rounds of the women's day rooms, he had been accosted by an old, toothless crone who wore her hair in bunches like a child.

'Why don't you play?' Her voice was plaintive as she gripped him by the arm: 'Why don't you play for us any more?' He had tried to prise her off, but her grip was surprisingly strong, and as she pulled him towards her he was enveloped in her mephitic stench of urine and decay. *Because you are vermin*, he wished to say. *Because you are old and useless and are not fit to live.* But he did not say this, since he himself could be temperate, he himself was a rational man. He shook her off and pulled himself up. 'I am sorry.' He straightened his jacket. 'I'm afraid I no longer have the time.' At this she began to cry, long and keening, before putting her hands over her eyes, throwing herself on the floor and fitting like a child. The nurses were soon upon her, however, and before long had her taken out and put her in the sleeves.

As Charles made to leave the room, he saw Miss Church, sitting very still, watching him, a book held open in her lap. *Miss Church* was number three on his list, but there was nothing to say they should be tackled in order. He crossed the room towards her. She seemed to shrink a little as he came near. 'Good afternoon, Miss Church. May I ask what is it you are reading?'

'It's . . . just a novel.' She gathered the book closer to her body.

'May I see?'

She passed it over with visible reluctance. He felt her eyes on him as he flicked through its pages. 'Where did you get this?'

'My father.'

'Indeed.' Charles smiled, closing the book carefully. 'I wonder, would you mind terribly if I borrowed it for a while?'

He could see her wishing to remonstrate, could see the conflicting emotions play out across her face, but he did not wait to see them resolve; instead, he thanked her, tucked the book beneath his arm and went on his way.

The next day he paid a visit to Soames's office.

'This was found on Miss Church's person yesterday.' He placed the book on the table between them, before laying out the information as plainly as he could: education had taken over Miss Church's body; even as they spoke it was laying waste to her organs of reproduction and of sense. From his very first readings of her notes it had been clear to him: she did not belong in this environment, but in living here for so long she had become an *antisocial unit*. She needed to understand the *true realities and duties of life*; only when this occurred would she be ready to be returned to her home. In brief, it was simple: *Miss Church should be deprived of her books.*

There was a pause in which the superintendent weighed the offending book in his hands and then opened it, letting it fall where it would and reading, as though in an act of bibliomancy, as though the answer might be found in its words, before looking up again. 'All right, Fuller,' he said, a little sadly. 'Consider it done.'

Charles nodded. He drew himself up to his full height, hands clasped behind his back. 'There's something else. You were right, sir. I'm afraid the double post is too much for me. Especially since my illness. I need to conserve my strength. Therefore, I wish to resign the post of bandmaster.'

Soames looked surprised. 'If you're sure, Fuller?'

'Quite sure.'

'Well, we cannot appoint someone else now, not when it's . . .' Soames plucked irritably at the collar of his shirt, 'not when it's so hot.'

Charles had thought of this: 'May I suggest, in that case, that the dances are suspended for the remainder of the summer? It makes most sense, does it not, for everyone's sakes, to reconvene when the heat is a little more tolerable?'

'Indeed.' Soames looked relieved. 'Quite so.'

As he spoke, Charles felt as though he was shedding skins. He felt infinitely lighter as he left the sombre, dark-panelled room behind.

He avoided the other men in the corridors. His contact with the staff was almost nil. At lunchtime he sat alone, scribbling into his notebook, and then after tea took himself upstairs to carry on his reading and note-taking undisturbed.

There *would* be a paper for the Congress. But it would be a markedly different paper from the one he had set out to write.

Even if there had been time for conversation, he had begun to see how inferior most of his fellow workers were: Goffin, for instance, who had stopped him in the corridor the other day and asked him straight why it was he had cancelled the rest of the season's dances.

'I thought that we were all getting along rather well.' The young man's head was bowed, hands thrust in his pockets, shuffling his feet like a naughty schoolboy. 'In the band, that is.'

He had put on weight, Charles noted, and a heaviness hung about his jaw. In five years' time, in ten, his moment would be past. He would have lost whatever fleeting attractiveness he had once possessed. Was this really the young man whose comments had so wounded him?

'I'm sorry,' said Charles briskly, 'but music resides in Mazeland, and I no longer dwell there. I have found my way out of the labyrinth. I have found my way home.'

Goffin stared, eyes popping, then nodded in a brief, frightened fashion before hurrying away.

Charles's violin sat silent and unplayed in the corner of his quarters. Each night, instead of practising, he sat at his desk and wrote. He was composing a letter to Churchill:

I see now, Home Secretary, that you are right. Sterilization is the only true course. It is a service, an inoculation for Empire. Without it, we will be overrun. My own experience bears this out. I, too, have been cloistered in here. I have believed that if we kept our lunatics safe, apart, and well fed, that with our home farms and our dances and our sports days and our musicals and our Mozart in the day room for half an hour every Monday we might also do them good.

I see now that my thinking was all the wrong side up. In keeping them here, in treating them well, we have cosseted them. We should be another Sparta, but since we cannot in all conscience leave children on the moorside to their fate, we should do the next best thing and prevent them from ever being born. It is a simple enough operation.

And here is the beautiful thing, the magnificent thing,

the thing of which I know you are abundantly aware –
these people will be <u>better off</u>.

Let the poor breed fewer and more productive members
of society. Think how many problems this would solve at a
stroke! Poverty would be halved – there or thereabouts.

I see now, Home Secretary, that it is the only <u>rational</u>
<u>course</u>.

He read back over what he had written; the question of
poverty was a salient one, the country appeared to be
teetering on the verge of collapse. Every day the headlines
in *The Times* grew more alarming. The strikes were spreading – millions of men were reported to have downed tools
across the south-east of England.

Medicines were in short supply. The patients were faring
badly in the heat. Despite regular cups of water, many of
them had the red crusty tongues of early dehydration, the
death toll had risen sharply, and many amongst the oldest
patients seemed to be giving up. Only yesterday, Charles
had visited the storeroom for some bromide only to be told
by the chemist that there was none 'until further notice'.

'What in God's name can you mean?'

The man had opened his hands and shrugged. 'The
strikes, Dr Fuller, the strikes.'

The leader articles were growing increasingly alarming,
yesterday's stating the country was *in imminent danger of
famine*.

The whole thing is as insanely foolish as it is wicked. The
trade union leaders talk of putting an end to poverty.
Are they really so hopelessly ignorant as to imagine that
destroying property, stopping trade and dislocating the

whole machinery of civilization is the way to benefit the poor?

Thank God for self-sufficiency. Thank God for six thousand acres and flocks of cattle.

Still, there was half the milk there had been this time last month; there was hardly any grass left on which the cows might graze.

On Friday, at the time when the dance would ordinarily have been taking place, Charles found he did not want to be in the asylum and so walked to Ilkley instead, and then up on to the moor from there.

A strange sight greeted him: the fields were blackened with people lying in the grass – whole families, it seemed, asleep in the sun, the one beside the other. As he passed through them, taking the path up on to the moor, Charles stopped, approaching a grey-haired man who was sitting a little way apart from the rest. 'Where have you all come from?'

'Bridlington.' The old man looked exhausted. 'But there's no trains coming back to Bradford, and so we have to walk. We're resting a while with the little'uns before carrying on.'

He seemed to be the only person awake of the twenty that Charles counted lying in that field. He was glad to get beyond them and begin his climb; there was something sinister about them, lying there in their black clothes, as though a factory floor had been shaken out. He was glad too when he reached the ridge line to see he was the only vertical figure across that great mass of moor.

The bracken was dry as tinder and the drovers' path

was sandy. Fissures had appeared in the earth. Charles imagined those people in the fields rising up. *Ten million men on strike.* He found it difficult to imagine ten million men, let alone ten million angry men. It was enough to overthrow any government, surely? He saw them, massed over the moor, packed in their blackness, lying on the ground, staring up at him, silent as he passed.

Sedition. *Sedition.*

A sudden report split the air as he crested the ridge line, and he fell to the ground, heart pounding. A shooter, up here on the moor? Were the shots meant for him? One of those men in the fields perhaps? There was silence, and Charles felt his breathing return to normal as more shots came, but further away now: the short shouts of men, the distant yap of dogs. The unmistakeable holler of beaters. *Of course.* It was the eighteenth of August – just past the Glorious Twelfth. They were shooting grouse. At the sound of more gunfire Charles propped himself on his elbows and watched white smoke rise from Wharfedale. The shooters were miles away; it was the stillness and clarity of the day that had brought the sound so close.

A fragment of that morning's *Times* came back to him: the King – reported to be shooting in Yorkshire, at Bolton Abbey. That was the direction the shots had come from; it could well be the King's shooting party he heard. Likely even! Charles stayed where he was, sitting amongst the bracken, staring out at the small grey puffs of gun smoke in the distance, before taking his water bottle from his pack and swigging from it, pouring a little on to his hand and rubbing it over his head and neck.

He knew there were troops stationed in London, in Hyde Park and Regent's Park and parks in the East End. He could picture them, sweltering in their bearskins and uniforms, bayonets flashing in the broiling sun. He turned to the west and shaded his eyes. There had been rioting on the streets of Liverpool, hundreds of thousands of men. Churchill had sent HMS *Antrim* up the west coast, and she was moored, west-south-west of where he sat, on the Mersey between Liverpool and Birkenhead. Over two thousand cavalry and their officers on board. It only took Churchill to give the order to fire.

Churchill's guns in Liverpool. The King's up here on the moor. Men in the streets.

> *On the idle hill of summer,*
> *... far I hear the steady drummer,*
> *Drumming like a noise in dreams.*

Chaos. He felt it, hovering at the edge of things.

There could be no sticking plasters now; the wound must be cauterized, root and branch.

The Feeble-Minded Bill would be the true revolution the country needed. In a generation or less there would be no industrial action. No workers plagued by unemployment or want. Enough jobs to go around. Such beauty to its simplicity!

A plan was rising within him, a bold plan, but a plan that, if it succeeded, might transform his fortunes along with those of the asylum, the superintendent, even the country itself. Sharston had the opportunity to become a different kind of hospital, one that specialized in prevention rather than cure.

Soames would soon see.

He had sent his letter to Churchill.

263

Charles stood and raised his arms to the wide blue sky. It was a time for bold action, time for superior men to step into the light.

John

LATE AFTERNOON AND THEY were working in the slaughter-house, a huge barn on the outskirts of the grounds. The butchers had gone home for the day, and it was the job of Dan and John to clean the tables and sluice down the cobbled floor. The air was thick with the sweet-metal tang of blood. Above their heads, the marbled, emptied carcasses of pigs swung from their hooks. Thunder rumbled in the distance, somewhere over the moor. Light came through high windows, but the glass was crusted with dirt, and the light fell murky and green. An attendant stood nearby: a young lad, smoking at the doorway.

John scrubbed at the stains on his bench. The water in the bucket at his feet was pink. When it had grown red and greasy, he threw it on the ground, where it ran down slanted cobbles to a drain, then he went and filled his pail from the pump in the yard.

He worked fast. The faster he worked, the more quickly his bucket needed changing, and the more often he went out. From the farmyard he could see the wood, see the edge of the field where he had lain with her. If he was quick, he might go back there. Even a minute would do.

Dan was restless. At each rumble of thunder he would nod, as though murmuring a kind of assent. He kept muttering, flicking glances over to the attendant. They worked in silence until the attendant stepped outside.

'There's a war coming, *mio Capitane.*' Dan's voice was low. 'That's what I'm hearing. A war.'

John looked up.

'A real one this time. Not just out there.' Dan jerked his head towards the door. 'Not just a tug of war on a cricket field. Not just those jokers, but a real war, real men, out in the streets. Liverpool. That's where to go.'

John nodded; he had heard it too. The papers that reached them, days old though they were, were full of it. He had seen the pictures: the men packed on to the streets of Liverpool. Hundreds of policemen on horses.

'It's time.' Dan balled up his cloth and chucked it on the stone slab.

'For what?'

'Moving on.'

'How?'

Dan put his hands under his armpits and gave a low whistle. 'You really asking me that, *chavo*? You really think I'm here cos they locked me up? You think I'm going to stay till I'm like those lads in there, sitting smeared in their shit? I'm only here cos I choose it. If I want to get out, I just go,' he waved his hand towards the open door, 'up, over and away. Like I always said.'

'They'll send men after you.'

Dan gave a low laugh, shaking his head. 'They won't find me though, will they? When I scarper, I'm gone. You should come with me, *chavo*.' He turned towards the door, where small pieces of seeds, or dust, the last shavings of summer, hung in the light. 'Wind's changed. I tell you, you'll be better sheltering on the moor than here. Death all around here now.' He turned back, eyes sharp and glittering, a challenge in them. 'This land is *us*, *chavo*. You

understand? We are the land. And these blind bastards . . .'
He shook his head. 'When men at the bottom have their
souls leave them, they end up in here. But when men at
the top do, they end up dangerous. What do you say, *mio
Capitane?*'

John regarded his friend: the deep lines of his face, his
fuzz of hair lit by the sun.

'Your heart's back now, *chavo*,' said Dan softly. 'Time to go.'

John looked away. He tipped his bucket on the stones,
watched its contents swirl and eddy down the drain. Water
and blood. 'Have ye some matches there, Riley?'

Dan palmed a box and threw it low towards him. John
pocketed them, lifted his pail and went outside.

As he bent to the pump, he took deep lungfuls of air. The
sky was low and grey, but the air was sweet. He lifted the
pump handle then let it fall, the water running over his
hands, washing away the blood.

Liverpool.

The brawling cacophony of the docks. The welcome he
had been given, men spitting and jeering as he stumbled
down the plank of the boat, half mad with fatigue, clothes
crusted with salt spray. The part of the city where the Irish
lived, and the men and women who lived there. The close,
stinking courts, the shifting, temporary nature of it all; all
of them waiting to get away, to America, to wherever the
hell, not understanding, or coming slow to the knowing,
that they were already as away as many of them would get.

The seeping disappointment of it all. Gathering in the
early-morning drizzle, hoping to be hired for the day,
punching and jostling to the front to get seen. Old men on
their knees for a job. The shame of it. The all-round shame
of it.

He might not know much about war, but he knew a little about Liverpool, enough to know he never wanted to go back.

Still, plenty of the men who were caged in those sheds with him, begging for work, would be out on those streets now. Slaking their shame with anger. The thought made him uneasy. Dan's words had got under his skin; he could not fathom where his allegiance lay.

His bucket was filled with water, and he carried it to the door of the slaughterhouse where the attendant was picking at his nail. 'Do ye mind if I take a minute there?' The young man shrugged, and John put down his pail and made for the low wall, his blood quickening as the place where they had lain came into view. A black scatter of crows was there now, the last of the gleaners, picking away at the stumps of the crop.

He saw her there beside him, heard again the way she had cried out. He had not thought a woman could cry like that, like an animal, with no thought of being heard. He saw her face, her white neck stretched, her eyes closed and then open wide and fastened on his, pulling him, until he could hold back no longer and let himself be taken down.

He did not need a war to come and remake the world; in her he could be made new.

And yet, beneath this he felt a great, growing unease. Dan was right. He was well again. His heart was back. And if he was well, he should not be here.

We should run, she had said. They had been free, and he had persuaded her to stay.

What had he thought? That the summer would last for ever?

John hoisted his pail and went inside, where the air was thick and close. Dan, whistling, did not meet his eyes.

Ella

SHE SEEMED TO TIRE more easily. Perhaps it was the heat, but it was harder to lift and wring the sheets, and to haul heavy baskets of wet clothes around the room. Often, when she looked up, Ella would see Clem's eyes following her, wide with a hurt that she did not know how to salve.

As Friday approached, though, Clem's mood changed. She barely let Ella from her sight, speaking excitedly of the dance and of the letter that would surely come. But it troubled Ella: a letter from John, speaking of what had passed between them, was too close a thing to share with Clem, and yet Clem was pining, looking forward to it as though she were starving and it was food.

At the end of the morning's work, Ella was happy to reach the day room where she could sit in her chair and close her eyes and think of him.

On Thursday she was woken by shouts.

'No!' Clem was screaming. '*No no no no no.*'

Clem and the Irish nurse seemed to be fighting. Ella scrambled to her feet. 'What is it? *Clem?*'

The nurse pulled away from the tussle, breathing hard, her cap askew. 'She's not allowed books any more.'

A low moan came from Clem. 'Give that back.' She lunged at the nurse, hands flailing, but the woman twisted away. 'Orders of the doctor,' she said, a sly triumph to her tone.

'Which doctor?' Clem's face was pale.

'Dr Fuller.' The woman took evident pleasure in the news.

At this Clem collapsed, quite suddenly, like a puppet someone had let go of, her skirts pooling around her on the floor.

'Clem.' Ella came to kneel beside her. 'They can't mean it. I'm sure it's wrong.'

'Leave me alone,' Clem said, in a hollow voice.

'Clem.' Ella reached out and touched her arm, but Clem pushed her off.

'I said *leave me alone.*'

At breakfast Clem did not eat her porridge, just two small spoonfuls before she pushed the bowl away.

'Aren't you hungry?' Ella had already finished hers.

Clem shook her head.

'Can I have it then?'

Clem shrugged, and Ella pulled the bowl across the table towards her.

At dinnertime it was the same: Clem took just a couple of mouthfuls of stew before pushing the plate away in distaste. This time Ella did not ask but reached for it and ate it gratefully. Clem hardly seemed to notice. At teatime she still ate nothing, and Ella was happy to take her bread and jam.

But when, on the second day, Clem did the same, Ella pushed the porridge bowl back. 'You have to eat, Clem.'

Clem was staring out over the room of women.

'I wonder if it hurts to live.' She spoke almost under her breath. *'And if they have to try. And whether, could they choose between, They would not rather die.'*

She turned her gaze on Ella. 'What do you think they

think?' Her tone had changed; a new chill edge had come to her voice. 'Do they think things will get better? Do they think they'll get out?'

'I don't know,' said Ella quietly.

'No,' she said, with a brief, bitter laugh. 'I don't suppose you do.'

'Clem,' said Ella again. 'You have to eat.'

'I'm not hungry,' said Clem. 'If you don't eat it, then they'll give it to the pigs.'

That Friday morning the matron made an appearance in the dining room, and hands were clapped for quiet.

'Tonight you are to go back to your wards. It has been decided that while this hot weather continues, there are to be no more dances. They will resume when the weather breaks.'

A silence, then the beginnings of whimpering from the assembled women. A distant thrum started in Ella's ears, as though she was suddenly underwater and all the sounds were strange. When she looked up, Clem's face was pinched, the blood gone from her lips. 'They can't do that.'

Ella didn't answer. Outside her, the world was tilting away. But Clem was already on her feet, voice raised, hands carving shapes in the air. 'You can't *do that*. We have to dance.'

Two nurses were walking quickly towards her.

'Clem.' Ella tugged on her skirt. 'Don't take on. They'll give you the sleeves.'

'Don't *take on*?' Clem spat down at her.

She did sit then, just in time, but as the nurses hovered at her shoulder she leant over the table towards Ella. '*Until the weather breaks?* Don't you see what that means? A month. Or more. Without any dancing.'

Ella saw it, but it was happening a long way away, beyond the tide of her blood.

Clem's eyes were wide. 'For God's sake, Ella. Don't you *care*? How long will it be without any *letters*?'

She wanted to say she didn't need letters. That she couldn't read. She wanted to say that what was written on her skin was stronger than a hundred letters could be, but the sight of Clem's white, wild face silenced her.

That afternoon, instead of lining up to be checked for the dance, they were put in the day room and made to sit in their usual seats. The heat seemed closer, the fractious, flitting chorus of the women louder than ever. Clem's voice was part of it now; she kept repeating the same few words: 'No dance. No books. No dance. No books,' staring at the air in front of her as her hands plucked in agitation at her skirts.

'Clem?' Ella said. But Clem did not look up or pause in her recitation.

'No dance, no books. No dance, no books. *Nodancenobooksnodance.*'

She turned her body away from the sight of Clem and shut her eyes. After a while, she slept, falling into a feverish dream in which she was back at the mill, and late, and Jim Christy, the pennyhoil man, was shutting the gate in her face, and she had her hands on the bars and was pleading with him to let her in. She woke to a tugging on her arm – Clem's face close to hers, and the day room drenched with woozy golden light. 'It's time for the dance,' she said.

Ella blinked at her. 'What dance?'

Clem grinned, baring her teeth; there were small flecks

of white at the edge of her lips. 'If they won't let us dance in the ballroom, then we'll make our own. We'll show them. We don't need stupid Dr Fuller and his *stupid* violin. Come *on.*' She yanked Ella by the arm. 'If you get up, then I'll play.'

'Wait.'

Clem made a small, impatient noise and turned on her heel. Ella stayed where she was, watching as Clem walked around the listless, sunken women, clapping her hands in their faces. 'Wake up! Wake up! One day we're all going to be dead.'

The nurse on duty was watching, but lazily, with half an eye, as Clem lifted the lid of the piano and played a few brief bars of a piece that Ella recognized, a beautiful piece, one that Dr Fuller had played. For a moment the notes hung on the air, until they crashed into clashing chords. 'If *he* won't play for us,' said Clem, 'I'll do it.' Next came the first few bars of a waltz, and then she was away from the piano and on her feet, clapping and singing. '*Da* da-da *Da* da-da *Da* da-da *Da* da-da.'

Old Germany was up, and Clem caught her, turning a hectic circle around the room. When they came close to where Ella was sitting, Clem span Old Germany around then let her go free. She turned to Ella, kicking her on the shin. 'Get up then. Go on.'

Clem grabbed her hands, and this time Ella allowed herself to be pulled to her feet. 'One day you'll be dead,' said Clem, and then leant forward, putting her lips on Ella's own. At first they were hard and bloodless, and then, as she pressed herself closer, they softened, and Ella felt the quick small flick of her tongue. 'Pretend I'm him.' Clem pulled back, placing her cheek on Ella's, whispering into her ear.

'Why don't you just pretend I'm him?' Then she span them off, singing tunelessly.

Ella tried to find her footing, but Clem was too fast and the spinning was making her dizzy. 'Stop. Can you just—'

'Stop bleating, would you, and *dance.*'

Clem's small, hard breasts pressed painfully against hers, the heel of her palms grinding against her own, until she hit the side of an armchair, and pain bloomed along Ella's hip. She wrenched herself away, the movement taking her on to the floor, the room spinning, giddy, queasy, until she vomited between her hands. When there was nothing left inside her, she managed to stand. Her eyes were streaming. The back of her nose and throat stung. She wiped her face and eyes with her sleeve. Clem was standing a little way away, breathing hard, her arms folded, a look of contempt on her face.

'I'm sorry.' Ella took a few paces towards her then faltered. 'I just felt sick.'

Clem made a snorting noise. 'Well, you shouldn't have eaten so much food at lunch, should you? That's what you get for eating twice.'

The next morning in the laundry, Clem was working on the other side of the room and so their paths did not cross, but at dinnertime, when Ella made her way over towards where she was sitting, ready to take her usual place, Clem looked up. 'What are you doing?' Her voice was very calm.

'Sitting down.'

'Not here.'

Ella's lips were dry. 'Why not here?'

'Because I don't want you to.' Clem's face was smooth.

Ella's cheeks scalded as she made her way to an empty

space on the far side of the hall. She felt tears wanting to come, so put the heels of her palms to her eyes and ground them out. All through dinner she kept her gaze fixed on her plate, but when she was finished eating she couldn't help but look up to where Clem was sitting, arms folded over her chest, bowl in front of her, staring out at nothing.

That was three days without food.

In the day room she saw immediately that they had removed the encylopaedia, and that, instead of the tall gold-backed books, there was only a length of bare shelf.

A high, thin sound came from beside her, and she turned to see Clem, standing very still, staring at the space where the books should be. After a moment, Clem took a couple of steps towards the bookshelf, reached out and ran her fingertip along the wood. *'I cannot live with you,'* she muttered. *'It would be life. And life is over there. Behind the shelf.'*

'Clem?'

Clem raised her head.

'I'm sorry.'

'Why? Why are you sorry?'

Ella gestured to the shelf. 'I'm sorry they took your books away. I'm sorry the encyclopaedia has gone. I'm sorry about the dancing.'

'Oh. Is that it?' Clem said in a strange, light voice. 'Is that all?'

The skin was stretched tight across Clem's skull. It seemed to Ella that while some parts of her were shrinking, others were getting bigger. Her jaw. Her forehead. Her eyes. Fear uncurled inside Ella.

'You have to eat, Clem. Please eat. If you don't, you'll get ill.'

'I already am ill.' Clem spoke slowly. 'I mean, really, Ella. You can't be that stupid, can you? Why on earth do you think I'm in here?'

'No.' Ella shook her head. 'You're not ill.'

Clem gave a short, bitter laugh. 'What do you know anyway?'

'I know you're not ill. And I know they'll put you in the chronic wards if you don't eat.'

'So?'

'If you go, then you won't come out again.'

'*If you go, then you won't come out again.*' Clem mocked Ella's accent. 'God, you're so *dull* sometimes, you know that? Don't you see? Who cares?' she said. 'Who bloody cares what happens to me?'

'I do,' said Ella miserably. 'You're my friend.'

Clem said nothing to that.

'Clem?'

'What?'

'Here.' She reached into her dress and brought out the letter, the last one he had given her, the one she hadn't yet heard. 'It's a new letter. I kept it from you. I'm sorry. Take it. I can't read it anyway, can I? You can have it if you want.'

Clem looked from the letter to Ella and back again. Her face was twisted and ugly with wanting. She was so hungry. Her hunger was frightening.

'Here.' Ella pushed her fist towards Clem. 'Read it, please. And then, would you help me write one back?'

Clem carried on staring at the letter but did not take it. Instead, she turned away, curling over herself as though protecting a wound. She began to shake. At first Ella thought she was crying, but when she finally looked up Clem's face was contorted, her mouth stretched wide. 'Why?' she said.

'Why should I help you write your *stupid* letter? I thought you cared about me?'

'I do.'

'Well, if you care about me so much you'll know when to bloody well *leave me alone.*' She was speaking so loudly that everyone would be able to hear.

Ella sensed movement in the room around them – saw the Irish nurse stand, come closer. She turned her back to her. 'Clem. Please.'

'Go on.' Clem was shouting now. 'Why should I help you? You're just a stupid, ignorant girl who can't even read. Why don't you tell him? Next time you see him? Next time you *dance* with him, if you can even call it that. Whatever it is you do with him. What is it you *do* with him, Ella? Why don't you tell him that you can't read? See what he thinks of you then? Your *man.* Your *John.*'

She snatched the letter from Ella's hand and waved it in her face. 'You've no idea what this says, have you? You think he'd like you if it weren't for me? If it weren't for *my* words?' Her lips curled back, and she was a snarling, spitting dog. 'How do you even know what he *wrote*? I could have made it all up. You wouldn't know the difference, you're so stupid. How do you know it's not me he likes after all?'

Ella reached up and slapped her across the cheek. Clem staggered backwards, hand to her face, gasping, then laughed, as though she were pleased, as though that was exactly what she had wanted to happen. Her cheek was bright red: the marks of Ella's fingers clear upon it. She was still holding the letter, crumpled now in her fist. Ella took a step towards her. 'Give that back.'

'Why should I?'

She grabbed Clem's hair and twisted it around her fist. 'Give it *back*.'

Clem cried out in pain, and as her hands went to her head the letter fell to the floor. Ella let go, clawing to pick it up, but arrived too late.

The Irish nurse had got there first.

Charles

IF HE RESTED HIS HANDS on the green baize of his desk, they did not tremble quite so much.

The crumpled letter was pinned by a paperweight at each corner. He read it again, slowly, mouthing the words under his breath.

Gradh Machree,
I barely know how to write to you, since now you seem to me a creature beyond any words.

There was a moment when I watched you, before you knew I was there. I watched your face as you stood beneath the tree. I hope you can forgive me. But there was no fear there, even though it was dark and the night was all around.

I will not write of our meeting. I cannot. Only to say, I believe the trees were our only witness. The trees and the fields and the sky.

You told me we were free. I asked you to stay with me. I think of this often, now. I told you once that you were made for flight. And so I believe you are. Forgive me for keeping you here.

It is my great hope that we will meet in the same way

again. But I would wish we would meet in freedom. True freedom. You were right. We must take our freedom now.

We will meet again. I know it. I know it as I know that my name is John or that I have five fingers on my right hand and I come from Mayo in the far west of Ireland. And these are things I know well.

And so, I look forward, mavourneen, greatly to that day, or that night.

Yours,

John Mulligan

The handwriting was careful, perhaps not that of a man who was used to wielding the pen, but the language was fluent enough, or, if not fluent, it made a virtue of a slight hesitancy. Charles knew there were board schools in Ireland, but there was something in this man's turn of phrase that could not be taught. Where had he learnt to write like that? And this girl – she was half feral. Surely she could come up with little in response?

'What does this mean?' He pointed to the letter, looking up to where Nurse Keane was standing before him.

The woman leant over the desk. '*Mavourneen?* That would mean . . . my darling,' she said, pressing her lip in a tight thin line.

'And this? . . . *Gradh Machree?*'

'I believe,' the tip of the woman's nose was turning red, 'bright love of my heart, Doctor.'

'I see,' said Charles. 'Thank you.' He dismissed her with a wave of the hand.

As he sat there, something occurred to him: that this was not the only letter; somewhere there must be a hoard of them, a cache. The girl must have them about her person somewhere. If he were to summon her here, force her to give them up . . .

He folded the letter and placed it on the mantelshelf alongside his sketches. If he were to summon her directly, the game would be up, and there would be no more letters. It would be more politic to wait and watch.

Along with delivery of the letter, the nurse had brought him news of Miss Church's disobedience. He requested an appointment with the superintendent at the earliest opportunity; Dr Soames received him in his room.

'It appears my idea has worked, sir. Miss Church has refused to eat for the last few days.'

The older man nodded. 'So I hear. And you take this to be a good thing?'

'I do, sir. She is reacting against her environment. Now her books have gone she cannot help but see what surrounds her. This is the first step towards her recovery. But it will not be easy; there has been a violent incident with another patient, a Miss Fay. A most unsuitable companion for a young lady. Miss Church has been violent with the nurses too it seems. One of them was badly bitten while trying to feed her.'

'I see.' The man nodded. 'Where is she now?'

'The infirmary. I think, sir, she must be fed by tube.'

'Indeed.' The superintendent looked hunched suddenly, old. 'You know I am a friend of the father, Fuller. Considering the . . . special nature of the patient, I wouldn't want to entrust such a job to just anyone. But I find I have little stomach for the task. Might I entrust Miss Church to your care?'

Charles wanted to laugh. Was the pun intentional? 'Of

279

course, sir.' He gave a slight bow. 'I should be delighted to carry out the feeding myself.'

When the patient was carried in by two male attendants, she was already strapped to the chair. She had grown noticeably thinner. Charles was shocked at the transformation but determined she would not see what he felt.

When she saw him standing, waiting with the tube, she thrashed about like an animal. A length of muslin was tied around her mouth – presumably to keep her from biting those around her – but it did not prevent the most terrible, bestial noises from escaping. The nurses took up their positions, two of the strongest on each side to hold the patient down and another freer to move about. As Miss Church was placed in front of him, the hands of the nurses became white with the effort of restraint. A nurse stepped forward and untied the gag, and almost as soon as she had done so the patient began to spit and curse.

Charles stood by, astonished, as the words spewed from her. Had it been in her all along, this propensity for filth? Or had she learnt it here from companions like Miss Fay? He could not but suppose the latter; still, the performance had to be seen and heard to be believed. It was like cutting into something fine – a good steak, perhaps – and seeing that beneath it was rotten and that flies had beaten you to the feast. When he had heard enough, Charles gave the signal to the nurse, who pinched the patient's nose with a clip. A sheet was tied beneath the chin. The patient was obstructive, tightening her lips, but Charles stepped forward and pulled them apart. He called for the steel gag, which he ran around the gums, feeling for gaps in the teeth. She twisted her neck wildly. 'Hold her, nurse!'

The free nurse moved to her head, and with two of them there the patient ceased her movement and he found a gap – cutting the flesh of the gums a little in the process, blood running over his fingertips as he prised the jaw open wide, then secured it tight. A low moaning came from the patient now, but the eyes were the only things that moved. He was reminded of the time he read her notes, of placing his handkerchief over those eyes so that he might not see. Now though, he did not need any such props, now he stared straight back and it was she who looked away first.

He brought all of his attention to the task in hand. Though such feedings happened in the asylum every day, it had been a good while since he had carried one out himself. First, he took the end of the length of India-rubber tubing and began to train it down into the throat. On the first attempt Miss Church gave way to a violent coughing fit, and the tube was expelled, but on the second try Charles was more careful, and after an initial gagging from the patient the tube passed through the throat and into the oesophagus, and there were no more convulsions from the chair. He placed the bowl ready on top of the rubber tube and called for the mixture. It was ready prepared, the same used for any patient who must be fed: beaten eggs and milk and vitamins added to the whole, altogether as much nourishment as might be had in liquid form, and really, he thought, as he steadied it over the opening of the tube and the patient's eyes grew wide, really, she was lucky they were feeding her at all. In Holloway, he had heard, they poured the mixture in through the rectum; punishment, not nourishment, was what was offered there. He could see the bared whites, the curve of the eyeball, the thin red veins lacing the sides. He began to pour. Silence. The only movement in the room the preparation moving from bowl to tube, the only sound the soft *glug* as the mixture went down. After a moment, the patient's body convulsed, and the nurse closest to him put a hand on Charles's arm. 'She can only take so much, Dr Fuller. It'll just come straight back up.'

He poured more slowly then, steadily, not stopping until the whole bowlful had disappeared. 'The mixture needs to digest,' he said when he was finished. 'And we'll have no vomiting tricks. Hold her down while I am gone.'

When he stepped out of the room and pulled the door shut behind him, Charles found his shirt was damp with sweat. He needed air. The infirmary was on the west side of the asylum, close to the men's quarters, and it was a short enough walk to a side entrance that brought him out overlooking the wood. Even at this early hour it was hot, and the heavy quality of the air felt wrong, like something rotten. He hurried towards the trees; let their green coolness envelop him. Fine spider's webs looped from their branches, filaments glistening silver. The first horse chestnuts had fallen and old leaf fall crunched beneath his feet as he walked. He made his way to a clearing and packed his pipe. Somewhere close by a twig snapped, making him jump. He cast his eyes about him but could see no one there. *The trees were our only witnesses.* Had it happened in here? In this very clearing perhaps? Impossible to know which trees had been witness to the sordid act. A small breeze came, ruffling the leaves in the high canopy, and Charles had the uneasy sense he was not alone. 'Was it you?' he said to the thick-trunked beech beside him. 'Or you? Or you or you or you?'

But the trees only stood there and said nothing in response. He was woozy as he made his way back to the asylum, and somehow the path he took was the wrong one, leading only to more trees, thicker now, darker, through which he stumbled, pushing through their branches, emerging in a bramble thicket, gasping into the light. When he reached the safety of the buildings, he turned and looked back. The wood was traitorous. He would not come here again.

The treatment room was empty but for one nurse sitting beside Miss Church, who stood as he entered. The patient was slumped in the chair. She appeared to be asleep. He approached her quietly. Looking at her lying so still, with her pale skin and her fine, light colouring, it was almost possible to feel tenderly towards her, to feel as though she might yet be unspoilt. She really was a most attractive girl. Then her eyes fluttered open. 'All done,' he said. Her expression had changed. There was something else there. Hate. He pulled on the end of the tube. It was strange to watch it come out. There seemed to be so much more length than had gone in.

Ella

IT WAS THE FIRST cool place she had been for months, and at first it was almost a pleasure to be down where the sun was tamed to a high, bright rectangle on the wall.

Her fury kept her hot though, wrenching and turning in the long sleeves, even though she knew it was useless, until she had tired and bruised herself. She conjured Clem's words, her twisted face.

You think he'd like you if it weren't for me?

How do you even know what he wrote? I could have made it all up.

Was it true? What would he think if he knew she had never read any of his words for herself?

She saw the triumph on the Irish nurse when she had claimed the letter, and she knew that she and John were in danger now. And she thought she hated Clem.

But then the cold began to seep up from the ground, and the strangeness of it all stole over her: Clem's dancing, her opened mouth, her searching tongue, and then her anger paled and cooled.

Was Clem down here too then, in the long sleeves? She could be in the next cell for all it was possible to know.

And she feared for her then. She wouldn't be able to eat, strapped in like this. Someone should tell them that she hadn't eaten. It would be six days, wouldn't it, without any food?

When they brought her back up, there was no sign of Clem or of the books. A new woman was sitting in Clem's chair, toothless and square as a box. She growled when Ella came near.

Ella took a seat on the other side of the room and nursed her swollen, painful arms, while around her the women fratched and cried. Outside, the sun shone, as though it still, after all these months, had something to say, lighting on the women's maddled faces, on the close, brown walls, the locked fireplace. On the piano, lying closed and heavy and still.

As soon as she could, she stood, went to the bathroom and made her way to the last of the stalls. But when she got there she saw the window had been replaced with green marbled glass. They knew. She climbed up on the toilet seat and put her eye to the pane, and a strange, twisted world became visible: brown grass, stretching; the stand of trees. The fields. There was no line of men though. The harvest was done. Whether the sun knew it or not, summer was coming to its close.

She pressed her forehead to the glass and groaned.

When she came back out of the toilet block, she threaded her way around the women to her seat.

'Whatisitthatshewants?'

'He'sburningburningburningher.'

Old Germany caught Ella's hand. 'Where is she?' Her face was plaintive. 'Where's my lovely? Where's my lovely to play for me?'

'I don't know,' said Ella, miserably, prising the old woman's hand away. 'I'm sorry. I don't know.'

Late in the afternoon the dog men appeared, and the old familiar fear rose in Ella: the chronic ward, the gawbers. With no music to cover it, the women's whimpering was loud. But sitting there amid the reeky stench and the yammering women, watching the men go about their work, something came to her, a thought that was clear and whole: she would go to the chronic ward. Go in with the gawbers. John was in the men's chronic ward. And the women's ward was surely where Clem would be. If she could not run, then she would stay. She would choose it.

The thought flamed in her blood.

It wouldn't be too hard to get there. She would simply have to do something bad. Start a fight. It would have to be vicious though, to make them send her there. Her eyes grazed the room and then tangled with those of the Irish nurse, who was sitting over by the door. The woman gave a brief, nasty smile, and Ella's blood quickened.

The next time the woman was close, she would grab her head and bray it against a wall. She didn't need a reason – although she had reason enough. It would better, in fact, if there were no reason at all, since that was more often the way of the women in here. Then the dog men could come and take her off, but they wouldn't have to carry her. She would walk between them with her head held high, knowing that what she wanted had come to pass. She clenched her fists around her thumbs.

But the afternoon passed and the Irish nurse was called away, and Ella sat, twined tight.

Tomorrow, she would do it. Tomorrow she would be gone.

But early the next morning, she was called to see the doctor.

Perhaps this was it, she thought, as she was marched down the corridors to his room. Perhaps it was already done. Perhaps it was him had read the letter. He was going to be surprised when she nodded her head and agreed that the chronic ward was the best place for her.

He was already there when she entered the room, standing behind his desk, hands clasped behind his back. He looked thinner than before. 'Miss Fay! Please,' he nodded to a chair, 'sit down.'

The large book was open in front of him, and she could see her page, the one with her picture on it, the wrong way up.

'I've been reading your file.' He drummed his fingers on the dark wood of the desk. 'And the more I read of these pages the more they tell me how well you've been doing here. Entry after entry acknowledges that you are a good, hard worker.' He threaded his fingers before him and looked her up and down. 'And now I have you before me I can see it for myself. Our food's obviously suiting you too; you look as though you've put on weight.'

He pulled out his chair and sat before her, turning the pages back.

'Not last week, there was a report by one of my colleagues that suggested that you should be set at liberty, pending a little further observation. Indeed, had this incident with Miss Church not occurred, you would have been sitting here around about now, visiting me for a review. And if you had passed that review, then we would have recommended you for release.'

His words hung in the air like strange dark fruit waiting to be plucked. Ella put her hands in her lap, making herself still, watching his pawky, cunning face. He was playing a game. He had read the letter and was playing a game. She needed to work out the rules of this game, and quickly, before it was over and she was beaten. *Think. Think.*

'Wouldn't you like that?' he was saying. 'Isn't that what you want? I seem to remember a day, not so very long ago, when we faced each other in this room, and it seemed to be what you wanted very much indeed.'

A coldness was creeping up her legs, as though it were coming from the cells beneath. 'Yes,' she said slowly. 'Yes, I would.'

Was it the right thing to say? She couldn't tell, but it was something, thrown into his path, something to slow this down. So she could think. Why couldn't she think?

His chin rose, his eyes narrow for a moment, and then that smile was back. 'Good,' he said.

Do you ever think that people are wearing masks?

'Witnesses report it was not you but Miss Church who started the incident in the day room. We are going to treat this as a misdemeanour. Providing all goes well over the next week, we will arrange for your release. Stand up, please, Miss Fay.'

She did so. He stared at her for a long moment, then shook his head and gave a quick, barking laugh. 'Goodness. Do close your mouth, Miss Fay. The door does not only go one way.'

Whatever the game was, she knew he thought he had won.

'What about Clem?' she said.

'Miss Church? What of her?'

'Is she on the chronic ward?'

Fuller closed the casebook, his mouth turning down at the corners. 'I'm afraid not, Miss Fay. Miss Church is far too ill for that. She is in the infirmary, where we are feeding her to save her life.'

'Her life?'

'Indeed.'

'But . . . you . . .'

'Yes?'

She wanted to rip his mask off, rip it so she could see the animal beneath. She was ready. She wasn't afraid. But she did nothing. As much as it was his fault, she knew it was also hers. She should have given Clem more. They were both of them to blame.

John

HE WOKE TO FIND three boxes of matches on his pillow, and before he was fully awake they were tucked in his sleeve and he knew: Dan was gone.

Seconds later, the ward was in uproar. Confusion daubed on the faces of the attendants. No trace of him, no broken window. No open door. John, along with everyone else, had no idea how he had done it; Dan had simply disappeared.

The men were locked into the day room and extra attendants were placed at the doors, and as men gathered in those close and foetid quarters, wild rumour spread. Dan had had the help of giants. He had been carried off by fairies. Had stolen a horse from the stables and ridden across the moor in the night. He had become a horse himself.

'It is true, John?' Joe Sutcliffe was in front of him. 'Is it true he turned into a horse?'

'I don't know, lad. I don't know about that.'

He might have done. He wouldn't have put it past him, somehow.

After several hours, the doctor arrived in the day room. It was weeks since they had been face to face, not since the incident on the cricket pitch, and John watched as Fuller moved his slow way around the room, speaking to each of the men in turn. He did not look to John, but it seemed to him he left him purposely till last.

'Mr Mulligan.' Fuller drew up a chair, brushed it with his sleeve and then sat down beside him. 'It appears your friend Mr Riley has disappeared.' The man looked thin. A restlessness to him. His cheeks hollowed out, a new, gleaming cast to his eye.

'Aye, so it does.'

'And you're going to tell me you have no idea where he is.'

'That's right.' John was sweating. He was not used to being inside.

Fuller smiled. 'I thought you might say that.' He stretched his legs out, letting his gaze roam around the room. 'It's a grand old life you chaps have in here, isn't it? I often wonder what you think up to amuse yourselves. You must have such an awful lot of time on your hands.' He turned back to John. 'I suppose I'm a little envious, to tell you the truth. I'm not sure what I'd do if I had as much time as you. Write, I think. More letters perhaps.'

John was silent.

Fuller frowned. 'You'll be lonely, no doubt, Mr Mulligan, if Mr Riley does not make it back?'

John said nothing.

'Well,' Fuller shook out his trousers as he stood, 'I should be getting on.' He smiled again, and, as though he had just remembered something, lifted his finger. 'One day, Mr Mulligan, or one night, we will meet again. I know it. I know it as I know that my name is Charles or that I have five fingers on my right hand and I come from Yorkshire. And these are things I know well.'

His words. His words in the fucker's mouth.

Fuller gave a jaunty salute. 'Till soon, Mr Mulligan, till soon.'

Charles

THE MONTH TURNED. September came. But though sunrise was noticeably later and sunset noticeably earlier, the thermometer refused to register the change of season and the mercury stayed stubborn at ninety degrees. The only tolerable time was first thing in the morning, and so Charles woke as early as he could, lifting his weights in the pink-hued cool before dawn.

Every day he fed Miss Church with the tube, but each day it grew easier; the patient was still recalcitrant, still chafed violently against her restraints, and the same vile invective poured when the muslin was taken from her mouth, but she was growing steadily weaker, and Charles no longer sweated when he carried out the feeding.

By the end of the second week the patient was different. When he took away the muslin, there were no words, and the head flopped awkwardly to the side. The face was covered in bruises, the gums tattered and bleeding. The lips chapped, as though the patient had spent time in a strong wind. A small line of spittle swung from the corner of the mouth.

Broken.

'No words today, Miss Church?'

With what seemed like a great effort, the patient turned her face to his. She opened her mouth and spoke in a low, rasping voice that he had to lean in to hear. 'What does it matter to you if I live or die?'

He might have laughed, so melodramatic was the question, but there was something in the girl's face – something so direct it demanded an answer.

'I'm afraid it does not matter to me at all, Miss Church, other than as your doctor. It matters a great deal to your family though, to your father and your brother. And it is for their sake as well as yours that I am doing this.'

He saw a small tear rise in the base of her eye. She blinked and it fell. Then she shuddered and closed her lids.

Good news, though, had come from the world beyond the asylum walls: the strikes appeared to have been broken; Lloyd George had brokered the peace. *The Times* reported that Churchill had left London for a holiday. This last was good and bad. Good, because the Home Secretary would now, presumably, have a little time for his personal correspondence, and bad, because if Charles's letter had not arrived at Westminster in time before he left, he might have to wait weeks for a reply.

Each morning he checked his pigeonhole, and each afternoon after lunch, even though it was out of his way to do so, he walked back to the administration block and checked again. After a few days of this, the porter raised his eyebrows. 'Waiting for something, Dr Fuller?'

'Evidently.'

But no word came, and as the days passed Charles began to wonder at what juncture it might be appropriate to write once more.

He had not been idle though; far from it. He had seized the initiative and written to Major Darwin and to Professor Pearson, making sure to take care with his wording but implying nonetheless that he had the tacit support of the medical superintendent in his plan to turn the asylum into a hospital: a teaching establishment that might lead the way in sterilization once the Feeble-Minded Bill had been passed. He had been surprised and delighted to receive replies from them both, urging caution but encouraging him in his plan. It wanted only a reply from the Home Secretary and he would be ready to present his case.

Then, on the eleventh of September, a day when the temperature had dropped by a blessed fifteen degrees, when the sky was thick with cloud and the mercury in the morning read sixty-nine, the letter arrived. A thick cream envelope with the stamp of the Houses of Parliament on its top-right corner. For a moment Charles simply weighed it in his hands, before tucking it into his jacket pocket, where it remained all day, close to his heart as he carried out his rounds.

As soon as the last patient had been seen, he hurried to his room. In his excitement he could not find his letter knife and so ripped it open, tearing it a little at the edges. The letter was short, and Churchill's handwriting was neat, with large spaces in between the words.

Dear Dr Fuller,
Forgive this tardy reply.

I thank you for your letter and for your proposal. I believe your scheme to be a fine one. Once the Act is passed, we shall need hospitals ready and able to specialize in such operations, and doctors who are willing to oversee them.

While I cannot, of course, condone any action that is still beyond the bounds of the law, your proposal to put yourself at the forefront of such a revolution is commendable, and I support it wholeheartedly.

I look forward to making your acquaintance at next summer's congress.

Yours,

Winston Churchill, Home Secretary

Charles sat, trembling on the bed. The future, *here* – in his very hands. He lifted the letter to his mouth and kissed the page.

He lost no time in requesting an audience with the super-intendent. When it came, he hardly spoke a word, simply laying the letter out on the desk, placing it beside those from Pearson and from Major Darwin, lighting the touchpaper and stepping well back.

The superintendent adjusted his spectacles and read each in turn. At first he seemed confused, and then his expression gradually darkened. By the end of Churchill's letter a high colour had entered his cheeks.

'My God, Fuller. What made you think that you could go over my head in this way?' His left cheek twitched with an odd syncopated rhythm.

Charles did not flinch; he had expected this. 'I am sorry.' He spoke smoothly, as though soothing a truculent child. 'I did not mean to go over your head. I simply meant to use my influence and contacts in the field of Eugenics to steal a march for our institution. The future is coming, and we can choose to be its pawns or its kings.'

He had rehearsed the speech in his mirror, imagining the superintendent's face as he delivered it. He watched the words land now. Saw the ripples they created in the wrinkled, puckered flesh.

'Go on.' The superintendent spoke quietly.

A quickening. The time was now. Charles laid out his plan in the plainest possible terms:

An inoculation for the body of the Empire
The Feeble-Minded Bill
Likelihood of law being passed next year
Following the American example
Dr Sharp, Indiana Reformatory
Parliament broadly in support
Leading the pack
Eugenics Society
Pearson
Teacher
Galton
Inspiration
Home Secretary Churchill
Ally
Friend

Charles paused at the end of his recitation – reminding himself to breathe. It did not do to show strong feelings in the matter. He was at all times, as he had hoped he would be, collected and calm. Perhaps he had embellished his relationship with the Home Secretary somewhat, alluding to a friendship and closeness that did not, as yet, exist, but *nothing comes of nothing* as a wise man once said. He counted *one . . . two . . . three*, as Soames gathered the letters towards him.

'Let me consider,' the superintendent said.

Charles managed to contain himself whilst he was inside the room but once outside on the lawn let out a small sound of jubilation. A passing nurse looked quizzically over towards him. 'Are you feeling well, Dr Fuller?'

'Oh yes! Yes! Quite well, thank you, nurse.'

The clouds built up over the course of the day, great swollen cumuli massing over the moor, bruised-looking in the changing light, rank after rank of them, queuing to drop their cargo of water. At his window that evening, glad of his jacket for the first time in months, hands thrust in his pockets, Charles believed he felt as an Indian must at the start of monsoon, scanning the pregnant sky for the first drops of rain.

There was a knock at the door, the porter, calling him downstairs. As Charles followed him through empty, echoing corridors, the asylum felt strangely deserted, the light appeared to have failed outside. Once inside the superintendent's room, however, on the western side of the building, the light was spectacular, compressed, almost phosphorescent.

The superintendent did not sit, and so Charles stayed standing himself, as Soames handed him back the letters with a curt nod. 'I assent,' he said quietly.

Charles nodded. *Comportment. Control. At all times control.* 'I believe posterity will thank you, sir. Once embarked upon this course, there will be no going back.'

The superintendent grimaced. 'In part, that is what I am afraid of, but you have convinced me to take the risk.'

'And I am extremely glad that you have done so.' He paused a moment, then: 'I had thought to carry out an operation soon,' he said, as lightly as he was able. 'A test case, if you like.'

'Oh?' The superintendent seemed listless suddenly, as though the matter had ceased to concern him. 'Have you any idea whom?'

'John Mulligan.'

Soames shook his head. 'I do not know the man.'

'An Irish melancholic, sir. He has been with us for over two years.'

'And why him?'

'He has no dependants. He is in the chronic ward. It is highly unlikely that he will need his reproductive capacities again.'

'I understand, but there are plenty of others who might—'

'No.' Charles shook his head. 'Mulligan. It *must* be him. It must begin with him.' His voice tightened. He stopped, made himself breathe.

Soames shot him a quick, severe look before seeming to crumple, as though he did not have the strength for what was to come. He took off his glasses and rubbed at his old, pouched eyes. And Charles saw, in an instant, that he was a man whose time was past.

'And you will write to the Home Secretary?' said Soames. 'Tell Churchill exactly what you are to do?'

Charles tucked the letters in his pocket. 'Yes, sir,' he said, 'I most certainly will.'

John

HE WAS OUT BY Mantle Lane when the weather changed, thigh deep in a grave.

The sky had thickened all day, and the temperature had dropped, but still the rain held off. Towards the end of the afternoon a low, insistent wind picked up and the first drops of water mottled the ground. John put down his spade and watched the sky, watched the wind tumbling the last few swallows that were left. Why had they waited? They should have flown earlier. Now their way lay through storms.

The rain came in earnest then, great shawls of water, drenching the parched ground, falling on the unmarked rows of the people who were buried six deep, pounding the raw hole he stood in, puddling around his feet.

He lifted his face to the sky, opened his mouth and drank. He felt how alive he was, and he thought of her.

After a moment, standing like that, he became cold, and the coldness struck him as a sort of brightness, as a strange, new thing.

Ella

THE DAY SEEMED TO crouch, ready to pounce. Ella stood by the window, staring out at the massed grey clouds, and spread her hands over her belly, feeling the warmth, the tightness there. She was becoming something new. At first, the thought had been a faint, distant thing, but now it filled her, the knowledge as present as the queasy, dizzy feeling that accompanied her all day. How long would it be before anyone else noticed? Two weeks? Three? Four? Her bulky skirts would hide it well. But nothing would hide her in the washrooms on a Friday afternoon. The staff saw everything then if they cared to look.

What would they do when they found out?

She remembered the woman with the birthmark – her mouth opening and closing around the words, *they kill them. They kill the babbies in there.* She could not think that was true, but she had seen women in the wards often; they would appear in the day room, heavy with a child, and the next day they would be gone.

Or might they kill it inside her instead? She sucked in her breath, clasping her hands across her stomach. It was possible – she knew. She had known a girl at the mill who went and had it done. Who came back grey-faced and slow.

Outside, the swallows were being thrown by the wind. Over the last few days she had seen them leaving, the skies growing emptier day by day. The family above the window had left, and now their nest, no longer a home, was just an empty clump of mud.

How did a child grow? She imagined a small person, the size of her thumbnail, like one of those curled leaves at the start of summer, with tiny hands and tiny feet and a tiny mouth. A child made of the fields and the blue night and of him and her. She ached to tell him. It had been a month since she had seen his face.

Was he out there now? If she thought hard enough, might he hear her? Might he come to know?

And what of Clem? Her words still echoed: *How do you even know what he wrote? I could have made it up. You wouldn't know the difference, you're so stupid.*

He was a man who loved words. If he found out she couldn't read, what would he think of her then?

Outside, the rain hesitated and then began to fall. Ella closed her eyes and pressed her hot belly, her cheek, against the cool touch of the glass. Perhaps she was afraid of this child, she thought, as much as she was afraid for it. And was it the fear, or the child, that was burrowing deep inside her now?

She thought of her mother, of the stroke of her hand on her cheek. Her mother was the first thing she had loved, and since then she had tried hard not to love anything at all. But she hadn't been able to help herself. She should have stayed safe. She had felt safe, for a moment, but it had been a moment in a wood, in a field, in a dream. There was no safety here.

Do close your mouth, Miss Fay. The door does not only go one way.

Would he really let her leave? Was he doing it to punish her?

Did it matter, in the end?

If he did let her, she knew, she would have to go.

Charles

HE WAS COMPOSING HIS reply to Churchill when the rain began to fall. A few small spots on the page through his open window, blurring the words he had just written. At first there were only those few first drops – as he moved the papers to the bed, where they would stay dry – then a pause, as though the whole world were holding its breath, and Charles's heart clenched, fearing that he might still be made to wait, and then they fell in earnest, turbid light drenching the room, turning it from grey to black.

That night he left his window open, sitting at his desk with a small lamp burning, listening to the rain drumming in the gutters. He could think of nothing but the operation ahead. He pulled his notebook towards him and scribbled.

The most important thing is to have access to the vas deferens. Thereafter two small incisions are made on either side of the scrotum. Then each vas deferens will come to the surface for excision. Both vas deferentia will be cut, separated and sutured to seal. On waking, Mulligan should feel pain, but not overwhelmingly so.

He made sketches of the area – of scrotum, seminal vesicle, bladder, pubic bone, penis. He could not help but sketch the organ he had seen that day on the cricket field; it was Mulligan's very genitals, after all, upon which he would operate, thick around the stem, the red tip engorged. Dr Sharp's testimony stated that he performed the operation without any anaesthetic, but this would be unlikely in Mulligan's case – the man would have to be knocked out with chloroform or ether; it would be the only way to carry it out without his knowledge. But then, in a matter of minutes, a first strike for a brave new world! And there was a peculiar poetic justice to it. Mulligan had nominated himself, had he not? That day on the scorched field, waving his penis at him. Pissing on his boots.

He went over to his barbells and began to lift, and as he did so he thought of Mulligan, going about his business, whatever that might be – his queer, sour relationship with that girl. Perhaps he was thinking of her now. Perhaps he was touching himself, his hands on his body, on that penis, grasping himself as he lay in his bed in the ward, spilling himself with no knowledge whatsoever of what was coming. Ten minutes would be all it would take. Ten minutes, and then generation after generation of corruption would be wiped out for good.

The thought was astonishing: clean, like a knife. Charles felt a stiffening in his loins, and he pulled at the weights, again, again, again. When he put them down, he was drenched in sweat and gasping, stripping off his shirt and splashing himself from the pitcher by the sink.

The weather had broken. The patients would be clamouring for the dances to start again. They would dance together, Mulligan and the girl. All unknowing.

Let them.

Let them have their last dance. Soon the girl would be gone, and Mulligan . . . well, Mulligan would be a different sort of man.

John

HE SAT CLOSE TO the front of the male lines, hardly able to stay on his bench. He had scrubbed himself in the washroom as best he could, but the linger of damp mud was still on him, its traces settled in dark lines across his palms. No fires were lit, and around him the other men were subdued, their voices low, as though damped by the weather too, as though uncertain as to what they should do in this grand, echoing room. A thick pall of smoke hung over their heads. The musicians were present on the stage, but Fuller was not amongst them.

Outside, the rain fell. It had not ceased for five days straight, the fields a quagmire now. His last week spent slipping and sliding in mud, the sides of the grave become yellow, sickly clay, as he was watched, constantly, by a leering Brandt. Dan was a raw absence in his days, but the thought of Ella was worse. The letter had been read by Fuller. Had the bastard found the store of them, his eyes raiding the rest?

He had heard nothing, but this only made him more uneasy. Was Ella being punished in his stead?

His foot rattled against the floor.

He was a fool. He had had his freedom and spent it, spent hers too – carelessly, like his father with his coins in the yard bars – had been greedy and blind, as though there would be days and days to live like that.

But now the women were coming, their voices bouncing off the corridor outside and his blood pummelling as he scoured the crowd, but as wave after wave of women entered the ballroom and she was not amongst them, his thoughts grew wild. She had been taken downstairs. They had hurt her, somehow. Fuller was there. He was punishing her now.

But then he looked back and there she was, and the sounds of the room around him fell away. Her face was turned, and she had not seen him yet. She moved slowly. Her hair – the last time he had seen it, loose and heavy and hanging over him – was tied in a tight knot at her neck, her gaze fixed ahead. Her hands clasped in front of her. A high colour flared in her cheeks.

He leant forward, willing her to look towards him. But she was moving away, slipping through the crowd to the back of the room, and he was losing sight of her already. He got to his feet, so that when she looked she would see him easily, so she would know he was here.

'Mr Mulligan.' A passing attendant gave him a push. 'Sit yourself down.'

He sat, and the air was jagged, filled with broken glass.

The first dance was called, and he stood again, waiting for her to make her way out of the benches towards him. But she remained where she was, eyes fixed on the floor. The musicians began to play, and the space between them was filled with moving bodies. He sat back, raked his hands through his hair.

The next dance was called, and the next, and still she did not look up. And he knew then that something had occurred. Something he could not imagine. That she must blame him for whatever had happened to her. But now he could not help it; he had to speak with her before the night was done, so he stood, counting the steps between them.

He stepped away from his bench. Pushing his way through the heavy press of men. Her head lifting now.

People pushing and jostling around him, finding their partners for the next dance. He was knocked off course and lost sight of her again, until he stood at the front of the female lines.

'Ella,' he called.

He could not read her face.

'*Ella!*'

She stood then, and made her way out towards him, but when she was still two paces away she stopped, the space between them churning. He closed it, stepping forward, reaching for her hand. 'What? Please God. What is it?'

She looked up at him, and her face was tight and pleading. 'Can't you see?' she said to him. 'Don't you know?'

'*What?*'

And then, with a great rising feeling, he knew, and reached for her, pulling her close. 'A child?'

'Yes.' She spoke against his chest, and her voice was desperate now. 'But I am leaving this place. They're letting me go free.'

He lifted her face to his, but her gaze escaped. 'I have to tell you . . .' she said. 'The letters . . .'

'What about them? Did he find them?'

'I can't . . .'

'*What?*'

304

When finally her eyes found his, he saw wildness in them, and fear, and hope. 'I can't read,' she said. 'Not really. Clem read them to me. She helped me. She read them out loud.'

He caught her face in his.

'I'm sorry,' she said. 'I'm so sorry. I didn't mean to lie.'

'Listen. *Listen to me* – you must not be sorry. Do you think I care? Do you think I care about this?' He held her face in his hands. 'You must go. Do you hear me? But send me word. Send me word where you are, and when I know how to find you, I will come for you. I will come for you both. I promise I will.'

Ella

IT WAS STILL RAINING on the day she left, falling fast from a low-slung sky.

She gathered her things before the other women were awake: a squashed flower, a swallow's feather, an oak leaf and a cross of woven corn. She put the feather on the bed, then folded the cross, leaf and flower into the small stack of his letters, and put the bundle beneath her stays, where it bulged, a lump before her heart.

She was dressed in her old work clothes; they had given them back to her last night: her black skirt, her blouse and her brown woollen shawl. They smelt of the past. Of animals and metal and the mill.

She picked up the feather, held its hard tip between finger and thumb, and traced a line across her palm:

Now, you must imagine, a bird with a wingspan no bigger than this, making the journey all the way across Europe, down to Africa, or even all the way to India and further east.

She hadn't seen Clem for over two weeks.

'What are you doing?'

She looked up to see Old Germany sitting on her bed, blinking in the pale morning, pigtails fluffed up around her head from sleep.

'Please, would you do something for me?' said Ella. 'When Clem comes back, would you give her this? She'll understand.'

She placed the feather in the old woman's hand. Old Germany stared down, then lifted it, inspecting it, rubbing it this way and that across her thumb. 'She's not coming back,' she said, in her small, light voice.

'What?'

'In the night. Creep creep. Her soul came and told me. It's leaving soon.'

'What do you mean?' Ella crouched before her. 'Where is she going?'

'Out there . . .' Old Germany waved the feather at the sky beyond the windows. 'But she's scared.' She frowned now, eyes narrowed, as if looking at something she did not want to see. 'It's a long way and she's frightened.'

Fear coursed down Ella's spine as she gripped the woman's thin, gnarled hands. 'What are you saying? What do you mean?'

But the old lady's face had changed. Her eyes were wide and blameless.

'Here,' she said, putting the feather in Ella's hands again. 'I think that you must take it back.'

Rain splayed itself against the windows as she walked the long corridor between two nurses, and it was as though her legs were moving despite her, despite the din and jangle in her head. In the administration block, with its green-ish light, they stopped. One of the nurses stood beside her while the other stepped into the doctor's room, from which low, mumbling voices came.

Beneath her feet, the tiled flowers, the black daisies. She had screamed when she first saw them. There was a scream in her now, but it was buried, a long way from her throat.

The nurse appeared again. 'There's a van going into Bradford this morning. You can travel on it.'

Ella nodded, mute.

They walked down the main hallway towards the ball-room and then took a different, snaking path through corridors she had never walked before. She thought perhaps they were in the men's quarters, that this side of the asylum belonged to them. Would he feel her if she passed close? Would he know?

Somewhere, she thought, there must be other Ellas, ones who were not staying silent, who were screaming and banging on doors and demanding to see John. To see Clem. To know that they were well. But those other Ellas would be locked back up, and so this Ella stayed silent, walking on.

They came to a side entrance where a van stood waiting, a delivery driver clad in a slick wet raincoat sitting up at the front.

'Go on then.' One of the nurses gave her a small push.

The air was hard and clean and smelt of rain.

Free.

She did not feel how she thought she would. She did not feel as she had felt that night, amongst the fields. A great numbness had come upon her.

'Have you no coat, lass?' The driver came towards her.

'No.'

'All right. Come on. Get in the back then.' He talked to her slowly, as if she were daft in the head. He moved around and opened the door, and she hauled herself inside, sitting down amongst sacks of grain. The van rocked as he took his seat above her, then the whip cracked and they were away. A smeared window showed the side wall of the building, huge at first, and then framed, with grey, puckly sky all around it, and then growing smaller, and smaller still. She put her hands to her belly and closed her eyes.

Free. This small hard word that felt so cold.

Could you live inside a word like that?

She banged on the thin wooden board between the driver and her. The van stopped, and she heard him climb out. He opened the doors, his face rumpled with concern. Behind him, the rain had stopped, and the sky was a thin, light grey. 'What is it, lass?'

'I want to get out.'

'We're not there yet.'

'I'm not going to Bradford.'

He looked around him and scratched his head. 'But there's nobbut grass and moor up here.'

'It's where I'm going,' she said.

When she climbed out, she saw they were on a high path, with drystone walls on either side, the land stretching far in both directions. 'This is right,' she said, making her voice steady. 'This is where I want to be.'

The man looked at her, bemused, then, 'All right then.' He tipped his cap to her. 'You take care.'

The van heaved and jerked away, and when it had gone, she was quite alone. She brought her shawl around her.

It was possible to see a long way – the fields and then the close, purple rise of the moor. The fields were filled with sheep, and the stones of the walls were hazed with moss. She walked to the walls and when she put her hands out to touch the moss it was soft and stained her fingertips green. It was quiet, and the air was still, but as she listened she heard the quiet was full of small, insistent sounds: the soft cropping of the sheep at the grass in the fields; the wind, which sometimes picked up and then died down again. The sound of water running, close by, and a strange sound, a sort of soft sighing, that she could only think was the earth itself. She climbed one of the walls and began to walk, finding a thin path at the edge of a field. She did not walk quickly. She did not know where she was going, only that she needed to climb; only that she wanted to be up high.

Soon the field gave way to wilder land, but the path remained, winding a white way upwards. The tussocky grass was wet. At the side of the path were bushes where tiny berries shone in great clusters, and she picked palmfuls and ate them, and now her hands were stained with purple too. As she climbed, the path grew narrower and was sometimes difficult to follow, as it crossed rocks slippery with water, and sometimes the water was a small brook she had to find her way across. She rinsed her hands and face and cupped water in her palm to drink, and the water smelt of the earth and the earth smelt of water, and it was good to have it in her mouth and on her skin.

When she reached the moor top, the sun was low in the sky to her left and the wind whipped her hair around her face and there was fear in her and sadness and hope. She thought of John. *Send me word.* She clasped her arms around her.

She would find somewhere. A farm. Somewhere they would need workers. She did not know how it would be. She only knew that she would live. That she would survive.

She thought of Clem. She conjured her before her, not as she had last seen her, but before – the lightness that was in her. The bravery.

She spoke her name out loud and wondered if Clem might feel it, might hear the sound her name made spoken in this high, free place. Then she brought the feather from her dress and held it and raised her arms. She tipped her head back, and as she did so the wind blew across the wide moor and passed through the feather, and her body hummed with it, as though she were an instrument, for the breath of some greater creature to pass through and make sing.

Charles

HE WAS UP BEFORE dawn. Fifty lifts on one side, fifty on the other, humming as he poured water into his bowl and soaped his face, his armpits. A tight but not unpleasant sensation seemed to have settled in his chest, the sort of feeling he would have as a child on the morning of a day at the beach – the sort of day when the pleasure of anticipation was almost too much to bear. He would need to be calm. It was the equinox, after all, a moment of balance, of poise.

The outside air was ionized, crisp, and as he walked out over the grass each dewdrop seemed to shimmer like a tiny pearl. Early fallen leaves lay in bright clusters on the ground. He paused on the lawn, taking deep, cleansing breaths. Autumn was here: playing to sense, not sensuality;

belonging to the rational mind; here was a season he could live in at last.

He made his way across the grass to the men's infirmary. The operation was scheduled for eight o'clock, and before that he had to carry out his feeding of Miss Church, but he had plenty of time yet to check that all was prepared.

Goffin was waiting for him at the door. He had been chosen for his bulk and for his strength, and Charles had briefed him, but barely. It didn't do to have him knowing too much.

'Good morning, Mr Goffin. Give me ten minutes, then meet me in theatre, please.'

The young man nodded. He looked uneasy, smoking quickly, his face yellow in the morning light.

Charles marched past the sick wards to the operating theatre, and once there, he unrolled his instruments, placing them carefully on to the small, wheeled table: a blade for shaving, a small pot of oil, a pair of scissors, two scalpels, three needles and then thin black thread for the finest of stitches. He brought a scalpel up and touched it against the pad of his thumb, pressing ever so slightly, then put it down again, satisfied it was sharp as it could be. From the tall cupboards ranged along one side of the room he brought out two small bottles of chloroform and a clean rag. These he placed on the table beside the instruments. There was a knock on the door, and Charles went to open it.

'Ah, Goffin. Come in.'

He handed a bottle of the chloroform and the rag to the young man. 'Now, you know to hold it hard against the nose and the mouth. The trick is to let no oxygen in. The patient will undoubtedly struggle, but the harder you hold it the quicker he will lose consciousness. And then *stay with him*. I want him watched at all times. Should it seem as though he is coming round, add more of the liquid to the rag and hold it against his mouth once more. But remember – too much and there may be cardiac arrest. Only apply more if he appears to be waking. Do you understand?'

Goffin nodded. 'Yes, sir.' He seemed agitated. 'May I ask—'

'No.' Charles spoke swiftly. 'You may not.'

Charles cast his eyes once more over the room, then made his way over to the women's side of the infirmary.

As soon as he entered, he sensed something was amiss. An absence. A distracted, jagged sense to the air. The matron was not there. Instead, a young, harried-looking nurse was in her place.

'Where is Matron Holmes?'

The girl shook her head. Her eyes were red and inflamed.

'I . . . there's been an . . .' And then the girl began to cry in great hiccoughing sobs.

'What? Speak up, girl. What?'

But the girl was useless, and Charles pushed past her through the doors to the female ward. When he arrived, he saw Miss Church's bed was empty. An indentation was present where her body had lain, but the sheets had been pulled away and the mattress was bare.

'Dr Fuller?' It was the young nurse, back again, hovering by his side.

'Where is Miss Church?' He swung round towards her.

She shook her head.

'*Where is Miss Church?!*' He was shouting now. 'She is *my* patient. She should *never* have been moved without my permission.'

'Please, Dr Fuller,' said the girl. 'Come with me.'

As they walked, every so often the young woman gave a small, muffled sob, but otherwise they were silent. The nurse took the lead, unlocking door after door, and after a few minutes the crying stopped and she appeared to have recovered her composure somewhat. Two, three corridors, and then down some stairs, and Charles seemed to sense everything as though for the first time: the cracks in the wall, the strange green colour of the paint, the mingled smell of ammonia and food, the distant taint of blood.

At the entrance to the mortuary, the young nurse stepped back, nodding him forward. Charles pushed open the door and stepped inside. The room was filled with a strange aqueous light, almost as though he was standing in a cavern at the bottom of the sea. Miss Church lay on the slab in the middle of the room, and from where he stood she might have been asleep. He made his way over to where she lay. Some careful person had brushed her hair so it coursed over her pillow, and a strange brightness seemed to emanate from her skin. Her position, with her hands folded over her chest, and the sheet pulled up to her chin, her hair like that and the sub-marine light, all added to the impression that she might have been drowned, but the bandages around her wrists gave the lie to that. He touched his finger to her cheek. Its coldness was a shock. He turned to the nurse. 'How?'

'A razor blade, Dr Fuller.'

'And how in God's name did she get one of those?'

'We don't know.' The young woman looked stricken. 'We think she might have had it on her all the time.'

Charles stared back at Miss Church's face, aware only of

a profound lack of surprise. 'When was she pronounced dead?'

'I found her this morning. About five o clock. Here.' She handed Charles a notebook.

From the viscosity of the blood we estimate that she cut herself around three in the morning.

The words were in Soames's spider hand. Anger flashed within him. 'Why was I not called?'

'I'm sorry, Doctor, but I called the matron, and she said Medical Superintendent Soames should be called instead.'

'I see.' He handed the notes back to her. Drummed his fingers against Miss Church's sheet. 'Quite so.' Damn. *Damn.*

He pulled out his pocket watch. Half past seven. If Goffin had done his work, then Mulligan would be ready. Everything was ready. The future was waiting to be born. 'Well then, I presume the girl's family have been informed?'

The nurse nodded.

'Very good. In that case, I can see no further use for my presence here. I'll leave you to watch over Miss Church.'

The nurse shrank a little from this last, but nodded. 'Yes, Doctor.'

Out in the corridor, he paused. Propriety suggested that he should speak to the superintendent immediately. There would be questions asked, forms to fill in. Miss Church had been in his care. But propriety could wait. Hang propriety. Propriety would not birth the future. Only boldness would. Only genius. There was no question of what should happen next.

He hurried back to the operating theatre. Once there, he

hesitated before entering, his breath rough and hard. *Calm. Calm.* He swung open the door and saw immediately that Goffin had performed his role: Mulligan was lying prone on a gurney in the middle of the room, his naked form covered with a sheet. The attendant was folding the last of the Irishman's clothes in a pile on a chair. He looked up as Charles came in. The sickly-sweet smell of chloroform pervaded the room.

'All ready?'

'Yes, sir.' The young man looked sweaty and distressed. 'He's been out for ten minutes now. Although . . . I think I might have used too much. He struggled. He struggled an awful lot.'

'Show me the bottle.' Charles snatched it from the table. 'For God's sake, man. You've used far too much.'

'Will he die?' Goffin was shaking now, his face on the verge of collapse.

'I sincerely hope not,' said Charles. 'Leave me.'

But Goffin only took a couple of steps before turning back. 'Please . . . Dr Fuller. Will you please let me know he's all right?'

Charles waved him away with a furious hand. *'Leave me.'*

Goffin was on the verge of tears. 'I'm sorry. I'm sorry. It was just . . . he struggled much more than I thought.'

The door closed behind him, and Charles was alone with the Irishman. Only the rattle of his heart. Only Mulligan's harsh breathing from the table before him. The smell of the chloroform was making him feel sick.

He lifted the man's wrist. The pulse was steady and regular. Thank God.

Next. What came next?

He had forgotten the steps of the operation. How many

315

times had he gone through them so that this would not occur, and yet now a thick, spongy feeling appeared to have invaded his brain. What was he to do first? He closed his eyes and it came to him: shave.

Of course. *Shave.* His eyes snapped open.

Sweat pasted his brow, and he was breathing hard again now. Hot. It was hot in here. The heat and Mulligan's ripe smell and the chloroform and Charles's own sweat made for a heady brew. He went to the window and opened it wide, taking several large gulps of air, and as a blessedly fresh breeze touched his neck his sickness lifted a little.

Now, he made his way over to the gurney and slowly began to peel down the man's sheet. First the torso and then the lower half of Mulligan's body were revealed. Charles's breath caught; the man's penis was curled over itself in its nest of hair, utterly soft and utterly defenceless. It seemed a different creature from the organ that had been wielded on the cricket field on Midsummer's Day. The testicles lay beneath it, slightly squashed, slightly hidden. He reached forward and lifted the man's member, moving it gently to the right.

Shave.

He picked up the razor and the pot of oil, and took the testicles into his palm. First, he rubbed a little of the oil on to the thin, almost transparent skin, then, pulling it taut, brought the razor across it. The hairs came away easily, leaving only extraordinary smoothness behind. When the testicles were clean, he moved to the pubis, and then the skin between the legs. There was fine, light hair on the shaft of the penis, and so he shaved there too.

He pressed a damp cloth to the area and then a dry one. He did everything with utmost care, astonished at the

316

tenderness he felt. He looked at Mulligan's face. He was ready. Everything was ready now.

And now the very air around him felt viscous, changed. He was overwhelmed with an emotion he couldn't quite name: a sense that he was partaking of a great mystery, that he was close to the source of life. It felt appropriate to say something. Gently, very gently, with one hand, he cupped the man's testicles, and with the other touched his cheek. He brought his thumb over the electric scratch of bristles, tracing the line of his mouth, and with the other hand he slowly stroked the soft, soft skin, as he began to speak, began to murmur that this act, though it might not seem so at first, was truly an act of creation, the creation of a better race. That Mulligan need have no fear. That Charles would be here beside him throughout.

A small choked sound came from the corner of the room. Charles turned slowly to see Goffin standing in the doorway. For a moment, Charles remained, in that viscous light, utterly calm, not thinking to move, one hand on Mulligan's cheek, the other cupping his member. Until the air seemed to change again, seemed to grow quite cold and sharp, and though he could not name the look upon Goffin's face, he knew he had never seen it on a human face before.

'What are you doing?' Goffin pointed at him.

Charles brought his hands away from Mulligan's body. 'How long have you been standing there?'

'Long enough.'

'Answer me. *How long?*'

'The superintendent sent me. He told me it was urgent.'

Charles adjusted his jacket. His cheeks were scalding now. He pulled the sheet back up to Mulligan's chin. 'The patient is ready. Stay here. Watch over him. Remember the chloroform. I will be back shortly.'

He held his head high as he left the room, but once outside the floor tilted beneath him as though he was on the heaving deck of a ship. He put his hands against the corridor wall to steady himself. Dear God. What had the man seen? How much had he heard? And what had he himself uttered, standing there, his hands on Mulligan's body? He could not remember. In truth, in that strange, honeyed light, he had no idea what he had said.

Anyone seeing that would think the worst.

Danger. There was sudden danger everywhere.

At Soames's office, he was brought up short at what greeted him.

He had expected the superintendent alone, a brief meeting to clarify the facts of the case, but Miss Church's father was there, seated behind the desk with his head buried in his hands. Soames stood behind him, a little distance away, the air hazy with tobacco smoke and an uneasy quiet.

'Gentlemen.' Charles nodded to them from the door.

Soames spoke first. 'Dr Fuller. As you can see, Mr Church has asked to be present for this interview.'

Charles turned and shut the door behind him. *Interview?* 'Yes, sir. Of course.'

He threw a furtive glance at the clock on the wall – quarter past eight. He stepped a small way into the room and planted his feet wide.

Soames eyed him for a long moment, then, 'As his daughter's chief medical consultant, the one to whom her care was entrusted, Mr Church, as you might imagine, has several questions to ask of you. I will leave him to do so, and then you and I will speak alone.'

Charles nodded. He clasped his hands behind his back.

Mr Church's shoulders were slumped, and his hands were stretched out on the desk, palms upturned, as though Charles might take whatever heavy thing weighed him down. 'How?' That low, sonorous voice was cracked. 'How did you allow this . . . to occur?'

'Superintendent. Mr Church.' Charles spread his legs a little wider. The thing was to take charge, not to be sorry, never to be sorry. A sorry man was a weak man. He cleared his throat. Beneath his jacket his shirt was tacky with sweat. 'I have been as shocked as anybody by this morning's news. But when a young woman is as determined and as cunning as your daughter was—'

'*Cunning?*' The father's face was twisted.

'Indeed. I am sorry to say I was informed this morning by the nurse on duty that she kept a blade on her person, for just such a purpose as this.'

'But . . .' Mr Church stared up wildly. 'Where did she get this *blade*? Why was she not searched? How, in God's name, was she allowed to do such a terrible, terrible thing?' The man's voice rose until it broke like a woman's and he was overcome, and the room filled with the sound of his sobs.

Charles stared. Other than on the wards, he had never seen a man weep like this. But Mr Church appeared to have no self-consciousness in his grief. Soames stepped forward, and Charles waited for the hand to come down on the other man's shoulder – *There, there, old chap, crying won't bring her back* – but the superintendent only hovered in the middle of the carpet, his face pale, his expression almost as stricken as that of Mr Church.

Charles threw a glance to the clock. Five minutes had passed since he had arrived in the room. How much longer would Mulligan stay under for? And Goffin. *Damn* Goffin. He didn't trust him, didn't trust him now to do his job.

Mr Church's sobs had become a little less vocal now. He was shaking, as though the force of his grief had been swallowed and taken within.

'Fuller?' The superintendent spoke sharply. 'Do you have nothing to say to this man?'

'Yes,' Charles cleared his throat, 'I do. With all due respect, sir, when someone is so bent upon their course, I fail to see how blame is appropriate or where indeed it resides.'

A muffled groan of pain came from the father.

Soames shook his head. 'No, Fuller. I am afraid that this is simply not good enough. The young woman was *entrusted* to our care. That she now lies dead in the mortuary I take to be our collective responsibility. That you show no sign of thinking the same I take to be a dereliction of duty. I will have no choice but to conclude that you no longer wish to work in a place where the care of other human beings should be your first priority and therefore say—'

'*No!*' Charles shook his head. 'You cannot do that. Not now. Not today.'

'I *cannot* do it?'

'You cannot.' He was shaking. 'I will not countenance it. I am in the midst of an operation. You know full well of what I speak. Everything is ready. Everything is prepared.'

The superintendent's face creased into a frown; he turned to Mr Church. 'Please, leave us, sir.'

The father rose slowly.

'*Wait.*' Charles put his hand out. The older man, bewildered, looked from one to the other. 'Mr Church, this girl, this daughter that you mourn for. What was she? Tell me. You think you knew her? Believe me, sir, had you heard and seen the filth that came from her in her latter days you would not be so quick to mourn. She was—'

'Dr Fuller.' Soames's voice was low. 'I warn you—'

Hang comportment. *Hang* politeness.

'Corrupted. She was utterly corrupted. Do you not see?' He could not stop the shaking. He did not care. 'Hereditary *taint*, Mr Church. Indeed, sir, one could even say it was your own fault for choosing to breed with a woman incapable of being a mother to her children—'

'Dr Fuller—'

'*No.*' He turned to the superintendent. 'Are you so conge*ni*tally stupid, Dr Soames, that you would choose to punish me for something that was inevitable? And in doing so deny this institution the opportunity to forge ahead? To *birth the future*?'

Turning from him, the superintendent picked up a bell and rang it sharply.

Charles reared his head as though he had been hit.

'Good *grief*.' A bark of a laugh came from him. 'What is the meaning of this? Do you mean to have me carried off?'

'It would appear that you may have to be forcibly re-moved from this room, Dr Fuller, yes.'

'My God.' Charles leant over the desk, incandescent now. 'Tell me, Soames, how will the future remember you?'

'I have enough to concern myself with, Dr Fuller, with the present matters at hand. Let the future remember me how it will.'

'Well, I'll tell you, shall I? As a weak man. A weak and a stupid man.'

'Dr Fuller. Let me tell you that you are doing yourself and your prospects no good at all.'

'My *prospects*? I assure you, Dr Soames, that my prospects are of the very best. I assure *you* that Home Secretary Churchill will hear of this.'

'Let him.'

The door opened, and two attendants appeared. Soames turned to them. 'Gentlemen, please take Dr Fuller away. I wish to see him escorted from this office immediately.'

The two attendants began to cross the room towards him. Charles put his hands up.

'Enough. *Enough.* There is no need for restraint. I will go gladly. I am not a patient, after all.'

John

BURNING. HIS FACE WAS burning. He put his hands to it and groaned.

A terrible sickening sweetness clung to him.

He curled on to his side and vomited, and when he had done, he lay, catching his breath, the upper half of his torso suspended over empty space, eyes and nose and throat on fire. As he came back to himself, he saw where he was – saw the space beneath him, the clean, spare floor – and in a swift, panicked movement pulled himself back up on the bed.

It was not a bed, though, but some sort of table. He was no longer in the ward.

He struggled to sit, limbs leaden, and in sitting saw that he was naked, his groin exposed. He had been shaved. Someone had shaved him. He stared down, stunned, unable to comprehend what he saw.

A sound came from beside him, and he turned to see the attendant was standing there – the young, tall one, and he remembered then being taken from the ward. Being told to sit on a chair, and then a cloth over his face, struggling to breathe. The wide eyes of this man as he pressed the rag to his mouth.

John lurched for him, but his legs did not obey, and he stumbled and fell from the table, limbs twisted beneath him.

'It wasn't me.' The man held his hands out before him. 'I swear . . . please . . . it wasn't me.'

'Who then?' John struggled to his feet, gripping the sheet around him.

The man shook his head.

'*Who?*'

'Dr Fuller.'

He could see more clearly now, could see his clothes folded in a neat pile on a chair. The table beside him set out with gleaming instruments. With tiny, shining knives. 'What the *fuck is this*?'

The man moved crab-wise towards the door. 'It wasn't me. Please . . . I promise it wasn't me. They made me. I don't know anything about it.' He opened the door and slid around it. John heard the sound of a key in the lock.

He roared and threw his shoulder up against it, but it did nothing but hurt him. He made to the chair that held his clothes, pulling on his shirt and trousers, buttoning them with thick fingers, stuffing his feet into his boots.

He was aware of a thick dread. In his body. In the sickly-sweet air. The shaved skin of his groin. He stood, pacing the length of the room. The door was locked. There was no sound in the corridor outside. The man was gone, but he would come back. Hold him down again. More of them this time perhaps. So many that he couldn't keep them off. They would hold that terrible rag to his face. And then Fuller would come and then – what?

He lifted his head.

He saw the window.

Open wide. No bars. Half disbelieving, he crossed the floor towards it.

The cool air of the day outside touched his skin; he sucked its cleanliness into his lungs. He saw a cobbled yard and then more stone buildings opposite. To his left, open country. Fields. The moor.

And everything shrank to this – an open window, the world outside. Beyond.

If he ran now, how would she find him?

But if he stayed, there may be no man left to be found.

For a long moment he remained there, unable to move. Until a sound came from the corridor behind, and he hauled himself up, scraping his shoulders as he pulled himself up and out, rolling on to the grass.

He could see the clock tower behind him, and knew he had been right – he was at the back of the buildings, close to the path that led to the wood and the farms, and the moor.

And so he ran.

He ran like he hadn't run for years, arms pumping at his sides, making for the stand of trees, the thickness in his head and his legs lifting as he moved.

And it was so long. It was so long since he had run like this.

November

1911

Charles

DISGRACE. THAT WAS WHAT his father had called it.

There was a poem, wasn't there? Shakespeare; they had had to learn it at school:

> *When in disgrace with fortune and men's eyes*
> *I all alone beweep my outcast state.*

Charles watched the lowlands of Yorkshire give way to the Midlands, the brown blur of autumn fields through the window of the train. He supposed, in a way, he had been outcast. But there were no tears. He couldn't imagine ever crying again. It was as though his blood had been changed. To mercury, or some other such substance. His fluids become the fluids of the superior man.

He had stayed two weeks in his parents' house. He had not ventured into Leeds.

That morning, as he left, it had been sunny, a bite to the air, the last of the leaves a deep, satisfying gold. He had taken a small trunk with only his most necessary books and a few clothes. He left his violin and his music in his childhood bedroom and knew he would never see them again.

He was going to London. He was going to a place that the future loved. He had money saved. No fortune, but enough to see him through for a good while yet.

The future was still coming; every turn of the wheels of the train affirmed it. Inexorable. Whatever had occurred, the future was always still coming. And whatever had occurred, Charles knew, this future was clean, unsullied and ready to be carved.

All one ever needed was a sharp enough knife.

Epilogue

Ireland 1934

John

HE PULLED THE LAST fistful of potatoes from the soil and brushed the dirt from their skin before throwing them in the crate at his feet. Then he lifted the heavy box on to his shoulder, steadying himself a moment before making back towards the cottage. Even now, after all these months, he could still feel the sway of the ship in him, the low pull of water beneath his feet.

The sun was bright, and he could see little at first as he made his way indoors, walking slowly through the kitchen, where he stacked the box in the dark pantry, taking four small tubers from the top and putting them on the deal table. He would eat them later, when he returned. At the sink he washed the dirt from his hands.

Through the window he could see the path that led to the lane and then to the small town three miles or so beyond. He had not known what he was looking for when he came last summer, only trusted he would know it when he saw it. And he had: the house was low and simple, but there was something welcoming in the slant of the roof. The thatch was good and would not need replacing for a long while yet. The barn wanted work, but nothing that was beyond him. And there was the position: close enough to the town, close to the sea. A hundred miles south of where he had grown up. An acre of good, fertile land.

At first, he had wondered if he would find it strange to have a house at all. To sleep between four walls. But he had taken to it without much fuss, and as the months passed he had begun to enjoy it. He was past fifty. It was time to plant himself.

He turned back to the room, and it pleased him to see the neatness of his kitchen; the fireplace with the hanging pots and pans. The bedroom, a simple chamber off the kitchen with a narrow single bed.

He took his jacket from the nail behind the door and a bag from the table and made his way out on to the lane.

Walking, he came to join the back of a small procession: a few carts with men at the front driving and smoking, women and children in the back tucked amongst sacks of flour and pigs. Young men and women wheeling bicycles. The light honeyed and thick. Dust was kicked up and settled again. Nobody moved very fast. He let himself fall into an easy rhythm.

Abroad, in his time on shore, he had seen the changes: London, Newcastle, New York, Buenos Aires, the swiftness with which things now moved. Had seen a war come and go, serving on the merchant ships. Seen machines replacing men. How the century was settling into mean, efficient lines. But here in Ireland, over a decade since independence, things still moved at the speed of a man. Or a man and a horse. It was fast enough for him.

The stream of people thickened as it neared the town, and the main street was thronged with people and animals. At one end the grocery shops, at the other the saddlemakers, the blacksmiths, the horses. He stopped at a good-sized shop that was alive with chatter, joining the queue for groceries, and when it was his turn bought flour and eggs, some currants, sugar and tea. He stowed them in his knapsack and made out into the sunlight.

A neighbour hailed him on the street: a red-faced farmer

whose land was close to his. 'Mulligan! Wouldja join us for a drink here?'

The man was standing at a makeshift bar, which was doing a brisk trade in porter, and he and his companions looked as though they had been drinking for a good while already. John made his way to join them, touching his hat in greeting. The farmer waved the girl over, and she brought a pint of porter for John, who stepped up to the table with a nod of thanks.

'This is John Mulligan.' The farmer introduced him to his drinking friends. 'He bought the Langan property back there.'

The men raised their glasses, made appreciative noises as they drank.

'How are you getting on out there now?' said the farmer.

'Oh aye. Well enough.' He took a sip of his pint. 'When the barn's finished, I'll be in the market for a horse.'

The farmer cast an eye over the animals. 'Plenty of horses out today.'

'Aye.'

'You're not lonely out there?' The farmer turned to his companions with a glassy wink. 'My wife's forever after getting him married.'

'Not lonely, no.'

'Plenty of young women out here now.' One of the other men leant in. 'Plenty of women for a fella like you.'

John took a sup of his porter and looked about him. It was true. The sun had brought them out in flocks, many with the modern look about them: skirts worn short to the knee, hair cut close to their heads. It made for a fine enough sight, but it wasn't for him. He smiled and shook his head. 'I think I'm a little old for that sort of thing now.'

The man who had been speaking leant forward again. 'You're never too old for that sort of thing, lad.'

John drained his pint, threw some coins on the table. 'Well, I'll be getting along there.' He shouldered his bag. 'Nice to meet you fellas.'

He saluted the farmer, turning to make his way down the street. Soon he was amongst the fray: young girls grasping chickens by the wings, showing their undersides to clutches of buyers. Young lads riding bareback on ponies through the crowd. Cows and goats and sheep and ducklings and the street thick with the sweetness of dung. The horses were at the far end, each with a small crowd around them: working horses, with young women grasping their harnesses, fine horses, horses with scabbed and matted manes. He saw a lovely bay mare that he thought might do. Next month, perhaps, if she was still for sale. The barn would be ready by then. When he had done a circuit, he made to walk back, cutting up away from the main street – past stalls with all manner of handmade spades and tools laid out. He cast his eye over them as he passed.

At the top of the road, passing the hotel, he stopped. A young woman was standing on the other side of the street. She had her head turned away from him. Her dark hair was tied in a knot at her neck. She was pale and pregnant, hands clasped around the swelling of her belly.

The young woman looked up, her attention caught by something just beyond him. And he saw her properly then: the paleness of her face. Her deep brow. The straight line of her mouth. The breath was emptied from him.

There was a shout, and a young child, a little girl, came barrelling down the road towards the woman. A man following. Slim and tall. Glasses. The man bent and lifted the child to the mother's face for a kiss, and for a moment the small family stood in the afternoon sun, almost as though for a photograph, or a still life, until the moment broke, the man touched the woman on the arm, she spoke to him and smiled, and they went into the hotel.

Slowly, John came back to himself. On the other side of the road was a pub, and he made his way towards it, and when he reached it he found he was breathing hard.

'Whiskey.'

He downed the dram, let its fire burn him. He lifted his head, saw his reflection in the glass behind the bar. The furrowed face. Eyes narrowed and lined from squinting at the sun. He was old. Somehow, somewhere along the way, he had become old.

That night he woke and did not know where he was. He could not see the stars, and so he panicked and shouted, tangled in his covers, until his hands touched walls and he understood. He pulled on clothes and walked outside, where he sat on the bench at the front of the house. The sky was clear – only a few rags of clouds trailing after the moon. He rolled a cigarette and smoked it, breathing as the thud of his heart becalmed.

For a long while on the ships he had insisted upon sleeping on deck. As long as he was in no one's way they let him. He spent years like that, wrapped in blankets. Not wanting to be enclosed by the things of men.

He stared out now into the blackness around him.

Ghosts.

He had thought he was done with ghosts.

When he had first escaped, he had seen her everywhere.

Every street corner. Every crowd leaving every mill. That was in his time of searching; always then, the balance of looking with the fear of being caught; with the need to make money and to live.

For days he had roamed Bradford, Leeds. He knew she had worked in the mills, and so he asked the women as they poured out from the gate, but none knew an Ella Fay.

He needed work himself, finding it in the flat farmland north of York, weeks digging turnips and swedes in filthy weather. Then, with some money in his pocket, he searched again.

That was when he went to sea. Dan had been right. No questions asked.

His first voyage a long one – Argentina and back. Colour and light and sound, and him torn inside and all he could think was that their child would soon be born.

On his return he searched the cities again. Manchester, Newcastle. At night he slept in boarding houses. Bolder now, he asked the foremen this time; anywhere a woman might work, he asked to see the names on their lists. He saw her all right. Over and over. A pale face in a crowd. But when he looked again it was never her.

He returned to sea, the years passed, and he moved through the ranks.

Il mio Capitane.

Dan had been right.

There were women sometimes. Sweet women who turned to him and held his face and asked so little of him that they broke his heart. But he still searched.

Until, at some point, he could not say when, he stopped searching. Stopped seeing her in the street. Stopped

336

thinking of her. Until his time at sea was more than his time on land. Until he felt himself become a different sort of man. Until years had passed. Until he had begun to grow old.

The next morning he woke early and gathered tools and wood. It was a fine day, blustery with sea breeze, the sunlight glancing off the sea in the distance, the Atlantic light pale and clear. He climbed the ladder up on to the roof of the barn and began to work straight away.

After a few hours, he was sweating. He stopped and rolled himself a cigarette, leaning back against the slanted roof, closing his eyes against the late-summer sun.

When he opened them again, he saw a figure coming down the lane towards the house. Moving slowly but purposefully, as though carrying a heavy load. She was wearing a yellow dress. He leant forward. Looked away. Then back again. Still she came.

He ground out his cigarette and climbed down the ladder, brushing his hands on his trousers. The woman had stopped, her eyes closed against the sun. She was smart, her print dress the colour of pale lemons. A hat placed at an angle on her head. She opened her eyes and he saw her hesitate, as though on the edge of cold water. She came towards the gate. 'John Mulligan?' she said.

The voice was different. Clear, somehow. And yet the face was the same.

He nodded, his blood in an uproar. He did not trust himself to speak.

'May I come in?'

He gestured yes, and she manoeuvred herself through the gate, making her way up the path towards him. Her eyes flicking to him and then from left to right as though to take it all in: the house, the land, the sky. He was aware of the weeds growing either side of the path, the hole in the roof of the barn. The overgrown garden, the tangle of the bramble patch. Himself. The weeds had grown there too. He passed his hands over his hair, then put them in his pockets. He took them out again.

When she was close, but still a few paces away, she thrust out her hand. A glove on it, despite the warmth of the day. He stepped up, and they shook.

'My name is Clemency.' An English voice. A crispness to it in the clear air.

He was aware of being looked at in the pale morning light by this young woman in her lemon-yellow dress. A reckoning. 'Would you come indoors?' he said. 'I have tea.'

She looked about her, and her eye fell on the bench. 'Might we sit outside instead? It's such a lovely morning.'

'Aye. Make yourself comfortable. Would you like the tea?'

'Yes.' She moved to sit. 'Please.'

The kettle had been hanging over the fire since the morning and so was warm, and he was grateful for it. He let it be a moment and went into the bedroom, where a mirror was nailed to the wall. His face had a streak of dirt on it. He rubbed it away. His shirt was damp in the armpits and the back. For a long moment, he simply looked at himself, adrift. Then he went back into the kitchen, where his hands shook as he poured the tea into mugs, and then milk. He carried them back into the sun.

'Would you like bread?' he said, as he put the tea down beside her. 'I have a little soda bread and cheese.'

'Tea is fine. Thank you.'

A precision in the way she spoke. You could hear the edges of the words. And the way she was sitting too. Neat, despite the bulk of her. Hands folded in her lap. Hair knotted at the base of her neck. Long, old-fashioned hair.

He felt he should not sit beside her, so he stood instead, a little way to her left. 'I saw you,' he said.

She turned to him, startled. 'When?'

'Yesterday. In the town. With your . . . husband and your child.'

'Oh,' she nodded. 'Yes. We're here on our holidays.'

'That's grand.'

'He's a schoolmaster. I am a teacher. Or I was before I married.'

'That's grand,' he said again, and then fell silent. *A teacher.*

He felt slow before this woman. Her mind quick. He could feel it landing on him, taking flight, landing again. 'How old is your little one then?' he asked.

'Two.'

'Ah.'

She put her tea to the side and – as though they irritated her suddenly – she pulled off her gloves. Threaded her hands in front of her belly. 'He told me not to come,' she said quietly. 'My husband. He doesn't know I'm here.'

He nodded. 'I see.' His mouth was tacky. 'And . . . why is it that you are here?'

She looked up at him, and her face was the face of another woman, a lifetime ago, and he wanted to get to his knees before her. And yet he saw the young woman in the yellow dress draw back.

She stood and looked around her. 'It's a lovely place you have here. Have you lived here long?'

'A year,' he said, gathering himself. 'No more.'

She nodded. 'And before that?'

'I was at sea.'

'And before that?'

'When are you thinking of?'

'Twenty-three years ago.' Her face tight.

He swallowed. 'Won't you sit down?'

She shook her head. Hands in fists at her side. She looked younger now. Scarcely more than a child. 'I have to know. Where were you then?'

'Yorkshire,' he said. He had nothing more to offer her than the truth. 'A place called Sharston.'

She put the heels of her hands to her eyes and gave a small sound.

'Do you know me?' she said, lifting her face to his. 'Do you know who I am?'

'Aye,' he said to her, softly. 'I believe I do.'

She nodded. 'I looked for you,' she said. 'I looked for you for so long.'

'I'm sorry.'

'Did you look for us? If you didn't, I'll go. And I'll never see you again. I promise you. But if you did, I have to know.'

'Please. Don't upset yourself. Sit yourself down. Your tea's getting cold.'

She sat again, but her eyes did not leave his. He saw her stubbornness and was proud. 'I looked,' he said to her. 'I looked for years. I looked until looking became . . .'

'What?' Her face was white. 'What did looking become? Tell me,' she said. 'I want to know.'

'I came to feel I should never find you by looking,' he said. There was silence for a moment, then, 'Where is she?' he asked.

340

Her face contracted. 'She's dead. She died three years ago.'

He nodded. He had known it somehow. Still, he felt the knowledge burrow its way into a soft, waiting place. He stored the pain till later. 'Was she ill?'

'For a while. And then it seemed she was getting better. But then, quite quickly, she was gone.'

Beneath his feet, a flower. Tiny. He leant down and plucked it. Turned it in his palm.

A sound came from beside him. The young woman was bent over herself now, her back shuddering. He wanted to reach out and touch her, soothe her, but he knew he did not have the right. So he waited until the shuddering was past.

The young woman lifted her face, blurred now with tears. 'I knew my mother had gone there, to the asylum to search for you. But whenever I asked, she said that there had been nothing of you there to find. That there was no way to know where you were. After she died,' she said, 'I went there myself. They treated me like a criminal. Said there was no record of you. No forwarding address. They said that you had just disappeared.

'My husband was furious. He hadn't wanted me to go. He never said so before my mother, but in private he'd said you weren't worth the finding. Any man that would leave a woman like that—'

Her voice fell away. John stayed silent.

'But that was not how she had spoken of you,' she said, softly. 'She had never spoken of you like that.'

'And how did she speak of me?'

'With love.'

The words, simple enough, entered him, a salve in them.

He saw her watching him. Did she think him worthy of them?

'Thank you,' he said. Then, 'She must have been proud. Of you. To be a teacher. To be – as you are.'

'She was.' The young woman looked away, plucking at something on her skirt. 'She loved to have me read to her often, when I was a child.'

He nodded.

'She kept your letters.' Her gaze on him again.

'She did?'

'She asked me to read them to her. When it was close to the end. She came to read herself, you know. A little. Enough. But still – she liked to have me read them aloud.'

He saw her then. Ella. In the ballroom. The last time.

I can't read. Not really. Clem read them to me. She helped me. She read them out loud.

The fear on her face as she spoke. As if that would have changed a thing.

'I'm glad,' he said softly.

'I knew then, once I read them, that I had to find you. That you weren't – what my husband said.' Her hands were in fists and she was speaking rapidly now. 'All I knew was what she had told me, and what was in your letters. I knew your name and that you were Irish . . . My husband is Irish. We come here every year, every summer, to visit his family in Galway. I knew from what you had written that you were from the west, and so I began asking. I would ask for a John Mulligan wherever we went. There are lots of John Mulligans, you know.' She lifted her chin, half-accusingly.

'Aye.' He nodded, a small smile. 'Plenty enough.'

'I took to asking everywhere. If we were in a village, I would go to the church. Look at the gravestones. See if there were Mulligans. It became . . . something I did. And then we arrived here, last week, and I asked in the post office. I was told there was a John Mulligan living alone out here. And I knew. I just . . . knew. I knew I had to come.'

Her face pierced him. So much of her mother was in it.

It was his turn to speak.

But now she was here, in all her living self, he found the words gone from him. Flown from his throat to settle in the throats of the birds, to hang suspended from the listening trees, to the sea, crashing its breakers at the edge of thought.

Breathe.

He put his hand to his chest. Felt the beat of himself there.

He knew where there was a store of words. Words that belonged to this woman. That she had been waiting a lifetime to hear.

'Wait.'

His heart was hammering as he went into the cool interior of the cottage. He bent and brought out a small suitcase from beneath his bed. Inside were papers, documents, the small collected stuff of his life: his merchant seaman's licence, his passport. A small sheaf of letters at the bottom. He lifted them, passing them through his hands until he found what he was looking for and took it back out into the sun.

'Here.'

She took it from him. 'It's for her,' she said.

'But you can open it.'

She opened it.

He closed his eyes as she read aloud.

Dear Ella,

It has been ten years now since I saw you for the last time. I remember your face. I will never forget your face.

I have written a letter to you every year on this day.

I do not know where you are, or what has become of you, and so I cannot send them. I will keep them till such time as I see you once more.

I am newly in England again. Today I will go to Bradford and then to Leeds and look for you. I think of you every day. Of you and of the child. Was the child born? Did the child live? The thought of a child growing up without a father or with a father that is not its own is more than a pain to me.

I am sorry I did not stay in that place. I can only picture you sending word – as I asked you to – and receiving nothing back.

But I had to run.

And when I ran I thought of you. Of your freedom. How you had given me that.

You are strong you have always been strong and if I think of you I feel you are alive. I hope that we might one day be a family. But wherever you are I send you my love. I work on the ships but I always return.

Yours,

Always,

John

The young woman looked up to him. She began to cry again, softly but insistently, the tears falling freely.

'Hush,' he said to her. And he brought her to him. 'All is well,' he said. 'All is well.'

*

The next day he shaved. Put on his finest shirt. He baked fresh bread. The morning light was the colour of lemons.

They arrived as arranged at three. His daughter, Clemency, first, holding her own daughter by the hand. He watched them as they came up the lane, hardly able to trust his eyes, but they were real enough: the little girl a sturdy thing, the husband behind, tall, reticent, but calm. When they shook, John saw that behind his spectacles his eyes were kind. They sat, and drank tea, and ate bread and butter, while the little girl played at their feet.

When they had eaten, he showed them the way to the sea. They walked the path through the meadows, emerging on to the strand, where the little girl shouted in delight at the sight of the water.

'You can paddle,' he said to her. 'If you like.'

The girl looked at her mother, who nodded and bent to take off her daughter's socks and shoes. 'Why don't you hold her hand?' she said to John.

He hesitated, but his daughter smiled. 'Please,' she said, 'it's all right.'

He reached down, and the little girl stared up at him. For a long moment she paused, as though weighing him up, until she slipped her hand in his and let him lead her to the water's edge.

The tide was in, covering the inlets, and small, fizzing waves broke on the beach. Gently, he lifted her into the shallow water. She laughed as the bubbling water covered her feet. He felt the astonishment of her presence, a miracle, unsought. The small, certain life of her beneath his hands.

They stayed there a while, as the water pulled back and then returned again, and again, undaunted by anything it found in its way.

Author's Note

Anyone who knows the West Riding of Yorkshire is likely to recognize the asylum in which *The Ballroom* takes place; it lies on the outskirts of the village of Menston and is known locally as Menston Asylum. The building opened in 1888 and was originally called the West Riding Pauper Lunatic Asylum, later West Riding Mental Hospital, then in 1963 it became High Royds Hospital, eventually closing its doors in 2003.

My great-great-grandfather, John Mullarkey, an Irishman, was a patient there from 1909, when he was transferred to the asylum from the workhouse. I found the discovery of his story to be almost unbearably moving. His notes describe a 'depressed' man who 'has had to work very hard and has worried over his work'. At the time of his admission, he was 'very emaciated and poorly nourished'. He never recovered, and died there at the age of fifty-six in 1918, while his son was fighting on the Western Front. This book is dedicated to his memory.

I researched extensively for this book, but I want to stress that, while the asylum provided the inspiration for my work, *The Ballroom* is a novel and is in no way meant to be an accurate representation of life or events at High Royds. For this reason, I have called my asylum Sharston, and it is a place crafted as much from the imagination as the historical record. John, Ella and Charles are wholly fictional characters.

Anyone wishing to know more about the history of the asylum could do no better than to start with local historian and photographer Mark Davies's online archive at www.highroydshospital.com. It was here that I first saw photographs of the ruined, spectacular ballroom at the asylum's heart, and knew I had to write about it. It was here, too, that I learned of the graveyard at Buckle Lane – Mantle Lane in *The Ballroom* – whose shared graves so terrify the patients in my novel. Mark has written two books on the history of the asylum, *The West Riding Pauper Lunatic Asylum Through Time* and *Voices from the Asylum*. He has also worked to restore the chapel at Buckle Lane as a memorial to those who lie in those unmarked graves.

Anyone who knows the West Riding may be surprised to encounter a working-class mill girl speaking Standard English. For the purposes of clarity I have chosen not to represent what would undoubtedly have been fairly thick dialect in the speech of Ella and the other Yorkshire characters. I have, however, used dialect words throughout, to which Arnold Kellett's *A Yorkshire Dictionary* was an invaluable guide.

Surprisingly little seems to be known about the history of eugenics in Britain. I was shocked and disturbed to learn of Home Secretary Churchill's enthusiasm for the sterilization of significant numbers of the British people. It was not just Churchill, though: the support for eugenics ran deep and across the political spectrum. Marie Stopes, the Fabians Sidney and Beatrice Webb and George Bernard Shaw were all keen supporters of the eugenics movement. For those wishing to delve deeper, the *Eugenics Review*, held on the open shelves at the Wellcome Collection, is a fascinating and troubling place to start. Britain was by no means alone in her enthusiasm for eugenics, however, and anyone wishing to read an overview of the period might begin with the chapter 'Questions of Breeding' in Philip Blom's excellent book *The Vertigo Years*.

Again, while my research was extensive, I have taken liberties with the historical record. Churchill, despite being an enthusiastic supporter of the idea of sterilization for the 'unfit', never, to my knowledge, wrote a letter like the one in the book. Neither, to my knowledge, did Karl Pearson or Leonard Darwin write letters to a doctor such as Charles. All of the quoted texts, however, from Tredgold's *Eugenics and Future Human Progress*, to the passages from the *Eugenics Review*, to the extracts from Leonard Darwin's lecture, are accurate.

The Feeble-Minded Bill was eventually passed in modified form in 1913 as the Mental Deficiency Act, which allowed for the segregation of the 'feeble-minded' without the crucial clause that would have enabled forced sterilization. The Bill had cross-party support, but there were a couple of prominent voices raised against it: the writer G. K. Chesterton, and within parliament the MP Josiah Wedgewood, both waged a campaign to modify the legislation. That Churchill's favoured policy was not in the eventual Act was a measured victory for human rights and can perhaps be put at the door of these campaigners. The Act as it stood was hardly admirable though, stating, for instance, that any woman giving birth to an illegitimate child while in receipt of poor relief was to be seen as 'feeble-minded' and would thus be liable for compulsory institutionalization. I wonder whether the dropping of the sterilization clause might also have come about because by late 1911 Churchill had moved to the Admiralty and by 1912 had his eye trained on very different horizons.

Acknowledgements

Of the many books I read while researching *The Ballroom*, I found the following most helpful:

Juliet Nicholson's *The Perfect Summer*, John Murray, 2006, offers an overview of that turbulent heatwave summer of 1911.

Maggie Newbery's vivid *Picking Up Threads*, Bradford Libraries, 1993, was one of the few accounts I could find of a working-class mill girl in Bradford in the 1910s.

Mark Davis and Marina Kidd's *Voices from the Asylum*, Amberley, 2013, is a moving record of those patients at Menston Asylum who ended their lives in unmarked graves.

Elaine Showalter's *The Female Malady*, Virago, 1987, gives an important account of the medical establishment's attitude to female patients at the time.

Arnold Kellet's *The Yorkshire Dictionary*, Smith Settle, 1994, was an invaluable guide to dialect.

Repeated visits to the Wellcome Collection, and to the asylum archives, which are held in Wakefield in West Yorkshire, were also vital for my research.

I owe thanks to many – but to these people in particular:

To Caroline Wood and Jane Lawson, my wonderful agent and editor, both of whom were patient, careful and enthusiastic midwives for the book.

To the teams at Felicity Bryan and Transworld Publishers,

but primarily my publicist Alison Barrow, whose care for her authors and passion for the wider world of books and readers is remarkable.

To my writers' group, the Unwriteables, still going strong after almost eight years. They read this book in chapter form over its two-and-a-half-year gestation and their intelligent responses are woven into the text.

To Thea Bennett, Philip Makatrewicz, Josh Raymond and David Savill, all of whom read the book at crucial periods and offered honest and invaluable criticism and support.

To Pamela Hope, always a key reader for me, who read this book swiftly, twice, when I most needed her help.

To Tony Hope, who accompanied me on a brilliant research mission to Bradford.

To my family and friends, without whose love and support the solitary work of a writer would be impossible.

And to Dave, always, for his love, laughter and light.

Thank you.

Anna Hope was born in Manchester and educated at Oxford University and RADA. She is the author of the acclaimed debut *Wake* ('A masterclass in historical fiction', *Observer*) which was shortlisted for the National Book Awards. *The Ballroom* is her second novel, and is inspired by the true story of her Irish great-great-grandfather. You can follow Anna on Twitter: @Anna_Hope.